SAPIENT FARM

Querus Abuttu

SCARY DAIRY PRESS, INC.
1071 BRITTEN LANE, #201
VENTURA, CA 93003
WWW.SCARYDAIRYPRESS.COM

Copyright © 2014 by Querus Abuttu
Cover art by: The Logo Team
Edited by: R.J. Cavender
ISBN: 0996052704
ISBN 13: 9780996052702
Library of Congress Control Number: 2014908849
Scary Dairy Press, Inc., Ventura, CA

All rights reserved. No part of this publication may be reproduced or transmitted in any form or by any means without the prior written permission of the publisher. All characters in this publication are fictitious, and all places in this novel are used fictitiously. Any resemblance to real persons, living or dead, is purely coincidental.

AKNOWLEDGEMENTS

My sincere thanks to my mentors, Timons Esaias, Tim Waggoner, Mike Arnzen, and Scott Johnson; my Seton Hill University critique partners, Gina Greenway, Joe Borrelli, and Stephanie Wytovich; my critique partners from Ventura Fiction Writers Guild, Broos Campbell, Mark Juric, Allison Cook, Wendy Larrivee, and Charlotte McLeod; my editor, R. J. Cavender; and my beta readers, Steven W. Booth, Ryan Harding, Leadie Jo Flowers, and David Day. This book would never have made it to electronic and/or paper print without the ideas and word-smithing of each writer, editor, and reader involved. I'm extremely grateful to all of you.

To Jim, Kira, and Sean,
for the weeks you did without me,
for each day you encouraged me,
for forever believing in me and keeping the faith.
I love you all so much!

TABLE OF CONTENTS

Aknowledgements ... iii
Prologue ... xi
One ... 1
Two ... 9
Three ... 15
Four ... 27
Five ... 45
Six ... 52
Seven ... 59
Eight ... 70
Nine ... 81
Ten ... 92
Eleven ... 103
Twelve ... 106
Thirteen ... 108
Fourteen ... 110
Fifteen ... 121
Sixteen ... 124

Seventeen ... 135
Eighteen ... 146
Nineteen ... 155
Twenty ... 162
Twenty One ... 176
Twenty Two ... 191
Twenty Three ... 200
Twenty Four ... 209
Twenty Five ... 216
Twenty Six ... 227
Twenty Seven ... 239
Twenty Eight ... 255
Twenty Nine ... 268
Thirty ... 284
Thirty One ... 297
Thirty Two ... 305
Thirty Three ... 315
Thirty Four ... 326
Thirty Five ... 337
Thirty Six ... 343
Thirty Seven ... 356
Thirty Eight ... 371
Epilogue ... 373
About the Author ... 375

The question is not, "Can they reason?" nor, "Can they talk?" but "Can they suffer?"
—Jeremy Bentham, *The Principles of Morals and Legislation*

PROLOGUE

December 24, 23:59

"Okay. Take a look. I've modified the germline cells, and the oocytes are ready."

"And the phenotype?" Miriam put on a pair of gloves.

"Difficult to say with absolute certainty, but it's a useful blend of what they ordered. The organs will be interchangeable, and the entire species should grow rapidly. The one thing I can't guarantee is... " Ben moved away from the microscope and let the senior scientist have a look.

"Yes?"

"How intelligent they'll be. The Cullers wanted options."

The room was silent for a moment except for the whirring of a nearby centrifuge.

"And the host is ready?" Miriam lifted her face from the microscope and peeled off her gloves.

"Yes, and, Em..."

"Yes?"

"Merry Christmas."

January 1, 01:03

Admiral Blandy bent over one of the young soldiers and examined him. The soldier had recently arrived from Afghanistan. His physique was that of chiseled flesh, save for where shrapnel had torn holes into his shoulders and ribs. He'd worked with the K-9 unit until three days ago, when a mortar blast inside Bagram Air Base had shredded his dog to pieces and turned the man's brain to mush.

Now, he was at the Landstuhl Regional Medical Center in Germany. The admiral examined the man's EEG results. There hadn't been any brain activity for days. None. And this soldier was just one among many.

Such a waste. How many more soldiers will we shuttle from the field? How many more will we transfer to this hospital only to pull the plug while the family watches?

The admiral looked around the ICU and counted the casualties. Each soldier was on a ventilator. Some needed new internal organs, like a kidney, liver, or heart. Others required skin grafts, brand-new blood vessels, and muscle tissue.

General Muttnic stood beside him and looked down at the soldier. "You really think it can be done?"

Admiral Blandy placed his hand on the forehead of the man lying in the bed. A breathing tube went past the man's mouth and into his throat. The machine whirred and beeped as it blew air in and exhaled for the soldier, who would normally be a corpse except for all of the lines in his mouth, nose, and veins keeping him alive. His body was still good. He could still be a good soldier.

"I *know* it can be done, General. Our scientists have assured me."

"And how do we do it?" The general's eyes stayed fixed on the man whose lungs were mechanically filled and emptied.

"Leave that to me. It's in the works. It will take a little time, but not as much as you think. This could be our first candidate."

Muttnic's stare focused on the admiral, and a spark lit inside his eyes. "If this works, we'll save billions. How long?"

Admiral Blandy suppressed a smile. "Nine months. Ten months tops. And you'll have what you need."

"What about his memories? What about his experiences? How are you going to grow those?"

"Provide me with as much information about him as you can. We will see to the memories."

Admiral Blandy turned away from the soldier's bed, preparing to leave, but the general grabbed at his sleeve. The words he hissed were so soft that the admiral almost missed them. "And the public? What of them? Can you imagine their moral outrage?"

"They can never know." He tugged his sleeve away from the general's fingers. "Their own families can't know. Not now. Not ever."

He pulled the curtain closed behind him, leaving the general alone with the soldier and the beeping machines. He made mental preparations to fly back to the States on the next airlift and decided to check on the Cullers' progress. There'd be hell to pay if they let him down.

Admiral Blandy opened his phone and dialed a number. "Get me Harper."

The Culler had better have good news.

The US military was plummeting into a sinkhole of failed war strategy and mandatory government cutbacks, which meant less funding for the Department of Defense. That meant less money for training military personnel and fewer operations in the Mediterranean and the Pacific. As the United States Navy's Surgeon General, he desperately needed a scientific miracle. And so, he continued to press the phone against his ear and wait for the voice he needed to make his wishes come true.

ONE

April 24, 02:45

The small lab was exactly what Miriam had wanted. It was in the center of a dead zone, just bordering the Badlands. No Internet, no phone service. Remote living on steroids.

Nights were cold. They had very little heat, save for the wood stove in the living room and a few space heaters to keep the chill from their fingers. Still, the Cullers made it possible to get most of what they needed, and the hills of South Dakota were gradually warming with the coming spring.

Now, the two of them huddled over a rotund figure, waiting for the outcome of their extraordinary efforts. The body in front of them gasped and grunted.

Miriam almost jumped when Ben leaned over and excitedly whispered, "It's coming!"

"Hush!" She wanted to enjoy the moment. No interruptions. She smoothed the yellow paper of her surgical gown flat over her lap.

They observed as a pregnant sow labored, the moment of birthing upon her. Her corpulent, pink frame stretched across a mound of golden straw and heaved with each strenuous breath. It was difficult to see in the dimly lit room, but bright lights only delayed the birthing process in mammals. Whitewashed flooring and walls made both the pig and the straw seem out of place.

The pig let out a pain-filled grunt. As they watched, little human feet poked through the soft vaginal opening, and then a pale, lifeless form flopped onto the floor with a sickening, wet thud. It stank of rusty iron and decay.

Miriam suppressed a sigh of disappointment.

A definite failure.

With gloved hands, she picked up the body and examined it. The dull blue skin on the baby was peeling back like the skin on an overboiled potato. She noted the concave head and a large gap that ran from above the upturned nose to below the bottom lip. The fetus had been dead for a while. She showed the malformation to Ben, trying to hide her dismay. Any show of emotion would demonstrate her lack of self-control, and she'd learned from harsh experience that a lack of self-control in front of anyone was unacceptable. *And dangerous.*

Ben took the body to an adjoining room. They'd do a more detailed examination on it later. Miriam stared at her partner's ponytail as he left and wished he'd cut the damned thing. He looked like a tree hugger or some kind of granola hippie, especially with the tie-dyed T-shirt underneath his lab jacket, but then again, he did come from California. When he returned, he repositioned himself on a short wooden stool, and they waited.

After two long hours and a total of nine births, the outcome was dismal. Two of the litter were stillborn. Seven more failed to survive the first hour of life.

An autopsy will help me understand what went wrong.

Miriam rubbed the growing band of tension over her brow. There were two more births to go. The initial ultrasound had confirmed a total of eleven fetuses inside the uterus. Oddly, it was the only ultrasound they'd been able to do. They'd tried several techniques after that, but something in the makeup of the amniotic sacs made the fetuses extremely difficult to see. The only things they'd been able to confirm were heartbeats, and it had been hard to determine one from another.

She chewed lightly on the wall of her cheek and waited for the inevitable. The pig grunted and wriggled, and an opaque sack emerged from behind her back legs and slid onto the floor.

Born in caul. Almost unheard of in the species. But then again, they're not completely pig.

Miriam tore the bag open with her fingers, and water gushed from the sack. The clear fluid had a musky, earthy odor to it, not unpleasant. To her surprise, instead of one infant, there were two, resting side by side. The babies weakly kicked their limbs and struggled to breathe. She rubbed both of them dry with a large towel, hoping the tactile stimulation would jump-start their nervous systems. After a few seconds, each of them emitted a faint stuttered squeal.

She picked up one of the new babies and squeezed a thin line of erythromycin ointment across each eye. There was an odd deformity that ran through the left side of the face, from the brow to the lower cheekbone, and it almost looked like a scar. It made the baby look as if it had survived a vicious brawl while in utero. She handed the medication to Ben and continued with her examination. This one was a male, and it was a good deal smaller than the other. Ben inspected the sibling. Their eyes met. He answered her unspoken question.

"A female."

Joy and pride thumped in her chest. She turned her attention back to the little male in her arms. A pink snout protruded from his face, and miniature piggy ears adorned his head. She scrutinized the newborn's extremities, and, yes...there they were—tiny fingers and toes, perfectly formed and remarkably human. His fingers seemed short, and the palms looked wide, but his digits flexed and curled just like those of *Homo sapiens*.

And at the top of his buttocks, right where the sacrum should be, was the tiny curl of a tail.

Two alive. One male and one female. Despite the failures in this litter, the overall outcome was acceptable.

As long as these survive.

She and Ben placed the newborns next to the sow's teats and allowed them to suckle while they recorded their findings.

A few hours later, Miriam removed the newborns from the warmth of their mother and brought them into the adjoining room. Fluorescent lighting overhead emitted a sickly blue glow, and the air was cold. The room stank of alcohol, formaldehyde, and piney cleaning solution. She placed the infants together in a makeshift crib, which was really nothing more than a large fish tank. They'd purchased it from a pet store in Rapid City, and now, it was filled with soft, fresh bedding. A heat lamp above them kept the tank warm.

"We need to finish up." Miriam averted her eyes from the pained look on Ben's face and began to prepare the formula for the infants. It was a superior combination of nutrients designed specifically for their optimum growth. A blend of proteins and enzymes their mother couldn't provide. All things considered, it was a good beginning.

"You did *what*?"

Harper tried not to cringe when the Surgeon General of the United States Navy yelled in his ear. He remained quiet until the admiral got it out of his system.

"What were you thinking? This is a top-secret project! And you moved them out of a quarantined area? To bumfuck...Where the hell is it?" Silence pounded on the line between intermittent static.

"South Dakota, sir. Pine Ridge Indian Reservation."

"And why the hell did you think that was a good idea? What made you think…"

Harper was amused. There was silence midsentence, which made the admiral sound like he was speechless. Harper imagined the man clenching his teeth together, with that little corner of taut muscle at the hinge of his jaw protruding underneath the cheekbones.

He must wonder how his top medical-intelligence agent, a man leading one of the United States' most important military research operations, gets the gall to pull a stunt like this.

Harper closed his eyes and focused on regulating his heart rate. Military personnel were so predictable.

People in power never want the public to know what they are doing. And the public doesn't care what the people in power do unless they make a decision that directly affects them.

"Sir, if you will, the best place for this project is in a natural environment. You said you wanted them to have basic memories. Stimulation of brain growth. They need to experience sights, sounds, and smells. That's what you're going to need to ensure their increased intelligence and to give them a well-rounded experience. In addition to providing replacement parts, of course."

The line was quiet again.

Plink! Plink!

The dripping water from the faucet in Harper's bathroom was an auditory irritation. A few more beats passed until the admiral spoke.

"The public can't know. No one outside this project can be aware of what's going on. You understand?"

Harper breathed in slowly, filling his lungs before he responded. It was the same kind of breath he took before discharging his firearm.

"Don't worry, sir. We've taken full precautions. And we have a number of control measures in place, in case of any...unforeseen problems."

Harper imagined the admiral's lower jaw shifting left and right to ease the tension in it. It was no accident that every leader in the military above the rank of O5 was a control freak. Harper was too. But there was a distinct difference between them. A senior military officer's desire for control was based on fear, power, and survival. Harper's need for control was grounded in logic, the simplicity of experience, and unadulterated habit.

"There better not be *any* problems. No ties to the military. You got that? And any communications between us, I expect to be wiped."

"Affirmative, sir." *Like always.* Harper listened to the connection die, took the device outside, and smashed it with a hammer before placing it in the incinerator. He was very good at destroying things. And he was getting better at it every day.

Ben felt his pulse quicken and rubbed his moist palms on the inside pockets of his lab coat. He knew what came next, but he still didn't like it. He walked over to the door and called to Chet. The security guard ambled up to the threshold, a hint of bounce in his step.

"You can take the mother out back." Ben cringed when the words left his mouth. Miriam routinely stressed the importance of destroying traces of their experiments. It was unfortunate he had cared for the mother over the past four months. Since Christmas, he'd fed and watched over her. They'd labeled her "Alpha-One," but Ben had gone so far as to nickname her Alphie. He had spent time petting her whenever he'd brought the animal her meals. She'd often nudged him with her snout, a comical gesture that told him she wanted her belly rubbed. A belly full of babies.

Collateral damage. The words in his mind weren't as convincing as he wanted them to be.

Miriam was determined to raise the infants as human, or as close to human as possible, which meant no more maternal pig feedings. She said it was important to avoid any animal-instinct triggers. With the way the infants were engineered, they wouldn't benefit from the sow's milk anyway. Chet suggested using the hog for food and said he'd share some of the meat with a neighboring family. Miriam thought it was a kindly gesture since the family had five kids.

It probably wasn't much different than euthanizing rats in the lab at the conclusion of an experiment. He'd performed that task hundreds of times.

Standard research protocol.

But he'd used sodium pentobarbital to put the rodents to sleep. This method was much more brutal. He tried to shrug off the thought. Death was death.

Ben looked over at the babies. The male piglet stared from inside the glass tank as Chet entered the room where his mother lay. The creature wrinkled its snout and let out an unearthly squeal. The noise kept going, like a screaming Tasmanian devil, and the male piglet's eyes brimmed with water. Little human fingers clenched tightly into fists.

Wow. Ben was surprised at the volume of noise the infant could generate. *The runt must really be hungry.*

In the next room, the guard yelled at the sow. The echo of his boots kicking porcine flesh bounced around the white cinderblock walls, and the mother's grunts of agony were audible.

"Get up, bitch!" Chet's voice was loud and harsh. Moments later, the mother pig scrambled from the birthing room to the outside door, with Chet following a few paces behind her. Both

Miriam and Ben jumped when a rifle blast boomed. It boomed again. And then once more. Abrupt silence enveloped them afterward, and the only noises Ben detected were the deliberate sounds of Miriam hooking up the video equipment to film the new babies.

They've killed our mother.

The girl squirmed next to her brother. It was difficult to see. Most of her surroundings were nothing but a blur. Her eyes stung, and the water welling up in them only made her vision worse. She felt her bottom lip tremble, and a question buzzed inside her head.

Why?

She nuzzled the cheek of her sibling and sensed his anger. They'd communicated silently inside their mother, but outside of her, it was much more difficult. Still, the skin beneath her hair prickled, and suddenly she felt afraid. Very afraid. But not for herself. No. Not for her brother. Not even for her mother.

Not anymore.

She was afraid for *them*. Those upright ones who smelled so sweet and placidly moved around this space wearing blinding white coats. Those upright ones who had demonstrated joy at their arrival and expressed excitement at their common bond of human fingers and toes. She didn't understand *why* she was afraid, just as she was unable to explain her innate intellect and awareness, but somehow, deep inside, she knew her fear would not be enough. Not enough to save them.

TWO

April 25, 09:26

The sky grew darker and more threatening across the prairie, and the clouds took on a greenish hue. Violent winds whipped across young field grasses, making them ripple in swishing waves.

Ben stepped onto the front porch to smoke a cigar. It was one of his few decadent pleasures. He pulled a Man O' War Ruination from his jacket pocket, humorously hoping that a man wasn't what he smoked. His fingers shed the clear plastic wrapper. It only took a moment to give the cap a snip, which opened the mouth end for him to smoke it. The blue flames of his torch lit the cigar with ease despite the storm winds kicking up.

Chet occupied one of the porch corners, his legs pushing back and forth as he rocked in a white wicker chair. Ben found it difficult to make conversation with the man. He was an oddity compared to Ben's own Californian ways, and Ben wondered why the Cullers had selected Chet as the primary security watch over their experiments. A native of Rapid City, Chet said he'd served several years as a US Army Ranger, which explained some of his odd behavior.

Ben took a puff off his cigar, enjoying the easy draw of the smoke and its dark, rich flavor. Chet just stared up at the clouds, his thick jaw chewing on what Ben assumed was a wad of his usual Red Man. As if on cue, the man spat a brown lump of slime onto the slats of wood. Most of it soaked into the roughened grains, leaving an irregular stain on the boards.

Ben ventured a few words. "Sky looks pretty dark out."

"Yep." Chet's voice sounded far away, like he was absent from the present. "There's a funnel cloud. Right there." He pointed to a blackened mass gathering in the sky. Ben noticed a small cone spinning slowly; the end of the tail reached halfway down to the ground.

"So, that's a funnel cloud." Ben worked to hide his growing apprehension, but his tongue felt heavy and his mouth had gone dry. He'd done his research. There was a greater risk of tornados in the springtime, but most of them were reportedly attracted to trailer parks. At least, that's what he'd read, though there was no scientific basis for it. Still, half of all deaths from tornados were of those who lived in mobile homes.

And there's not a trailer park for miles.

But the truth was that Ben knew more about surfing Pacific waves than tornado weather, and he took in the full measure of Chet's distant gaze.

Chet spat out his tobacco, unwrapped a piece of tinfoil, and chuckled before he bit into his snack.

A pork chop sandwich.

"Don't worry, Doc. I'll let ya know if ya need to run for cover." Brownish-red sauce dripped down the corner of his mouth, and he snickered. Ben suppressed a shudder. Chet was the epitome of what Ben had pictured of the people in South Dakota: checkered flannel shirt, faded jeans, rounded beer belly, and a cowboy hat. He even wore an enormous brass belt buckle, adorned with a grotesque buffalo-skull design.

The dude could be cast right into an old Western.

Ben strolled over to Chet, puffing on his cigar. He reached into his pocket and, despite his inner reluctance, handed Chet one. The security guard palmed it, grinned, and stashed the gift in his jacket.

"Thanks, Doc. Hey, where's your woman?" The chill in the air didn't keep the heat from rising to Ben's cheeks, and he fought the urge to make a snide retort. He stared through Chet's steely gray eyes and tried to imagine burning the optical nerves in his sockets.

"I told you that she's not *my* woman. She's a fellow scientist, and a very good one at that."

"Yeah. Sure." Chet wiped his mouth with the back of his hand. Ben's stare had no effect.

"She's inside, feeding the...pigs." Ben wondered why he shied away from calling them babies. They weren't designed to be animals. Why did he still think of them that way?

The military will treat them like research projects, no matter what you call them.

"Ah. Now, if the girlie were barefoot and pregnant, then she'd be of some real use." Chet met Ben's stare and then looked back at the sky. Ben was trying to come up with a witty response when he noticed Chet's face had turned gravestone gray. The man jumped up from his chair.

"Shit! We've got trouble! Tell that lady friend of yours to run to the cellar!"

Ben looked in the direction of the funnel cloud, and what he saw electrified his nerves like a jolt from a loose-wired wall socket. The spinning cloud had touched ground and was moving their way.

Chet reached over, grabbed his shoulders, and shook him hard, placing his messy mouth right in front the scientist's face. "Doc! We don't got much time! We gotta get below!"

Chet's words finally pierced Ben's brain.

Holy shit!

Ben ran to the door, and his fingers fumbled as he worked to punch the numbers on the cipher lock, a protection he and Miriam had put in place to keep prying eyes out of the lab.

Bursting into the room, he saw Miriam sitting in a rocker with one of the babies in her arms. It was sucking greedily from a bottle. Milk drizzled from its snout after it startled from the bang of the door.

"Run to the cellar, Em!" Ben could barely get the words out.

Behind him, the twister roared.

Miriam looked up from the baby girl she held in her arms and focused on Ben's reddened face and windblown hair. Before she could chastise him, Chet bounded in behind her partner. "Now! Now!" The sound of his voice was muffled by a howl like a freight train growing in the background. Wind whipped into the room, blowing over bottles and scattering papers into the air.

Ben bellowed a word at her. "Tornado!"

Miriam felt as if her blood were draining from her body. She made a quick assessment. All of her research notes were here. She hadn't kept them anywhere else. She'd carefully recorded everything in her paper journals, as well as on her personal computer, which sat just across the far side of the room.

The babies. The priority is the babies.

She lifted the infant to her chest. "Grab the male!"

Ben ran over to the sibling and whisked him up. Miriam scooped as many journals as she could into her other arm, fumbling to hold them and the infant close to her chest.

"Get the laptop!" She could barely hear her own voice now over the increasing roar of the twister bearing down on them.

"For Christ's sake, people! Move! Move out!" Chet headed toward the back door and ran outside to belowground shelter.

Ben went to the computer, ripped it away from its cord, and ran on ahead of her. Miriam stumbled over a chair, but kept the baby safe in her arms. She dropped one of her journals and went after it. The wind pushed her into a wall as she grabbed at the pages.

"Leave it!" Ben was already stepping through the back door. Wood splintered and moaned. A large gust of wind slid a lamp across a table and smashed it against a wall. Miriam scooped up the journal, tucking it under her arm, and barely made it outside. The house groaned and shook madly.

"Here!" Chet held the shelter doors open. A dark hole in the earth yawned before them, ready to swallow the fugitives whole. "Hurry now!"

Miriam stumbled down the porch steps and fell to her knees. Ben set the laptop on the ground and helped her up, keeping a grip on the infant in his other arm. Through her fear and anger, she heard herself growl, "Get below!" Together, they raced toward the shelter. Behind her, she heard debris fly through the air and crash against walls. Glass shattered. The house was coming apart.

Miriam started down the shelter's rickety set of stairs before realizing Ben's arms held only the male baby. She turned to look over her shoulder, and the shock of what she saw made her heart sink. The laptop was still sitting on the grass by the porch steps. She started to go after it, but Chet pushed her back down into the shelter.

"You can't, girlie—not now." He closed the doors overhead with a bang and shoved an iron bolt into place. Miriam pushed against him, determined to save the laptop, but Chet's thick arms wrapped around her, holding her firm. She struggled against him, dropping her journals. And then, the wind of the twister screamed above them. The cellar doors shook furiously, and there was no other choice but to retreat down the steps into the darkness of the earth.

Miriam's eyes watered with anger and frustration. She shook Chet's arms off her. She'd be damned if she would let the men—least of all, Chet—hear her cry. All of her data was on that rectangular piece of technology. They'd backed it up on a hard drive. A hard drive that was still inside the house.

The baby fought inside the grip of her arms, and she realized she'd been squeezing it too tight. She relaxed her hold on it. Though she couldn't see the infant, Miriam still looked down, and the thought occurred to her that it might be the last of its kind.

"I'll never get the genetic code right again," she mumbled.

So many years. So much time. Whisked away with the wind. When the opportunity comes, how will I start over?

The baby struggled once more, and with a sudden flash of inspiration, her despair evaporated and a wave of satisfaction and resolve took its place. She brought the infant to her face and nuzzled against its ear.

At least I have a female.

THREE

April 25, 12:07

Deafening silence replaced the roar of the tornado, and Chet tossed open the doors after waiting a few moments. Miriam emerged from the cellar and felt her knees wobble. Her heart hammered against her ribs as she took in the devastating sight before her. The concrete foundation had survived, as well as some of the cinderblock wall of the lab, but the rest of the house was a mishmash of chaos. Panels of wood, soundproofing walls, furniture, papers, and household items lay strewn under a pile of matchstick boards—large pieces of what might have been the roof.

They left the babies in the cellar, nestled on top of Ben's wool jacket, and shut the doors once more. Miriam stumbled over to the debris and spied a pair of red underwear pinched between two pieces of broken plywood. She grabbed the piece of clothing and stuffed it in her jeans pocket, then her hands reached out to start combing through the rubble, a faint hope of locating remnants of her research surging within her.

I need to find the laptop! And the hard drive. Maybe something survived.

She couldn't imagine what would happen if the information she'd stored fell into the wrong hands. Miriam didn't relish breaking the news of her loss to the Cullers. But, she also knew they monitored the airwaves and computer traffic. They'd discover if someone found the laptop and hacked into the information. Still, the thought of someone accessing her work gnawed at her, and she immediately started digging into the mess until she felt the pressure of a hand on her arm. She whirled, her nerves raw and her body ready to throw a punch, but she stopped before connecting with Ben's gentle face.

"We'll get a recovery team out here, Em. If there's anything left in this mess, they'll find it." He was trying to be logical, which she found oddly amusing; she was usually the rational one. But he had a point. She looked around at the destruction and shrugged her shoulders. "I'll stay and recover what I can. You go call it in." Chet was standing nearby with his hands in his pockets, chewing his tobacco, and surveying the mess. He hocked brown slime on the grass. "Take him with you," she said.

Calling it in presented a problem. Both of their vehicles, one a Chevy pickup and the other a cheap Toyota four door, were sitting upside down on the prairie. Neither was drivable. The closest house was two miles away. Ben and Chet started off down the dirt road, carrying Miriam's hopes that the residents had a phone or might be willing to drive them to town to make a call. She wasn't sure how they'd get back, but Ben was resourceful. At least he'd had his wallet on him when the tornado hit.

———

Harper had just settled down for an evening of well-earned sleep when one of his cell phones rang. His black satin sheets moved around him like a rich pool of oil. Across from him, Man

Ray's "Prayer" glowed softly with the help of an accent light. The picture reminded him of many things: peaches, humility, orgasms, and the fact that some people weren't too far from sticking their own heads up their asses. When he identified the phone that was ringing, he clenched his teeth. He never got a call on this line unless something was wrong. When he had the cell in his hand, he pressed the button, placed the phone to his ear, and waited.

"We've got a situation." It was one of Harper's fieldmen who kept an eye on the projects.

"What's going on?"

"A twister hit the lab. Looks like everything's been leveled."

"And the team? Projects Eleven-Juliet and Eleven-Kilo?" Harper sat up and gripped the phone, pretending the man was standing in front of him and he had hold of his throat. It was irritating to have to ask for details.

"All safe, sir. They made it to the underground shelter just in time."

Harper would bet his ticket to the Underground that they owed their lives to Chet. The man was a royal ass, and the military had used him up and spat him out dry in Iraq, but despite his unconventional and crusty ways, Chet was a man who got things done. Harper had allowed himself the pleasure of smiling openly earlier in the day, when he thought of Miriam dealing with Chet. She would never know it was him who had put both of them together. She barely knew who the Cullers were. Harper could bank on the fact that she didn't really care as long as they funded her beloved research. Without even trying, she was helping his plans come together seamlessly. In the future, she'd be doing far more for him than she'd ever suspect.

"If you find anything important, make sure you bring it to me."

"Yes, sir!"

Harper's thumb pushed the off button. One stroke of bad luck, and a stroke of good luck. The research lab was destroyed, but the projects were intact. If he could find anything of Miriam's research, he'd hold it for safekeeping. Her knowledge, and that of her partner Ben, was one of the few things that managed to keep them employed. Miriam was wise to store her information on a self-contained computer or in handwritten notebooks. But as much as he loved the woman, there would come a time when the Cullers wouldn't need their lead scientist any more. His boss had made that clear.

Harper felt his eyes sting. Just a little. Miriam had been an excellent trainee. One of his best. Her future wasn't going to be easy, but there'd be a time when she'd have no worries. He'd have to see to that personally. After all, he owed it to her.

The Cullers arrived to clear the wreckage, and they did it in less than three hours. Miriam watched closely as they sifted through and removed the debris. They recovered her purse and a few more notebooks, along with fragments of her hard drive. After looking them over, she reluctantly handed the pieces back to the recovery crew and hoped the Cullers could somehow extract her data.

Ben seemed doubtful about allowing them to take the pieces. She tried to reassure him. "If they recover anything, there isn't a scientist in the world who can make sense of what's inside." He raised an eyebrow at the remark, and she added, "Even if they did, it wouldn't do them any good." It staved off his questions and protests for a while. And there was still the matter of her laptop. It was nowhere to be found.

After making some local inquiries, a Lakota man agreed to rent them his house for a couple of weeks. Miriam paid him five thousand in cash—more than most tribal members made in a year. She told him not to ask questions, and he agreed. The man was gone the instant she paid him. He didn't even bother to pack.

May 16, 17:05

Miriam stood on the front porch of the small house. Judging from the inside of the place, she guessed the middle-aged owner was bound for a cheap hotel and some rounds of gambling. Old lottery scratch tickets lay on the floor of the living room, and casino flyers littered the top of his kitchen table. His garbage was filled with empty Budweiser cans and several dead bottles of Jack.

Despite their isolated surroundings, Miriam knew they would have to leave the house soon. Lucky for her, the Cullers had transferred more than enough funds into her account to keep their project going. The organization was quite interested in providing for their developing product. Unfortunately, they also expected a greater degree of control over their investment. Yesterday, Miriam received a phone call that requested that the scientists move their location to the West Coast.

With the funding, they were expected to travel to California and live somewhere in the countryside—at least at first. They would stay there until the children were too grown for her and Ben to handle. And that day wouldn't be long in coming. Even so, she was anxious to see what her little pig-humans could do and gauge their full potential.

I haven't even thought of a proper name to call them.

But then, why did that matter? They would be the *only* ones of their kind, unless Miriam could find a way to breed or clone them.

Ben picked up another laptop for Miriam in Rapid City, but the Internet was difficult to come by so far out in the country. They'd have to put in a satellite dish, and they wouldn't be there long enough. After searching online at the town library, Ben located an abandoned vineyard outside of Bakersfield where they could move their research and stay for a while. Miriam put Chet to work planning proper security for the premises. Neither she nor Ben could afford to let any aspects of their research leak out to the public.

Unfortunately, Chet knew almost everything there was to know about their research. Either they'd have to take him with them or find a way to dispose of him. She didn't like that the Cullers left her to clean up their messes. She was a scientist. Not an assassin. Not anymore.

Miriam had broached the subject to Chet and had offered him the option of traveling to California and setting up a security system for the vineyard. At first, Chet had been reluctant, but then he seemed to have sensed his true bottom-line alternatives. He wasn't as dumb as he made out. When she had given him a creative list of employment options, he'd jumped on board to say he would work for them without any questions.

"Hell, the only reason I saved yer hides was because of what you pay me. I wouldn't get near so good a job here in South Dakota," he had said.

Chet was a practical man, but dangerous. Miriam kept a close eye on him while holding him at arm's length. She didn't like the way he looked at her, especially when they were alone. He was shorter than her, but stockier. More muscular. In a physical struggle, she'd be at a definite disadvantage.

There was only one way she could take him down, and he already knew she carried a Glock. The gun was a gift from her long-time mentor, Harper, and though she was no stranger to firearms, she'd been surprised when she had opened the case he'd given her last year. "You might need it." It was all he had said, which, for him, was a mouthful.

And she just might need it. She remembered a day Chet had come up behind her in the kitchen and slid the back of his hand across her hair.

"You dye your hair red, or is that natural?" He'd said it kind of cocky, touching her like he had the right. She'd brushed his hand away and told him to go tend to the security system outside, her fingers already stretching toward the black metal in her holster. The memory of how he'd laughed when he had walked away made her shiver. She knew his kind.

Miriam was a graduate from the Medical College of Virginia, or MCV, as everyone called it. In her youth, her hometown was filled with farmers and good-ole-boy Virginia yahoos. Most of them were the kind of men who were difficult for a woman of intelligence to stomach. The weekend barn keggers, drunken rides along winding country roads, and clumsy fumblings in the back of Ford flatbeds during hunting season. She had spent long nights dreaming of getting away from the place, its stink, and the persistent blare of whiny country music. Chet reminded her of all those things even though she was miles away from her birthplace. He, and his kind, disgusted her.

But, the man is good at what he does.

Miriam's gaze swept over the grassy lands in front of her. The tan Dakota hills were pockmarked with multiple dirt mounds that spanned the landscape—a testimony to the continuous burrowing of little prairie dogs. The furry animals scampered from hole to hole, playing in the sun, popping up their heads, and standing like stone before squeaking at danger when a hawk flew overhead. Fear, as well as constant vigilance, kept most of them safe. It was the arrogant animal, or the ignorant one, that ended up in the claws of the raptor.

At least I didn't waste my time on those farms.

Some of the boys back home had taught her how to shoot. She'd learned a lot about shotguns, rifles, and pistols in her youth. And she'd learned how to fight from a boxing pro that had lived just a few miles from her house. Her mother had disapproved of the lessons, but her stepfather, a deputy sheriff of the county, had been keen on her learning how to defend herself.

Miriam's accomplishments hadn't stopped there. She'd learned to drive a mean tractor and had fed cows at four in the morning, practicing discipline and never shirking her duties. Not that she'd had much choice. And on the day she turned eighteen, she'd packed her bags and unceremoniously left home. It was the middle of her senior year, and not even her mother's tears had stopped her. If anything, they had spurred her on. She never regretted leaving.

Ben poked his head out the front door. "Miriam? It's time to feed them again."

Miriam gripped the front-porch rail, noticing how the white paint was peeling from the once-sturdy wood. Eventually, the frail ends would break, leaving the wood raw and exposed.

Dear, gentle Ben. He should never have become a research scientist.

The man was ten years younger than her thirty-eight, and he was absolutely brilliant. He was at least six feet tall, and his thin, lanky frame seemed so frail it would break. But he jogged every morning and stayed in shape. Miriam admired his discipline with that part of his life, but she wished he'd apply himself more to the hard sentiments of science. He was too soft, especially for what lay ahead. She'd seen the pain on his face the day Chet took the mother pig out back and killed it, and she suspected Ben prayed over every animal he'd ever euthanized.

I wonder if he has a clue how much harder this job is going to get.

She knew Ben loved the challenge of science and enjoyed the rebellious nature of this project, but he had no understanding of how twisted the experimental rabbit hole was going to get. The upside of putting up with his weakness was she knew he wouldn't get in her way. Not when it mattered.

Miriam followed her partner back inside, and her eyes took in the life of desperate poverty that graced the intestines of the place. There wasn't even an indoor bathroom to use. A small building in the backyard, with a toilet seat that sat above a hole in the ground, served as their latrine. The smell of it crawled through the open kitchen window and permeated the air when the wind blew just right. Which was often.

California is looking better all the time.

They both headed toward the kitchen where the babies waited. In just a few days' time, they'd grown rapidly. Regular pigs doubled their body weight the first week of life, and Miriam swore these little ones were determined to beat that record. Instead of a large fish tank, they now stayed inside a wooden pen that Chet had constructed. It was sturdier than commercial ones designed to keep human children corralled, and it took up most of the floor space in the room.

Baby pigs typically took a little less than four months to mature, but in just a few days, these crossbreeds looked more like toddlers, with the exception of their defined porcine faces. They crawled on hands and knees with legs that were almost human, except shorter and stockier. Their facial features were slightly different from their animal counterparts. Each of them had a snout for a nose, but they had human-looking lower lips. And their eyes were large, expressive, and framed with long, beguiling eyelashes. The male infant, despite being the runt of the two, had quickly surpassed the growth of his sister, and now, he was bigger, chunkier, and ate ravenously at every meal.

As they entered the kitchen, both scientists stopped cold. In the middle of the children's pen, the male infant held a large rat. His thick hands were wrapped around the animal's torso, his mouth blatantly gnawing on the rodent's head. Blood dripped out of the male's maw in a long gooey trail, which ran down his chin. He pulled a hard suck, his lips overlapping the rat's eyeballs and ears, his own eyes closed in the throes of what seemed like ecstasy, and he squeezed the body as if it were a tube of toothpaste. The female sat on the far side of the pen, watching her brother with her jaw open and sheer horror etched on her face.

"Hey! Hey, stop that!" Ben rushed over to the male, leaned across the pen, and yanked the dead animal from the infant's hands. Its fur was drenched with saliva, and the almost-severed head of the rodent flopped over to one side. The male stared up at Ben, his icy glare causing the scientist to flinch.

Miriam noted Ben's reaction and squatted down in front of the male baby, curious. "Where did you get that?" The infant swiveled around and turned his back to her. He seemed rather put out.

"So, you're hungry." Miriam stood up and went to the refrigerator.

In just a few days, the little ones have already outgrown their formula diet.

That worried her a little. She tried not to show it. Piling some lunch meat onto a plate, she placed the dish onto the linoleum floor in the center of the pen. The male turned suddenly, dashed over to it, grabbed the meat in fistfuls, and gobbled it down. The female just watched him, not moving a muscle.

"Ah, so the little guy is greedy. No worries, Petunia." Ben scooped her up out of the pen and took a turn at the refrigerator, opening it up. "What would you like?"

The fridge had little to offer in the way of food options. A bit more bologna was left in an opened package, and there was milk and orange juice, hot dogs, and coleslaw. A container of potato salad sat on the second shelf. To Ben's amazement, the baby pointed with her right hand to the potato salad. She grunted with the motion.

"Seems we have an herbivore in our midst." Ben chuckled, and he noted the odd tone that had crept into his voice. When he glanced over at Miriam, she showed no surprise. His partner's face was as calm as a southern summer pond.

Her behavior is odd compared to her brother.

As an experiment, he moved his hand over to the hot dogs, but the girl insisted with her finger pointed at her desired food. He pulled out the potato salad.

Ben moved to the table with the plastic container. But the female shook her head furiously and pointed to a drawer. She stretched her finger to where they kept the silverware. He moved toward the drawer and opened it up, and of all things, she reached down with her left hand and grabbed a spoon. For a brief moment she seemed happy, and Ben brought her to the table while she played with the item.

He popped off the lid as the female sat in his lap. Ben was blown away when the girl took the spoon from him, fumbled with it at first, and then gripped it tightly, digging into the mix. She removed a dollop of the salad and brought it to her mouth, then ate the heaping scoop in one big bite. She did this again and again, until the container was empty. Her little snout was smeared with yellowish residue, and a few flecks of celery remained between her teeth—teeth usually removed from baby pigs at birth, by farmers.

I'll be damned; it looks like she's smiling! Ben looked over at Miriam after this confounding display.

"You guess she's been watching us eat and putting the idea of food and silverware together?"

Miriam looked from one infant to another, slowly shaking her head. Her silence made him feel as if he'd tumbled on the face of an easy wave and wiped out in front of a crowd. He shrugged his shoulders and tried to think of something witty to say, but what came out of his mouth only highlighted the obvious.

"Something tells me we're going to need a lot more food."

FOUR

May 23, 14:02

Planning the trip to California required some strategy. Miriam needed to rent a U-Haul, or some sort of large truck that they could keep the infants in overnight as they travelled. U-Hauls, however, were not known for their luxurious accommodations. The front seat could hold the three of them, but their seating arrangements would be less than desirable. Particularly for Miriam. She couldn't stand the thought of Chet sitting next to her on a multihour trip. She would never feel comfortable trying to take a nap beside that Neanderthal.

Ben offered a suggestion. "Maybe we could rent a car, too. Take turns driving?"

Clearly, Ben wasn't thinking. Miriam wouldn't trust Chet driving the U-Haul at all. What if he took off with the little ones? She imagined that he'd given it a thought or two—how much they were worth.

"No fucking way." The words sounded harsher than she'd intended.

"All right. You don't have to swear." Ben seemed hurt. In the past, he had pointed out that she never liked his ideas. Which was mostly true. Luckily for her, he was gullible and easily pacified, even when he had a differing opinion. It was part of why she liked him as a research partner. It was so easy to persuade him to accept her viewpoint whenever there was a disagreement between them.

"Sorry." She softened her words. "But, I mean we can't take any chances. I don't want to let those babies out of my sight."

"Well, what do you want to do?"

"Sending Chet on ahead of us was another idea you had. We could do that." Miriam tried appeasing Ben this way, making him believe his idea had merit. Which it did. Just a little. What she worried about most was that Chet would flap his tongue around strangers. He liked his whiskey, and if he drove on alone, she knew he'd eventually stop at a roadside bar. And then, he'd drink. And after that? She preferred not to think of the potential fallout.

In the end, Miriam purchased a nice, shiny pickup, a black Ford F-150, and presented the keys to Chet during their pizza dinner, jingling them in front of him with a matador's flourish.

"We need you to have that security system ready when we arrive. Do you think you can handle it? You've got just two days."

He grabbed the keys from her fingers with gusto. "Sure, babe. Just for you." He gave her a sly wink.

It was all she could do to keep her skin from crawling out of the room without her.

"Just be sure not to talk to anyone about our research. Understood?"

Chet grinned at her as he got up. It was his only response. In less than an hour, he was heading out the door, stuffing a wad of cash into his front pocket. Fresh bills Miriam had given him for gas money and food.

"You need to be there in two days," she called after him, hoping her emphasis on the deadline would keep him away from the beer.

"Hey, don't worry 'bout a thing." He tipped his cowboy hat and disappeared through the doorway. They heard the truck roar as he spun its wheels down the dirt road that led into town. He'd still have a ways to go before he reached the interstate.

"Okay. We need to pack," Miriam told Ben as they got up from the table, glancing at the two infants munching on pizza remnants. "And we need to bring food."

---

24 May, 22:00

Ben took his turn driving. It was over an hour since they'd passed the Utah state line on I-70. The town of Green River was just forty miles away, and Miriam was feeling the first pangs of hunger. She hoped they could find a fast food place to pull over and grab something hot to eat. Even a greasy hamburger would taste good right now.

"All I'm saying is we need to call them something. Saying 'hey precious' is getting a little old now, don't you think?" Ben had nagged her on this topic since they started the trip.

Miriam slowly inhaled and reminded herself to be patient. "To name them is to get too close to them. You learned that when you worked at NIH." She was growing weary of the discussion. He seemed hell-bent on naming their experiments, and she had to admit she hated calling them pet names, too. There was nothing that the little beasts could particularly answer to, and they were obviously ready for some increased challenges to their intelligence. How could she study their potential without calling them by name?

Thing One and Thing Two.

Ben plied her. "C'mon, Em." He looked over at her, his brown puppy dog eyes doing their pitiful act, trying to influence her on just this one thing. She decided to give in. It was a small victory she could allow him.

"What would you call them? Hypothetically, of course."

"Well, I'd name the male Gevurah, maybe Gevu for short. It's from Kabbalah, meaning strength or power."

Miriam tried not to roll her eyes. It was like him to pick something esoteric. Still, she had to admit she was interested in his thought process.

"And the girl?"

Ben seemed excited that she was actually listening to him. "I thought maybe something that matched his and, yet, went with her personality." He paused, then continued. "I want to call her Binah." Ben's eyes focused intently on the darkening road. He made it appear as if he was being hypervigilant, watching out for little critters that might bound onto the highway, but Miriam knew he was really waiting for her approval.

"And Binah means..."

"Understanding. She is quite that, don't you think?"

"Gevu and Binah." Miriam let the names roll off her tongue. As she did, a strange little shiver tickled its way down her spine. The children were named. So be it.

Ben glanced over at her again and tentatively smiled. She smiled in return, thinking about how easily he was won over, but when she looked back to the road, her senses screamed.

"Ben! Look out!" A large pair of glowing red eyes rose up in front of them in the darkness, and then several more floated up from the ground.

Ben hit the brakes. "Shhhhittttt!" He swerved and plowed past the sea of glowing orbs. The U-Haul hit a ditch and flipped over on its side, skittering to a halt. Dust and dirt surrounded them in a swirling cloud and started to settle over the windshield and side window.

"Em! Are you okay?" Ben's body was against the window closest to the ground. Miriam was hanging over him, dangling from her seatbelt. She took in a breath, and Ben immediately felt a surge of relief. She coughed.

"What was that?" A drop of her blood hit him on the face.

"My best guess? Elk. Quite a few of them. Jesus. They came out of nowhere." Ben unbuckled himself, then reached up to try to free Miriam from her restraint. It was close quarters. In the back of the U-Haul, they could hear the babies yelling—no, only one was yelling; the other was screaming.

Gevu and Binah! Miriam was surprised at how quickly she'd already accepted their names. She had to get out of the vehicle and check on them. Ben freed her from the seatbelt, and she landed on the window next to him. At least the front seat of the truck was wide enough that it allowed for some movement.

"Push me up, will you? I'll roll the window down, and we should be able to get out." Ben helped her reach up to the passenger door, and she was thankful the glass hadn't shattered. She cranked the handle until the entire window was open, then she crawled out and waited to grab Ben's hand as he came through the makeshift exit.

There was a nasty gash across his forehead, probably where his head had hit the steering wheel. The blood drizzling into her eyes let her know she'd been injured too. She wiped her forehead with the back of her hand and stared at the red smear across her knuckles. It didn't seem very big. She must have hit her head on the dashboard.

Ben stumbled toward the back of the U-Haul, yelling amid the pigs' vocalizations. "It's all right, guys! Don't worry!" He started to turn the handle to the door and almost laughed at the words printed on the back of the U-Haul. *Moving Made Easier.* He gripped the metal, expecting some difficulty, but the handle twisted with ease.

Obviously the advertisers for the company didn't think about possible encounters with elk when they came up with that slogan.

He desperately hoped the roll-up door hadn't become too damaged from their unconventional landing.

Miriam was standing beside him. Calm. Watching.

Nothing ever seems to get her overly excited.

Ben pushed at the door, having to shove it open on its side. It moved a little, but it was difficult to budge. The children had quieted down, but at least one of them was crying softly. He glanced at Miriam, whose mouth was set into a tight, expressionless line. He tried again and was able to budge it a little more. Putting as much of his weight as he could against it, he finally pushed it open enough to get inside the truck.

The children's crates were secured with cargo straps and had held up beautifully despite the crash. Each of the little ones had righted themselves, with Binah on the side closest to the ground and Gevu directly above her. Apparently, Gevu had evacuated his bowels sometime after their landing, and Binah was soiled with his excrement. She was sobbing softly, and Gevu glared at him. Coolers of food and drink were none the worse for wear, but their suitcases and a few other boxes filled with notebooks and other research materials they'd salvaged from the tornado were strewn all over the side of the U-Haul, which now served as the floor.

Ben called back to Miriam over his shoulder. "They're okay, Em!" She didn't answer him. He went back outside, only to discover Miriam was trying to make a call on her phone.

She gave him a disgusted look as she faced him. "No service." A car whizzed past them, traveling in the opposite direction, hurtling down the road at breakneck speed. It didn't even slow down.

"We've got two units in place. One near the truck, and one with the U-Haul."

Harper listened to the report from the junior man on the other end. "Make sure they maintain contact. When Chet arrives in Las Vegas, send in the extra unit."

"The extra unit, sir?"

Harper gave the junior man the contact information and then ended the call. After years of working with Chet in the army, Harper knew just where he'd go. He patted the battered laptop that sat on his desk. All of the information on it was still intact. Despite a few setbacks, things were going well. Very, very well.

"See to the little ones. I'm going to get us a ride." Miriam realized, after the fact, that her voice sounded harsh. Ben didn't deserve her anger. The truth was she knew what she had to do, and she loathed being slave to her gender.

Yes, it was the new millennium and men took less kindly to helping stranded women than they used to, but she reasoned that if a traveling man saw her in distress without a male counterpart, she'd have more luck catching a ride.

I hate this.

She walked over to the highway. Ben disappeared inside the truck.

Miriam stepped out on the road and readied herself, preparing to flag down the next oncoming driver.

What will I do if someone actually stops? Her brain whirled in a vortex of various options, and some of them weren't pretty. A few minutes later, a large tractor trailer came barreling toward them. It was traveling in their chosen direction. Miriam took a chance and stepped out into the middle of the road. The truck blared its horn at her and then began to slow. The plight of their U-Haul was clear; the man couldn't miss it. But he didn't stop. Instead, he edged by her at reduced speed, a mike from his CB radio in his hand. He pointed to it. "I'll call up the county mountie to help you out!" His voice disappeared into the roar of the engine as he rumbled by.

Damn it! That's the last thing we need. Police. Miriam tried not to let the panic that pulsed in her gut get to her. She spotted the headlights of another vehicle headed toward Green River. It slowed without provocation, and an elderly man stuck his head out of a silver GMC pickup. It had a cab on the back, which suited their needs perfectly.

"Can I give you a hand?"

"Yes, please!" Miriam's heart thumped in her throat. She couldn't let him see Gevu and Binah. Hopefully, her gun didn't look too bulky strapped underneath her shirt. She didn't want him to shy away simply because she was carrying a firearm. He pulled up behind them and parked the truck.

He jutted his chin toward the U-Haul. "That's some nasty business. And so far away from the city."

Miriam managed to curl her lips into a grateful smile. "We've got just a few things in the back. If you wouldn't mind, we can load them up and catch a ride with you to Green River."

The man reached up to scratch the side of his head, which was decorated with a well-worn baseball cap. The Salt Lake Bees emblem was proudly displayed on the front.

"Gee, miss. I wasn't planning on going that far."

She gave him a distressed and pleading look. The best one she could manage. "I'd be happy to pay for gas, if that's okay. My partner and I really need to make it to somewhere safe for the night."

As if on cue, Ben emerged from the truck, a couple of suitcases in hand. The man got out of his truck, eyeing Ben, probably making a quick assessment of him. Ben had an affable look that immediately won over just about anyone that met him. He strode up to the man.

"Wow! I'm really glad you stopped. We were in a bind, that's for sure." He held out his hand in a friendly gesture, the headlights of the man's truck making Ben's simple smile glow. The man reached out a hand. "Name's Emmet. Emmet Fisher." They shook hands.

"Emmet, we've got a few things that with your help, we could load up into your truck."

Their plight was evident, and clearly, Emmet didn't think they'd harm him. Apparently, his chivalrous attitude won out. "Back of the truck's empty," he said, "and I got no place in particular to be right now. See'n as you're willing to pay for the gas, what can I help with?" He started to approach the U-Haul.

"No. Please. Wait here." Miriam held out her hand. "Ben and I will get our things."

Ben lugged the suitcases over to the back of the cab while Miriam went into the U-Haul. She grabbed a box and came out again, still wondering how she would get their odd little infants past the Good Samaritan. Emmet leaned against the truck and waited as they loaded the rest of their gear. All that was left was Binah and Gevu. She gave Ben a look as she walked up to Emmet and started conversing with him.

"We've got a particular bundle Ben will have to ride in the back with, if it's okay with you."

Emmet drew away from her for a moment.

"It's not illegal, is it?" There was a sudden edge of concern to his voice, which Miriam knew she needed to squelch.

"No. Not at all." She faltered for a moment trying not to tell the man too much. "My partner and I have couple of small animals we need to transport. Their crates are ruined, and I need him to watch them. That's all."

Emmet seemed relieved. "Well, miss, I'm a farmer. What kind of animals?" He watched her face closely. It was clear he was a bit suspicious.

"Pigs. Young pigs," she said truthfully, hoping the honesty in her voice would calm his anxiety. "We keep them as pets. They don't like strangers, and this crash has got them pretty scared."

"Huh. You don't strike me as the pig type," he said looking her up and down. She felt a bit awkward and self-conscious in her blue designer jeans and bloodstained Jones New York white blouse. "Suit yourselves." Emmet climbed back into the driver's seat and waited.

I'll bet he's wondering what he's gotten himself into.

Miriam followed his lead and climbed in on the passenger side. Just then, Ben emerged with two rounded lumps of blanket. One bundle was squealing and struggling. Miriam turned to Emmet.

"Could you shut off the headlights? Just for a moment?" Emmet eyed her quizzically, but he complied, and as soon as Ben was past the window, she signaled Emmet it was okay to turn them on again. "The bright lights, you know." It was a lame explanation, but Emmet seemed to accept it.

"I'll help fasten them in," Emmet said as he climbed out of the front seat and headed toward the back of the cab. Miriam opened her door too and followed him on the other side of the vehicle.

Ben was inside, holding two gray-blanketed lumps. Miriam kept Emmet's attention on her as she assisted him, praying the animals would stay hidden completely, but just then, a little snout poked out through a fold of fabric despite Ben's best efforts to keep them covered. Emmet grinned. "Aw. Cute little thing... "

Miriam cut him off as she pulled down the top window of the cab. "Yes. But troublesome when they're not in their crates. Let's hurry please, Emmet."

Emmet cleared his throat and turned the handle to secure the door. He tapped on the cab. "You let us know if you need anything," he called to Ben, then he and Miriam walked up to the front of the truck. They climbed in, and Emmet turned the key. The truck roared to life, and he eased back onto the highway. They had just started down the road a couple of miles when a police car raced by them. Emmet furrowed his brows as the vehicle passed, but they drove on in silence for a while.

"You get into town, and you'll find a tow service that can help you out," he said. His eyes were fixed in front of him. It was clear he felt the situation was awkward, and Miriam was no good at small talk. She hoped the miles would fly by.

―――

May 25, 01:06

A few country songs later, they pulled into town. What Emmet called a city was a far cry from the definition of the word, but it would have to do. She'd talked him into dropping them off at a motel. The neon sign of the Sleepy Holler flickered off and on as he waited for Miriam to check in and get a room.

"Can you back up?" Miriam pointed to a door on the ground floor, and Emmet turned the back of the cab toward the room. She got out and walked over to his door. He was preparing to get out and help them unload. "Don't worry. We've got it." She handed him three fifty-dollar bills. Emmet's eyes went wide. "Well, thank you." It was obvious he hadn't expected that much, but he took the cash without a protest.

"Just give us a minute, will you?" Miriam gestured for Emmet to wait, and she opened the cab and grabbed one of the bundles from Ben.

"How was your ride?" she muttered. She grasped the squirming load under her arm, then carted it to the door and slipped the key into the lock.

"Miserable. Thanks for asking." Ben followed just behind her. Miriam turned the key. Her bundle kicked violently, and the infant dropped from her arms. And there was Binah, crying and uncovered for the whole world to view. She placed the blanket over her quickly, hoping Emmet hadn't noticed Binah's very human appendages. They rushed to take the babies into the bathroom, and Ben shut the door. When they returned, Emmet was standing outside of the truck. He looked pale.

"You guys okay?" He studied the ground after he asked the question and shuffled his feet a bit before he looked back at her. "I can help you if you'd like. Make it a little quicker."

"Sure," Miriam said. She tried to act nonchalant. Deep inside she had a suspicion Emmet had glimpsed their secret. If he'd seen Binah, well—she didn't want to think about it, but the thought came anyway.

The Cullers aren't near enough to help me. And Ben can't. Wouldn't. Won't. He can't know.

Miriam turned and smiled at Ben, and they unloaded the rest of the truck. It took only minutes. She checked her cell phone. Finally, she had service.

Then, she said, "Ben, why don't you get the animals settled? I'm sure Emmet won't mind letting me off at the convenience store just down the road. We need a few groceries." She flashed her damsel-in-distress look at Emmet once more, hoping the ploy would work.

When he agreed, she lifted her eyes to the sky and praised Watson and Crick. They both climbed into the front seats, leaving Ben to stand at the entrance to the hotel room with a bemused look on his face. Emmet turned the truck back the way they had come. The convenience store she'd spotted wasn't too far away.

Miriam looked over at Emmet and studied him. He had a face full of wrinkles, but it was creased with more smile lines than those of worry, sadness, or anger.

How much of Binah did he see?

"It's been a tough time, Emmet."

"I can imagine."

"Do you mind if we drive a little further with the windows open? I really need to shake off the effects of that crash."

"Sure thing," he responded, bobbing his head just a little. He didn't glance her way but seemed to be in deep thought.

"Our animals drive us a bit crazy," she ventured after a few minutes. "But they're very special to us."

"I can see why," he said. She raised an eyebrow, and Emmet went on. "I saw you drop that little one. Didn't seem right."

"How do you mean?"

"Those little hands and feet. They're not normal pigs, are they?"

She squeezed her eyes shut for a moment, and when she opened them again, her chest felt heavy.

"Can I trust you, Emmet? Do you want to hear a story?"

Emmet's eyes flickered with interest. "Yeah, sure."

"Pull over here, at this little road, and I'll tell you."

Emmet turned the truck onto a winding dirt road and rolled to a stop.

"Do you mind if we walk a bit?"

Emmet shook his head. They got out of the truck and stood on the road, both taking a moment to gaze up at the stars. The sky was packed with them. She told him about their experiment at NIH and how they'd brought the mother pig to the Indian reservation. She told him about Gevu and Binah, and their trip to California.

"And you must promise to tell no one. It's really important. Do you understand?"

Emmet's eyes were wide with interest the entire time she'd confessed her role in the experiment. "Sure," he said. "Seems like you folks have been through a lot." They turned to go back to the truck, but Miriam stopped and reached out to him. He held her in a hug, perhaps hoping to comfort her.

"I'm so sorry, Emmet."

She watched him gaze down at her and took note of the questioning look that crossed his face. "Sorry for..."

He never finished the sentence. Her finger pulled the trigger, the muzzle flush against his body, almost silencing the shot. He crumpled to the ground. She finished the job with a shot against his right temple and left his body on the dirt as she marched back to the truck. It took only moments to drive within cell phone range.

She dialed the numbers, and the line picked up. No voice came across on the other end. Despite hearing only the crackling sounds of static, she gave a brief report.

"U-Haul crashed. Projects in danger. Green River, Utah. Dead end ten miles out. Cleanup requested." Once she'd included the directions, the phone line became eerily quiet.

Now, what do I do with the truck?

She decided to drive it and park close to the convenience store, being careful to stay clear of any possible video cameras. The Cullers would confiscate the tapes anyway if they found Emmet's truck there, but she didn't want to take any chances.

She wiped her prints clean from the steering wheel, dialed in the truck's position, left the keys in the ignition, and then entered the store and went shopping. She wondered if there was another truck rental place in town. Hopefully, they could find something to take them the rest of the way to California. After picking out some sandwich meats, bread, milk, and cereal, she checked her items at the counter, grabbed her bags, and started to hitch a ride back to the motel.

It was only moments before a local police car pulled over toward her. A friendly looking gentleman, no more than twenty-five or so, rolled down his window and asked her to get in. "We don't normally do this kinda thing, but it's a slow night," he said.

Miriam started to turn down the invitation. Her hands were trembling. She wondered which decision would be more conspicuous—declining the ride or accepting it. What if he discovered she was the renter of the crashed U-Haul just a few miles out of town? He'd certainly start asking her questions on their ride.

"No, really, I'm okay..."

"Ma'am, I insist. There are all kinds of lowlifes traveling these highways. Let me keep my conscience clear."

She looked thoughtfully at his police hat and his radio on the dash. He even had a computer sitting near the front of his seat.

"Sure." Miriam breathed in deep, flashed him her teeth, and tried not to succumb to the tension headache building across her brow. Not only would she have to make up a story for Ben about what took her so long, but she was going to have to play the game with Dudley Do-Right. Just as she was getting ready to climb into the car, a call came over the radio.

"Car seventeen. Car seventeen. Possible one-eighty-seven at South Wilford Road. Please respond."

The policeman looked at her wistfully. "I'm sorry, ma'am. Gotta go." He turned his car around and headed back in the direction that she had come from. The Cullers hadn't arrived in time.

Shit.

As she caught the glow of the hotel lights in the distance, she began making up a story to tell Ben, hoping to Einstein that something would help pull her out of this one. She had to protect Gevu and Binah at all costs.

"She called in a cleanup, sir. But we were too late to respond."

Harper's junior man described the situation, and Harper caught himself clenching his teeth and deliberately relaxed his jaw. It was then that an idea sparked in his brain. "It's okay," he said. "Just get her a vehicle. I'll handle the rest."

"But, sir... "

"I said I'd handle the rest. You got a problem with that?"

"No, sir, but the police..."

"It will work in our favor if we need it too. Just do as I said."

"Yes, sir."

Harper's lungs sucked in air slowly, and then he exhaled. It was time for him to exercise, but he'd make another call first. He pulled out a new cell phone, and he scrolled through a few numbers until he obtained the one he wanted.

"Foster," the man on the other line answered.

"Emery County Sheriff?" Harper already knew the answer; formalities were tedious, but it was the name of the game.

"You got him. Who's this?" The voice had a hard edge to it, despite the long, drawn-out syllables.

"Agent Reznick. FBI."

"Got proof of that?"

"Sure." Harper noticed a bit of dirt under his fingernail and picked at it. "I'll fax that on over to you along with the rest of the documents."

"What documents would those be?"

Harper let his face relax. His voice needed to sound confident. Self-assured. "Your murder case. Old man in Green River. Emmet Fisher."

"How did you know?"

"Like I said, FBI. Your suspects are the same suspects we're investigating. This is a federal matter now. Our agents will be there soon to take over."

"How do you know who we have as sus—"

Harper cut him off. "Two travelers in a flipped-over U-Haul. One male. One female. That about right?"

The line was silent for a moment. Harper heard the man blow his nose. "You got it right."

"As I said, this is a federal matter now. I'm sending two men over, and they'll take your statement, as well as any reports from your staff. I'll fax the documentation in just a minute." Harper was at his computer clicking away as he spoke.

"We ran prints through CODIS and came up with a match."

"I know." Harper guessed what was coming next. They always thought they had more information than he did.

"You've identified who the suspects are?" The sheriff's voice sounded a bit surprised.

"Dr. Miriam Wetzel and Dr. Ben Skylar." His staccato voice didn't even sound like him for a moment. Too rehearsed. He mentally kicked himself. "They're under investigation. Probable kidnapping and theft of government property. Our staff is on it as we speak."

Harper gave him the agent's name and got ready to hang up.

"Don't you need my fax number?"

"I've already got it." Harper hung up the phone and faxed the information he'd prepared just in case such a scenario arose. It was all going perfectly. Better than he'd ever dreamed.

"Dear, dear, Miriam," he whispered under his breath, "I taught you not to trust anyone. Not even me."

FIVE

May 24, 22:00

Chet loved the neon lights of Las Vegas. Something about their wild, electric glow sent a thrill through him. The pulsating colors were a drug—utterly hypnotic, and suddenly he was more relaxed, easier than he'd felt in weeks. Riding along the main Vegas drag in the brand-spanking-new Ford F-150 made him feel like more of a man than he'd felt in years. He was instantly young and had a rising hard-on from the sensations hitting him all at once.

The pressure from the roll of cash in his front pocket pulled at his mind. He'd driven a long way, and fast, without stopping, just to have the time he wanted in the proverbial Sin City. His throat was parched, and he longed for an ice-cold beer and a shot of Irish whiskey. The wind from the open window blew him kisses filled with scents of the high-roller world.

And I'm gonna drink that beer, damn it. I've got plenty of time to sail into California before the science geeks get there.

And there was the matter of the pigs. He didn't know how, but he would find a way to sneak those two freaks away from their owners. All he needed was some time and a well-crafted plan.

Fetch a good bit of greenback, those little freaks of nature would.

He'd have to be crafty in how he did it though. The geek skirt was just a woman, but she was a smart woman nonetheless. Smarter than her wimpy-assed partner, that's for sure. He'd almost busted a nut watching the alfalfa-eatin' sissy try to smoke a cigar that day of the tornado, imitating what he thought was a real red-blooded man.

Stick to yogurt and tofu, boy. Chet shook his head. *Yeah, it takes all kinds to make the world go round, but the world would spin smoother if all the wimpy-assed faggots just got the fuck off.*

Chet chuckled at his own inner wit as he passed by a cluster of hookers on the corner, and his semihard erection grew firmer and pressed against the wad of cash in his pocket, sending a shiver of pleasure up his spine. Totaling the amount in his head, he figured he had at least a thousand bucks sitting there. Fuck it. He'd stop for the night. He had time. And he had the money.

"A stiff drink, a loose lay, and call it a day." True wit. And women liked a smart man. He winked at the girls and grinned. The Ford pulled to a stop, and he opened the door. A buxom, black female sporting a lavender tube top and golden shorts riding up past the curve of her butt cheeks slid in on the passenger side. She was rocking a pair of high-top black boots. Her Afro hair was full and round, and it shimmered when she turned her head. He kept the door open and jutted his chin to her friend.

"How much for both of you? For the next couple hours?"

"You enough man for two women, honey?" The black woman placed a long red fingernail against his face. She traced it alongside his jaw. He grabbed her hand and pulled it down between his legs. "Let's find out, shall we?"

The second girl, a fair-skinned redhead with hair flowing straight down the middle of her back, slid in as well and gave him a pretty smile. "Four hundred for each of us, big man. Are you down for that?"

It was a Tuesday night. He knew the hotel would run less than a hundred midweek, and he'd saved a bit more cash over the past few months to cover his expenses.

"Come to papa."

He pulled around a corner and into the parking lot of the Rocket Hotel. It was home of the infamous Pinko Taco, a little Mexican restaurant and bar decorated with neon Pepto-Bismol lights. Fluorescent trim of pink paint framed the walls of the building. He loved staying here. It was one of the places he itched to go whenever he hit Vegas and had the time. And he was going to make time now, damn it. *He* was worth it.

Chet sauntered into the hotel, a girl on each arm. The clerk signed him into a room with a king bed for the night. He liked that description. King bed. And tonight he *was* king, with a couple of hot bitches on his arms for luck. He didn't mind shelling out the dough. In Vegas, these ladies were safer than the usual street traffic. The business wasn't exactly legal in Las Vegas proper, but Clark County had legalized it and good pimps made sure that their merchandise was clean. He'd heard many of the girls had to get regular STD checks just to keep up with surrounding competition. Besides, he always played safe. Too many trips to the medic when he was in Korea had taught him to wear a glove if he wanted pussy love.

"You ladies mind downing a drink or two before we have some fun?" He tugged at their elbows, his question more of a statement than a choice. They went along with him, the pouts on their faces telling him that they hoped he had the money. To make them feel comfortable when they got to the bar, he flashed his cash as he made his order.

"Jameson. Straight," he told the bartender. "Three fingers. And for the girls, whatever they want." Both women ordered mimosas and gently sipped their round. Chet hammered his drink back and ordered another. The girls weren't much on conversation. So much the better. He'd make sure they pleasured him, kick them out afterward, and then take a nap. Later, he'd eat some good food and get back into the truck and drive.

He eyed the Afro woman. "What's your name, honey?" A third drink was in his hand in just a matter of minutes, and the girls started rubbing on each other's thighs, increasing his excitement. His eyes lingered on their breasts and their too-tight shorts riding up their firm, rounded asses. He was about to grab them both and take them to his room when he heard a rich feminine voice behind him.

"No fucking way! Chet! That you, Chet?"

His tongue pressed against the side of his cheek. *Shit. Not here. Not now. Where the* hell *did* she *come from?*

He turned in his seat, and sure enough, there sat Stella in all her glory. She'd changed over the past couple years. More wrinkles on her face, and maybe a boob job because her tits looked fuller. Still, she was as attractive as ever, with her long blond tresses done up in a bun of ringlet hair. The girls sitting beside him started to look pissed. They raked their eyes over Stella and then stared back at him.

"We doin' this?" said the redhead. "We're not hanging out for free."

Stella sidled over to him. Her stature was a good deal shorter than the leggy girls he'd brought to the bar.

"You slummin', Chet? Let the fish go back to the street, baby. I can do more for you in a night than either one of these loose twats."

She flashed them an evil smile, and in response, the black woman's hand jetted into the air, ready to smack a set of red nails across Stella's cheek. But Chet's reflexes were faster. He caught and gripped the girl's wrist midstrike, gently kissed it, and put it down at her side. In one fluid motion, he pulled some cash out of his front pocket and handed each one of them a hundred-dollar bill.

"Beat it," he said, his tone bordering magnanimous. "You both got plenty of time to catch some more business."

The redhead leaned her mouth against his ear and gave it a long, sensuous lick with her soft pink tongue. "You're gonna regret it, big guy. Woulda' been the time of your life."

"No doubt. No doubt." He chuckled with a catch in his throat, openly letting her see his regretful grin, and he copped a quick feel of her breasts before she turned to go. Afro girl spun around and wiggled her buns against him. It was the most she could do for a hundred bucks.

"Thanks for the drink." She winked at him, and together, the girls sauntered to the door, hanging on each other like ardent lovers. They stopped just inside the doorway and pressed their lips together while running their palms up each other's crotch line. Chet thought he'd explode at the sight of them feeling each other, and he soaked up the moment, visualizing pink and black pussy and how he would have screwed each one of them till they screamed.

His eyes lingered on them until they walked out the door, then he looked back at Stella. Her little pout was predictable. Full lips pursed outward, betraying a hint of impatience behind them. At least he knew what he could do with that pout later. From the look on her face, he was certain of that.

Chet also knew Stella was a force to be reckoned with. The last time they'd worked together, they'd cleaned out a few high rollers at a casino in Glacier Peaks. She was both beauty and brains wrapped up into a tight little package. And he bet himself that if the cash potential was right, he could talk her into helping him for a fraction of the total take on the snotty-nosed animals. Then he could pay back some of the debt he owed. Hell, maybe pay it all back. Until then, there was no way he could return to his hometown. He missed Sturgis.

Chet gave Stella a winning grin.

"Hey, babe, don't sweat it. Those girls got nothing on you. I was just taking time to admire the view." The rhyme came out before he realized it. Damn, he was clever.

"And what about now?" She stuck out her chest, the cleavage of her white, pearly boobs parted slightly under the low-scooped blue dress she wore. His hands itched to squeeze them, but he played the game and looked into her sapphire eyes. He noticed her pupils were large. Dilated. She seemed genuinely happy to see him. He was gonna get what he needed. His eyes drifted down again to her breasts.

"View's definitely improved." He stared at her hardening nipples just underneath the fabric and thought about how this trip had become six-hundred-dollars cheaper. "Come to my room for another drink. You can tell me what brought you to Satan's playground."

"Who needs another drink, baby?" Stella was amazing. She didn't skip a beat as she caressed his neck. It was probably habit, but Chet felt a twinge of suspicion. Most people would want to catch up on old times, find out what had been going on in each other's lives and so on before getting down to rocking the sheets. Stella seemed roaring to plow past the formalities and get to the pillows. Or maybe the shower. She'd always liked it in the shower.

Gotta keep an eye on this bitch, as always. But he liked that she was a double-dealing, two-timing cunt. Stella served only to reinforce his opinion that there were two kinds of women. The kind you married and the kind you used for pleasure. The science-geek lady didn't fit into either one of those molds, but one day, he was determined to make her fit. With that thought, he couldn't help but let a smile leak out and smear across his face.

Chet knew that in a few minutes, when he was riding Stella, he'd be picturing the science whore beneath him and fantasizing what he was going to do with her after he took away her prized pigs. He'd let her know exactly what kind of woman she really was.

Chet grabbed Stella's arm.

"Oww!" She gave him a sharp glance, wincing in a moment of pain. She seemed to hesitate.

"Sorry, baby. It's just that I need you in a bad way, and I want you now."

Stella's mouth parted with his words, and a little breath escaped from her lips. Chet placed his hand on the small of her back, and he guided her from the room. Together, they headed to the place where he'd be king for a night. And as they moved, Stella chuckled softly like a woman who'd won a prize.

SIX

May 25, 05:02

Binah peered over at her brother. The cold tile floor was uncomfortable. In their exhaustion, they'd napped for a while, but when they woke, they realized they were still trapped inside a place the White Coats called a *bathroom*. Binah looked over at the large white trough. It had a silver spigot on the end and shiny handles. It was similar to what Dr. Wetzel had bathed her in before. The doctor, she remembered, had called it a *tub*; and over to her left, stood what she knew was a sink. What perplexed her, though, was the white bowl next to her. It was shorter than the sink, almost oval in shape, and it held water that sat too far down at the bottom to easily get a drink. She stood on her legs and pushed herself up to look inside. It smelled of some type of chemical. She drew back in distaste.

"What do we do now, Gevu?" Binah said softly under her breath. Her brother was examining the doorknob of their prison. He didn't immediately acknowledge her, but after a few heartbeats, only said, "Wait."

Binah sat on the tile floor and fidgeted. Dr. Wetzel had left with the man in the truck a while ago, and Dr. Skylar was in the large part of the room, just on the other side of the door. There was a noise coming from inside, but it wasn't Dr. Skylar's voice. The sounds in the room varied, changing over time, much like some of the pictures and noises she'd seen when both the doctors looked at the thing they called a *laptop*. She crawled over and sat at the door, staring at Gevu, and he stared back at her for a moment. His thick eyelids and big round snout gave him a brutish appearance. She could tell from the look on his face he was already up to something.

Do I look the same as him? She found herself wondering about her own features as she observed her brother. Something about him was rough, arrogant, and dangerous. They'd shared their mother's womb. They'd shared their very birthing sack, but after their birth, that was when their sharing had stopped. Still, she thought something in Gevu seemed to realize he needed Binah, and although he was kind to her sometimes, she sensed his occasional platitudes were only to get her to cooperate with his plans for stealing food or other wild antics when he needed her help. And she needed him, too. She learned from him things she wouldn't think of herself. As far as she knew, he was the only other existing creature of her kind. It was a pathologic symbiosis at best.

At their old house, the one they'd lived in for a couple of weeks after the tornado, Gevu had made it a habit to take food from her whenever the White Coats weren't looking. She found it funny he insisted they call them "White Coats," because they hadn't worn white coats since the first days of their birth. And Binah hadn't said anything about him taking her food. As a matter of fact, neither of the children ever said a word. Not to the doctors. But after just a few days of living in the new house, they'd begun to practice talking White Coat language between themselves.

When the White Coats weren't around, Binah and Gevu perfected their speech, mimicking their guardians. There were always careful to avoid being heard, or filmed by those little black boxes Dr. Wetzel set up in front of them. Both of them instinctively knew that was how the White Coats watched them when no one was around. Binah spoke in a soft, whispering voice; Gevu uttered his words in low gravely tones. Both of them realized their alliance was necessary, but neither trusted the other.

Her brother used his voice once more, this time almost teasing.

"Let me see your hands." Binah hesitated a fraction of a second, then held them out to him. His fingers traced her palms. Gevu's hands were much bigger than hers, and when he stroked her thumb, she tried not to shudder. His touch was like coming into contact with cold boogers or poo. Gevu looked back at the doorknob.

"Want to try something new?" Her brother was using his coaxing voice. The one he knew she couldn't resist. When Gevu used his voice like that, she knew he was issuing a challenge, which often led to something they probably weren't supposed to do. Each time she succeeded in one of his challenges, she felt a thrill inside her that she couldn't explain.

"What?" She was curious to see what he had in mind, though she'd already grasped that it had something to do with the doorknob. They were both too short to reach the shiny metal, but they'd seen their guardians turn the knobs several times before.

"Get on my back. See if you can turn it." Gevu followed the order with a sharp whisper. "Do it *quietly*." He turned his back to her, gesturing for her to climb on up. She felt awkward at first and fell off a couple of times. Her toes accidentally poked him in the eye once when her foot slipped, which caused him to growl low under his breath. She tried again, and she found that once she balanced herself, she could grasp the knob with a bit of difficulty. Turning it proved to be a feat, but once she realized all she needed to do was twist it to the right, she was able to make it turn. Then she lost her balance and fell off once more.

Gevu turned toward her for a moment, a devastating look of anger bubbling up on his face, and then he seemed to visibly make himself calm down. "Again," he said.

Binah exhaled in frustration. She was in need of a diaper change. Dr. Skylar had placed fresh diapers on both of them before their ride in the truck, but unlike Gevu, she'd waited to evacuate her bowels. She hadn't done it in the U-Haul. And she hadn't removed her diaper, unlike Gevu who felt the need to be "wild and free" at any opportunity. Even now, her brother's clean diaper was in the middle of the room, discarded with disdain, right next to a fresh pile of his poo.

"Hurry up," he goaded her. "That thing you're wearing stinks." His nose wrinkled with disgust. Binah pretended to ignore his comment and crawled up on him again, determined to turn the knob this time and perform the magical deed that the White Coats did so effortlessly. If she could master this, then she'd be a step closer to being just like them. And she would succeed in doing something that Gevu couldn't do—not yet.

Binah's palm grasped the knob once more; her fingers slid against the surface, but she still managed to grip it well enough to make it turn. Then, she turned it further. Then a bit further. And suddenly, they heard it. *Click*! First, she pulled back on the door ever so slightly, but it didn't budge. Then, she remembered that some doors required pushing to open them. She pushed forward ever so gently, and the door opened. Binah almost fell over in surprise and unrestrained glee. She'd done it! She'd actually opened a door.

Dr. Skylar rested atop a large platform covered with a garish-colored fabric, which was decorated with red squares and multicolored triangular designs. It looked soft. Inviting. How she wanted desperately to be up there with him, curled up on that softness. Both of the children observed the man for a moment and noticed his deep, regular breathing. His eyes were closed.

"He's sleeping," Binah whispered as she climbed down from Gevu's back.

"Yes." Gevu stood up on his hind legs, using the door as a prop. "Let's try the next door."

Binah felt her throat constrict, and she moved backward just a little. The door across the room led to the *outside*. It was a place Dr. Wetzel had said they were never to go alone.

The trip here had been scary and exciting enough. Riding in the truck was interesting, feeling every bump as they rode along on the road. And the rollover they'd experienced had been extremely frightening. When Dr. Skylar had taken them into the back of the strange man's truck, they'd been able to peek out from the blankets as he held them, but they could only see darkness and a few passing lights. Only when Dr. Wetzel had accidentally dropped her before entering this room had she gained a glimmer of understanding about the greater, larger world *outside*.

It was only a brief glance of course, but she'd caught sight of cars sitting on top of a large black surface, and several doors to a building a few levels high. She'd seen lights and the glow of a sign with sharp, blazing colors, a total contrast to the usual white lights. And the smells! So different. Some appetizing and some repugnant. But mostly there were smells that made her mouth water. And now, she realized that she was hungry. It seemed like a long time ago since they'd had their last meal. If she was hungry, then Gevu must be absolutely famished.

Binah crawled over to the platform where Dr. Skylar was resting. Dr. Wetzel called him *Ben*, though she'd told Binah and Gevu his name was Dr. Skylar. She didn't understand why they should know him as one name and Dr. Wetzel called him another. It was confusing.

She turned her face toward the sound of the voices. They were coming from a square, picture-shaped box. What did they call it? She remembered. A *TV*. On the screen, White Coats, like Dr. Wetzel and Dr. Skylar, were talking. Only they weren't wearing white coats. A female seemed to talk right to her, and behind her was a group of males wearing hats and bulky coats, holding a long, thick hose that shot out massive amounts of water. It seemed like they were trying to put out a fire. She knew fire. They'd had a fire in a woodstove at the house where they had lived before. But the fire in the picture was much bigger and burned all over the outside of a building. Binah sat transfixed at the sight until she felt a slight pinch, and she jumped at the touch.

Gevu's head moved in front of her face. "Door," he whispered under his breath, cocking his head in its direction. Binah looked at the door that led to the outside. It seemed huge. Bigger than the one they'd opened before. But instead of a knob, there was just a simple handle.

It can't be that easy. But something inside her couldn't resist giving it a try.

Binah crawled on all fours over to the door. Instead of following her, Gevu used the big platform Dr. Skylar slept on to pull himself up, and then, with what seemed like a concentrated effort, he moved his legs across the floor while he stood upright and held on to the platform. When he reached the end of it, he took a couple of steps with his back feet before he dropped on all fours. He had a triumphant sparkle in his eye. Binah was sure he'd decided to practice his upright walking just to show he had a different edge on her. Since she could open doors, he wanted an achievement of his own.

"Door." He jutted his chin up.

Before she could move, the handle jiggled and the door pushed open. Suddenly, Dr. Wetzel stood before them. She gazed down on them with a hardened look, and then her eyes flickered over to Dr. Skylar.

"I've got food," she told them, placing the bag on the platform where Dr. Skylar rested. She pulled out a package, opened it, and put it down on the ground. With the rustling of plastic bags, the sleeping scientist woke and rubbed his eyes. He looked down at the two of them.

"What were you thinking? Leaving them to roam around free while you were sleeping?" Dr. Wetzel seemed overly agitated, and Binah couldn't figure out why. She wondered what had happened to the man she'd left with in the truck earlier. The man hadn't come back with her. At least there was food. And Gevu seemed happy. He tore at the slices of meat Dr. Wetzel placed in front of him, and Binah sat quietly waiting for her meal. She sniffed the air and then noticed the faint odor of blood. It was ever so subtle, but it was enough to make her shiver and remember the rat her brother had killed. The blood smelled fresh.

SEVEN

May 25, 07:00

Stella hadn't taken much convincing to come with him, and she'd been good company on the morning ride so far. Chet stared out of the front window as he drove, taking in the view. Since passing through Barstow, the red and gold colors of Utah had changed into the low flat brown and sparse dull green of desert. In a couple of hours or so, they'd be at the new farmhouse.

Stella's feet were propped on the dash, a pair of pale blue jeans hugged her fairly trim legs, and the pink nail polish on her toes glittered at him from her well-manicured feet.

Chet snuck a glance over at her again. His eyes roved from her face to the curve of her breasts and then back to trace her handsome neck and jawline. She gazed out at the dusty brown of a barren land, and with the window down, the wind fluttered through her hair and sent streams of it across her cheeks now and then. She tucked a few loose strands behind her ear and caught him staring at her.

"Watcha thinking about, babe?" Her voice wasn't coy, but it had a knowing sound to it. It was like she knew what was going on inside his head. She probably thought he was a bit crazy or that he was exaggerating about the pig gig, but she'd see soon enough. She'd see the bacon babies were real, and he knew her pupils would dial up dollar signs the moment she set eyes on them.

Chet decided to talk a little, just to help win her confidence. After all, the last time they'd worked together, everything had gone sour. It was in Cheyenne, Wyoming, before the days of cell phones and easy text messaging. How was he supposed to have known that she was going to bring the high roller back to his room before Chet was done casing it? He'd needed to know more about the man before he battled him at poker, and Stella was supposed to bed him and talk him into playing a game later that night. When they'd walked in to the room in the middle of his search, things had gone downhill from there.

Oh, he hadn't gotten caught. No. He'd been clever. Stealth was a training gift from the army, and it came in handy even now. But his security buddies saw him leaving the man's room via the videocam, and they'd searched him the moment he'd returned to the floor. Finding nothing, they'd kicked him out with a warning not to come back. So much for friendships and occasional bribes.

Not wanting his indiscretion to impact his pending jobs, he not only left the building but also left town. Unfortunately, that meant leaving Stella.

Now, she was being a good sport about it. Really good-natured. It was odd for her, and the lack of any anger directed at him nagged in his brain. But their meeting had been coincidence, hadn't it? He mulled the thought around in his head.

Chet answered her question. "I'm thinking about how we're going to explain you to your new lab-rat employers. You don't work for the Cullers, and both the science geeks will be suspicious if they see you on the farm without an explanation." Stella just looked at him for a moment.

"We'll think of something, babe." She gave him a winning smile.

"Yeah, we will," he said as he reached out and ran his hand along her thigh and then up to the warm vee of her crotch. She smiled at him again and laughed, low and throaty, then turned to stare back at the California wasteland. He never once saw the bitterness congeal around her eyes.

———

Ben tried to make sense of what was happening. Miriam had come in with an armful of groceries, and the children were scampering inside the room free as birds. He clearly remembered he'd shut the bathroom door well, but somehow, Gevu and Binah had managed to open it. It seemed like days since he'd been able to get a few hours of rock-hard shut-eye. He must have conked out solid.

How could I not hear them fumbling at the door and moving around the room? Thank God Miriam walked in when she did.

But Miriam seemed angry. She probably thought he'd let them out of the bathroom and then fallen asleep. He'd have to explain to her later that the children had done it all by themselves, but now didn't seem the time.

"Gather everything together," she said, as her eyes darted around at a couple of open boxes and a random bit of clothing strewn across chairs and a table. "And keep an eye on Gevu and Binah this time. I'm going to pick up a car."

"You've got a vehicle already?" Ben wondered how in the world she had managed to get everything together so quickly. But Miriam was like that. She made plans and rounded up things faster than anyone he'd ever known. She must have called the Cullers, and in their efficient manner, they were delivering her some sort of transportation.

"Just get the kids ready." Her knife-edged voice made him flinch, and before he could respond, she'd stepped out the door, banging it behind her. Ben got up from the bed and slid the deadbolt home, then twisted the lock.

Let those little guys try to open that. When Ben turned around, he caught Gevu and Binah watching him intently.

Only four weeks old, and they already seem so capable. So aware. Of everything.

The scientist in him was anxious to test their intelligence and get a better handle on their developmental abilities. He packed their meager belongings back into boxes and then grabbed a journal, sat on the bed, and started writing.

The male appears more outgoing. Dominant. Neither animal...

Ben paused and erased the word *animal*. What should he call them? He doodled in the margin, sketching a bizarre cartoon of a human with pig snout, ears, and tail. Swine. Human. Swineman? It would do for now.

Neither swineman has attempted vocal communication, human or otherwise. Communication between each other is primarily done with a series of grunts and physical motions, sometimes involving the hands. It is unclear at this time if they have the capacity for speech.

Ben stopped writing and looked down. Binah still sat in the middle of the floor, staring at the bag of groceries on the bed. Gevu had gobbled up all of the food on the floor. Ben looked inside the bag and pulled out some cheese, a can of beans, and a bag of mixed salad. There was also a pack of diapers and baby wipes. And then he noticed the smell coming from Binah. He put his notebook down and picked her up for a diaper change. Gevu sat in front of the door, diaperless, studying the doorknob.

Study all you want, buddy. You can't tackle that yet.

He changed Binah's diaper, set her down, and then went to the bathroom to dispose of the mess. Gevu's pile of dung and discarded Pampers greeted him on his way to throw the soiled diaper in the trash. He held his breath and cleaned up the mess before the rustling of plastic on the bed caught his attention.

"Binah, I'll get your food in a minute." Ben came out of the bathroom while he was talking. Gevu had managed to climb up on the mattress and was now actively eating the block of cheese, plastic wrapper and all. Ben ran to the bed.

"Hey! Save some for your sister, little guy." Ben reached out to pull the cheese away from Gevu, but the little beast's mouth snapped at him and then caught his hand, gripping it fast.

What the hell?

Sharp teeth sank into his flesh, and when he tried to pull back, he felt the persistent grind of the animal's incisors in his skin.

"Oww! Shit!" He used his other hand to pry Gevu's mouth open and freed his injured palm with some difficulty. He went to the sink to wash it and wrapped it in a towel. When he came back, Gevu had finished the cheese, the bag of salad, and a full pack of Oreos.

"Don't do that, Gevu! It's wrong to bite. Next time you'll be punished. You understand?"

The pig looked at him defiantly, seeming satisfied with himself. Ben needed to talk to Miriam about how they'd discipline them in the future. Simple verbal admonishments obviously didn't work. They needed to be clear how to reward acceptable behavior and how to teach them what was unacceptable.

Binah still sat on the floor, only now her eyes were watery and her lower lip quivered. "Guess it's beans for you, baby." He pulled out a tray from under a couple of coffee cups, popped the top on the can, and dumped them out. Then he went over to Binah, picked her up with his good hand, and took both her and the beans into the bathroom and shut the door. When he returned to the bed, Gevu was rooting through the groceries again. He looked up, and Ben thought he saw a rather-pleased glint in the pig's eye. Swineman. Pig. Animal. Whatever. The little dude had sharp teeth and a belligerent attitude. And he wasn't sure how he was going to handle the creature. Not yet.

May 26, 11:00

Stella made some coffee and sat down at the kitchen table. It was strong. Black. Just the way she liked it. She looked at some of the security systems Chet had recently installed. He was good. Very, very good.

But I'm better, old friend.

Her cell phone buzzed. She flipped it open. An unidentified number. She answered the call and put the phone to her ear.

"We need to get in and set up our own visuals and sound. Can you manage a delay of about thirty minutes?"

"Leave it to me." Stella closed her phone and deleted the call. Then she put on a red tank and a pair of jeans and slipped on some shoes. The sun gleamed in the turquoise sky. It was a glorious day.

Chet pulled out the last few yards of electric wire, ran his gaze along the fence line, and surveyed his work. The sky was the brightest blue he'd ever seen, and there wasn't a house for miles.

Damn I'm good.

The electric fence was gonna be perfect. When most animals experienced the initial jolt from those wires, they never tried escaping their confines again. He knew that much from raising pigs in his youth. And he had wired the entire perimeter around the house and electrified the doorknobs inside the home to boot. A flip of the switch, and those stupid little piggies would get a nasty jingle.

The corner of Chet's mouth turned up as he envisioned the porkers' surprise the first time they felt electricity slam through their bodies. His right hand reached for his belt. Doorknobs and fences weren't the only place they'd feel pain. If he had his way, he'd make them squeal like they never had before. God he hated pigs, and these little shits were worse. They cantered around like they dared to be human. A childhood of shoveling pig shit, dealing with their stink, had put pigs at number one on his animal hate list. There were other reasons too. Ones he didn't care to relive. Chet patted his Taser.

Old Tom Swift here will rock your bodies till you puke.

"What are you mumblin', babe?"

Shit. Stella had come up behind him, and he hadn't even noticed. He was losing his touch.

"Just checkin' my handiwork. I'm gonna flip the switch in a minute." Chet fingered the wire, pushing it out toward her. "Wanna give it a try?"

Stella let out little laugh and gave him a coy smile.

Damn, she looks nice in them tight blue jeans.

She whispered against his ear, her breath tickling the little hairs that grew just along the lower edge of his lobe. "You're enough live wire for me."

Stella slowly unbuttoned the top of her pants. Her thumb and forefinger pulled down her zipper, and she turned her backside against him, shook her hips out of her jeans, and kneeled on all fours in the tall, pale grass. She tossed her long hair over her shoulder. Chet let his eyes linger on the heart-shaped outline of her bottom, then with a downward flick of his zipper and an almost inaudible thud of his knees, he was pushing forward and plowing her soft, pink fields. He sowed his seed in her, again and again, until he was empty. Until he was spent.

Stella looked forward, moaned, and tossed her blond tresses in the air. Her hips thrust against Chet with what she hoped he'd interpret as lustful vigor. Meanwhile, she searched the vacant hills in front of her. Her eyes drifted down toward a set of large brown rocks. A flicker of sunlight on glass confirmed what she already knew. *They* were watching. Recording every move. In her younger years, she might have been embarrassed, but she was long past that point. Today she was simply doing her job, and she hoped they did theirs.

"What happened to your hand?"

Ben knew it was no good trying to hide his injury. He'd cleaned up the wound and washed it as best he could. Pig bites could be nasty—some of the nastiest, depending on where the animals had been. But then, these animals weren't really pigs, were they? *Swinemen. Porci-sapiens. Were their bites any different?*

"Your boy, Gevu, bit me."

Miriam's lips tightened, and she scowled at the pig. He looked up at her, scratched his head with his fingers, and showed his teeth in a quirky smile.

"Really?" She crouched toward him. Gevu nuzzled her hand with his nose. "He doesn't seem like the biting type right now, does he?"

"Try taking food away from him when he's eating."

"Ah, well. That explains it. Get the boxes in the car. Mazda van. Blue."

"Don't you think we should talk about this? He almost cut to the bone..."

"No. Pack up. We've got to go."

Ben wondered why she refused to address the problem right now. Gevu's behavior was a dangerous sign, and they should agree on how to correct any future issues. Still, when Miriam was pressing forward to reach a goal, it was futile to talk to her further. He made a mental note to bring it up later, and carted their notebooks and some blankets outside. The minivan had a back hatch that was big enough for the twins. The windows were heavily tinted in the back. No one could see in, but they could look out. Perfect.

He returned to the room. Miriam was holding Gevu in her arms, just barely. In just a day, it seemed as if he'd put on a few extra pounds. Ben picked up Binah. She was much smaller and lighter than Gevu now.

"Let's go." Miriam wrapped Gevu in a sheet and placed him into the back of the Mazda. "Stay here," she told Gevu. "No stupid shenanigans. I don't want to stop by a pet store and get two more crates."

Ben observed Gevu's face as Miriam talked to him, and he involuntarily shuddered. There was cold calculation in that creature's eyes. Ben set Binah beside Gevu. Her large hazel irises ,dotted with flecks of green, reminded him of cool brooks running gently through the forest, sunlight flickering on the water's surface the canopy. There was nothing there but gentle trust and kindness. He shut the hatch. Miriam was already in the driver's seat.

"We've got to get out of here. Get your seatbelt on."

Ben wondered why his partner was in such a rush. Sure, they'd wrecked the U-Haul, but their insurance would cover it. The Cullers had found them another vehicle. So, why the hurry?

Miriam pulled out onto the highway. After five minutes of driving toward the California border, three cop cars sped by in the opposite direction, headed into town. Ben looked over at her, but her face didn't twitch. He leaned over and turned on the radio, but only managed to pull up a local radio station.

"Looks like we've got a choice of country, or a static-filled Top 40." Ben twisted the knobs slowly in grim determination. Miriam hit a small pothole, and his hand twisted a bit further than he'd intended.

In other news today, police are on the lookout for a murderer in the town of Green River. Early this morning, a man's body was found in the middle of Wilford Road. He reportedly died from gunshots to the body and head. No bullet casings were recovered from the scene. The man was identified as Emmet Fisher. Sixty-eight years old. No suspects or motives have been connected to this crime. Police warn the homicide might be the work of someone passing through and ask all citizens to report anything strange or unusual that occurred last night.

The radio droned on, but Ben didn't hear the rest. He stared at Miriam. In just moments, he realized he was pressing himself against the passenger side door.

"Did you know about this?" His mouth felt stiff, as if his jaw refused to work properly.

Miriam remained quiet.

"Damn it, Miriam! Did you know?" Ben was trembling. He knew their work was serious, but he hadn't expected people to die for it.

She inhaled and let out a big breath, but she kept her eyes on the road. She didn't look away once. "Of course I knew. It had to be done. The Cullers are good. They take care of everything."

"Then, you didn't have anything to do with his..." He wanted to hear her say it. He thought he knew Miriam, but now he wasn't sure.

"I had to call it in, Ben. He'd seen Binah."

"What do you mean, you *called it in*? Does that mean you didn't kill him? Tell me." Ben felt his heart beat hard in his chest.

A car whizzed past them from the opposite direction. One cloud crept over the sun. It was the only cloud in the sky.

"I didn't kill him." Her voice wasn't convincing. And she hadn't even glanced at him when she said the words. He closed his eyes and tried to decide what he wanted to believe. He'd flip a coin later. Statistically, it would be easier.

EIGHT

May 27, 18:00

The minivan bumped along a gravel road just a few miles outside of Bakersfield. Miriam found it amazing that the twins managed to sleep through the rough ride. They'd been extremely quiet most of the trip, and she was thankful. Eventually they'd have to learn to abide by her rules and how to properly behave, and at their rate of growth, she'd be handing them over to the Cullers in no time.

Google Maps proved useful up until they passed through Bakersfield and arrived on the outskirts of the city. Long rolling fields of dry brown-and-green grasses alternated with hills of tall pines and cottonwood trees that greeted them along the way. On the way toward Glennville, there was a sprinkling of homes near the road. Most were small farmhouses. Miriam recognized some of them as manufactured homes and others as old farmhouses, whose surfaces had once worn white paint but were now gray and weathered, flecked with traces of snow. Their surface blended into the landscape like a deer in a winter forest.

To the right of them, the mountains of the Sequoia National Park bounced in and out of view. Wildflowers dotted the open tracts of land, and the scent of juniper drifted through the air.

The late afternoon breeze from the window felt cool and light, and Miriam let her thoughts wander as the vehicle rolled along the road.

"There should be a turnoff to the right soon." Ben was trying to make sense of the printed directions, looking ahead and then back to the map, but Miriam drove on without concern. They crossed over a small creek and passed by more open fields, then more trees.

Miriam startled at the sound of the window rolling down behind her. She hadn't touched the button. When she checked in her rearview mirror, just in the seat behind her sat Gevu. His nose was tilted into the air. His eyes were closed. She hadn't even heard him crawl out of the back.

A few seconds later, she glanced in the mirror again. Binah sat on the other side, just behind Ben. Miriam watched as Binah tentatively pushed a button. Nothing happened. Binah pushed another button, and her window lowered. Binah stuck her nose in the air, a reflection of Gevu on the opposite side. They seemed so happy that Miriam decided to let them enjoy the view. They were in the middle of the country, crossing a swath of farmland, and if they passed anyone, the passengers wouldn't be sure what they'd seen, if anything. Both Gevu and Binah's heads barely reached the bottom of the tinted windows. And Miriam was going to have to trust them eventually. The children would be adults before any of them realized it.

Miriam spotted a piece of yellow ribbon tied to a stick, just a few feet from a right-hand turnoff. "There."

Ben put his papers down, conceding the map was useless at this point. This road was even bumpier, and the minivan jiggled and jumped. She could have sworn she heard the children giggling.

The exterior of the house wasn't quite as nice as what was displayed in the picture on the Internet. It was an older two-story farmhouse, in the middle of large, grassy fields filled with wildflowers and surrounded by wire fencing. Just up the hill sat a fairly large barn. Miriam pulled into the driveway, got out of the van, and opened up the passenger door on her side. "Here, Gevu. See what you think of this." She scooped him up and put him on the grass. He sniffed the mix of brown and green plant life and then pressed his nose into the ground. Ben followed her lead, taking Binah out of the vehicle and letting her roam free for a moment. She simply sat and gazed around, seeming entranced with her new surroundings.

The bang of a door startled them all, and Chet ambled down the stairs, already at home in his adopted environment. Miriam didn't miss the addition of the Taser to his belt.

"What's that?" She pointed to his new sidearm.

Chet grinned at her. "Glad to see you too, Dr. Wetzel." Miriam set her stare on him, knowing he'd get the message. She still wanted an explanation. "It's just an extra precaution, that's all." He patted the device like an old friend. "It'll pack a wallop but still leave any trespassers able to answer questions." She wasn't quite satisfied, but she decided to leave well enough alone for the moment. She picked up Binah, and Ben grabbed Gevu—but not before Miriam noticed the little snarl that twitched at the corner of Gevu's nose and mouth. All together, they entered the farmhouse.

Chet took a great deal of pride in showing them the security system he'd rigged for both the house and its perimeter. He demonstrated the doorknobs he'd electrically wired to deliver a nasty shock whenever the system was engaged. Next to the door was a panel with two different bulbs. "Green is A-okay," he said. "Red, and, well, you won't wish you were dead, but the jingle you'll get will zap you outta your shoes."

Ben eyed the panel dubiously, but Miriam grudgingly approved. If the twins had mastered doorknobs, as he'd explained on the rest of their ride, then they needed a way to keep the little ones contained. Years of science and research gave her vast experience in both animal and human behavior. They'd soon learn the meaning of the colors if they didn't listen the first time.

The control panel to the system was in the kitchen, located just inside the pantry. And on the wall above the kitchen table were cameras and viewing screens. More cameras and screens were set up in the living room right next to the TV. Chet showed them how each of the screens were set up to view the children's rooms and other rooms throughout the house, as well as various places in the yard and the barn.

Miriam had to admit that Chet did a bang-up job. Even Ben seemed to approve of the work. She approached a panel, with Binah squirming in her arms, and motioned for Ben to come closer. She noticed how Gevu focused his attention on her. Miriam pointed to the panel. "Gevu. Binah. See that panel right there?" The little ones turned their faces in the direction of her finger. "The light there is green, which means it's okay to use the knob." The twins looked back at her. "Chet, flip the switch." Chet went over to the pantry and flipped a control switch, and the green light at the top went out and a red light underneath blinked on.

Miriam continued her lesson. "The light is now red, which means don't touch the doorknob. If you try to touch it when it's red, it will hurt you." Chet flipped the switch back to green. Both of the children seemed as if they were processing the information. Miriam placed Binah on the floor, and Gevu immediately squirmed out of Ben's grasp, causing him to drop to the ground. Gevu stood on his back legs for a moment and then took a couple of steps before he returned to all fours. Miriam was pleased he already showed a capability for walking, but she didn't miss the fact that the child looked intently at the pantry and then gazed once more at the panel next to the door.

Just a few weeks old, and they're growing so fast. Time to get them started with lessons so we can assess their potential. "Chet, engage the front door and back door."

"Yes, ma'am," he said as he complied. His congenial tone took her by surprise. He was being almost polite, which led her instantly to wonder what he was up to. But the Cullers trusted the man for some odd reason, and he'd done a great job. She had nothing to complain about—at least not yet.

Miriam opened the kitchen door. "Gevu. Binah. Let's show you to your rooms."

August 1, 07:00

Each morning, Binah was amazed at how much her body had changed. In a week, her squat baby body had lengthened, and her pink, fleshy legs had thinned and straightened, becoming more muscular and toned. In three weeks, she'd grown to twice her infant height and had gone from walking to running around the house, dashing away from Gevu's rough-and-tumble ways. Her brother always wanted to wrestle, and his body grew more rapidly than hers. And when it came to mealtime, he managed to put away twice the amount of food she did.

By the middle of the sixth week, her flattened nose was much larger, and her pink ears were wider. It seemed that Miriam brought her new clothes almost every other day. Binah seldom wore anything more than once or twice.

For the most part, daily lessons were exciting for Binah. She and Gevu learned to read and write, and best of all, they spent time learning to use the computers. In the evening, she and her brother watched movies on history and science channels and other films that dealt with a multitude of other subjects. Each of them developed preferences to certain specialties in their learning, and the White Coats seemed to notice and adjusted their lesson topics to highlight their intellectual abilities.

Dr. Skylar taught Binah chemistry, biology, genetics, music, and other arts, such as painting, while Gevu tended more toward learning mechanics, engineering, and weaponry, which Dr. Wetzel readily took time to explain to him. By the end of two months, they'd mastered several lessons and passed a number of challenging individualized tests, but the most difficult and frustrating time of all was when the White Coats tried to teach them to speak.

The only rooms in the house that had no panels with red and green lights were the bathrooms and the closets. And the only rooms that had no cameras, as far as Binah could tell, were the closets. When the White Coats seemed occupied, Gevu would bring her into a closet at the far end of the house, and they would quickly practice their speech.

"You can't let them know we can talk," Gevu told her gruffly again and again. "It's the one thing we have that they can't know about."

"Why not?" Binah felt both guilty and sad to keep this ability a secret. Dr. Skylar was so knowledgeable, and she had a number of questions she wanted to ask him. "It seems silly not to let them know we can speak. We could learn so much more at a faster pace."

"We are learning plenty." The anger that grew in Gevu's voice always made her tremble. "There will be a time when it's right, but not until I say. It's like playing cards. You don't show everything in your hand."

Binah thought she understood, although part of her disagreed with him. *What difference would it make if the White Coats knew they could speak?* As she asked the question in her mind, she realized it really was significant. Human speech was the ultimate form of communication. Once they showed the White Coats that they could speak, they'd be much more threatening. Much more dangerous. They would be equal to all mankind.

And so, Binah endured her daily lessons in speech. Dr. Skylar and Dr. Wetzel sat in front of them both when they were in the kitchen during mealtime, flashed picture cards in front of them, and encouraged each of them to form the words that matched the pictures. She and Gevu responded with guttural sounds, squeaks, and squeals equal to what she considered open lies, and each day, she was tormented with the look of disappointment that filled Dr. Skylar's eyes. But the White Coats taught them sign language too, and through that and writing words, Binah learned to ask questions, although the process felt slow and clumsy. At least it was easier than just typing questions on the computer. She knew speech was faster—easier—overall. And she longed more than anything to converse with someone other than Gevu.

In the afternoons, Binah and Gevu were allowed to go outside. After a week's time, she knew the name of every insect and each species of tree and flower that grew on the edges of the small field that surrounded the house. Her nose was tantalized with the smells of cedar and juniper that permeated the air.

Gevu seemed to enjoy his daily lessons as well. He eagerly studied computer science and various schematics, and Dr. Wetzel would take him to the barn nearby where they worked on a car engine and other forms of machinery.

Then came the day that Binah heard a sound she hadn't heard in weeks. Not since her birth. The sound was that of gunfire.

It wasn't difficult for Gevu to keep up his charade. He eagerly absorbed new information as rapidly as Binah, although his interests lay in completely different areas. And Dr. Wetzel responded to his interests and taught him efficiently. He learned sign language so completely and signed so fast that by the end of the week, Dr. Wetzel seldom responded to his questions using sign but verbally answered his questions instead. That suited Gevu just fine.

During their daily oral-language practice, he appeared to struggle with his vocalizations and hoped the enjoyment of his deception didn't play out on his face. Dr. Wetzel seemed patient at first, and then became more demanding with passing days. It was as if she realized he could utter the words and was frustrated that he wouldn't perform the monkey trick for her. Yesterday, he realized that Dr. Wetzel was almost as calculating as Gevu himself. She held a picture of a car in front of him. "Car," she said.

Gevu snorted, and growled in the back of his throat.

"You can do it, Gevu. I know you can." Her usual clinical voice softened, as if coaxing him like a child. She'd reached out her hand and touched his. Soft. Warm. Compassionate.

Then he remembered it was the same voice that had ordered his mother's death, and he'd pulled away. That was a mistake. Dr. Wetzel, instead of acting surprised, went back to the lesson with an air of triumph in the undertones of her voice. He'd betrayed something in his abrupt action, although he was uncertain as to what.

Today, he was looking forward to going to the barn again with Dr. Wetzel. He munched on some crispy bacon, wiped some grease from his chin, and shoveled some scrambled eggs into his mouth. Would he learn about a new mechanism or perhaps be tested on how to put together the generator they'd taken apart the afternoon before? Binah sat across from him, eating a toasted bagel and fresh fruit salad. The sunflower-printed tablecloth lent a cheery air to the room, and the golden light of a new day poured through the window.

Dr. Wetzel finished wiping down the counters and put away the last dish in the drying rack. "You guys finish your meal, and then we'll get started." She walked out, and Gevu heard the upstairs water running. Dr. Skylar was probably taking a shower. It was something they'd learned not long after they had arrived. How to bathe every day. How to stay clean.

Monkey tricks. A couple of days ago, he and Binah watched a film about animal intelligence and saw researchers working with chimpanzees. The animals were learning rudimentary skills. While he watched their actions, he suddenly put many things together. He realized he and Binah were just an experiment. They were precious to the White Coats, but experiments none-the-less. And why were they using him and his sister? He was determined to find out. Gevu would discover their goals before he ended their pathetic lives, just like they'd ended the life of his mother. But before he did that, there was another human at the top of his revenge list.

Chet entered the room.

"What's up, piggies?" Chet shut the kitchen door and grinned at them as he swaggered over to a nearby counter. He pulled out a plastic coffee tumbler from a cabinet, filled it with coffee from the half empty coffee pot, and leaned his back against the marble and watched them eat. "What's the matter, little beasties? Cat got your tongues?" He took a sip of his coffee and mumbled just under his breath, "Oh yeah, I forgot you're only dumb animals, just like your mother. Heh, dumb." He chuckled a bit with his last words, as if he'd told a good joke.

Out of the corner of his eye, he saw Binah signing. *He's an asshole, Gevu. Don't give him the satisfaction.* But Gevu's blood was boiling. The man that had shot his mother dared to bring it up, right here, right now. He forced himself to look out the window. Binah reached across the table and held his hand. Chet walked over to the table, paused a moment as if considering exactly what he wanted to say to them next, then strolled back over to the counter.

"Gevu! Binah! Lesson time!" Dr. Wetzel's voice called from the study room. Gevu got up before Binah, determined to leave the room before he lost self-control. He stalked past Chet, reached the doorknob, and started to twist it. His ears picked up the sound of a click after it was too late. A violent jolt buzzed down his arm and shook his body. He fell to the floor, his muscles contracting, his hand refusing to let go, his mouth clenching tight and body contorting with the painful sensation. Binah sprang toward him. Another little click sounded in the air, and he let go of the knob. He looked up at Chet. Every cell in his body wanted to tear the man to shreds.

Chet whispered, "Just so you know what that red light feels like." He closed the pantry door and took another sip of his coffee. "And don't get any ideas about telling the science geeks." Chet lifted his chin toward the ceiling where, just near the table, a videocam hung. "Because it never happened."

Gevu stared at the camera. Just over the lens, a small piece of duct tape blocked the all-seeing eye. "And this..." Chet touched where a rectangular box with a handgrip was holstered on his belt. "This will give you three times that jingle if you ever cross me." Chet walked behind the camera and pulled off the tape when Gevu and Binah stood up, then he pushed past them, opened the door, and left.

Gevu's hatred boiled up from the pit of his stomach. How he longed to place his hands around Chet's head and twist it one hundred eighty degrees. He was sure he could do it if he got the chance.

He hadn't expected Dr. Wetzel to teach him about weapons, so, the other day, he'd pulled up a picture of a rifle on his computer and searched for more information on several other types of firearms. The next day, in the barn, Dr. Wetzel had taken her

Glock out, showing him how it worked. They'd taken it apart, cleaned it piece by piece, and put it back together. He hadn't asked to fire it, and she hadn't offered, but, oh, how he really wanted to learn now.

NINE

"Do you think they realize we're watching their every move?"

"Not yet. But they will."

"What do we do then? How will we explain it to them?"

"We won't. By the time they realize what's involved, it will be too late."

"Too late for what?"

"Rank has its privileges."

September 18, 07:30

Gevu knew all he needed was time, but he was growing impatient. He felt the urge to do something more, to *be* something more, and the White Coats weren't doing a lot to help him progress. But he'd also learned a secret to dangling them on a string: act just smart enough to keep their interest, but not so smart that they'd be wary. He didn't want them to begin listening to his conversations with Binah or dissecting their every move.

Dissecting. He remembered the day when he had found out what that word meant. As best as he could determine from brief interludes of CNN and peeks at the MSN on the computer when the White Coats were away, they'd been at the farm in California for about three weeks. He'd opened up a frame on the computer to the "Dictionary" app Dr. Wetzel had on her screen. The word had been used in conversations between them sometimes, and he'd wondered what it meant. *To methodically cut up (a body part or plant) for the purpose of studying its internal structure.*

Dr. Skylar had brought the term up sometimes when he discussed his previous job working with rats. Gevu remembered Dr. Wetzel hushing him, checking to see if they were listening. He wondered what else the doctors had dissected. Other humans? Pigs even? The thought didn't sicken him. It only made him curious. He'd like the opportunity to take a human apart. One human in particular was on his mind.

He tried to look up the word "pig" on the Internet, but nothing other than photographs showed up on the screen. Then he tried several other words he'd heard. Pork. Nothing but a blank screen with a little cyber ball that showed the computer was constantly searching. Swine. Just the tiny "searching ball of death." There had to be other words; he just didn't know them. It was as if every link to their genetic design was denied.

In this place, he and Binah had their own rooms and their own beds. They shared a bathroom down the hall, where they'd each been potty trained. It hadn't taken long. Neither of them liked the stench or the feel of their own excrement across their backsides. And although Gevu had once made a habit of taking his diaper off, he soon realized the mess it made inside his own room. And he discovered he didn't like his own smell interfering with the details he could gain without it. His sense of smell gave him more information than eyesight.

Gevu stared at the doorknob. He'd get that bastard, Chet. One day, he'd have his revenge. And the human would beg for mercy. But he wouldn't get it.

Gevu looked up at the video camera tucked into the corner of the ceiling, and then his eyes flitted over the hidden microphones he knew were camouflaged in his room. His lamp. Behind the frame on a picture. They thought he was stupid. So much the better for him.

The doorknob buzzed, and a little light on the wall turned green. He waited a moment, and then unhurriedly strode over on two feet and opened the door. Gevu was so much better at everything now. He was twelve weeks old, and he could already walk, run, climb, and solve complex puzzles. His muscles bulged all over his body, and he was as tall as Dr. Skylar. Dr. Wetzel had bought him extra-large shirts and two pair of large, roomy pants. The clothes were bigger than Dr. Skylar's, though that wasn't saying much.

And there was more that Gevu could do too, but he didn't let *them* know.

White Coats. The name helped him remember his mother's murder. He made Binah call them that too, whenever they conversed. He wouldn't forget. *They* wouldn't forget. Not now. Not ever. Not until they were dead.

Gevu sniffed the air. Dinner was almost ready. Whenever Dr. Wetzel made beans, they had ham on the side. And he loved ham. There was something about tearing his teeth into the meat that was oddly satisfying, although he preferred fresh blood. After the rat, and after tasting Dr. Skylar's blood, Gevu had made the decision to find food more to his taste.

The farm offered a whole plethora of rats for him to eat, and then there'd been the chickens that belonged to their neighbors two miles down the road. Chet really thought his little electric-wire fence could keep him inside. Gevu had leapt over that thing easier than an Olympic jumper over cow shit.

Killing the neighbor's chickens had given him real pleasure. Their fear. Their screams. He loved the blood. And the ultimate was knowing he was doing wrong. It thrilled him. And no one would have suspected him if Dr. Wetzel hadn't seen that feather lodged between his teeth. So, now, he was grounded. Couldn't leave the house. And perfect little Binah still got to go outside.

But, no, she's not perfect. Not so little either. And for her, it's really just a matter of time.

―――

Binah felt restless. She shifted her weight as she sat on the grass and was barely able to stay still. Something was different. Something new was happening. Her genitals were swollen, and they throbbed. They ached. Not to mention the thin, milky mucous saturating her groin, making her underwear moist in a way that was almost pleasant, but very weird. It wasn't something she was used to.

She felt her legs. They were so much longer, stronger, and leaner. They were thicker than human legs, but they'd grown quite shapely. She was taller than Dr. Wetzel now. It gave her a bit of pleasure to look down at the scientist whenever she walked up to her.

"Binah! Dinner!" Dr. Wetzel's voice echoed easily across the field where Binah sat gazing up at the evening sky. Thick layers of clouds were turning into a lovely mix of gold and purple against the western ridge of mountains. The air smelled of new-mown hay, fresh-turned earth, and the beans Miriam must be cooking. She wasn't hungry. It was odd, because she was almost always hungry when it came to mealtime. And Dr. Wetzel's beans were absolutely excellent.

Dr. Skylar came up behind Binah, sat down, and gave her a gentle pat on the head. He'd been cleaning out the barn, making sure it was organized. She hated that she had to play the part of a mime. Gevu insisted on it. Twelve weeks after her birth, she was almost fully grown. Almost a woman. She should be able to converse one-on-one with Dr. Skylar and speak with him as an equal. Share ideas with him. Ideas that Dr. Wetzel never bothered to discuss with him.

After a few moments, Binah realized she could feel Dr. Skylar's body heat. It emanated from his skin like a comforting blanket, and Binah felt the intense urge to rub up against him. She leaned her head on his shoulder, and her genitals quivered. She ached to touch him. Rubbing up against him felt *good*. She pulled back and stared at his face. He turned to look at her, his large brown eyes so intelligent. So expressive.

I could make him love me. Her pig features wouldn't matter to him. She sensed he was attracted to her in a way he wasn't sure of himself, and she decided to walk over to the barn. She hefted her weight forward, stood, and made slow, easy strides toward the building's doors.

"Where are you going? Dr. Wetzel has dinner ready, and then it's time for some more studying."

Binah gave him a pleading look, as if she wanted to show him something, and continued toward the barn. Dr. Skylar let out a breath of exasperation, then got up and followed her. They entered through the large doors, and the smell of sweet hay only heightened her arousal. She moved farther into the barn, near some bales of hay, and he followed. Then, she turned toward him and tried to place her hands on his shoulders, but succeeded only in reaching the top of his chest. Tentatively, then more boldly, she started to rub her groin against him.

Dr. Skylar drew his hips back in shock. "Binah! No!" But she reached her arms around him and hugged him tightly. Her strength overpowered his struggle to move away. She gyrated her genitals against his thigh. As she did, she realized how delicious it felt. But she wanted more than this feeling. Something much more.

A week ago, Gevu had made her look at pictures of male and female human anatomy. They'd watched what was called "porn" on some of the videos they'd found on Dr. Wetzel's computer, and they'd learned how humans mated. Then they'd watched YouTube videos of how cows, dogs, and monkeys mated, a method that was crude and awkward in comparison. Gevu had kept his eyes glued to the screen. Binah had crept away to her room afterward, the images never leaving her mind.

Now, Binah's growing appetite for something she couldn't explain took over. She moaned and grunted to express her desire, and a slow look of understanding spread across Dr. Skylar's face. She lifted her skirt a little, removed her underwear, and then smoothed her fingers down from his shoulder to grip his hand. He looked bewildered as she brought his palm to the lips of her vagina. Her genitals were sopping wet. Drenched. Her juices were practically dripping on the floor.

Dr. Skylar tried to draw his hand away, but she held him there, pressing his fingers into her. He tried to pull away once more, and she still held him there. Then his arm relaxed, and she heard his heavy breaths. She sensed he was gradually accepting what was happening. He'd explained a little about human and pig physiology in some of their lessons. He had to have known she'd go into heat one day.

"Binah. I—I can't," he stammered. But she was pleased she could feel a stiffening of his flesh against her. His male organ was growing large and hard beneath the fabric of his slacks. All he had to do was drop his pants, kneel on all fours, lift her skirt higher, and bare her bottom, and she knew she'd be satisfied. Binah placed one hand on the button of his pants. Dr. Skylar looked around furtively. "No." But he wasn't really fighting any more. Her thick fingers reached in and drew out his penis, and she watched his flesh respond to her touch by jumping up slightly in her hand. Dr. Skylar's eyes closed, and he moaned.

Binah stroked his erection. How she longed to call him "Ben," and in her mind, she did just that. *Ben, help me be complete.* She pulled him down onto the barn floor and placed herself on all fours. She felt him kneel behind her.

She felt the head of his penis touch her wet, slippery skin. "Oh my God. What am I doing?" Ben said with rapid, heavy breaths. Then he pressed his warmth into her. Binah's whole body shuddered, and she bit back a yell of pain mixed with joy.

Yes! That's it. That's what I wanted...needed...and Ben! Ben is my first!

She felt Dr. Skylar grip her hips as he moved deeper into her, then out and in again. The aching and burning sensation she'd felt in and around her genitals subsided and then gave way to a furious desire for him to go faster, and harder. She wiggled her backside furtively against him, and he seemed to sense her desire and pounded into her with fast and furious thrusts.

The feel of his sex moving inside her overwhelmed Binah. It was a thrill beyond measure. The intense wave of it was indescribable, beyond any words she had the capacity to summon in thought or in English, and her body shook with a pleasure she hadn't known it could feel. Then, she felt his flesh expand even larger, and with three long, furious thrusts, she suddenly felt a warm sensation fill her and heard him groan. He made a few more gentle thrusts and then bent over and hugged her. At this very moment, she was happy, more complete than she'd ever felt in her life, and she wanted the feeling to last forever.

Something clattered against the floor, and the shock of the sound caused Dr. Skylar to rapidly pull out of her. They both whirled around, and there stood Chet, a rake at his feet and a shit-eating grin spread across his face. In his hand he held a cell phone. It was aimed at them, and with a deep, sickening feeling, Binah knew he'd been filming them. Filming them! Chet, that evil, loathsome slime, had video of her most sacred moment. She snarled at him. The bastard seemed not to notice.

Chet spit some tobacco juice toward them, and the sticky, brown substance landed just a few inches from Binah's behind.

"Well, Doc! Didn't know you had it in you. When you're done, you wanna let old Chet have a turn? Maybe you'll watch us before you climb on again?" Chet guffawed as the scientist stood up and fumbled with putting on his pants.

Binah was furious. How dare Chet interrupt them! She was surprised that she felt more anger than embarrassment at being caught and filmed in the act of mating. And she hated Ben for not doing anything. He just stood there, like a confused idiot, instead of decking the hired hand.

Chet walked over to the doctor. The Taser he carried like a side arm was obvious on his belt.

"Make you a deal, Doc. I'll keep your little bestiality habit a secret for a price." He raised the cell phone up for emphasis as he said it. "Don't you worry. Your little science lady won't need to know she's not enough woman for you. Or should I say *animal*."

What did Chet mean? The man's words hit Binah's ears like a hot iron skillet as she searched Ben's eyes. Did Ben mate with Dr. Wetzel as well? No. Not her sweet Ben.

"Binah, don't listen to him."

A giant pressure Binah couldn't explain welled up in her chest, threatening to make the bands of her ribs explode. She stood, pulled her skirt down over her bottom, and raced out of the barn as Chet's cruel laughter followed her across the yard.

Her ears felt as if they were burning in fire. Yet, despite the embarrassment, all she could think of was Ben.

Dr. Wetzel can't have him. She doesn't deserve him. Ben made love with me. Me! And the video. Shit. No one can ever know about the video.

Ben's semen dribbled down Binah's right leg, first warm and then turning sticky and cold, and she tried to think of where she could go at the moment. Dr. Wetzel was in the kitchen probably, eating with Gevu. Binah decided to go in the front door, head up, and get into the shower. But when she opened the door, she found Gevu was just coming down the stairs. He turned his head and stared at her as she raced up the steps past him, and she heard him sniff the air.

Binah knew he could smell Ben's scent on her. He'd know what had happened, and at that moment, her fiery anger congealed into fear. She continued running up the stairs without looking back. Gevu would never forgive her for what she'd done. And as far as Ben, well, Gevu would have no mercy.

"Give me that cell phone." Ben held out his hand and tried to keep it from shaking.

Chet continued to smirk while watching Binah run off. "Won't do you no good." He rocked back and forth on his heels. His face was smug.

Ben was perplexed for a moment, and then he understood. "You didn't."

"Not to a public account. Just to somewhere private for safekeeping."

"Chet, you can't do this. The Cullers will have you..."

"What? Fired? The way I figure it, if you blow the whistle, we all get exterminated."

"So, what do you want?"

"I'll let you know when it's time."

Ben knew Chet had him by the balls. There was nothing he could do. Not yet. He'd have to bide his time. Maybe find a way to steal Chet's cell phone and figure out where he sent the video.

"Ben! Binah!" Miriam's voice was more insistent. Ben imagined Miriam was getting frustrated because she'd actually gone to the trouble of making dinner and no one was coming. *Binah. Oh God. I need to see how she's doing.*

Ben started to say something else, but the man was gone. He was good at that. Stealthy. Sneaky. And Ben was going to pay a huge price for letting his guard down. For getting caught up in the moment.

Something small and shiny was resting on top of the hay where Chet had just stood. Ben reached down to pick it up. It was Chet's cell phone. Ben opened it, and the screen immediately glowed. Staring him in the face, as the phone's wallpaper, was a pic of Chet grinning while Ben had sex with Binah in the background. The cell phone buzzed. A text came in. Ben pressed the button.

Animal-fucking faggot. Keep this phone with you. I'll tell you when I need you. Meanwhile, enjoy the mammaries.

The cell buzzed again, and in came a picture of Binah's breasts. Somehow, he'd got a shot of Binah naked, and he'd managed to capture all six of her breasts.

Ben snapped the cell shut.

"What have I done? Holy shit, what have I done?"

He headed toward the house, but he wasn't hungry. He wondered if he'd ever have an appetite again. A breeze lifted his hair and caressed his face. An owl hooted in the distance, its haunting voice echoing across the field.

Ben stopped walking and looked up at the two-story home. The owl wasn't in a tree. It was sitting on their house. He'd grown up believing owls were messengers of death. His grandma always told him that if an owl sat on your roof, someone was going to die. Someone you knew.

TEN

September 22, 02:00

Gevu's room was dark, but he knew exactly where the surveillance camera was. He slipped on a pair of loose jeans, threw on a T-shirt, then sneaked toward the mechanical eye, reached up, and placed a piece of duct tape over the lens. Despite his hatred of Chet, at least the human had taught him a thing or two.

In seconds, he'd cranked out his flashlight and quietly padded over to the door. It took moments for him to bypass the electrical wires on the panel near his doorknob, and then the light turned from red to green. Studying electricity and schematics, in between his regular lessons, had definitely paid off.

Easier than they'll ever know.

Gevu had some exploring to do, and this time, he was after much larger prey than chickens. He could smell an animal farm just a few miles away, and when he'd asked Dr. Wetzel more about the place, she had dismissed his questions. It was time he found his own answers.

His hand turned the doorknob slowly. Quietly. He crept down the hallway and down the steps, taking care to avoid the floorboards he knew would squeak. When he reached the front door, he pulled the tools from his pocket and bypassed the next panel. Then he was outside in the crisp, clean air.

Gevu sniffed the early mist that covered the open fields. The scents he inhaled were strong. But it wasn't just the smell of the dewy grasses and fresh-turned earth that caught his attention. He caught the odor of the farm he'd noticed a few times before. Earthy. Manure-like. And for a second, he thought he heard something that sounded like screaming. The sounds were distant, very faint, but there was terror in their muffled echoes. Gevu struck out in that direction and then broke into a run. When he reached the tall electrified fence, he easily vaulted over it and kept on running.

Pumping his muscles at full speed felt right. Felt good. He stretched his legs and settled into a rhythm, wondering what he would see. Would it be more chickens? He loved the taste of fresh chicken. He shivered at the prospect of slurping up their warm blood. Or perhaps another type of animal. One larger, more tasty. The possibility caused him to salivate.

As Gevu grew closer to the odor, it became so thick and heavy, so revolting, his stomach lurched. Despite the stink of it, he felt driven with a mad curiosity. He crossed a field and then an asphalt road. He passed a large sign that read *Greenfield Farms* in large block letters, and in the distance, there were several rows of one-story, white buildings. The structures were long, and the windows were made of frosted glass. It was impossible to see inside. There were only small openings at the tops of the windows, just as wide as the span of his two hands, which ended before the wall met the roof.

What is in there?

The stench of the place was overpowering. Gevu slowed as he approached and walked around one of the buildings. The sounds from the creatures inside were familiar. He heard several squeals and grunts; they were noises that tickled his memory. His mother had made identical sounds. He and Binah even made utterances that resembled these.

Were there more like his mother inside these houses? The thought both excited and sickened him.

A low rumble startled him from his thoughts. An enormous truck bumped and clattered in his direction. Near the building sat a variety of farm equipment and a tractor. Gevu hid among the structures and watched as a lean human male wearing a baseball cap and baggy T-shirt got out of the passenger side of the truck and opened the doors, then opened the back of the truck and pulled down a ramp.

"Hurry up!" The man on the driver's side sounded impatient.

"Get out here and lend a hand then." Baseball-cap man was now entering the building. Gevu crept closer so he could see. He heard a smack of something striking against skin.

"Move, bastards, move! Fucking pigs. You'll be ham by sunrise." Another smacking sound, and then another, and then several animals stumbled and ran on all fours up the metal ramp. Their faces were similar to his own, and their soft, furry nostrils were wet, pink, and sniffing the air. He touched his nose and realized his lips were trembling.

Pigs. Ham. Gevu had heard every word, but he was just beginning to comprehend what the man had meant. He'd eaten ham. They'd let him eat pig meat, when he hadn't even know what kind of food he'd swallowed down. Anger welled up inside him, and the only thing that kept him from erupting was the fact that he wanted—he needed—to see what happened to these creatures.

What seemed like hours must have only been minutes until the men closed the gates and pulled up the ramps. Baseball-cap man shut up the building and secured a lock on the front of the door before jumping back into the vehicle.

"We got several runs to do tonight. Let's go," said the driver.

They both slammed the doors to the vehicle, and before they could take off, Gevu sprinted and hopped onto the back of the truck by clutching at the top corner of it. From there, he scrambled to the top and hung on. No one heard him over the noise of the animals inside. Gevu clung tight, determined to see what was going to happen to the pigs.

They traveled down the road for just a few miles and then pulled up to a large building where machinery hummed. The animals inside the truck were restless. Some cried. Some squealed. Gevu pulled at his ears as he helplessly listened to them. The men got out of the truck and opened the back. The ramp slid down, and the pigs scuttled helplessly into the building. Some of them collapsed and tumbled over each other in the process. The men whipped and prodded them with long sticks until they got back onto their feet again.

On the other side of the entrance, Gevu saw a man wearing a mask over his face. He helped shuttle the animals inside, then the building doors started to close.

Gevu eased over the edge, slipped down one side of the truck, and ran to a dark corner of the building.

"Did you hear something?" One of the men turned his head toward Gevu's hiding place.

"What are you expecting? Coyote? C'mon, we've got a lot more runs to go." The man with the baseball cap climbed back into the truck, and they drove off.

Gevu waited until he was sure they'd be unable to see him, then he walked around to another part of the building. More screams emanated from inside, but there were no windows. His body shook uncontrollably as he searched for an entrance. A single door, alongside a wall, was barely cracked open. Outside of it sat several small benches, and the sickly smell of old cigarettes rose from a large red can. He gently pulled at the door and stuck his head inside. There was a corridor, a place for hand washing, and boxes of masks and gloves. A rack of white plastic jackets hung nearby.

He put a mask over his face, grabbed a white cap and stuffed his ears underneath it, and then pushed a hardhat over it all. A small mirror above the sink let him check his profile. He could pass for human. He hesitated before he put on the largest white jacket. Did putting on one of these turn him into one of them? Would he become a White Coat? Become what he detested? He pulled his arms through the sleeves and buttoned up the front.

Gevu walked down the corridor. A human female came through a set of double doors, passed by him, and gave him a strange look. She was covered with blood. Slick and fresh. She tore off a piece of white fabric that was particularly soiled and threw it in a garbage can. He watched her for a moment and then headed for the doors.

"You're missing your apron. You'll need it on the kill floor." She pointed to a box that held similar coverings, and then she continued down the hall. Gevu picked up the one of the aprons and tried to figure out how to put it on. He remembered the woman had had part of it tied behind her head and another part tied behind her back. He guessed the largest portion of fabric was meant to protect his chest. He put the apron on quickly, then stepped through the double doors. Nothing could have prepared him for what he saw. The sounds of machinery mingled with squeals of fear.

This was the kill floor. This was where his kind died. Oh, yes, he was human too. He realized that. But he'd been raised in a pig womb, born of his mother, and suckled on her breast, if only for a moment. He felt more compassion for these helpless creatures than he did for humans. What did Dr. Wetzel tell him humans were called? *Homo sapiens*. And, Gevu, with his knowledge, his superior growth, his massive body-build...what was he? *Porci sapiens?* Dr. Skylar called him a swineman. Gevu felt his upper lip involuntarily twitch at the thought.

Machinery whined. A brown-skinned, burly man pulled a pig toward him, and it rolled on a conveyor belt. He placed the pig's leg up to a hook, which mechanically gripped it and hoisted the animal up into the air. The pig struggled as it stopped in front of another man who pushed a metal implement against the animal's head, right between the eyes, and then, suddenly, the pig stopped fighting. It was either unconscious or dead. Gevu couldn't tell which.

Gevu watched this maneuver a few more times, his breath rising and falling, faster and faster, until he pushed himself to move on. At the next station, another human used a knife to slash along the place where the pig's front leg and neck met. Gevu was startled at how the blood poured out of the animal in a thick, heavy stream. The pig started thrashing, and he realized the creature was still alive. They'd only stunned it, allowing its heart to pump blood from the body until it died. His knees felt wobbly, and he almost dropped to the floor.

All of them stunned and then bled out to die.

Gevu followed a carcass to the next processing station, where each body was dunked in a vat of boiling water and transferred to another conveyor belt. The bodies were rehung, and they swung in an aerial line of morbid processing, their heads hanging down, their feet spread apart. Each carcass stopped in front of a human that inserted a pistol-like implement into the pig's rectum. After that, the pig was moved to a machine that sawed its belly from chest to groin, and Gevu stepped back just a bit when he saw a gray mass of intestines spill from the corpse.

"Está bien?" A voice yelled behind him in Spanish. He'd studied a little Spanish. He turned briefly to look but raised his hand to signal he was okay. "Si," he said. The person behind him nodded and continued on, his appointed task keeping him moving with his duties. Gevu walked along, following the carcass. Many smaller Mexican women and men were cutting the organs of the pigs away from the body. Heart. Lungs. Liver. Despite Gevu's interest, he felt lightheaded. His world started to spin around him, and he realized he needed to leave.

"Hey! Hey you!" A larger man down the line cocked his head in Gevu's direction. His heart thumped in his chest. This was too much. He knew all about it now. He knew what humans did. What they'd made him eat. How could they? *They* were the animals. *Humans* were the beasts. Humans were cruel beyond anything he had ever comprehended. He turned and ran away, and then ran faster when he heard the footsteps in hot pursuit.

Someone else yelled, "It's one of those PETA fanatics!" A man stepped in front of him. Although the worker was wide and burly, Gevu pushed past him, a mere human was no match for his strength. He was superior. He was stronger than they could ever hope to be. The door he'd entered earlier caught his eye, and he pushed through it easily. Early morning air greeted his lungs, the smell of blood and steaming entrails replaced once more with the stink of excrement.

He sprinted toward the long white buildings he'd seen earlier. There were shouts behind him, and the sound of a truck revving up its engine. Gevu kept running, his lungs sucking air, his muscles screaming. He had to get to the white houses before the humans caught up to him.

It was not just the White Coats who made his kind suffer. It was all of the humans, and their desire to corral intelligence. Their desire to effectively neuter any form of life that posed a threat to their egotistical existence was testimony to their cruelty. These weaklings worked to keep his species helpless and vulnerable. They raised farm animals for their pleasure and consumption. And Gevu decided he would be their savior.

Gevu tore down the road, the momentum of his fury bringing the farm buildings closer. A pair of high beams framed him against the early twilight, and his shadow grew in front of him with increased intensity. He broke away from the pavement and jumped over a rough wooden fence that divided the grassy land. He headed for one of the long buildings furthest from the road. The truck slowed, and then, as if his pursuers realized exactly where he was running, they roared toward the animal housings with renewed vigor.

When he reached one of the end buildings, he grasped a lock on the double doors. Its housing was firmly bolted onto the wooden door. Blind with anger, red with fury, he wrapped his thick fingers around the lock and pulled with all of his might. The lock's housing budged slightly. He pulled again, and the entire plate that held the lock ripped away from the door.

The roar of the truck engine grew closer, but Gevu ignored it and allowed his eyesight to adjust to the scene before him. Several hundred pigs in various pens stood wallowing in their own excrement. Their faces turned toward him. Eyes dull, almost lifeless. He rushed to a gate, lifted the metal latch that helped to hold them captive, and threw it open.

The pigs just stood there. Some didn't even bother to rise to their feet. He entered their pen and growled in a loud and furious voice. "Move! Move!" Pigs scuttled here and there. A few made for the gate. He dashed out of the pen and headed for another. He unlatched the gate. Just as he started to pull it open, he heard a gunshot, its report briefly causing him to relive the day of his mother's death. He remembered his own experience firing a gun. Gevu unlatched another pen and dove among a group of pigs as bright lights flickered on. The animals grunted. Some squealed. He turned his eyes toward the door.

Four large men crowded at the entrance.

"We know you're in here! Best show yourself now. You're trespassing, and we don't need a reason to shoot you dead. Right here. Right now!"

Gevu crouched low between two very large swine. The scuffle of their boots on concrete was barely audible among the anxious grunts of disturbed pigs.

Four of them. Two at the door. Two walking toward me. Which one has the gun? And what if there's more than one firearm? Gevu caught sight of their shoes. He gathered himself together into a compacted ball and sprang over the gate toward the two men closest to him. He connected with one man and knocked him down, then landed and rolled to the side. With a quick glance, he realized it wasn't the man with the weapon. Gevu lifted his head, and looked directly into the end of a double-barreled shotgun.

"Hold it right there, you pansy-assed bastard! Take your mask off." An older, black-haired human, flecks of gray highlighting the sideburns of his shortly cropped hair, smacked the barrel of the gun against Gevu's hard hat. In a moment of pure reaction, Gevu seized his opportunity. He grabbed the barrel and lifted it to the ceiling while he stepped straight toward the man. In one brutal motion, he shoved the butt of the shotgun into the man's throat, which caused his fingers to let go of the weapon. The black-haired human crumpled to the ground.

A faint grunt from behind warned him of his other attacker, and Gevu swung the gun around like a baseball bat. The end of it connected with a younger man's head, and the sound of bone crunching sent a wave of pleasure through Gevu. Blood splattered on the floor, and the iron smell of it thrilled him.

Two down. Two to go. The two men guarding the door stared at him in shock, and both of them turned and ran. Gevu followed them into the open air of near dawn. Both men were running for the truck. He aimed at the larger one and pulled the trigger. The man went down, bright blood flying out from the center of his back.

The other man hollered and started to stammer as he reached the vehicle and climbed into the driver's seat. "Oh God, oh God..."

Gevu deliberately stalked up to the truck and pulled the door open just as his victim dropped a set of keys on the floorboard. He leveled the weapon at the man's head and enjoyed watching the man's face. The whites of his eyes grew excessively large, while his pupils shrank down into ebony pinpoints. His mouth opened into a large "O," but Gevu pulled the trigger before the human could beg or scream.

It was amazing to see what the weapon could do to a human skull. The windshield ran scarlet and gray with globs of flesh rolling down the glass like snot from the nose of a four-year-old child. Gevu admired his own handiwork. It was beautiful. Fragments of bone littered the dashboard. And nothing could have prepared him for the unimaginable high. He spied a box of ammo on the passenger side floor.

Nice. Very handy.

Gevu leaned over the dead body and grabbed a handful of shells. He pulled back with his prizes when heard a cell phone ring. Gevu cocked his head and fished the device out of the driver's front shirt pocket. He flipped it open and pushed the green button. An excited voice on the other end inquired, "You guys okay? Did you get him?"

"Yeah. Got him." Gevu barely managed to reply without laughing. He folded the phone and tossed it onto the corpse's lap. Then he headed back to the building. What was it he'd learned about loading shotguns? Break action versus pump action. This one was a break. He opened it and shoved two more rounds in the barrels as he strode back into the building. The man he'd struck in the throat was still on the ground gasping for air. The one he'd clubbed on the head remained unconscious.

Gevu bent over the first man. "Please," the man gasped while clutching at his neck. "Help me...please..."

"Oh yeah, I'll help you all right. You wanted to see my face, remember?" Gevu pulled down his mask and removed his hardhat and head cover. The man's eyes went wide, and his apparent shock made Gevu smile.

"I've seen what you do to my kind. It's time for us all to get even." Gevu stood up, stepped back, and aimed at the man's face. "Eat this." The resounding blast was sheer joy.

The wristwatch on the new corpse beeped. Gevu was running out of time. They'd soon realize their men had failed to haul him in. The other man was still unconscious. Gevu observed his arm twitch just a little. The hilt of a knife protruded from the comatose man's belt, and Gevu strode over to him, reached down, and pulled it free. The blade was a good four inches long and sharp.

Should've attacked me with that, buddy. You might have stood a chance. Gevu thought about the line of pigs hanging in the slaughterhouse, and his anger turned to ice. In one smooth motion, he bent down on one knee and plunged the knife into the side of the man's neck, slashing down to his shoulder bone. Blood spurted out against Gevu's face, and he licked the sticky warmth while the man's arms and legs jerked furiously. A pool of blood gathered beneath the body.

At that moment, Gevu decided he'd be more than the savior of his kind. He would be God. God was a master over life and death, and before he was done, that's exactly what he would be.

ELEVEN

September 22, 05:59

Miriam's cell phone rang about the same time she heard a creak of a floorboard downstairs on the front porch. She looked at the clock on her nightstand. Almost 06:00. She flipped open the phone while listening for the sound of the front door to open, but she only heard the songs of birds waking from slumber.

"Dr. Wetzel." She strained to hear if there were any other sounds in the house.

"Miriam?" a voice said on the other end.

"Harper? Is that you?" Her brain shook off any leftover sleepy haze, and she heard the upstairs bathroom door close. Then the water pipes in the farmhouse groaned and shuddered. Echoing sprays of water hit the walls of the tub. It was an odd thing to hear this early in the morning.

"Miriam, it's time to bring them in."

Her heart thumped inside her chest, and her palms grew moist. She tried to control her reaction, but in the absence of anyone who could see her, she didn't mind that the muscles around her left eye twitched.

It's too soon. We need more time.

She was about to argue with him when Harper continued. "We've had to call out another cleanup crew. Seems your boy caused some havoc just down the road. He found a pig farm this time. It wasn't pretty."

Miriam clenched her fist tight, squeezing her fingernails into her palm. The pain helped. She wouldn't allow tears to form in her eyes, although both Gevu and Binah were her life's work. At this point, she couldn't imagine anything worse than losing them. Yes, there was a higher cause she needed to rise to, but all of that research!

Damn it all to chaos theory! And so much left to be done.

"They wanted a killer. I guess I trained him well." She was proud that her voice hadn't trembled a note. It was calm, cool, and steady.

"Let's just make sure that he doesn't scrub you and Ben before you get him here."

"We knew the risks." She dismissed the threat but clutched the phone as if it were a life preserver. It was reassuring to hear his voice, although she was glad he wasn't standing in front of her. Her emotions were easier to control when she didn't have to look at him. "I'll handle it. Don't I always?" She knew Harper trusted her, and she'd never known a smarter or more capable man. No other human being could live up to the beauty she found in him. He was kind, but lethal. Quick thinking, but calculating. Well-spoken, but brutally honest. He was all that she would have ever wanted in a man.

Except, we can never be together.

The line went dead. Miriam slipped out of her T-shirt and underwear and used a sheet from a box of baby wipes on her nightstand to conduct some early morning hygiene. Then she dressed in a pair of jeans, threw on a bra and a clean shirt, and grabbed more wipes before she crept downstairs to take a look at the door. The light was still red, but she detected a tiny trace of blood on the panel. Miriam took a fresh wipe and cleaned it away. After a quick trip to the kitchen, she padded to the front door again, where the light now gleamed green, and she opened it. The sweet smell of freshly mown hay tickled her nose as her eyes scanned the porch floorboards. It was barely day. But, yes, there on the very edge of the bottom step, a smear of reddish brown told the story. Another pass of the damp cloth in her hand, and the blood was gone.

Oh, Gevu. Why couldn't you have waited?

He'd been bred for killing, but not like this. She inhaled a deep breath and let it out slowly. How much time did she have? Just a few hours? Maybe. After another trip to the kitchen and a flick of a switch, she headed upstairs to her room. The bathroom door was shut, the water still running. Miriam gently pulled out her duffel, and before packing, she texted Ben and told him to get his things ready. Hopefully he'd do it quietly and not alarm the children.

Children. How long had it been? Just a few short months? No, Gevu and Binah weren't children anymore. Not by any means. But it seemed just yesterday when they had been created in the lab. Only days ago when Harper had told her they had surgeons who could do what no one had ever done before. That her experiment would be unprecedented. She'd done her job, and now it was their turn. And though she'd never doubted Harper in the past, she couldn't help but wonder if he knew what he was doing by bringing them back right now.

Lambs to the slaughter.

She hoped the lambs that were waiting were ready.

TWELVE

September 22, 06:00

Binah had difficulty sleeping, and she tossed and turned in between intermittent waking. When she did sleep, she dreamed of nightmarish faces she'd never seen before. Faces that stared into her body as they bent over her. She dreamed of White Coats, sterile walls, and bright white lights, like those that had blinded her the day of her birth. Long silver needles chased her down endless hallways, and her screams echoed against the corridor, growing louder and louder. She flinched when she ran into a dead end and thousands of needles pelted against her body. Her eyelids fluttered open. Someone was in the shower. Her clock read 06:00. She looked at her door. The panel light was green, which was odd, given the early hour. The White Coats usually weren't up until 07:00.

Curious, she rose and straightened her flannel lounge pants. Her overly large T-shirt was rumpled from slumber. She opened her door and listened, then moved to the top of the stairs just in time to watch Dr. Wetzel wipe off the panel and then go through the front door. Something had happened, although she didn't know what.

Binah sniffed the air. The distinct odor of blood wafted from the bathroom. She shuddered. *Gevu, what have you done?*

She moved back into her room and shut her door, then went to her bed to wait. Her light went red again. Despite the noise coming from the shower and the groan of the water pipes, she heard Dr. Wetzel return to her room, and a slight rustling in the next-door closet told her the White Coat was doing something unusual. In the bedroom on the other side of her, she heard Dr. Skylar moving, and gentle sounds emanated from his room as well. The shower water stopped, and for a few long minutes, all was silent with the exception of a gentle scraping sound against one of the walls. Then the White Coats resumed their soft noises, and Binah could only sit on her bed and wait for whatever came next.

THIRTEEN

September 22, 08:20

Their morning routine wasn't the same as it had been. Binah's light stayed red until well after eight. When her panel light turned green, she went to the bathroom and then walked downstairs. Dr. Skylar and Dr. Wetzel sat at the table sipping coffee and talking with Chet. Chet's gaze flickered over to her, and he got up from his chair.

"Reckon I'd better go and get the truck ready." He pushed past her in the doorway without saying anything else, but his close proximity prompted her hair to bristle.

Bastard.

Binah looked back to the table and signed to the White Coats. *What's going on?*

Dr. Wetzel slid Dr. Skylar a sideways glance before she answered. "New plans today. We're going on a road trip."

Where? Binah signed nervously.

Dr. Wetzel got up to get more coffee. "You and Gevu have surpassed all that we can teach you," she said. "It's time for a higher level of training."

Binah looked at Dr. Skylar. *Ben, what is it really? What are you not telling me?*

Dr. Wetzel continued talking. "Eat some breakfast, then get dressed and pack your things. I'll put a duffel bag on your bed for you."

Ah, they were packing this morning.

Binah looked at the ceiling and signed to Dr. Skylar. *Gevu?* Her fingers spelled his name with rapid motion.

Dr. Skylar avoided making eye contact with her, and she sensed he felt as if they'd done something very wrong that day in the barn. Mating with him had come so natural. How could he ever see it as wrong? If only Chet hadn't found them and been so vile.

"Gevu's probably still sleeping," Dr. Wetzel answered. "And that's okay today. A little more sleep won't hurt him. Just an extra hour or so before we get started."

Binah went to the cupboard and pulled out a box of Cap'n Crunch. It was one of her favorite cereals. She got a bowl and filled it, poured almond milk into a glass, and took her breakfast to the table. Her spoon dug into the dry cereal, and she placed a scoop of it in her mouth. She sipped on the milk and enjoyed the way the cold creamy liquid swirled around the squares. Eating it this way always kept the cereal crunchy and didn't let it become soggy from sitting in the milk.

While she ate, Binah observed a fly stuck between the window glass and the screen. It bumped and buzzed, desperately trying to find a way out. Then she looked down to examine a dead fly on the window bottom. A casualty of prolonged captivity. She and the buzzing fly had one thing in common. They were both in a prison with little hope of escape.

What the fly needs is someone from the outside to give it some help. She lifted the window up, and the insect flew free, zoomed around her ears once, and then landed on her cereal. She didn't brush it away like she might have normally, but let it take off and land again on her food several times while she sat in deep thought.

FOURTEEN

September 22, 09:10

Chet quickly made his way back to the trailer on the far side of the farm. The place was near enough to the barn but not close enough for the science geeks to notice he had a lady. He'd decided to keep Stella a secret, and she had seemed content to sit and wait until it was time to kidnap the beasties.

Chet stood in the doorway to the bedroom and stared at Stella for a moment. She was still sleeping. Damn, that woman was a real piece of work, and he'd enjoyed having her around while they planned their kidnapping.

Fucking stupid-ass male pig. The animal had taken the wind out of his sails, causing problems before he was ready to act. He'd just have to make do.

Adapt and survive.

He had the truck transport ready with the proper crates in the back. What they'd never suspected was that the truck wasn't for them. He'd use it instead, take the animals, and make some money. Chet had contacts ready and waiting. And the Cullers, well, the Cullers could go to hell. Even Harper. They all treated him like a dumb-fuck farmhand despite the fact he had skills. And he now realized he could make much better pay working on his own. As one of the meanest mercenaries on the market, he was a commodity that would draw top dollar. He had contacts. Wealthy contacts.

Chet went over to the bed, reached down, and shook Stella's shoulder. Her back was to him. She smelled of that perfume he loved. What was it? He looked on the nightstand. Secret of Venus, with just a hint of oil of patchouli. She moaned for a second but still stayed asleep. He sat down on the edge of the mattress and shook her shoulder a bit harder. "Stella, wake up. We gotta go."

Stella rolled over and reached out to him. "Come here, baby. Let me kiss you." He bent down, and she gave him a long, lingering kiss. Damn if she didn't make his dick hard just by breathing on him. But he couldn't do anything about that problem right now. They didn't have much time. The geeks were going to be ready to go soon, and Chet planned on being long gone before they realized what was up.

"What's going on, baby?" The sleepy look in her blue eyes dissipated, and her gaze was clearer, more awake.

"It's time to take our show on the road." Chet cupped his hand around one of her breasts. "But, tonight, I swear to you, you'll be screaming for God over and over. How's that?"

She smiled at him with that coy purse of her lips. "Sure, baby. And I'll be wet and ready."

Chet got up and walked out the door. He had a lot to do, but damn if it didn't feel better knowing he had a hot woman to come home to.

Binah had packed most of her things. There were just a few of her paintings in the barn that she needed to get. They weren't particularly good, but they were ones she was proud of. She'd donned a black baby-doll T-shirt, extra-large, and a size-fourteen pair of black jeans. She'd cut a small hole in the back for the curlicue of her tail. Gevu typically covered his tail, but her pants were tighter, and she felt freer and more natural that way.

Binah opened the front door to make her way to the barn. Heavy, thick fingers grabbed her shoulder. She spun around. Gevu stood there, his eyes boring into her.

Where are you going? he signed.

Barn, she replied. *I smelled blood again this morning.* Then her hands moved rapidly. Accusingly. *What did you do?*

He averted his eyes from her and stood there for a moment. *Look up "animal slaughter" under Google. You'll figure it out.*

Her face fell as she processed what Gevu was saying. She suddenly understood all of Chet's vile jokes. She felt her heart beat wildly against her chest. All this time, with all they'd learned, and the White Coats hadn't told them.

We're leaving.

Gevu scowled.

She continued. *If you want any of your projects from the barn, you should get them.*

Gevu did nothing, but she could see him clench his jaw as he headed for the kitchen.

Binah walked down the steps of the porch and made for the barn. She inhaled the scents of grass and trees. After only a few weeks, she'd learned to love it here. Her first real experience with being outdoors. Her lessons. And mating. By her calculation, she should be in heat again soon. How was she supposed to deal with *that* every month?

She opened the barn door, went over to her makeshift easel, and picked up the canvas. It was done in acrylic paints, so the picture was dry. Oil paints took too long to dry. With the number of insects that swarmed around the building, they sometimes got stuck in the peaks of sepia, sienna, ebony, and olive that she loved to use.

A tube of red acrylic paint sat near her most recent creation, an abstract piece of art that only she would understand. Pink swirled against pieces of wooden fence here and there, and a palm and fingers flared out, screaming, "Stop!" in body language, blood dripping from the wrist. It was the most morbid piece she'd done so far. She'd put the image to canvas right after her latest nightmare.

"Well, well, what do we have here?"

Binah's heart twisted in her chest. She'd hoped not to run into him again this morning.

I was just leaving, she signed. She picked up the canvas and headed toward the barn doors.

He moved in front of her. "Now, Miss Piggy, you don't need to go. Let's visit awhile." He took the painting from her and tossed it on a bale of hay. She pushed him away. He flew back, hitting the ground with a thud. Her anger flared and rose to a furious boil. Here was the man who had shot their mother and abused Gevu, and he had ruined her most precious moment with Ben. She was pretty sure every cell in her body hated him.

Chet got up laughing, his hand going to his hip. "Well, well. Got some fight in you after all, eh? I'll show you just what I think of that." He pulled out his Taser, and Binah moved back. Chet spoke as he aimed at her. "This little piggy went to market..." Suddenly, blinding pain caused her to fall to the floor, every muscle in her body contracting. She was unable to move for just a few seconds. But those excruciating seconds were all that Chet needed. She watched him take out another weapon, a black pistol. She tried to run, but a large needle pierced her flesh when he pulled the trigger. She opened her mouth to scream, but only a grunt issued from her lips just before everything went dark.

Gevu did have a couple of things in the barn that he wanted to bring with him. One of them was a Lamborghini Miura engine, one of the toughest car engines to work on. It was the greatest challenge Dr. Wetzel had given him. He'd taken it apart and put it back together easily—twice. He wasn't sure where the White Coats were moving him to, but he was pretty sure he'd have to leave the V12. He wanted to see it one last time and grab a few other things.

The air was crisp and smelled sweet. Dry grass and dirt crunched underneath his feet while his thoughts scrolled through memories from last night. Despite all of his research and reading, he'd never once thought about what humans did to pigs. Sure, Chet had killed his mother, and Dr. Wetzel had given him the order. But there was some other reason, wasn't there? He hadn't considered that humans used pigs for food. What were he and Binah meant for? Why grow their swineman kind at all? Certainly not for food. For some weird experiment? He knew the White Coats were studying them, but there were so many unanswered questions.

Gevu entered the barn, heard a muffled noise, and then caught the scent of something he'd smelled once before. It was heavy, rich, and musky. *Sex.*

He slowly crept around a stall, and what he saw was unthinkable. Binah was asleep or passed out, lying on her stomach over a bale of hay. Her pants were around her knees, and Chet was kneeling on the ground, pumping his dick into her, fast and hard. Gevu moved a little to the side so he could see Chet's face. His expression was one of pure hatred as he gunned into her again and again. And all Gevu could do was watch in fascination. The man was raping his sister, and he was watching. And Gevu realized, oddly, that he had an erection. Still, he did nothing. He felt compelled to see what happened next. He was paralyzed.

Chet pulled out of Binah, and then forced himself into her anus, grinning when he saw a little trickle of blood seep from the ring of her bottom after a few violent thrusts.

"You'll never know what hit ya, baby, but you'll be walking sore for days, that's for sure." He chuckled as he fucked her. A few more groans, and he banged up against her flesh and pressed himself there, grunting and moaning. Chet stood up a moment later, walked over to Binah's face, and shook his dick over it. A thin stream of urine trickled onto her head.

Gevu's fascination was gone, and his strange curiosity was sated. His outrage burst into a furious explosion, and his muscles bolted into action. He let out a primal growl and charged at Chet. Before Chet knew what had hit him, Gevu threw the man against the barn wall, fracturing some wooden boards. He ran forward, pinned him against the boards, and pummeled Chet with his fists, pounding blows of hatred he'd harbored for the man these many months.

Chet pounded him right back, but Gevu was stronger. Chet's body curled down into a squat with his hands over his face, and Gevu kicked him until the man ended up on the floor, his boots facing Gevu's head as he tried to ward him off. Gevu grabbed a boot, pulled, and twisted it past his hip. Chet's thigh was now in front of his head. Gevu opened his mouth wide and clamped down on Chet's leg, the quadriceps firm and chewy between Gevu's teeth. The jean material gave way like the skin of an apple in Gevu's mouth. Gevu pulled his head back, bringing a sinewy chunk of Chet's muscle with him, and ignored the man's howls of pain.

Excellent! He ground the meat between his teeth. *The taste is excellent.* Muscle tissue and blood roll around on his tongue, and he savored the flavor a moment longer. He was ready for another bite when Gevu heard a click, and suddenly, pain coursed through his body. Gut-wrenching paralysis dropped him to the ground.

Funny thing was, Chet was incapacitated too. The electricity coursed through his body even as he'd pulled the trigger on Gevu, and now they were both lying on the floor waiting to regain their muscular ability. Chet smiled at him and wiggled his fingers. Gevu tried desperately to push his muscles to move. Nothing. Chet aimed another firearm at him, but this one was different. "Thanks for saving me the trouble of rounding you up, Porky. You know all that stuff I just did to your sister? Well, you'll get a good dose while you're sleeping too. And when you wake up, you can tell her all about it."

Chet dragged Binah to the truck with some difficulty. His leg hurt like shit, but his adrenalin pumped energy into him and helped to numb the pain. The delivery vehicle was one he'd worked on for a couple of weeks now. It was intended to transport the animals, and he'd designed it for the scientist bitch in order to take the piggies to the research facility on the military base.

He placed Binah in the back, inside a specially designed pen. From the head up, her features looked very much like that of a standard pig except for the longer shock of hair on her head. He'd situated the crates so they sat at the back of the truck bed; if there were an inspection at the base's gates, the guards wouldn't get close enough to see her human features. Now, the strategy would benefit him just in case the police stopped him for any reason. If he had to open the back, all they'd see were pigs.

Chet texted Stella to help him with Gevu. Damn, his leg was killing him. The animal had not only bitten him, he'd taken a small chunk of muscle out of his thigh. Chet had placed a tight-pressure bandage on the wound to keep it from bleeding, using a piece of torn T-shirt, but he'd need medical attention soon to make sure the wound healed okay.

All in all, he felt satisfied. The injury had been worth it to screw that pretentious little piggy that acted like her shit didn't stink, and to take down the big guy who thought he was human. *Better* than human. Let the buyers deal with the little shits. He'd take their money. The next morning he'd become a Canadian. Stella would go with him, and together they'd live high on the hog. Chet smiled at how his own wit entertained him in moments like this.

High on the hog. Heh.

Stella flipped her phone open. She didn't wait for a voice. "What do you want me to do?"

"Let him keep going. We need to find out who his buyer is. It's important. We'll step in when we need to."

"Got it." She shut the phone. Her shithead prince waited, along with his bestial carriage. In her opinion, midnight couldn't come soon enough.

September 22, 09:51

Ben was in the shower when he thought he heard a voice yell somewhere in the distance. He shut the water off for a minute or two, but he didn't hear anything more. He twisted the water back on, and the hot jets pummeled his back. His mind dove into the problem of transferring Gevu and Binah to the research facility on the coast at Point Mugu.

It bothered him to lose the one-on-one interaction he'd had with the subjects, but since Gevu's rapid growth and the development of Binah's maturity, he had to admit he felt a bit of relief. Things were getting out of control. Miriam hadn't told him what happened, but he'd find out soon enough. After Gevu's chicken episode, he guessed it was something similar. Something that could potentially lead law enforcement to the farm. Ben just hoped Miriam knew what she was doing. More than that, he hoped he knew what *he* was doing. He couldn't afford to make any more mistakes.

"Let's ride, baby! Ride!" Chet pulled the truck out from the side of the barn and adjusted his hat. It didn't matter now if the geeks saw him or not. He had money, the piggies were in the vehicle, and he had Stella. And what were they going to do? Report him to the police? Nah, his biggest worry was the Cullers. No doubt they'd been keeping tabs on the house and goings-on. Good thing he had his woman to help him out. She was Bonnie, and he was Clyde, only he didn't plan on dying.

He pointed the truck toward Interstate 5. Los Angeles was just a few hours away. There he could disappear, meet his contact, and get rich. He could fly out of LAX, and he'd never have to work in the United States again. Stella flashed him a smile, and he gunned the truck down the road. It was going be heaven living like a real man. A house. A woman. And some place with peace and quiet. He guessed he ought to break the news to Stella while they were driving. She'd be surprised, but he had no doubt she'd come with him. She'd come this far, hadn't she? Her cell phone rang. She looked at it and placed the phone back in her pocket.

Chet was suddenly suspicious. "Who's that?" She hadn't received a phone call since they'd been together these few weeks. Her phone messages were always empty. He'd made sure to check. No texts. Nothing. And now she gets a call?

"Nobody," she said. "Old friend I keep trying to ditch." She hit the delete key.

Chet was quiet as he drove, and he turned up the KUZZ, Bakersfield's best country-music station. He was processing a lot right now and trying to decide what to do. Perhaps meeting Stella wasn't coincidence after all. Perhaps she was a plant. But if so, by who? Tim McGraw started singing, "I'm better than I used to be," and Chet sang along. And as he did, he realized he meant every word.

Harper hung up the phone and crushed it on the floor under his heel. He focused on one of the many computer screens in the room. One in particular caught his attention. The tracking beacon blipped along the map, and the satellite view was clear. He walked over to the screen and used his hands to adjust the view. "Side cameras?"

"Coming up, sir," one of his men said. In moments, he could see the entire vehicle close up. Just a basic white delivery truck with a magnetic sign stuck to the side. *Greenside Farms*. Pictures of cows, pigs, and chickens all standing happily together. Big fucking harmony.

General Muttnic frowned at the picture and sat forward in his chair.

"You sure this is going to work, Harper? We can't let them escape."

"Absolutely, sir. You have my word. They'll be in the facility quicker than you can say *Porco Rosso*."

"What's that supposed to mean?"

"It means you won't have time for a nap or you'll miss everything."

FIFTEEN

September 22, 10:11

"Binah! Gevu!" Miriam stood with the front door open. Nothing stirred. The air was eerily still. She'd checked the videocam earlier and hadn't seen any movement in the building. A floorboard creaked. Ben was pulling on a shirt as he came down the stairs. Miriam caught a glimpse of his well-cut stomach muscles just before the cloth covered them. She hadn't realized he was in such great shape, which was odd because she knew he exercised every day. She'd been so caught up in her research that she hadn't really taken the time to notice.

"I'm still packing. Can you run up and check on them? I don't see them on the screens, and both of them went to the barn to pick up some of their things."

Where is Chet? He should be dismantling the equipment.

"Sure." Ben didn't bother with shoes. He stepped outside and crossed the small field to the barn. Miriam closed the door, went upstairs, and brought her bags down. The Cullers would be here soon to help Chet remove any indication of their stay here. They'd take care of Chet too, she suspected. *Couldn't happen to a meaner guy.* She supposed they'd known what they'd be dealing with when they took him on.

The front door burst open. "They're gone." Ben was breathing rapidly as he stood at the threshold. "Gevu and Binah are gone. And there's no sign of Chet or the truck."

"Shit!" Miriam hadn't thought Chet would be so stupid. He'd decided to make a fortune with her fucking research. She'd suspected he was capable of rash behavior, but she didn't think he'd try something like this. Not under their very noses.

He must have realized the Cullers wouldn't let him go alive. With that thought, she wondered how long she and Ben had before the organization decided the same for them.

They couldn't. They don't have an inkling of how to recreate the project.

But what if they did? That would mean her and Ben's days were definitely numbered. Once Gevu and Binah were in the hands of the military, officials probably thought they could easily clone them.

Not so easy. They won't have that extra sprinkle of pixie dust. Miriam felt a self-satisfied wave of pleasure ripple across her chest. It paid to keep some information inside the head and nowhere else.

"Miriam!"

She looked at Ben, realizing she'd been staring into space. "Get the car keys. I'll be right behind you," she said.

"Truck or van?"

The black Ford would probably be faster, and it could take tough terrain if was necessary.

"Truck."

Ben pulled the keys from where they hung in the hallway and ran out to the Ford.

Miriam dialed a number. Thank the spirit of Nikola Tesla, at least she'd thought to put a tracker on both trucks as well as their van. No one answered. *Fuck! Harper where are you?*

Miriam hoped Chet hadn't gotten far. He would head for the highway. Maybe for the city.

Son of a bitch, I knew we shouldn't trust him.

But Harper had trusted him, and Harper didn't make mistakes. If this was a mistake, it was the first time she'd ever known the man to miscalculate. The thoughts buzzed through Miriam's head like hornets in a nest on fire. And like the hornets, all she could do was move fast and hope that the devastation didn't overtake her.

Miriam grabbed the keys from Ben as he was opening the door to the driver's side.

"I've got this. You navigate."

Ben ran over to the passenger side, and they both strapped in. She handed him a computer tablet, already set with the map and tracking the vehicle. He looked surprised, but he accepted it and immediately studied the face of the screen.

Pedal to the floor, Miriam peeled out but kept her cell phone in her hand. She probably wouldn't need the map, but what if Chet took a detour? And where the fuck was Harper? She scanned the ridgeline, the forests, and the sky wondering if the Cullers even had a clue.

SIXTEEN

September 22, 10:42

"So where we headed, babe?" Stella realized Chet had been quiet the past few miles, opening his mouth only to sing an occasional song or two.

Chet glanced over at her and smiled as he stared back at the road. "Los Angeles. Some guys are gonna give us a big payday."

"What then? What about the scientists and that military group you told me about? What's their name?"

"The Cullers? Oh, don't worry about a thing, sweet cheeks. I got it all covered." He seemed to hesitate for a moment before he reached down toward the floor and pulled out something black and shiny. His hand reached for hers, and she gave him her palm. "Colt .45. You remember how to shoot, right?" Stella handled the weapon carefully and tried to make sure she looked comfortable, but not too comfortable.

"It's been a while." She didn't bother to tell him she liked this firearm better than the M9 Berretta. The trigger was easier to squeeze, and she didn't have to worry about the slide catching on the web of her hand. Stella checked to make sure the weapon's safety was on and popped open the magazine to see it was full. Seven packed in. One already in the chamber. "Jesus," she said, happy he didn't know about the pistol in her purse. "You really think we're going to need this?"

Chet reached down, pulled out four more loaded magazines, and set them down beside her.

"You can bet our lives on it."

Binah regained consciousness first. Her head throbbed with a powerful aching, and her mouth felt dry. The moment she realized her hands and feet were tied and that she was enclosed inside a wooden box with only her head sticking out, she started to panic. She wrenched at her bindings, but her hands didn't come free. Chet had used some sort of plastic tie around them, and the more she struggled, the more the pieces bit into her skin. A little bump and jump of the floor let her know she was in some kind of vehicle, but it was too dark to see. Only a few strands of light seeped through the back door.

The vehicle hit another bump, and her buttocks slapped against the floor. Binah's face burned with anger and embarrassment when she realized her pants were around her knees. She was helpless to readjust them and could only endure the cold floor against her bottom. And her bottom hurt. Binah tried to remember what had happened. She'd gone to the barn. She'd run across Chet. Then suddenly she understood what had happened. He had electrocuted her, tranquilized her, and raped her while she was unconscious. Why would he have done such a thing? If she ever got free, Chet would pay.

A low growl rose in the shadows beside her. Gevu was coming to. When he was completely awake, he was going to be furious. If he managed to free himself from his bonds, Chet's minutes in this world would be numbered; she'd seen Gevu kill. She personally hated the idea of ever taking a life, but something odd flickered inside her skull, and if Gevu just happened to get free and try to kill Chet, Binah wasn't sure if she'd lift a finger to stop him. Her brother groaned again, and his breaths became ragged and deep. He let out a roar that shook the walls of the truck. Then Gevu made more noises, as if he were struggling.

"Gevu!" Binah tried to reach him with her voice. "Gevu!"

He quieted for a moment. "Fucking bastard."

"He raped me, Gevu. I can feel it. And my..." She wasn't sure it mattered to him, but she continued. "My pants are around my knees."

"I know." Gevu took some deep breaths and then struggled against his bonds again. The plastic strips apparently held tight. "I can't get loose."

Binah kept quiet for a moment, the wheels in her head turning. How did he know she'd been raped? Had he been there? She didn't want to know the answer. Not yet.

"Where do you think he's taking us?"

Gevu was silent. A long minute went by as the truck jiggled and roared.

"To market." And then silence claimed them both once more.

Ben held the computer tablet steady and focused on the map. Miriam was driving like a madwoman. He hadn't known she could do the things she did behind the wheel. They came to a turn in the road, and she drifted around the corner like a professional driver. "Careful, Miriam!" An orange Corvette rolled past them, barely missing her front bumper. Its horn blared with indignation, but it kept going.

"How far?" Her words sounded tight, as if she had pressed them through her teeth.

"Ten miles maybe?" Ben looked at the map, the little blip on the line growing ever closer. "It looks like we're gaining ground, though."

A whirring sound passed above them, and Ben looked up. A small, black helicopter was flying just overhead. "Chopper!" He was surprised, but he'd suspected the Cullers were watching them all along. With an experiment this hot, how could they not? And he'd done everything they'd asked, including a few genetic modifications he wasn't permitted to tell Miriam about.

That was something he'd had a hard time coming to terms with. He'd met with the admiral. What was his name? He pictured the man's deadpan face. *Blandy. Name like the face.* The admiral had asked if he could do it. When Ben had said that he could, he'd been told to make the changes and keep his modifications quiet. There had been a threat in the admiral's voice. A tone that had made it clear his life, and Miriam's, depended on his silence.

Ben could live with dying for doing what was right, but he couldn't accept being the cause for Miriam dying too. There wasn't a day that went by that he didn't want to tell her what he'd done. Because it might change everything.

Shots came from the chopper overhead. The sound of bullets piercing metal rang against their eardrums. Miriam's eyes widened.

"They're shooting at us!" Miriam looked at her phone once more. She frowned. Ben gathered she didn't like what she saw—or, rather, what she didn't see. Instead of slowing to a stop, Miriam pushed the pedal to the floor and zoomed down the road even faster.

More shots came from the helicopter. Bullets pierced the back of the roof, barely missing them, and then the right rear tire blew out. "Miriam, you've to got to stop!" Miriam ignored him, swerved, and tried to keep going. He grabbed her arm, hoping to reach through her fury by touching her. She glared at him fiercely. "We have to keep moving!"

"Em, we've got to stop! The tire's damaged. Can't you see? It's what they want. They want to get there first." He paused for a moment, then said, "Do you know why they want to get there before us?"

Miriam looked as if she wanted to bite her lip. Her facial muscles twitched as she pulled the truck to a stop. Nothing but brown farmland and a few houses dotted the countryside. Her muscles visibly relaxed as if she'd turned on a switch. "Get the spare tire," she said. "We're wasting time."

Ahead of them, the chopper flew southwest, toward the horizon. Ben couldn't help but feel chills prickle down his spine. The wind was changing, and it didn't feel good.

"Just a few more miles." Chet barreled down the southern asphalt of Interstate 5 as fast as he dared to go. The last thing he needed was to get pulled over by a black-and-white. He was mildly surprised the lab geeks hadn't found him yet. *Not so much as a fart of trouble.* The fact he hadn't encountered any resistance made him uneasy. He looked over at Stella. He expected her to be nervous, but instead, she seemed relaxed. Every now and then, he caught her checking her side view mirror.

"See anything?" Chet looked at the rearview too, but maybe Stella had noticed something he hadn't. Was he too trusting? She hadn't pulled out her cell phone once, which was reassuring, but that phone call nagged at him.

"Not a thing, babe." She tucked a flyaway piece of hair behind her ear. "But it's weird, isn't it? When I saw them, I just knew these guys were—well—important. Seems as if there'd be..."

"What?" Chet was interested in what she'd say. He wanted to trust her. After all, he had plans. And she'd become part of them. He'd handed her a weapon. Granted, it was one that didn't work, but she wouldn't know until she tried to pull the trigger.

"It just seems too easy," she said. "You trust these guys we're meeting with?"

"Not one ass hair. Nope. That's why you've got that." He pointed his chin toward her gun.

Chet turned off the highway and made for East 4th Street. He'd find out sooner or later exactly who was on his side.

The rotary blades kept turning as Harper and two other men got out of the chopper. He knew LA's finest weren't happy about giving way to his request for a landing on their helipad, but fuck them. At least he had some military muscle to back him up.

He called over a handheld radio. "Cars in position?"

A voice answered back. "Waiting on you, Chief."

Harper and his men headed downstairs. "Don't let the others get too close. Wait for my call." He ignored the indignant looks from the surrounding PD. He half expected a challenge. Even half hoped for it. He hadn't done hand-to-hand in a while, though he expected these newbs were far from up to the task.

A uniform on the first floor took him out the back door. "*Los Angeles Times* is across the street. Keep a low profile. We can't sneeze without them hearing," he advised.

"Thanks," Harper replied, though he wanted to ignore the man.

You never know who you're going to need on your side.

He and his men slipped into a vehicle with darkly tinted windows. Chet was too predictable, which might make him seem less threatening. But Harper knew that simply wasn't the case. From now on, until he had the cargo, things were going to be much more dangerous.

Miriam wove in and out of interstate traffic, fighting to regain the precious minutes she'd lost. An RV puttered in front of her in the left lane. She honked her horn and flashed her lights, hoping the driver would move over. All four lanes were blocked with slow-moving drivers.

"Son of a bitch!" The RV finally moved over. She passed the mammoth vehicle and saw a gray-haired couple conversing and laughing amiably. It was an effort to repress the urge to roll down Ben's window and remind them the left lane was the fast lane, not memory lane. But why take her anger out on them? She wasn't angry with them. She was afraid, afraid of losing her research, and extremely pissed that the Cullers had dared to slow her down.

Who the fuck do they think they're dealing with?

"Looks like they're headed toward the river," Ben said. Miriam hoped that the map on the screen was accurate and that Ben was steering her right. Once they got off the highway, Chet would be difficult to find. Especially if he managed to duck his vehicle into one of the abandoned warehouses along the way. She couldn't afford the time it would take to locate him. The Cullers could be engaging Chet at any minute, and if they did, one of her babies could be hurt.

The corners of her jaw hurt, and she realized she'd been clenching her teeth. *Damn it, Gevu!* When she got him back—and she would get him back, she'd make sure he understood what his little stunt cost her. She'd make it perfectly clear.

"Turn here."

Miriam barely made the turn in time, rounded the corner, and was dismayed to find they were stuck in the middle of traffic. Cars were bumper to bumper with nothing to do but inch between stoplights. "Damn! Damn! Damn it!" She pushed through a yellow light just as it turned red. Blue and crimson suddenly flashed behind her, and a siren started to squeal. "No. Fucking. Way." The cop car followed closely behind her. She pulled the vehicle to a side road, and the police car raced by her. Two black SUVs with darkly tinted windows followed closely behind it. Miriam pushed the truck forward and up onto the sidewalk, turning the vehicle around to follow.

"Miriam! What are you doing? This is a one way street!"

"Hang on." She pulled around, drove up on the walkway, and sideswiped an oncoming car. Despite the honking horns and yelling, she kept going and put the truck back onto the main street. She was several cars behind the black SUVs, but she instinctively knew the direction they were going. And come chaos or oblivion, when they arrived at their destination, she was going to be there too.

Gevu wriggled his wrists against the plastic zip ties and realized two things. One was that he and Binah weren't on their way to a slaughter. If Chet had wanted them dead, they would have been dead already. Which meant they were valuable.

Two, even if he did get loose, he had no way to survive. There was nowhere for him to go, and he didn't know the territory where they were being transported. He might be caught too easily. Never mind Binah. She'd want to make a peaceful approach toward the humans. Stop and make friends. His sister was so naïve.

Maybe he could make a break for it. Try to hide.

No. Let this play out. See who's involved.

"We've stopped!" Binah sounded nervous.

He snorted. Why did she insist on stating the obvious? *Hard to believe we were born from the same mother.* Binah was so different. She was his polar opposite. He couldn't understand her affection for the White Coats. Especially since he'd told her what they did to pigs. Even though they weren't exactly pigs, they weren't human either. At least pigs were strong, smart, and true to their nature, while humans were puny, weak, and untrustworthy. If the humans hadn't abused and dominated the swine species, what kind of animals might they have evolved to be?

Something better. Gevu's bonds were now loose against his wrists. He could have snapped them at any moment and made a run for it. Instead, he sat quietly and waited.

"Gevu?" Binah sounded worried. His simpering sister actually acted like she cared for him, and maybe she thought she had feelings for him. But he knew she feared him more than anything. He'd seen to that. Well, she was the closest to family he'd ever have. At least for now. There was nothing to do but make the most of it.

The back doors of the truck opened into the dim light of an underground building. After so much darkness, the lights from the ceiling made him squint.

"Ah, little piggies. You're awake." Chet's boisterous voice echoed against the walls. "All the better for the sale."

Gevu overheard snatches of a foreign language in the background. It sounded oriental. *Not Japanese. Korean? No. Chinese? Maybe—yes, but rough. Not Mandarin.*

The beam of a flashlight struck his eyes, momentarily blinding him.

"Mr. Ching. Delivered as promised."

A shadow of a man grunted behind the light. Gevu listened carefully to the words. If he remembered the syllables, perhaps he could research it later.

"Show me the rest of them."

Chet hesitated and left Gevu's line of sight for a second, a motion that removed the beam of the flashlight out of his eyes. His vision adjusted. Several Asian men stood there. Six or seven. Maybe more around the corner. He spied a tattoo on one man's forearm. He didn't know what it meant, but he memorized the stroke of the characters. As he did, he realized Binah was doing much the same. She wasn't panicking. Maybe she had more strength in her than he thought. The flashlight's beam blazed into his eyes once more.

"Pardon me, Mr. Ching, while my associate here keeps you company." Gevu couldn't see the person, but he could smell her perfume. Rich with a woodsy scent he couldn't place. He could smell blood too, and Gevu salivated at the thought of how good Chet's flesh had tasted. He bared his teeth as Chet came near him, unbuckled a hinge to his box, and swung a panel out. Chet didn't respond to his sneer but did the same to Binah's box. Their hands and feet were fully visible.

From the shadows behind Chet's light, Gevu heard a voice. "Impressive." The men talked among themselves in their language excitedly, and he could have sworn he saw one or two of them bow in his direction. Chet's sweaty stink permeated the air. After the men took a long look, the filthy human closed the panels on the boxes and latched them.

"Give me the money, and they're all yours." Chet winced as he got down from the truck, a move that gave Gevu some satisfaction.

"You were not followed?" A pause filled the air. From somewhere above them, Gevu heard the rumble of a vehicle passing overhead.

"Hell yes, I was probably followed, Ching-man! Listen, I took the risk. I pulled off my end of our bargain. Give me the money." Gevu detected the sharp edge in Chet's voice. Chet placed the flashlight on the floor of the truck, and Gevu heard a click. One he distinctly recognized. Chet had a pistol. Another click echoed next to Chet. Whoever he was with was armed as well. Gevu felt the spring-loaded tension in the air.

"I see," came the thickly accented voice of Mr. Ching. A man with a large rectangular case came forward and moved between the two figures. Chet was easy to spot because of his cowboy hat. The other man opposite him must be the leader. The man in the middle must be a nobody. A hired hand. "Four million, as agreed," said the leader, Mr. Ching.

Chet's shadow motioned with his weapon. "Open it."

"You dare disrespect me? The count is correct." There was disbelief in Mr. Ching's voice. Two figures near him in the background raised up what appeared to be firearms. Gevu found the whole scene rather comical.

"Not trusting of anyone, Ching-man. Don't take offense."

The man between them bent down, and the rectangular box opened. "That's good enough," Chet said, and he motioned with his weapon for the man to get up. The rectangular object was snapped shut. "We'll be on our way. Forgive us for taking one of your vehicles."

"You cannot!"

"Oh, but I can, Ching-man. And I will. And you better get moving. I'm betting this vehicle's got a tracker or a bug—maybe both, and I gotta get the hell out of Dodge." Chet and his partner moved away, and the doors to the truck closed, plunging him and Binah into darkness. Just when he thought he'd probably have time for some shuteye before the next boring event, he heard several shots. An enormous wave of pleasure washed over him. Biding his time was working perfectly.

SEVENTEEN

September 22, 16:03

"She's close behind us, sir."

Harper listened to the words through his earpiece and issued an order. "Keep her covered. Allow her to enter, but only five minutes after our crew has gone in. I don't care how you do it, but we need those minutes."

"Roger that." His earpiece was silent for the moment. He'd ordered all communications to be kept to a minimum in order to keep the channel free.

"Status?" Harper was in the rear SUV, and he hadn't spotted where Chet had taken the truck. The tracer wasn't picking up. The signal was scrambled and hard to pinpoint.

"Just a block away from the Chinese Consulate, sir. They went through a gate and disappeared." Taylor was a good man. Reliable and adept.

"Send us the location. They're probably underground. Sardano?"

Harper's driver looked at him from the rear view mirror.

"You'd best make sure your firearm is ready."

Sardano stared back out at the road and started rubbing his fingers along the edges of the steering wheel. If Harper didn't know better, he'd think the man's mood had just improved. Perhaps it had.

———

Stella's shirt was damp beneath her armpits, and she felt a few beads of sweat trickle down from her brow. She'd checked her cell phone three times. No messages. No communications. When Chet had stood at the back of the truck talking to a group of what Stella assumed were Chinese Mafia because of their oriental eyes, their bad-ass look, and the fact they were near the consulate, she'd tried to call Harper, but the number she'd punched in went directly to a recording.

We're sorry, but the number you have dialed is no longer in service.

"Fuck your service," she said. She noticed in the rearview that Chet was coming to get her. She threw her phone in her purse.

"Need you, baby. Bring your things. Keep your iron ready."

Stella threw the extra magazines in her purse and slid the bag over her left shoulder while hefting the pistol into her right hand. She held the barrel down, careful not to point it at anyone, but she knew an observer could see she carried it with confidence. Chet climbed into the truck, showed the men Gevu and Binah, and then slowly emerged and closed up the doors. He threw the keys to the man he'd been talking to earlier and walked in reverse toward one of their sedans.

"C'mon, Stella. Back up easy. We're taking the consulate car. Diplomatic immunity." Chet chuckled, but Stella felt far from laughing. Harper was supposed to be here. She hadn't bargained for a shootout at the Wing Chun corral. A crash sounded overhead. The Asian men in front of her looked up at the ceiling.

Chet turned his head and yelled at her, "Run, now! Run!" They both dove for the car. Chet opened the door and twisted the key sitting in the ignition as bullet rounds pierced the glass in front of them and the windshield fractured. Stella pulled out her gun and aimed it out of her half-open window. Her finger pulled the trigger, but the gun didn't go off. She checked the weapon's safety as more bullets pinged against metal. Safety was off. *Damn it!* Chet had handed her a bum gun. Which meant he suspected her of being a traitor. Which meant she had to be extremely careful.

"Drive!" Stella felt like everything was moving in slow motion. The Chinese were firing at them; she and Chet were leaving the truck with the pig experiments inside. Harper and his men were breaking through the barrier on the floor above them, and Stella was sitting next to a man she loathed more than any other.

I will blow my cover before I get on a plane with him.

Chet floored the vehicle and grazed two Chinese men who'd run toward them. A black SUV barreled into the underground parking deck and screeched to a halt. Their sedan leaped away from it and barely missed swiping a second SUV as it came down the ramp.

Harper. Stella stared as it went by. She didn't know for sure, but if she were a betting woman, and she most certainly was, Harper was in that vehicle and pulling all the strings.

"Yeehaw!" Chet was acting like a tweeker after a fresh hit of meth. They'd barely escaped with their lives, and he was high as a kite. Time for his reality check.

"Chet, where we going, babe? We can't fly out of here, if that's what you're planning. Not with this money and the firearms we're carrying." She made her best pouty face and tried to look nervous. She didn't have to work very hard. Everything had been planned up until this point. The Cullers knew who the buyers were, but instead of arriving on time and dispatching Mr. Yeehaw, they'd botched it, which had left her alone to fend for herself.

"We are gonna drive for a little bit, ditch the car, and pick up a new one. Then we're driving to Vancouver. From then on, sweet cheeks, it's just you and me." Chet grinned at her, and she tried to smile at him convincingly. She looked out the window and pressed her lips together. She still had her purse, which meant she had one working pistol. And Chet was injured. He reached over and ran his hand up her thigh.

If there's an intervention planned on the Culler side, then it better happen soon. If it didn't, then Stella swore she wouldn't take it lying down anymore. She'd become the mother of invention with a four million dollar bounty.

Harper's SUV pulled up just as the consulate sedan pulled away from the scene. One look around, and he knew just what had happened. Chet was gone. And Stella. *Shit.* He gave the word for additional men to tail them and turned his attention to the Chinese. The consulate was only a block away. This was a parking deck near an abandoned warehouse. But most of these thugs weren't from the consulate. All but maybe one or two were from the streets. Which probably meant a gang.

Harper stepped out of the SUV, his empty hands raised level with his shoulders. "Lower your weapons, team." When his men pointed their barrels at the floor, the well-dressed and obvious leader of the group made a hand motion, and the members of the Asian group either pointed the barrels of their guns at the floor or holstered them.

Each step was measured in terms of appropriate assertiveness and mutual respect as Harper approached the leader. "My name is Harper." He made a short bow. "I'm afraid there's been some mistake. This is federal property." Harper jutted his chin at the delivery truck as he said the words.

The well-dressed Chinese man gave a curt nod with his head. Harper noted it wasn't a customary bow. "My name is Mr. Ching. Mr. Wah Ching. I believe we have a misunderstanding. This is Chinese property, bought and paid for, and you are on Chinese soil. Surely you haven't failed to notice this parking deck runs just underneath our building?"

Harper fought not to roll his eyes. *Mr. Wah Ching?* What idiot would use the name of a well-known Chinese syndicate as a cover? Surely the man realized how ridiculous he sounded. Harper switched tactics to gauge the man's intelligence and background.

"These were not your option to buy. They were not for sale." Harper continued in Mandarin. It was one of many languages he spoke fluently.

The man in front of him frowned as if Mandarin were not his preferred dialect. That told Harper something. This man was not government. But he wasn't mafia either. He looked more traditional.

"Perhaps, given the circumstances, we can come to an agreement?" Harper uttered the words this time in perfect Teochew. He was rewarded with a bow comparable to the one that Harper had given him.

"Please tell me what it is that you had in mind?" It was clear Mr. Ching realized he was not going to win this round.

"Payment equal to the sum you've recently parted with." Harper's opponent started to frown. "Plus fifteen percent interest for your inconvenience in this misunderstanding." It goaded Harper to give this man more money than he came with, but Projects Julia and Kilo were worth every dime. Worth even more than the military realized. They'd come to understand soon enough. Then, it would be too late.

"Done." The man graced him with one word of his revered language.

"You will trust me to make the appropriate delivery." Harper said the words as a statement, not a question. He pulled out a disposable cell phone and began to walk toward Mr. Ching. Immediately firearms pointed again in his direction. He kept his arms raised, blatantly showing the cell phone. Mr. Ching nodded for Harper to come closer. "One time use. Send the account number, and then you can dispose of it."

Ching took the device and seemed satisfied. He held out the keys to the truck and said in English. "An exchange of trust."

Harper took them and bowed once more to the man. The leader spun on his heel and returned to another waiting sedan, and his men piled into cars and drove away. Just a few more minutes, and Harper would have exactly what he'd needed to know.

A black Ford F-150 came careening down the ramp. It screeched to a stop. Miriam jumped out of the truck. Her eyes were wild.

"Where the fuck are they, Harper? And what the fuck are you doing here? What *do* you think you're doing?"

Harper held out the keys to the delivery truck and dropped them into her palm.

"Don't lose them again, Miriam. We'll be watching." He made sure to use the knife-edge side of his voice when he spoke. It needed to be clear that she must never take these projects for granted. Still, he felt his jaw clench as he returned to his vehicle. He hated seeing the conflict and hurt on her face. But that was only temporary. In his world, change was an everyday occurrence. And on some days, it happened more rapidly than others.

Chet pushed the pedal to the metal as he gunned the sedan through traffic. Even if he lost the Cullers in town, the car probably still had some kind of Chinese tracker. He wouldn't get out of LA alive. He tried to think hard how they could get another vehicle. An ambulance passed them, and an idea came to him. He took a couple of turns and pointed the car away from the interstate and sped down 3rd Street.

"What are you doing?" Stella was wide-eyed. Instead of heading out of town, he was going farther into it. They'd get caught in traffic. The only question was, by whom?

"Trust me, babe." A car screeched to a stop in front of him, but he managed to swerve around the asshole just before a Waste Management truck could clip him in the rear.

"Damn it! Are you crazy? Where are you going?"

"Cedars-Sinai." He could have pissed his pants when he saw the look on her face. She was so bugged out she wasn't thinking. "Remember Vegas? '97?"

He had a space of open road and was making the most of it. The hospital complex was just ahead. "Damnedest thing, Los Angeles hospitals," he continued. "Did you know they have fucking *valet*?"

"No way."

"Oh yeah."

There was a pause. The corners of her mouth rose. Good. She remembered.

"You'll drop me off?"

"Yep, and you'll pick me up."

"I'll circle around clockwise when I leave."

"You got it. Don't keep me waiting too long."

She smiled at him. Right now, he was feeling like a million bucks. Four million, even. With a steady woman to boot.

Ah, life is good. Very, very damn good.

Stella tried not to bounce with joy. She twisted her hair and put it up in a neat bun. Professional. She'd done it before. She could do it again. It's not like they looked at what you were wearing.

Chet dropped her off at the corner, then drove up the ramp of the parking deck to one of the patient garages. Stella walked half a block, still carrying the briefcase, and found the ground-level entrance. Her timing had to be good, or this wouldn't work. She was lucky that most days her timing was good. *Except in Cheyenne.*

Two young men were at the counter. They talked as they waited for another car. They didn't wait long. A BMW convertible pulled up. Luscious metallic red. One of them took the driver's keys and drove away. That left just the one. Every cell in her ovaries spun the wheel, and she prayed to Lady Luck.

She spied a blue Jag. Normally, a car like it would stick in someone's head, but they were a dime a dozen in this area. She confidently strode up to the young man, the large briefcase hanging easily in her hand. The boy's nametag read, *Joey*.

"Hello again," she said. "Thank *God*, that is over. The board can be such a pain."

He gazed at her, and for a moment, his brow wrinkled. She let her musical and bubbly laughter wash over him. "Oh, now, you surely haven't forgotten me?"

His eyes questioned her, and he rubbed his chin. She noticed the stubble on his face. The quick groom of his hair. She could smell the ketones on his breath and the faint hint of mescal. "Oh, Joey, that late date last night doing tequila shots must have kept you up too long!" She laughed, this time politely. Her heartbeat remained steady. It must not quicken. *It's all in how you act. He must* believe *you know him and that he knows you.* "Could you be a love and get my car. I lost my ticket, but you remember the blue Jaguar coupe? I think it's parked in the back?" She pointed over to the far end of the lot. His eyes followed her finger, and with a ripple of pleasure, she saw his expression change. He'd made his decision. He knew her.

"Ah, yeah. I mean, yes, ma'am. I'll go get it, Ms...?"

"Joey, you *are* touched today. Really? It's Ellen, remember? Ellen Stewart. I'll forgive you because it's only been twice, but don't you forget me next time. I'd like to tell the board about how well you're doing." She made a playful pout. Before she knew it, he was flashing her a smile and running for the car.

Stella stood at the counter, turned around, and changed her demeanor. At the same time, she reached back and changed her hair. A conservative ponytail, swept to the side. On the counter was a clipboard. She picked it up.

C'mon. C'mon! She desperately needed the next car to come along.

Not red. Not electric blue. Please. Please.

It was like having a single bet on seventeen black. She could hear the ball bouncing as the wheel kept turning.

Tinkity, tink, tunk, tin, tink.

A silver Lexus drove up, and a fluffy woman emerged, dressed in what was surprisingly an Alfred Dunner ensemble. Large floral-print top. Pull-on black pants. *Probably from Macy's. Maybe even JCPenny. She's not too high-end. Speak plainly. Candidly.*

She put on her best business face. Pleasant and helpful. She used a cheery voice. "Park your car for you, ma'am?"

The woman's face melted with gratitude. Part of Stella felt guilty, but only a small part.

"Thank you." She handed her the keys. Stella spun around to the counter in time to see the blue Jaguar inching its way to the exit. She pulled a tag from the counter and handed it to the woman.

"Emergency room?"

The large sign on the road made it clear, and the arrow was obvious, but Stella could see the Dunner-clad woman looked worried. "Right that way, ma'am. You can't miss it."

"Thank you." Then the woman's face started to crumple, and tears beaded up in her eyes. "I'm sorry..."

No, fucking no. No. Don't do that... Young, naïve Joey would be pulling up any minute, and she'd have to make a quick getaway on foot. How far would they get before they got picked up?

Thinkity, tink, tunk...bop...bop.

The wheel was going slower and slower.

Stay. Calm.

"No worries, ma'am. The hospital staff is wonderful. You and your loved one will be just fine."

The woman dressed in the pink-and-golden-flower print gave her a tremulous smile, drew herself up tall, and headed in the direction of the emergency room. Thankfully, she didn't look back. Stella grabbed up the briefcase, tossed it in the car, and slid inside just as the blue Jag rolled up to the exit. She put the keys in the ignition and hit reverse, pulled out of the lot, and put the car into drive. A horn blared at her. She'd run a red light. In her rearview mirror, she saw young Joey running after her.

Tink. Bop. Bop.

She should have gone left, but instead, she pulled into the right lane. The next red light stopped her. One car in front of her just sat there. Stella chanced a look to the left. Chet stood there at the crosswalk. He spotted her, and his head drew back in surprise before his eyes turned into daggers and stabbed right through her. She knew he'd expected her to make a counterclockwise turn, but she was on the other side of the road. He trotted purposefully across the lane. The light turned green, but he was pounding on her window.

"Stella!" She didn't look at him and pressed the gas pedal, pulling away from his storm of curses. The road was miraculously free and clear. The next light was green. And the next. She saw his body recede in the distance.

Tunk!

Number seventeen! Lady is a winner!

"You're not out of this yet, girl." She swallowed the knot that had been building in her throat and drove as fast as she dared. There was no way she could let her guard down. She'd have to ditch the car soon. Ms. Dunner might be having a bad day, but at least she'd get her car back. And Stella, well, she was closer than she'd been in years to being free.

EIGHTEEN

September 23, 12:01

One of the lesser-used entrances of the Point Mugu base was straight ahead on Los Posas Road, just after the exit for the Pacific Coast Highway, which veered off along the beach and past Point Mugu Rock. The road snaked along to the gold coast of Malibu and Santa Monica, and Ben regretted that his surfboard was still back East. He'd love to explore Neptune's Net, a famous surfing spot. Or even go up to Rincon, a sacred niche for surfers. It had been a long time.

Maybe the base has a surf shop.

Ben daydreamed about waves. The naval base's coastline was renowned for its barrels when the swells were right, and only military personnel, or people who knew military personnel, were allowed to go there.

Ben rolled the truck up to one of the two gate guards checking base passes and IDs. The guard bent down to examine Ben's vehicle pass, as well as his identification.

The man's cheek bulged out as he stroked it with his tongue. "Whatcha got in the back?" Ben tried not to hold his breath. He looked in the rearview mirror. Miriam was right behind him in the Ford.

"Just a delivery to the research center. Couple of pig specimens."
Please just let us through. Please just let us through. Damn, the old Jedi mind trick would really come in handy right now.

"We went to security level delta a couple of hours ago. I'm gonna have to search your truck before I let you through." The guard looked as if he were trying to gauge Ben's reaction.

Ben felt trickles of sweat roll down from his armpits, but he tried to stay calm. God, he really didn't want to be doing this. He couldn't lie to save his ass, and now he was going to have to give it a go. Miriam would find it amusing if she knew how much he was squirming.

Time to man up.

"Sure." He made a smile and hoped it looked genuine. *If a person has nothing to hide, then they smile and joke.* He'd read several books on body language and studied videos on microexpression. But it was all theory and no practice. Now it was time to put the psychological bullshit to the test.

"Pull over to the side."

Ben continued to wear his happy face as he drove the truck to an area of pavement designated for vehicle inspections. He watched another guard wave Miriam through the gate. She drove straight ahead and didn't even glance his way.

Two armed guards ran long poles with mirrors on the ends of them under his truck. A military dog sniffed around the vehicle, his handler walking behind him. Ben watched them in his side mirror. The dog reached the back of the truck, and his ears flattened against his head. A low growl emerged from his canine throat.

"Open the back of the truck?" The guard phrased it like a question, but it was most certainly an order.

"Sure." Ben couldn't think of any jokes or light humor to put the man at ease. He only hoped Gevu and Binah behaved. He and Miriam had checked on them before they left LA and given them water and a snack. Now was not the time to expose their experiment, even if this were a military base. And there was a risk of media exposure, since journalists lurked everywhere, even here. There was always a cameraman waiting for a plane crash, and in these days of a tanked economy, they stalked military bases frequently, ready to report any hot story they could find.

Ben got out of the vehicle and opened the back. Gevu and Binah's heads were visible in the shadows, while their plywood boxes hid the rest of their bodies. Binah snorted. Gevu wrinkled his snout and bared his teeth. The dog pressed its paws up to the bumper and barked wildly, his neck bulging and threatening to burst from his leash. Binah and Gevu grunted and rattled in their holding area.

"Settle down, boy! Settle down." The guard pulled back even as the dog forcefully strained forward. It took a good deal of strength to haul him off the bumper. The dog lunged toward the truck again. "Shut the door," the guard ordered. Ben closed up the back, but not before Gevu flashed him a wink. He sure hoped the guard hadn't seen the sly move.

"Carry on," he said.

When the gate was no longer in his rearview, Ben let out a breath of relief. He'd thought for sure something was going to go wrong. But then again, things had already gone wrong or they wouldn't be here. At least not yet.

He thought about Binah. He'd never be able to explain to her why he didn't tell her everything. Never be able to make her understand why he continued to move forward with what he had to do.

He caught up to Miriam. Her taillight signaled she was turning left, and he followed her past an airfield and past a fuel farm made up of several huge white tanks containing JP4 and JP5. They drove along a road that meandered through a wildlife preserve filled with a variety of birds, including pelicans. A number of seals lay on the sandy banks of a watery inlet, soaking up the warmth of the sun. In a matter of minutes, they were parked in front of a gray three-story building that was perched close to the wild waves of the ocean. It took a moment for Ben to realize why the building looked so strange. It had no windows.

Miriam was not prepared for what happened once they arrived. A squad of men dressed in black immediately filed out of the building and went to the delivery truck. She got out of the Ford just in time to hear one of them order Ben to open up the back. Two men pushed a cart behind the vehicle. Her skin prickled.

How dare they? Without permission? She moved rapidly to where they were already loading Binah and Gevu into the cart. One of the men broke away from the group and came toward her.

"Come with me, Dr. Wetzel. Our men have got this."

"Under whose authority?" A fire was raging inside her. Who would dare touch her research without her permission and act as if her children were nothing more than pieces of meat?

"That would be me."

She didn't have to turn around. She knew the voice. "Harper."

He placed a hand on her shoulder. "They will take good care of them. We have things to discuss."

She composed herself before she turned around. Her mentor wore dark sunglasses, which made it impossible to read his eyes. Ben stood beside him, anxiously watching as the armed men rolled Binah and Gevu out of the truck and into the building. Before she could protest, the men and her children had disappeared.

"Follow me." Harper headed for the building. She looked at Ben, and he shrugged. It seemed she had no choice but to walk with him. What had she thought? That they'd arrive and let her take control over all of the aspects of her hard work? That was exactly what she'd thought. She should have known better.

When they reached the building, Harper punched in a code on what appeared to be a blank panel, then ushered them through a set of sliding doors. They walked along a nondescript off-white corridor, which smelled of fresh paint, and after a couple of left turns, they arrived in front of a very large elevator. Enormous metal doors slid open, and they stepped inside. The building was about three stories high, but there was just one button. He pushed it, folded his hands in front of him, and stood quietly.

The elevator lurched, and she felt the platform descend. Several agonizing minutes ticked by. She wondered why pain and discomfort had the excruciating power to slow time down, while moments of happiness passed in a flash before one could really savor them.

Harper never looked her way. Although he stood stiff as a statue while the elevator sank below ground, she knew he was evaluating her. He'd look at the videos of her later and try to read her, no doubt. She wouldn't give him the satisfaction of betraying more than she needed to. It was clear he was here for one thing, and one thing only. To pry information from her.

How much does he know? Anything he could read, hear, or see, he'd use against her. He would have had his specialists pull as much data from her hard drive as possible. She kept her breath even. Steady. There was one place he couldn't go. One place he'd never access, and it was there that she held the key to what he really wanted to know.

The elevator came to a halt and opened up into an enormous tunnel. A shuttle waited for them. It looked like a large golf cart. Harper stepped forward and motioned for them to get in. The hall was just as busy as similar main hallways of the Pentagon.

Other shuttles passed by. Soldiers in formations of four or six walked in step. Civilian men and women with security badges stood at a small coffee bar, sipping their drinks from steaming cups. The scent of cappuccino filled the air, and her stomach rumbled. How long had it been since she'd eaten? Yesterday maybe?

She climbed into the vehicle. "We'll get you settled in your rooms and bring you something to eat," Harper said. His voice was short. Unemotional. *Damn my body!* He'd obviously heard her stomach growl. She glanced at him, a number of questions bubbling inside her. *Your rooms? They were going to stay here? For how long?* Part of her suddenly wondered if she'd ever be allowed to leave.

The driver of the cart didn't say a word. Ben's leg jiggled nervously up and down. Miriam sharply inhaled with impatience, and then she consciously made her breath slow and even again. They rode along the tunnel, which gradually sloped down. More minutes crawled by.

Where the hell *are we?* The tunnel floor rose up at an angle then leveled off. She smelled salt water before she saw it. A huge bay opened up in front of them. It was a giant cavern. And in the middle of the spacious bed of water in front of her sat a submarine.

She'd heard the channels near Point Mugu were deep. Deep enough to run a submarine through. She'd never suspected such a base could lie here. They had to be deep under the nearby mountain, she realized. There was a reason for all of those radio antennas on top of the mountain. And there were constant operations on San Nicholas Island, which was just off the coast. Now she wondered what lurked under that small island as well. Was there a concealed city beneath it where the test missiles were launched? Lost in thought, it took her a moment to realize they'd stopped in front of another elevator. "This way" was all that Harper said, and when the doors closed, they started up.

This place is enormous. Miriam and Ben walked side by side as they followed Harper into a softly lit room filled with a number of radar and video screens. Men and women sat at desks in front of each one, listening through headsets and typing on keyboards.

"I believe you know Admiral Blandy." A tall, lean man with salt-and-pepper hair, shaved high and tight, strode over to Miriam. He wore what navy personnel humorously called "aquaflage." The digital dark- and light-blue uniform allowed him to blend in with the surrounding room, with the exception of the two stars on his collar.

She looked up at him and held out her hand. "Sir."

He grasped her palm firmly, attempting to turn his wrist over hers in the political "upper hand." She resisted and ensured that the shake was strong and even. He pursed his lips and left his eyes on her face for a heartbeat before he turned to Ben. She noticed Ben had no inkling of handshake protocol. The admiral gripped his hand and turned it over easily. "Good to see you both. Let's go to the conference room, shall we?" He started to put his hand on the small of her back, and she stiffened. His arm moved away from her as if she'd set up an electric force field. Somehow, she was sure she could hear Harper's chuckle.

Bastard.

They entered a room with a rectangular table. It was ebony and long enough for twenty or so people to sit around it comfortably. Black ergonomic chairs stood at attention along the edges. On one wall, several screens monitored identical scenes like the one's she'd seen in the control room. On one screen, she saw Binah and Gevu. They were in a sterile, white room with a dividing panel. A bunk bed sat on each side of the space. There was a bathroom on Gevu's side of the room.

Admiral Blandy gestured for them to sit and took a seat himself.

"As you can see, Projects Eleven Juliet and Eleven Kilo are quite comfortable."

He paused as if waiting for any questions or objections before he moved on.

"We'll accelerate their training now, of course. And they need to be tested. I've got to say, despite the slaughterhouse incident, it looks like you've done an amazing job with them. Highly impressive. If all goes well, we're looking at surgical procedures in just a few weeks."

Miriam was stunned. All of her research. All of her work.

"There's one thing that's not clear though, and it could be a problem."

"What would that be, Admiral?" She mentally told her body not to flush and willed any rising color to stay away from her cheeks. She knew what was coming.

"We need to know if they can speak. They must have the capacity for language."

"They already sign flu—" she started.

"You know what I mean," the admiral interrupted. His voice held an impatient edge that caused her to bite back anything else she wanted to say.

Harper swiveled close to her, and Ben stared at the table in front of him.

"We need you to get them to talk, and to do it openly. No more closet talk."

She wondered why she felt so irritated that he was pressuring her for this. She'd known all along that this was a goal of the research, but it was one she'd ignored for a while. After all, the children were growing, walking, and learning rapidly. But speech was necessary for them to communicate and demonstrate their full skills. She glanced over at Harper, and her eyes flickered over to the flat-panel screen that showed Binah and Gevu inspecting their room.

"Leave it to me," she said. "I'll take care of it."

It was clear to her the only way she'd remain with her research was by participating fully in what the admiral wanted, and for once, she wondered if the military agenda was the same as the Cullers'. At least, here, she'd have virtually unlimited access to top-secret files. She'd do what they wanted, but her own research took priority. And if anything failed, there'd be the backup plans. She had information that none of them knew, and she'd use it to gain an advantage if necessary.

Right now, my greatest enemies are time and Harper.

And she had to find a way to beat them both.

NINETEEN

September 24, 14:28

For the first twenty-four hours, Gevu continued to keep silent around the White Coats, as did his sister. He knew they were being watched continuously. After some sleep and a meal, they were escorted to a room where they had to lie down and stay still inside a large tube while a machine fully scanned them. He was told not to move. The only way he managed it was to visualize that he was hunting humans, stalking them before the kill. Once he fixed his mind on that fantasy, the hour flew by.

When they returned to their room, he worked with Binah so they could communicate with each other using the sign language they'd learned, while secretly developing nuances within it that only they understood. It wasn't long before the White Coats caught on.

The door slid open, and Dr. Wetzel walked in. She hadn't worn a white coat since the day of their birth, but now it covered her body like gladiator armor. Gevu suppressed a growl. He signed to Binah. *See?* Her face visibly crumpled in front of him. Instead of feeling pity, he enjoyed a deep satisfaction. It was time she finally saw them for what they were. It was time she stopped mooning over Dr. Skylar and came to terms that he was simply a White Coat. It was time she realized they were all the same. Their mission was to suppress the strong, belittle the intelligent, and squash any threat to their mighty existence. Their motto was research for research's sake; to hell with all life that tried to get in their way.

"We know you've been communicating using vocal language," Dr. Wetzel told them as she walked with slow, deliberate steps around the room. Gevu looked down at the traces of the milk gravy and biscuit he'd had for lunch and his large, empty cup, which had once been filled with fresh orange juice. "Our MRI and CT scans show that your brains are functioning on a very high level. In particular, they indicate a capacity for speech."

Dr. Wetzel squatted in front of Gevu, and she reached out and ran her fingertips along his jaw. His mind created a pleasant vision of what it would be like to grab her hair and bash her head against the floor. He wondered how her flesh would taste. Maybe he could even crush her skull, crack it open like a walnut, and eat her brain.

He'd read that humans considered cow tongue a delicacy. Gevu imagined chewing on the White Coat's tongue and devouring it with relish. He'd swallow Dr. Wetzel's lies and what she thought was a superior language. The truth was their pathetic vocalizations paled compared to what he and Binah could do.

Gevu noticed his sister looked conflicted. Confused. He used the little motions he'd taught her. *We have no reason to trust her. No reason to speak to her.*

Dr. Wetzel tilted her head in recognition of the communication between them and pressed her lips into a thin, fake smile. "Your vocal cords are complex, but definitely designed for uttering more than a grunt or a snort." The room was silent except for the hum of the harsh fluorescent lights overhead.

"If I can't get something out of either one of you, then this research study will be over. That means, frankly, you won't live out the year." Binah cast a sideways glance at him and opened her mouth. He gave her a sharp nudge, which made her shut it again. His jaw hurt, and he realized he was grinding his teeth.

Binah, don't. It was just the slightest motion of his fingertips and a twitch of his ears, but regardless, the scientist seemed to understand.

"Very well." Dr. Wetzel tapped her fingertips against her thigh. "I really hate to lose the two of you." She moved toward the door and placed her hand on her security badge. She hesitated only a moment before swiping it through a groove on the wall. The hesitation was just long enough to glean a response.

"What will happen to us?" a squeaky voice croaked. Gevu felt sick to his stomach. His entire life was a bet at a tough poker game, and any advantage he had was just obliterated. *Almost.* Dr. Wetzel spun around, visibly pleased, though not much surprised.

Miriam crouched down toward Binah's face and looked deeply into her eyes.

"Nothing. Not for a while now." She tried to make her voice sound soothing. "You've just bought us all several months. Maybe years."

A twitch at the corner of her mouth betrayed how much she'd like to openly savor this moment, and it caused Gevu's temper to ignite in his chest. He suppressed the urge to roar at her. If she thought she had complete control over them, he'd show her that he knew better. And if he had his way, he would show her much more before she took her last breath.

Miriam spun on her heel and left. The door slid closed behind her. Gevu's anger threatened to go supernova. Still, he disciplined himself and said nothing.

"It's a new beginning," he heard Dr. Wetzel say just outside the door. He stared at Binah, who looked triumphant at giving away one of their most precious secrets.

You are so stupid, sister. So naïve. But he knew that, no matter what, the tides had turned. From here on out, there'd be no going back.

You'll talk soon enough, Gevu. And when you do, you'll answer to me. I made you, and I can break you. But deep inside, Miriam knew she could never destroy him or allow anyone else to threaten his existence. He was unique, as was his sister. And there was much more research to be done.

Binah has finally braved her brother's wrath. Miriam's self-satisfaction lasted only a second.

"So, they can talk." Harper stood next to Ben in the adjoining room. He sounded as if it were exactly what he'd expected. She had never told him she'd heard their hushed whispers when they thought they were unobserved. No one other than she and Ben had known about the surveillance of the closets in the farmhouse. *Obviously Harper knew too. How?*

But of course he would have kept close tabs on the government's prized possessions. Now she realized he'd known everything all along.

"But you knew that already." Her tone was matter of fact. She kept it level and worked not to let any inflection of irritation taint her voice. But with him, she always felt at a disadvantage.

You're always one step behind, Miriam. When will you learn you have to think three or four moves ahead of him?

Harper didn't deny his knowledge of Gevu and Binah's speaking ability. He didn't even miss a beat with his next sentence.

"It's time to start their testing." He turned to leave. Anger welled up inside her, and her fingers were trembling. This was *her* research. She wouldn't let him waltz in here and take over what she'd worked on for years perfecting.

"Harper!"

He stopped, his perfectly pressed suit as gray and steely as the eyes he used to bore into her. "They're not yours anymore, Miriam. They never were. They belong to the military, and your job with them is done."

"My job is *not* done."

"Yes. You're right about that. You've got a lot more work to do for the military. The admiral wants clones. I trust you can handle that. Yes?" It wasn't a question. And she knew damn well she'd never walk out of the compound alive if she refused. Any warmth she'd ever felt for her mentor slipped away with the metallic voice and stare he'd just used on her.

"Don't I always handle what you need?" Instantly she regretted the bitterness in her tone. It betrayed her feelings. It let him know he'd gotten under her skin.

"This is not for me, Miriam. It's for your country. And for the world." Harper walked out the observation room door, and Miriam pierced the back of his head with her stare until it closed behind him. Her gaze swiveled to Ben, who'd remained characteristically silent. Instead of looking down or away, he returned her look with a concrete resilience she'd never sensed in him before.

"You can't do it, Em. You can't let them take Binah and Gevu."

Miriam didn't say anything. She'd known all along that the funding came through the Cullers via the military. Now she understood that Gevu and Binah might serve a higher purpose than supporting her breakthrough research of providing a steady supply of military replacement parts. Whether he knew it or not, Harper had just confirmed that he needed her for more than a military agenda.

And she wouldn't have time to discover the full extent of what the children could do. Apparently the Cullers were on a tight schedule, and time was a commodity she didn't have anymore. Oh, she'd start their fucking clones all right. It was the only way she knew she'd survive long enough to get out of this mess. *I'll create their little monsters, and when the time is right, I'll...*

"Miriam?" Ben's voice was soft. Insistent.

"Let's go to the lab. We've got some work to do." Her voice sounded sharper than she'd intended. This time she found it difficult to meet his eyes. Not because she felt awkward. Not in the least. She just didn't want him to suspect her next move. The less he knew, the better. The better for her. And for Gevu and Binah.

In the depths of the Los Angeles sewers, Chet found a temporary place to hide in a small room that ran parallel to the subway. He hadn't wanted things to go this way, but it was time to figure out what to do next. Why had Stella turned out to be such a fucking whore? And why had he expected any less? Oh yeah, she was a looker and sharp as a tack, but she'd always been a weasel. He looked down at his crotch.

"Failed me again, boy." And though he blamed his losses on the voracious appetite and naïvety of his hungry prick, he realized he missed Stella. Damn, she was good to have around. Despite the stink of the sewer and the overpowering stench of rotting meat, bubbling feces, and decaying garbage, he could smell Stella's perfume when he thought of her. Its mysterious, woodsy quality. Secret of Venus and that hint of patchouli that breezed on the air with an undercurrent of sensuality. And then he remembered the scientist woman, and her fragrance of roses, which reminded him of classy boudoirs and satin sheets.

    His sexual appetite grew with his fantasies, and although his surroundings were disgustingly putrid and filled with the vile attributes of a discarded life and defecation, his prick grew hard. He wasn't sure which would come first, but he'd make Stella pay for betraying him and Miriam would feel the heat of his fury from between his legs. Not all weapons were guns or knives. The weapon he carried with him was always ready, and he was excellent at using it.

TWENTY

October 13, 06:30

Each day, their lessons had begun immediately after a quick breakfast of cornflakes and juice. Some tests were physical. Others included the most complex problems she'd ever dealt with. She and her brother were getting stronger mentally and physically. They'd demonstrated intellectual abilities far beyond those of their captors. Binah had never failed to wonder at the purpose of each instruction and test.

She was using a microscope to observe a particularly lovely biological specimen they'd given her, when the guards came for Gevu. The moment they placed their hands on his shoulders, he tossed them back against the walls. "Get off me!"

Binah inhaled deeply. Her brother was the smart one, but at times like this, she doubted the depth of his intelligence. The guards put some distance between them and pulled out their weapons. Two Tasers and a dart gun.

"Just like the humans do. Yeah, buddies, you're all wimps without mommy's and daddy's guns."

Binah watched Gevu crouch down and hurtle his body toward them. She flinched as she heard the predictable buzz of the electric gun and the little pop that announced the release of a tranquilizer dart. Gevu's muscles first contracted from the force of the electricity then went flaccid from the medication in the dart. They dragged him away. Binah pressed her lips together and looked down at the floor. *Why does he always choose to do things the hard way?*

She heard the whisper of the sliding door again and glanced up. Dr. Wetzel was walking toward her, accompanied by two more guards.

Where is Ben? Why doesn't he come? Doesn't he want to see me?

"Good morning, Binah." Dr. Wetzel's lips curled up into a plastic smile that reminded Binah of a hideous doll she'd played with a couple of months ago. It had been a used thing, with matted hair and a missing eye, one of many toys the White Coats had brought them to play with. "We've got a field trip to go on before we continue with your testing."

She led the way from the room, and the two guards flanked Binah as they walked along a labyrinth of corridors. The lighting and the smell in the air changed. Where there had once been more of an electronic and antiseptic odor in the air, she detected sweat, pungent odors of human feces, and other scents she couldn't identify. Dr. Wetzel opened a door with her badge, and the sudden and overwhelming stink almost dropped Binah to her knees.

In front of her were several hospital beds. On each of them rested a comatose human. They had plastic tubes in their mouths and tubes leading to their forearms and wrists. Tubes also connected to their stomachs and their bladders. "What are they?" She'd never seen such a thing.

"Soldiers." Dr. Wetzel ushered her to one of the nearest beds. A young woman rested there. Her long blond hair was tied neatly to the side of her head in a ponytail. She was attractive for a human. Well built. Fit.

"What's wrong with her?" Binah couldn't fathom how such a lovely young woman could be consigned to a place as horrible as this. Condemned not to move. A machine at her bedside pumped air into her lungs.

"Her brain is dead. And she's missing a kidney. Hazards of war, Binah." She made a sweeping motion with her hand. "All of these young people have suffered the same fate. Their bodies live on, but who they are is gone. They will never wake up."

"That's horrible. Can't you do something for them?" Tears welled up in Binah's eyes. She imagined having a loved one like Ben stretched out, unresponsive, on one of these beds. Did each of these soldiers have a brother, sister, mother, or father waiting for them somewhere?

"A few months ago, there was nothing we could do for them." Dr. Wetzel gripped the side rails of the bed they stood beside. Her knuckles were white, as if she were holding it very tightly. "But now there is something we can do."

"That's good. It's horrible knowing how much their family is probably suffering."

"You think so? What if I told you that the only way we can help them is if you agree to help us?"

Binah's heart skipped a beat, and she started to back away.

"What do you mean? What does any of this have to do with me?"

"Not just you, Binah. You and Gevu. You both will help these soldiers live again."

"How can we do that?" Binah took another step backward. She instinctively sensed that she didn't like where this conversation was going, and yet she knew she was being shown the true purpose of coming to this place. She looked around at the dozens of bodies that lined the large room. Nurses tended to them. Machines pumped fluids and food into them. Orderlies turned them and cleared away excrement.

Dr. Wetzel took a few steps forward and grabbed Binah's hand. She brought her back to the side of the bed where the female soldier lay. "Binah, how would you like to live inside a human body such as this? Take a good look. It's young. Attractive. Imagine being able to be with a man in the natural way that a woman can be with a man. Maybe even have children."

Natural. Was what she'd experienced with Ben unnatural? What did Dr. Wetzel know? Had Ben told her everything? She snatched her hand away and felt heat rising to her cheeks.

Dr. Wetzel's eyes widened for a microsecond, and a look of understanding crossed her face. It was gone the moment Binah blinked her eyes. She looked down at the foot of the bed where the soldier's name was printed on a tag. It read, *Captain Alice Spann, 101st Airborne.*

"I brought you here so that you might understand why we need to do what we are going to do." The White Coat drew herself up, and her face became stony. Resolute. "In a couple of weeks, both you and Gevu will undergo a procedure. The very first of its kind. When you wake up, you'll find yourself in this woman's body. Your brain. Your consciousness. All that you are will occupy this form, and her body will walk again. She'll be a good soldier again."

Tears pricked at the corners of Binah's eyes. She couldn't stop her body from trembling. *No! They could not! How? Why would they dare?*

Binah spread her fingers across her abdomen as she glared at the doctor. "What about *this*? What are you going to do with the rest of me? Eat it?" There. She's said it. Dr. Wetzel would understand now that she knew about their atrocities to animals, to *pigs*.

"No, Binah." The woman lowered her head for a second, and when she looked up, what she said next was flat and cruel. "We're going to use the rest of you for replacement parts." She gestured toward the other bodies filling the room. "Some of them need skin grafts, a heart, or a liver. Your body will be used to help these soldiers heal. To help them live."

It was a simple reflex to run. The need to survive pumped adrenaline through her arteries like oil through an Alaskan pipeline. The enormity of what Dr. Wetzel had just told her set her mind reeling. What she proposed, in effect, was a death sentence.

Worse than a death sentence.

Binah staggered back in the opposite direction. Her feet slipped on the smooth tile, and she collided with a metal table filled with instruments she didn't recognize.

She fell to the ground, the contents of the table spilling across the floor. In a desperate moment, Binah caught sight of a small blade on a green stick. She recognized it from her biology lessons. A scalpel. She palmed the item and managed to hide it as the guards helped her up. It would do no good to fight here. She realized that.

"I need the bathroom," she gasped. "I think I'm going to be sick." They escorted her to a nearby toilet and stood outside while she made fake retching noises. She placed a foot on the bowl of the toilet seat and gingerly pushed the scalpel up into her vagina. The plastic that covered the blade kept it from cutting her, and she hoped the instrument didn't fall out while she was walking.

Dr. Wetzel was waiting for her when she came out. Binah attempted the best apologetic look she could muster. "I'm sorry, Dr. Wetzel. This was all very unexpected. It's not every day that you hear that your lifelong wish is going to come true."

The White Coat's eyes measured Binah from head to toe, her eyes just a little wider. Binah couldn't tell if the doctor was pleased with her evaluation, or if she'd managed to fool Dr. Wetzel into thinking that she approved.

"Good girl. Now let's get back to your testing."

Once again, Dr. Wetzel led the way. Back through the corridors of sterility and chemicals. Back to the glowering military guards who were all too disdainful of her and her brother.

What would it feel like to live inside a human body? Would Ben love me more if I occupied the form that lay spread on that bed like a stunned animal waiting to be sacrificed? And with her brain in that body, would she control her own life? Probably not. She was an experiment. She would die an experiment. Her existence was meaningless unless she managed to take her life into her own hands.

The scalpel wiggled in her vagina as she followed the doctor into the room where she'd be tested. She sat in a chair and thought about the blade and how she might use it for her freedom. Dr. Wetzel left through a sliding door once she seemed certain Binah was secure in her seat and strapped in for her testing. And as she watched the doctor go, Binah smiled. She would be free, one way or another. There were worse things than death. She realized that now.

October 13, 17:05

It was a hell of a long shot, but Chet was willing to roll the dice. Mr. Ching had been so interested in getting his hands on Gevu and Binah that he was betting his life the old man would still take a risk. *Besides, what did the chink have to lose?* He followed a few of the tunnels in the proper direction and found his way back to the right place, just two blocks from the consulate.

"Okay, balls to the wall, or ya got none at all," he hissed through his teeth as he made himself step out into the street. Camera on the corner. Another facing the consulate. He walked toward the front door with both his hands up.

"I need to speak to Wah Ching!" he yelled at the top of his lungs.

Chet paused on the street corner, just a few steps away from the consulate door. Nothing. No movement anywhere. A blue car cruised by him, the rap music pumping from it probably hitting a two or three on the Richter scale. His hopes faded like the tunes that had filled the air only a moment earlier. It was almost dark.

Another car rolled along the street in front of him. A black sedan. Hope surged into his chest. He hadn't lost the game. Not yet. It slowed to a stop in the middle of the road, and the back door opened. A spine-numbing shock came with the first solid blow that hit his back, and then his brain seared with pain before the last light of day tunneled and faded into nothingness. He was shoved forward into a giant abyss, and the fall seemed endless.

Don't lose the game...

October 13, 22:07

Stella was finally free, and she held the world in the palm of her hand. Or at least in a briefcase. She decided to keep with Chet's plan. Canada looked real good right now. And she wouldn't need credit cards or any traceable object for a good long while. She'd just have to be careful. Take care that she wasn't ripped off until she could get to a town where she could set up a new identity.

Her one weak link was the car, which she had ditched as soon as possible. She'd taken a cab to a used car dealer. Cash under the table had bought her a vehicle without any questions, and soon she was rolling north on the Pacific Coast Highway in a sky-blue Sonata. Taking the coastline seemed safer than the interstate.

They'll find you, a little voice nagged at the back of her head. "No, they won't." She said the words out loud hoping that saying them would make it so. Her fingers turned the dial and found a radio station with some tunes she could enjoy. *Anything but country.* Lady Gaga's "Born This Way" hit the airwaves on 104.3, and she opened all the windows of her car and turned up the volume. *He'll find you.* The voice nagged again, and she tossed her head furiously to stop the inner chatter.

Canada was a big country, and she had money. A few cars snaked along the road in front of her, but she made herself drive slow and easy. She planned to take a few days, maybe camp at a park or a cheap motel. The longer she took, the more confused the Cullers would be. They'd get the police to help search for her at the state lines, and she hoped to throw them off. Let them think she'd traveled east or maybe south.

The next stop, she promised herself to purchase some hair dye. She'd make an okay brunette. Maybe she'd cut her locks too. How far did the arm of the Cullers reach? They had a ton of technology, but she was nothing to them. A drop in the bucket.

Except you've got four million dollars, and you know about the pigs.

Okay. Not a drop in the bucket. Gold bars in the bucket. Goddamn pigs. What was the big deal, anyway? She'd kept her mouth shut. They didn't need to worry about her.

You're kidding yourself, girlfriend.

She drove until she hit Oakland and then found a little motel. Two story. Dilapidated. The kind some people tend to rent by the hour. If anyone were looking for her, they'd probably be scoping out the five-star hotels. No, she'd lay low here and stay cool. Risk the potential bedbugs. She was in survival mode. Then again, these days she was always in survival mode. That's why she'd agreed to work with the Cullers in the first place. When Chet had ditched her in Cheyenne and she'd tried to get away—and failed, the Cullers had offered her an alternative to prison time. She'd done as they asked and trained hard, letting her hatred for Chet fuel her fire. But she was finished with them now. No more spying. No more undercover sex. She was tired of being a puppet.

After she checked in, she sat on the bed and looked at the clunky TV. The motel was so cheap that it hadn't gotten with the times. The room looked like a throwback from the seventies with its garish wallpaper, neon orange standup lights, and carpet decorated with red, yellow, and green circles.

I need a drink. She pulled some bills out of the briefcase and stashed it under the bed. *Just one or two beers, then a good night's sleep.* She'd be on the road again before sunup.

The motel clerk gave her directions to a skanky bar around the corner. *Big Joe's,* the neon sign read. She walked in and strolled up to the bar. "Gin and ginger ale. Two shots of gin."

The bartender smiled at her. He was an older fellow with a round Buddha belly and a shiny bald head. "Sure thing." He handed her the drink, and Stella took in the rest of the bar. An older couple sat in one corner talking gently. The man had his hand placed over the woman's fingers. Stella's heart melted for a second. What would it be like to be in love again? It had been years since she'd had that feeling.

Across from the bar was a billiards table. A multitude of scratches and dents were testimony to it having seen better days. Several men in leather jackets, with beards and bandanas, were shooting a game. She remembered the motorcycles outside.

Bikers.

A familiar itch came to her fingertips. It had been so long since she'd played.

"Hey, blondie! Play a game?"

Shit, she'd forgotten to color her hair. The box of hair color was still in the grocery bag in her room, unopened. She'd have to dye it tonight before she went to bed.

The man who'd spoken to her was tall. Lean. His biceps grew out of a leather vest that hung loosely around his frame. Underneath it he wore a tie-dyed tank.

Only in California.

She took a couple of long pulls from the straw in her drink and batted her eyelashes. "Well, I don't know…" She hoped her hesitation sounded convincing. They'd likely think she was a tired traveler. Some simple city lady.

The rest of the men joined in and cajoled her into coming over to the table.

"You know how to play, right?" A guy with skulls on a bandana worn around his head leered at her.

"A little. Solids and stripes, okay?" She took a pool cue and played after the initial break. She scratched. "Ouch. It's been longer than I thought, boys."

"Another round for my partner here!" Tie-dyed-tank man was getting brave. Their opponents put in a stripe. "Guess you and me are solid, babe."

He put his hand on the small of her back, and she tried not to flinch. Instead, she pursed her lips. "I'm afraid you'll lose this one because of me." And they did lose.

She was on drink number three when she let all hell break loose. She was playing straight up to sixty and never stopped after the break. Each ball found the pocket she called. They racked three more times. None of them ever got a shot. The table was silent when ball number fifteen went into the side pocket from an impossible angle.

Skull-bandana man looked her up and down when she picked up the money. "Boys, I think we just got played and played real bad."

"Hey." She tried really hard not to slur her words. If they thought she was drunk, they'd see her as easy prey. "You guys asked me. And I told you the truth. It's been a while." She couldn't tell if their eyes sparkled with hatred or admiration. Maybe a little of both. She folded the bills, pocketed them, and for a brief moment, she felt good. Real good. She'd showed them something they'd talk about for ages.

When she stepped outside, she realized her mistake. *They'd talk about it for ages.* Bikers were friends with truckers, and truckers shared stories over the airwaves. Every step back to the motel seemed as if it was in slow motion, even though her mind was racing faster than wild dogs after a housecat.

She pulled the key from her pocket and opened the door. She'd have to sleep hard and wake early, color her hair, and get on the road. When she turned on the lights, she realized all her worry was for nothing. Two uniformed men stood in front of her, their guns pointed at her face.

A man in a suit came up behind her. He handed her a phone with a real-time link. Harper's face filled the screen.

"You took a hell of a drive, Stella," he said.

"Yeah, well, I thought I was running for my life." *Did they find the money?*

"We've got the perfect place to put you in protective custody. And don't worry about the money. It's in good hands, right where it belongs."

The men led her out of the room, and she looked wistfully at her blue Sonata as they drove away. *Freedom, left to rust in a parking lot.* And all of her hopes and dreams remained there to corrode with it.

October 14, 02:00

Jesus Fucking H. Christ! Chet tried to open his eyes only to find they'd been taped shut. His head felt like ten thousand maniacs had pounded on it with two-by-fours. He tried to speak, but a piece of cloth had been stuffed into his mouth and some kind of adhesive held it in place. Apparently, the Chinese had a million and one uses for duct tape too. A wave of nausea went through him, and he gagged. Bile rose up into his throat, and since the normal exit was blocked, it leaked through his nostrils and burned like shit.

Voices spoke in Chinese, or at least he guessed it was Chinese. They surrounded him. Finally, someone spoke to him in English. A female.

"Mr. Idiot," she said. "You unwisely came back. Our superior is thankful you allow him the honor of ending your life." A punch socked him on the side of the head. His yells were muffled, and he gagged on the rag again. He tried getting up, but he realized he was tied to something hard and unyielding. Another punch landed on the opposite side of his face. *Maybe this wasn't such a good idea after all.*

"Where is the money? Where is the woman?" Laughter surrounded him. He felt like a fool but understood that was the point. He'd take the beating. Of course, he had no choice. Some part of him banked on the fact that Wah Ching's curiosity wouldn't let him die without saying why he'd come back.

Something hard struck his kneecap, one, two, three times and then landed with full force on his femur. Bile rose into his throat again and poured out his nose. He felt it clinging to his nostrils, and he tried to inhale and snort it out. He failed. Its warmth grew cold, and the wet gobs of snot stuck to his face.

Bring it, fuckers. You don't know what I know. And you won't get what you want without me.

"You lucky you haven't eaten solid food in a while," the feminine voice continued to goad him. "Maybe you be choked and dead by now. Would be so sad to deprive our superior of ending your life." Fingers reached out and grabbed his hair and tossed his head back into the hard surface behind him. Through the sour bile, he caught the scent of jasmine.

Chet's mind whirled. *Think, man, think.* He grunted and tried to move his fingers. He was rewarded with a hefty blow to his hands. Tears welled up in his eyes, but the tape sealed them in.

"Stop!" The voice was commanding. Self-assured. Mr. Wah Ching had said the words in English so Chet would know he was there. "I assume you have something to tell me." Chet nodded his head vigorously.

Jasmine-scented fingers pulled at the edges of the tape over his mouth and then ripped it off in one violent motion. He coughed, bent over, and tried to hawk the rag out. He failed and gagged. Sweat trickled down his neck, and he imagined how he must look. Dirty. Unwashed. He was sure he stank. In a flash, the cloth was removed from his mouth, and he sucked in a wave of cool, life-giving air.

"I know where they are," he rasped. His throat was on fire.

There was silence except for a low rumble overhead. So, he was back in the underground parking lot.

"And that concerns me, why?" Chet imagined the man picking dirt from his fingernails as casually as he would squash his brain on the floor.

"You still have a chance, if that's what you want, Ching-man. You can own them." Another blow connected with his head. He could taste the blood now and felt a gash on the inside of his cheek. A harsh rebuke in Chinese poured into the air, and he imagined several apologetic bows in the Ching-man's direction.

"Respect will minimize your pain," the man continued. "Still, I am intrigued. Tell me more."

The tape was ripped from his eyes, but he couldn't see due to the tears. Everything was a blur. One thing was for sure: he was going to look funny with no eyebrows or eyelashes.

Chet took another deep breath and spilled what he knew. Most of it, anyway. After he was done, his bonds were loosened, and he rubbed his wrists.

"My men will take you to where you can wash," Mr. Ching said. "Once you've cleaned yourself, we will talk more."

He watched a couple of figures walk away, and he remained motionless as the footsteps receded. He heard a door open and shut. That was the cue for the real beating to begin.

TWENTY ONE

October 17, 06:30

"It's today or never," Gevu mumbled at breakfast. "Tomorrow we're scheduled for the transplant. I'll kill them all before they put my brain inside a human."

"Shhh." Binah hissed over her spoon. She took in a mouthful of cornflakes.

"You still have the scalpel?"

Binah nodded almost imperceptibly. Gevu's eyes flickered to the camera. She was so careful. So damned cautious. His sister gave the White Coats way too much credit. The soldiers, too. Everyone here was confident to a fault. And they could not imagine what he had planned.

One of the guards moved toward him, and then another. Breakfast was over. He could feel his hairs bristle as they got closer. He leaned in and whispered in her ear. "Two," he said. Then pushed his breakfast away. He hoped Binah was ready for the breakout of a lifetime.

Binah stared at Gevu's back as he stalked through the steel door, flanked by soldiers. He was almost twice their size. Tomorrow Ben and Miriam would let the soldiers take their brains from their bodies and place each into a human form.

But not if we escape. Not if we get away.

Her cornflakes smelled stale. The milk soured in her stomach. She pushed the rest of her food toward the center of the table. Her appetite was gone.

"Better eat up," one of the guards sniggered. "Nothing for you after six this evening. Tomorrow you'll feel and taste in a whole new way."

The other guard grinned, and then the mirth on his face evaporated. "It doesn't seem right, putting pig brains into our own kind. Our guys served in Afghanistan. They shouldn't end up in some freak experiment."

Both of them talked in front of her like she didn't exist. Like she was just an animal. No feelings. Not human. Not worth a smidgen of decency or respect. She'd done things neither of them could ever dream of doing. Her intelligence exceeded that of any human here—except maybe the White Coats, Dr. Wetzel and Ben.

Would they watch the surgery? She had no doubt Miriam would. But Ben? How could he?

Maybe Gevu is right. Maybe the time has come for us to stand up for ourselves. To take our lives into our own hands.

It wouldn't be easy. Even if they did make it out, where would they go? How would they hide? Their physical features and faces were an immediate giveaway that they were "freaks of nature."

She thought of the scalpel she'd hidden in her quarters and reached behind her ear where she'd discovered a tracking device resting inside her subcutaneous tissue. If she pressed deep enough, she could feel it, but she didn't dare do that here. They'd notice, and she didn't need them noticing anything except her compliance. She and Gevu had talked about taking them out weeks ago, but they never got the opportunity.

Lull them into thinking you've given in, that you've accepted your fate.

Binah dropped her hand and simply smiled when a female medic came through the door and gave the signal to take her to the testing room. Binah looked around at the steel tables, the plain walls, and the doors and wished for flowers, the scent of pine trees, and the beautiful flicker of stars overhead. This would be her last day here, or she'd die. She refused to continue her life as a caged animal. Even in a human body, she'd still be caged. Limited in what she could do. Bound by the needs of this government. Assuming she survived.

Miriam sat in front of the screen and watched Gevu and Binah eating breakfast. She took note of their brief conversation. Words too soft to pick up on audio. When the soldiers came for Gevu, she observed his reaction. Just before he'd left, he said something to his sister. In doing so, he unwittingly signed one word with his hand. *Two.* Old habits die hard. She continued to watch Binah and saw her hand reach behind her ear. She stroked the tissue there before she put her hand down.

No.

Miriam hit the playback button. Then did it once more. As she watched their brief exchange, she became absolutely sure of what she suspected. Her darlings were, as crazy as it seemed, planning to escape. And she knew what time. She just didn't know how. One thing she did know: when the hour came, they wouldn't be alone. She would be there.

Across the other side of the room, ten large containers held the clones of Binah and Gevu. Five from her. Five from him. The general and the admiral were pleased she'd given them their weapons. Their precious means for saving lives. And Harper, well, he could go to hell, which was where she was sure he'd come from in the first place.

Ben held up his security badge, and the door opened. He crossed the threshold to another door, bent, and pressed his eye to the retinal scan, and the entrance to the lab slid open wide to let him through. Miriam sat in front of the surveillance screen, staring at the picture of two empty chairs. She didn't seem to sense he was even in the room. He walked up behind her and placed his hand on her shoulder.

"Em?" Her entire body jumped as if a bolt of electricity had just coursed through her. She turned and regarded him, her expression intense. Thoughtful.

"Sorry," he said. "I didn't mean to..."

"Where have you been?" She stood up from her chair and walked across the room, the scent of roses trailing behind her.

She always favored that perfume.

Miriam stopped in front of their cloning project, and the artificial uterus in one container wriggled just a little.

"What's wrong?" Ben felt as if something dark was building a web in her brain.

Miriam said nothing at first. She put her hand out to the container and ran her fingers along the outer surface.

"Pixie dust," she said, as she inhaled a deep breath and dropped her head.

A chill went up Ben's spine. Perhaps now was the time to tell her. He'd held up his end of the bargain with the admiral, but tomorrow the time for secrets would be over.

"Pixie?" He decided not to ask. It was now or never. "I've been wanting to talk to you about something." Ben waited a couple of pulse beats, and then a deluge of words poured out of his mouth. He told her about additional genetic manipulations he had been coerced to make. The true reason for growing swinemen. Miriam just stood there and listened. She didn't move a muscle. But as he finished, her eyes turned cold and glittery, and then she did something he didn't expect. She laughed out loud.

October 17, 19:04

Gevu was exhausted by the time he returned to his room.
More of a prison cell than a room. A sanitized cage.
Reflecting on his life so far, he'd decided that his entire existence was that of a prisoner. A life of captivity. And he suffered the penalty for no other crime than being born a research experiment. He had been condemned to incarceration for an eternity and reduced to a mere pile of replacement parts for damaged humans because of a tweak of spliced genes. And tomorrow, he'd be a brain donor.

Today they'd exercised his body in every way imaginable and tried to push it to the absolute limit. Running, tumbling, lifting, and fighting. But they hadn't succeeded in exhausting him. Then they'd placed electrodes on his head while he performed a variety of intelligence tests. He'd passed every one in record time. Or so they said. The cheers now going on in the room next door made him assume that they were testing Binah, too. He wasn't sure what their exclamations meant. No one had cheered for him during his ordeal.

Tomorrow. The mere thought of his brain being forced to occupy the body of a pathetic human male sickened him. Made him queasy. He was determined that tonight he and Binah would either escape or die. He'd rather end his life than be condemned to exist in the body of a human. *Homo sapiens.* There was nothing sapient about them in his opinion. They were stupid animals. Much less intelligent than he. And weaker.

And what galled him more than anything was that they were the ones responsible for his creation. But if nature could create something as dull and thoughtless as a human, a stupid organism that still managed to dominate the surface of the Earth despite its weakness, then was it too farfetched to consider that humans could actually create something greater than themselves? The question nagged at him, and he tucked it away in the dark recesses of his brain. He'd answer it later, when he knew he'd exhausted all of the possibilities. When he knew he'd dominated them, ruled them, and destroyed them, and when, in the end, the answer wouldn't matter. And that simple thought put him at peace. For the time being.

October 18, 01:15

Binah woke. She wasn't sure how she'd calculated the time; she didn't have an alarm. When she opened her eyes and looked at the glowing numbers on the clock that hung on the wall, fortunately, the moment was perfect. She dug the scalpel out from the tiny hole where she'd hidden it in her mattress. Removing her transmitter had to be first thing. She covered herself with the blanket and felt for the invisible-but-palpable chip just behind her ear. It didn't take much effort to put the blade in the right place, and she was amazed that she didn't feel a bit squeamish with what she was about to do. Instead, she found some comfort in slicing her skin and removing the chip.

It was an awkward process, and the smell of her own blood assailed her when she fumbled for the chip beneath the skin, but there was gratification in removing the source of the White Coat's ability to track her. To spy on her.

The transmitter was tiny, and she almost dropped the device in her bedcovers when it slipped between her blood and her fingers. She shoved it under her pillow and then got up to go to the bathroom. Of course their room was monitored, as was everything in her life. Her heart raced. She'd taken steps to change that forever. After tonight, she'd either be free or dead—free either way, and she'd no longer be a puppet. She was tired of being a thing on a string, responding to the bidding of her own creators.

But what about Ben? He hadn't come to see her. Hadn't lifted a finger to rescue her. Instead, he'd participated in transporting her to this place and left her in captivity. He'd never told her he was sorry for what he was doing. Her insides felt reduced to rubble. The trust, the joy she'd gained in mating with him, in being with him was like flowers on fire, singed to ashes. And there was no promise he could make that would revive that joy.

Binah glanced at the cameras on the ceiling. The watchers would see her creeping to Gevu's bed. It might seem suspicious, but she had no other choice. She was lucky that the bathroom was on the other side of Gevu's cot. When she slipped him the scalpel, he'd have to find the microchip on his own. Remove it by himself. She didn't see that as a problem. On her way to the restroom she stopped ever so briefly at Gevu's bed and bent to kiss him, simultaneously sliding the scalpel underneath his pillow. Then she went to empty her bladder.

No telling how long this will take. The clock was almost at the two. She wondered what Gevu had in store, but she chose not to worry about it. They were in agreement. Escape or die. And for her, she decided death was not an option.

Gevu was amazed. His sister had actually done it. He knew she had because he could smell the blood the moment she'd made the first incision on her skin. And now the scalpel lay just under his pillow. His hand reached for it, and he pressed just behind his ear to find the chip. He cut the skin a little, then had to cut deeper, but his fingers extracted the locater without much difficulty, and he shoved it under his head.

That will buy us some time.

But he knew the time would be mere seconds. Minutes if they were lucky. But that was all he needed.

He heard Binah climbing into her rack on the other side of the room. It was about time she'd grown a pair. Together they'd be an unstoppable force. Together they'd find a way to beat humankind down to the place that they deserved.

He glanced at the clock. *Almost two.* Gevu took a deep breath, gasped, and then started to cough. He coughed even louder, as if a spasmodic fit had taken him over. Binah rose from her bunk and came to him with a glass of water. He sipped but continued to cough harder, then harder. His face turned red and puffy, and he started to drool. He rose from his bunk and then fell to the floor.

"Help!" Binah cried. His sister stared at the cameras as Gevu twisted and convulsed in a spasm. He'd made sure his hands were bloody and pressed them to his face so it seemed as if the red stains were coming from his mouth. The door opened, and two guards came in. One approached him. Binah looked down, and Gevu gave her a wink. He had everything from here. Right now, given the circumstances, he was master. He was in control.

In a flash, he leapt up and lunged at the guard. A solid punch to the solar plexus knocked the wind out of the man, and he crumpled to the ground. The other man retreated toward the door, hoping to escape, but Gevu was faster. Another swing of his fist, and the second guard was down. Gevu sucked in the sweet air of success. The door was still open, and Binah stood on the other side, motioning him out.

In his mind's eye, Gevu imagined what it would be like to pummel the human into squishy hamburger. To pound him until the lights in his eyes went dark. To take his own porcine teeth and sink them into the muscle fibers of the human's arms and legs, to peel back his flesh from the bone as carelessly as a human ate chicken wings or thighs on a football night.

"Gevu!" Binah was calling him, and he shook off the vision. *There will be a time. There will be* my *time.* But right now, escape was the priority. He raced past Binah, and they locked the door shut.

"One thing to take care of..." With Binah behind him, he burst into another run down a long, narrow corridor to a door where retinal scans and fingerprints were required for entry. They were flimsy barriers, and besides, he'd mapped out almost the entire facility in his head. From maps to walking the corridors and observing computer configurations, this underground base was an open book to him. He knew the room where he had to go first and the exact location of the secret elevator shaft. He tore past their defenses and ripped the doors from the walls. He wasn't prepared for what he saw next.

Dr. Wetzel and Dr. Skylar stood before them, right in front of the experiments he'd heard the humans whispering about. The look in their eyes was resolute. No matter. Whatever they did, the end would be the same.

"Move." He barely acknowledged their presence. He prepared for a fight and looked at their hands. They were empty.

No Tasers, no guns, no tranquilizer darts. Then they did the unexpected. They moved out of his way.

In front of him lay ten enormous tubes, each with a fetus that resembled his own form or Binah's. Clones. He didn't know how he knew what they were. He just did. And the White Coats were simply moving out of his way? Didn't they want to protect their experiments? Weren't they part of this entire military operation? Dr. Wetzel raised an eyebrow as if to say, *Now what?*

Gevu walked up to the artificial uteruses, and Binah shuffled behind him. He observed the sleeping fetuses, and a wave of deep emotion washed over him. They were innocent. They were the beginning of his species, grown from the greed of science, harnessed by the desires of military force, and designed to serve under the domination of mankind. But still, they were his kin.

He paused only for a second before his fist curled into a massive ball of fury and plunged into one of the tubes. He pummeled the little life that lay flopping on the ground until it resembled nothing but a smear. Binah cried out, but he blocked out her voice, isolating himself from any reason she might try to impart to him.

Die! Die! It was all he could think as he smashed more of the thick glass and then pounded his knuckles onto each of their heads until they resembled squashed Play-Doh.

It was Dr. Wetzel's voice that snapped him out of it. "Gevu! If you want to get out of here, if you want to be free, we've got to go now!"

Gevu looked at the yellow-green amniotic slime and the red-pink flecks of flesh and blood that covered his hands. He realized much of his anger was spent. For now. He'd build up a fire in his gut when he needed it and take the house down if he had to, but there was one way out his captors didn't know he had access to.

"This way!" He hurled himself from the room, aware of Binah, Dr. Wetzel, and Dr. Skylar behind him. To his left, the sound of numerous footfalls shook the walls. He veered right and turned down two corridors until he stood before an enormous set of steel doors. He yanked off the panel beside it and used his teeth to skin some wires, and his fingers twisted them together. The doors activated and slid open.

He crammed his body inside and pulled Binah in with him. There wasn't enough room for all of them. Dr. Wetzel shoved Ben forward. "Go!" The doors shut, and Gevu couldn't help but wonder what would happen to his good little doctor. He hoped she survived. He really did.

The doors opened up, and they stepped out of the small building. Large radio towers surrounded them, and up above, a canopy of twinkling stars dotted the sky. One star in particular blazed in the sky, a tiny trail of light following behind it. She remembered reading that this was the year of the comet ISON 2. It wasn't supposed to be visible this early, and she was puzzled, wishing she'd had more time to learn about it.

Binah looked down on a smattering of building lights, a runway, and the ocean. In the opposite direction, a winding highway disappeared behind the miniature mountain on which they now stood. The elevator doors closed.

"We've got to go! They'll be here any minute!" Binah felt useless stating the obvious, but *this* was the extent of Gevu's plan? Escape, only to be captured once again? Sirens began to blare near the airstrip at the bottom of the hill. She realized it was Point Mugu Airbase, and several Jeeps were passing through the gates and headed up to the top of the mountain where they stood. Binah stared at the vehicles headed their way and then looked at Gevu. He seemed calm. Almost satisfied.

Ben grabbed her arm and yelled, "Let's go, Binah! Maybe we can make it..."

Gevu gripped Ben's shoulder and pulled him away from her. "Wait," he said.

"For what?" Binah was confused. Why did Gevu want them to wait? She had never seen Ben so animated. He looked afraid and angry. She was almost touched. Perhaps he cared for her after all.

"We need transportation." Gevu looked around at the sound of a vehicle approaching.

A Jeep rounded the corner, and a spotlight shone on Gevu. Instead of dodging it, he headed straight for it and plowed into the bumper like it was made of putty. The vehicle rolled, twisting the front tire and making it no longer drivable. Two men in the front seats attempted to remove themselves from the upside-down crash.

Another Jeep bounded over a pile of brush. Binah shouted with alarm, "Gevu!"

"If at first you don't succeed..." This time Gevu simply walked toward it and put his hands out. The Jeep crashed into the palms of his hands, and the driver's and passenger's heads smashed against the dash. Gevu ran over, unbuckled them, and threw them to the ground.

"Step right..."

The sound of a gunshot pierced the air.

"Hold it!" The voice was Harper's. Binah spun around. Dr. Wetzel stood next to him. They both had firearms aimed at her. Probably real guns. Real bullets. She guessed neither was a tranquilizer because she recognized Dr. Wetzel's Glock. More men arrived in Jeeps, and desert dust filled the air. In minutes, they were surrounded.

"We can't afford to let you go. You know that." Harper's voice was steady, but Binah knew it wouldn't make a difference. They'd come this far, and if she understood Gevu well enough, they weren't going back. Not at any cost.

"You going to shoot me, human? After all you've done to get me here? I don't think so!"

Gevu whirled around to a nearby Jeep. The men in the other vehicles leveled their weapons at him, but before they could fire, Gevu ripped the driver out of the seat and threw him into the air. The passenger waited only a second, then bailed and ran.

"I'll shoot if I have to. It's not my preference, but the security of this country comes first." Harper edged a little closer to Gevu as he yelled. Binah had no clue how the man planned to capture the huge monster that was her brother. Then, she realized he was only stalling for time. The number of lights from the military base at the foot of the mountain had increased, and Binah heard the sound of helicopter blades starting up.

Gevu growled at her. "Binah, get in!" Could she and Gevu get away so easily?

She climbed into the Jeep. Harper's gun continued to point at her brother, but Gevu ignored him and barked out orders. "Skylar, get in the driver's seat."

"We can't let them go, Gevu. They won't get far." Harper sounded so sure.

Gevu leapt toward the next vehicle, but the armed men were ready. They aimed their M16s and fired at Gevu's chest. Binah screamed. He fell to his knees as his flesh tore away from his ribs, and blood splattered on his face. Incredibly, he got up again.

"Cease fire! Cease fire!" Harper ran to Gevu, but her brother threw himself forward, wrenched a rifle from one of the men in the Jeep, swung it around, and knocked them both in the head. Then he threw it to Binah. It landed in her lap. He tossed a handgun to her as well, and then bellowed as he plunged to the ground falling on top of Harper. Gevu turned his head and looked at her, his eyes glazed over but burning with anger.

"Put it in gear! Get ready!" he gasped. Gevu's chest made a sucking sound, and dark liquid poured out of his mouth. Harper was grunting beneath the overwhelming weight of her brother, and Dr. Wetzel just stood there, silent, pointing her gun.

"Come with us!" Ben held his hand out to Dr. Wetzel, but she shifted her muzzle and shot at the man who was aiming at them from the other vehicle's driver seat. He slumped over the steering wheel. Dr. Wetzel screamed at them manically, lowered her gun, and dropped to her knees. "Go, asshole! Get the fuck out of here!" Ben paused for a second, but then he put the Jeep in gear and pressed the pedal to the floor.

"No, don't leave him!" Binah couldn't bear the thought of leaving her brother behind. Ben hesitated when she yelled, but then he gunned the Jeep forward, spinning up clods of dirt down the road. There was more gunfire behind them, and Binah screamed again. She'd seen the blood. She knew her brother was dead.

Miriam stared at the retreating taillights. The tires kicked up so much dirt that the thick cloud of dust made it hard to see. She looked back toward Gevu, but he was gone. *Holy shit, Ben was right.* Harper lay on the ground, gasping for breath. The magnitude of Gevu's weight pressing on top of him had caused him to pass out. Her boy weighed well over four hundred pounds. Now Harper was coming to. Miriam took advantage of the time she had and ran to the radio attached to the dash of the lonely Jeep.

"This is an order from Dr. Miriam Wetzel! All hands, stand down. Hold position at base! Patrols, pull back!" She only hoped they would listen, and she dropped the mike. Her feet slipped on Gevu's blood, and she stumbled on her way back to Harper's side. Her shirt was damp from sweat, and her hands were trembling. *Where would they go? Would they get away? Holy Banneker, I have no idea what the hell will happen to me.*

When Harper had found her at the base of the elevator after Gevu and Binah's escape, she'd made a great show of pounding on the metal doors in anger and frustration. At least the emotions she'd felt were real. But how much had he really seen? How much did he know? Should she take her chances and run now, or see how it all played out?

Miriam didn't get a chance to decide. Harper's hands suddenly lashed out and struck her across the face. She fumbled for her pistol and realized she must have dropped it on the ground somewhere. He pivoted upright, grabbed her around the neck, and squeezed her throat tight.

"You bitch. You knew. And you let them go." He dragged her to the elevator doors and pushed the button.

Going down. Oh, she was going down, all right. For her, there would be no escape. No freedom. Her decisions had ensured she'd go through hell. And hell couldn't have a better overseer than the man with his forearm pressed across her windpipe.

TWENTY TWO

October 18, 03:23

How could Binah leave me? How could she betray me? Gevu's thoughts raced faster than he could stumble through the brush. He'd meant to hop into the back of the vehicle after fending off the attackers. Instead of waiting for him, Dr. Skylar and Binah had left without him. He expected the scientist to turn tail and run, but not Binah. She was his sister.

He'd never forgive her. Not for this. They were the only two of their kind, and she'd decided to go her own way. Decided to leave him. She should have had the strength to make Ben wait. And she'd never last out here. She hadn't explored the world like he had. She wasn't strong like he was. Didn't have his willpower. Binah would fail. He would survive. Not only survive, but succeed. Pity.

The full moon helped him see where he ran, but its light was a detriment as well. The humans would hunt them both down. Helicopters, dogs, trucks. He imagined there was a number of things they could do to track him. Gevu reached behind his neck and rubbed the spot where he had cut to remove the locater chip. He was surprised to find it had almost healed.

Were there any more chips? Or were the humans so saturated with the idea of their own superiority that they never considered that Binah and I would escape?

He thought about the shots he'd taken to the chest and felt the spots as he ran. They were hardly bleeding now, and the flesh had almost knitted back together. Was it a miracle? Had he really taken such a devastating blow?

Well, none of that mattered now. He'd think about that later. He was free right now, and he needed to stay free. His feet pounded the dirt as he ran up a hill and headed for the scent of salt and water. The ocean waves sparkled in the moonlight. Next to the sea, he could make out the zigzag of the Pacific Coast Highway. He'd find transportation, and he'd head for the city. There were places he could hide, and perhaps, one man he could bargain with. His only problem was that he didn't know how to find him.

First things first. Gevu ran toward the beach. When he got closer to the shore, he ran a few more miles. A small ranch-style structure rose up to meet him. He read the sign out front. *Neptune's Net.* The windows were dark. All closed up in the wee hours of the morning. Across the street, on a cliff right by the ocean, sat two vehicles. A Volkswagen Beetle and a large van with a few surfboards piled on top of the roof. Not a person stirred near them.

On a hill, he heard voices, and an odd, pungent smoke tickled his nose. Gevu felt a deep sense of relief and a bit of euphoria as he made for the van. He only hoped the humans were going in the direction he needed. If they weren't, then he'd find a way to convince them otherwise. He doubted that would be a problem.

"There." Chet pointed at a figure moving along the scrub brush on a nearby hill. He was pleased his guess had paid off. The animal was a bastard, but his sheer size and his smarts led Chet to consider the pigs would try to escape once they knew what Harper really had planned. He was glad Ching was patient, coming here night after night. Waiting was hell, and each day that went by without a sign of escape made him anxious. It was interesting that Ching insisted on being there. Every hour was painful as the minutes ticked by, but they'd finally hit pay dirt.

He paused a moment and looked at the team surrounding him. Not just Chinese. There were other Asian mixes there. Ching-man was the obvious standout among the crew. He alone wore a finely tailored suit. Modest, but chic. Two men beside him held tranquilizer guns, and they shifted their feet slightly now and then. A telltale sign that they were nervous. They should be. Chet had firsthand experience of the damage the brute pig could do. The animal had grown large and strong in just a few months, and even though he was only a pig, Chet knew from experience he was extremely dangerous.

Ching-man pursed his lips just a little. It was hard to tell if the man was pleased or perplexed. The Chinese man held out his hand. "Wait," he said to the team. They watched Gevu cross the road and climb into the back of the van. Long minutes passed by before two men and a woman walked up to the vehicle and got into the front seats. The headlights popped on, and the van reversed, then pulled out onto Highway 1 and headed toward Los Angeles.

"Follow," Ching ordered.

Chet wondered why Ching had waited. His prize was right there, and now he was letting him get away. No matter. Chet's personal freedom was secured. The one thing Ching wouldn't do is backpedal now. The man was a textbook on decorum and honor. Something Chet admired to a certain extent, although he found the methods impractical. Men with honor got fucked. It was just a hard and simple truth. They lived by a code that the rest of the world considered a cold sore, and most folks couldn't wait till the blight faded into nonexistence so they could forget about it. The trouble was that the festering sore came back now and then, but Chet knew it would go away with time. It always did.

Their two-car team followed the van along the highway. It was just after Malibu that the vehicle swerved madly and then careened onto a rising embankment that flanked the sea. The driver and passengers piled out of the van at breakneck speed, yelling and screaming as they went, and it rocked back and forth before Gevu exploded through the back doors. He crouched low and looked around as if uncertain what to do next.

Ching spoke into his headset. "Now." Two black sedans pulled up around Gevu, and he stared into the glaring whites of the headlights. Ching got out, but when Chet made as if to follow him, the man flashed his palm. "Stay" was all he said, and he shut the car door.

Chet felt like a dog meant to do the master's bidding, and he didn't like that feeling at all. He was his own man and called the shots. He was not the kind of man who took them. Not since Kuwait.

He watched as the fool of a chink strode up to Gevu, bowed, and said something he couldn't hear.

Idiot. Gevu was twice the man's size in bulk, and the animal towered over him. *Pig-Hulk. Pink instead of green.*

"You're gonna get it now," he muttered. This was when he expected the pig to tear into the Chinaman. Chet would normally have enjoyed the prospect, but he hadn't gotten paid in full yet. He was a grasshopper's butt hair away from going against the man's orders and placed his hand on the car door handle when the most dumbfounding thing happened. Gevu turned around and quietly got back into the van. One of Ching-man's men climbed into the driver's seat, and before they knew it, they were headed back into town.

How the fuck did he do that? Sure, their captive was only a pig. An excessively large, dressed-up pig. But a dangerous one with muscles, bulk, and teeth. A killing animal that had blasted a couple of people away only a few nights ago.

And Ching just says a few words to him, and the pig does what he says? His curiosity got the better of him, and he had to ask. "What did you tell him?"

A long silence hung in the air and made Chet think the chink wasn't going to answer, but then the man spoke. "I said that I can help him." Ching put a hand on his arm, and Chet felt a sharp sting before the world became blurry. His eyesight started slipping from one scene to the next, and nothing made sense.

Slipping. It was, maybe, the last concept he'd remember for a very long time. Perhaps forever.

It took the patience acquired from all of his ancestors, but Mr. Sun Heung held on to his dignity and poise. It was bad enough to have to endure the faux name of "Wah Ching" for the sake of anonymity. At least the crude American had, despite his indecent behavior and atrocious manners, managed to return *the being* to him. It made it easier, albeit not much, for Heung to realize that the oaf had no idea who the sacred being was. And it was of little consequence if the imbecile understood or not. His only hope on the ride back to his headquarters was that the hamburger-and-fry eater would not make a futile attempt at conversation. Americans were incredibly inept at good conversation—so much so that even trying to attempt a strategic dialogue was exhausting and exceedingly irritating. He was pleased at his decision to drug the man for the return trip back. The ensuing silence was bliss.

It took forty-five minutes to reach the garage. The van parked, and the two black sedans pulled alongside it. Heung didn't even want to look at the American, but he gave the man a brief glance meant to compel the barbarian to listen to direction. "Wait."

The illiterate dolt bristled, but Heung acknowledged the emotion like it was an irritating mosquito on his arm. He'd be dealt with later. In whatever manner *the being* decided.

He shifted and got out of the sedan, mildly amused that his own palms were damp. It wasn't every day that one had the opportunity to meet a god. The van doors opened, and the one the Americans called Gevu crawled out of the back and stood before him. Heung bowed lower than he'd ever bowed to anyone in his entire life.

"This way, honorable one."

The god said nothing, but followed close behind him, and Heung was nearly in the throes of ecstasy. He alone had discovered the true god, and his future lives would be protected as long as he cared for him and nurtured him. As long as he allowed no one to do him harm ever again. And Heung would see to that personally. He would be his protector, as well as help him with his vengeance.

They came to a room, and Heung bowed low once more as he opened the door for the pig.

"Your room, *Zhu Bajie*." Heung held his breath as he dared use the real name of the most honorable one. It was the name of the one he'd followed all his life. The one he'd searched for with a fervency that Buddhist monks use to search for their reincarnated teachers.

The god only tipped his head in his direction, but it was in respectful acknowledgement, which was all Heung needed to know this moment was real. This spectacular being was truly divine, and all of his hopes and dreams came together. He knew he would serve *Zhu Bajie* until his last living breath. But until then, he had gifts for the god. One of them sat ignorantly in the parking lot. If *Zhu Bajie* were to discover his Buddha Nature on Heung's watch, he had to be careful and guard the god vigilantly. Guard him and guide him to his destiny.

But am I worthy of this task? He shook his head in order to bring him back to the present moment. Of course he was. He was the chosen. He alone had the knowledge and the power to find the god and lead him where he belonged.

Heung was beyond the crossroads of the life of simple humanity. Instead, he'd accepted a life with a god and the subsequent achievement of ultimate realization. Heung was pleased with his choice.

He whispered softly to his attendants. "Prepare his meal." Three young men left. The transformation of *Zhu Bajie* was only a matter of time, but Heung recognized its proximity. He wondered about the god's sister. But she was of no consequence. A mere aberration in the intricate web of fate. When the time came, he would help the god decide what her end should be too. Until then, he would serve the one. The true Pig King. And no one who thought they were anyone would stand in his way.

October 18, 05:34

Ben drove along the back roads and thought about Binah as the car curved toward Ojai. By some fantastic luck, the road was clear going down the mountain, and from there, he knew this area better than anyone. His family had a secret mountain cabin in the hills. One they hadn't used in years. It was once a place for growing premium weed, and he thought about his own "bud trimming" years in the hills beyond town. A carefree place where he'd smoked almost as much as he'd picked.

Things were different now. His parents were dead, and the cabin had been vacant for a number of years. He'd returned to it now and then when he had needed peace and quiet, but he never expected that he would use the place to harbor an escaped scientific experiment.

The entire ride, Binah said nothing. She seemed lost in her thoughts. He suspected she felt devastated at losing Gevu and probably worried that they were going to get caught. This was the first time she and her brother had ever truly been apart. *And now she thinks he's dead.*

Ben had no idea how to tell her the truth. After all that had happened, he was sure she was in shock. He started to say something a couple of times, but when he glanced at her face, her snout pointed to the sky, eyes shedding tears that rolled along her cheeks. The words just wouldn't come.

There will be time enough to tell her later. But how much time? He thought about his career. The research he'd done with Miriam. It was all so fantastically warped somehow, and what had passed as months seemed like lifetimes ago. Not to mention, he could never go back and take the place of the man he once was. A young, respected scientist. Now he was a criminal. A wanted man. If not wanted by the law, then hunted by the Cullers.

The Jeep pushed deeper into the California mountains, and the roadways twisted and switchbacked like an angry rattler. They never met an oncoming car, which didn't surprise Ben. Not many people ever came out this way, and they'd been on his land for a few miles now. The road took a sharp dip into a hidden valley nestled next to a slow-moving creek and some green cottonwoods. The first rays of the sun were just peeking over the top of the sage-covered hills, and the sweet chirps of western bluebirds filled the air.

Binah sat up and looked around. "Where are we?"

"Home," Ben said. He tried to feel optimistic when the word passed his lips, but a sense of unease settled over him as he gazed around at the place. He couldn't remember if he'd ever told Miriam about his land. Nothing else in his recent background linked this place to him, but eventually, a determined organization like the Cullers was sure to find out where they were hiding. And he wasn't certain what to do about that. Not yet.

TWENTY THREE

October 18, 11:26

Chet woke. Groggy. Unfocused. He raised his hand to scratch his face, and realized his wrists were shackled. He looked with confusion at the cuffs attached to a chain on either side of him. Each one was fixed on opposite corners of the wall. His body was naked, and he could barely move. The concrete floor was damp on his buttocks, and in the middle of the room was a slotted drain much like those in the center of showers. One bare bulb glared at him from the ceiling. It lit the center of the room easily, but kept the corners in shadow.

A camera, mounted on the ceiling at the far corner of the room, pointed its lens at him.

"What the *fuck*, Ching-man?" He yelled at the top of his voice, knowing the chink had to be watching him. "We had a deal!"

In response, a steel door on one of the sidewalls opened. What stood in the doorway made Chet's stomach crumple like a crushed beer can.

Gevu. Fucking bastard. Fucking freak. *Why was he here?* Their places should be exchanged. The pig should be chained up instead of him, and Chet was supposed to be on his way somewhere. Anywhere but here.

Gevu strode into the room wearing an enormous red-silk robe that fluttered behind him when he moved. Otherwise, he was naked too. Giant rolls of muscle and fat undulated with each regal stride. Two female attendants followed him. In the shadows just past the door, Chet could make out a dark figure standing there silently. "Ching, you bastard!"

Gevu shed his robe and handed it to one of the women. "Take off his cuffs," Gevu said, and Chet struggled. The giant pig grabbed his throat with one expansive hand and squeezed. The pressure was unbearable and made him gasp for air. The two females unlocked the restraints from his wrists then retreated to the door. The man in the shadows barely moved except to shut the giant steel portal behind them.

Chet choked against Gevu's grip, and saliva dripped down his chin. *Damn fucking bastard is huge!* He squirmed and kicked out, hoping to connect with the brute's balls, but the pig threw his knuckles hard into Chet's belly while maintaining his grip. He wheezed and tried to cough, but he could only manage a strangling sound.

The pig placed his mouth against Chet's ear. "It's not going to be as easy as you think. No, human, you won't die right away. Just piece by piece."

He couldn't believe it. The animal could talk! How long had he been able to communicate with words? Did the Cullers know? Did the military know? The bitch doctor sure knew how to keep her secrets. Chet made an attempt to inhale, but without any air, the room started to grow dark. Gevu chuckled. "Surprise," he said, and then the beast opened his mouth and settled it around Chet's ear, crunched his teeth closed, and pulled.

Chet tried to scream as he felt the agonizing, burning sensation of his flesh being torn from his head. Hot blood squirted down his neck, and the stink of iron filled the air. He kicked. He punched, cried, and fought with every bit of strength he had left.

There has to be a way to get free.

Gevu dropped him on the ground. Chet stumbled, sucked in some air, and ran a few feet. He turned to face him and looked up. The beast's grin was the most horrific thing he'd ever seen. His own blood was smeared across the pig's mouth, and pieces of flesh from his ear were stuck between his teeth. Chet looked around the room. There was nowhere to run, and for the first time in his adult life, he felt scared and utterly defenseless.

October 18, 12:02

Harper strode down the corridor, taking pleasure in his ability to move in silence. The walls here echoed horribly. Each noise that hit their surface made it extremely difficult to walk up on anyone without them being aware.

He tried to push thoughts of Miriam deep into the recesses of his brain. What was done was done. She'd been his loyal trainee and a highly valuable operative. Now she'd gone rogue.

So much wasted talent.

Miriam was willful, self-centered, and couldn't see beyond her own research agenda. It was his task to remind her that the research was not hers. The military had paid handsomely for what it had ordered, and they'd provided her with the joy of performing an innovative study. She would be useless to them unless she accepted the path they needed her to follow. And it was up to him to make her useful again. Until they got what they needed.

He stopped at a door and placed his hand on a panel. A blue light glowed from it as the sensor scanned his palm and fingertips. The door slid open. Miriam sat on a long slab that protruded from the wall. Her knees were drawn up to her chest, and her hair fell loose around her shoulders. If her lips weren't pressed so tight together, she'd almost be pretty. He shook off the thought.

Harper walked over and handed Miriam her security badge. Her eyes flickered with surprise, then the fire in them dimmed.

"What's this supposed to mean? I let your prized project get away, and suddenly you are giving me back my privileges?"

"Not all of them." He sat down beside her and showed her his computer tablet. "Right now, Utah state officials and federal agents are out looking for you." On the screen was a news story about a man who'd been shot to death just east of Green River. Suspect drawings, rendered by a law enforcement artist, looked just like Miriam and Ben.

"There's nowhere to run, Miriam. You leave here, you're a wanted woman. We won't be able to save you from going to prison."

"A threat, Harper?"

"A promise. Did you know Emmet's brother was a deputy sheriff? I imagine he'd like to find you and bring you in himself. Dead or alive."

"What are you saying? That you know I won't leave because I'm suspected of a murder?"

Poor Miriam. She always simplified the things that needed to be complex and complicated things that were actually very simple.

"That's exactly what I'm saying. Now, as soon as you're done moping, I believe you have a lab to clean up. See if you can salvage anything."

"And if I can't?" She straightened her shoulders and raised her head in a regal pose as if she were challenging him.

"Then perhaps we'll have to hand your body over to the authorities. It would, of course, be a shame." He thought he saw her shiver a little. She always had to work so hard to cover her emotions. She'd do much better if she just relaxed. But he wasn't going to tell her that. Not now. He had to read her body language as much as possible in the next few days. If anyone could find Project Kilo, she could.

October 18, 14:15

Two agents stood behind Stella, and in front of her, she viewed the aftermath of Gevu and Binah's breakout. Broken containers were strewn across the room. Slimy, red flesh lay smeared on the floor. The heavy smell of decay had set in, and it made her gag repeatedly. She tried breathing through her nose, but it didn't help much. She didn't know how the agents tolerated it without a flinch.

Whoosh.

The door opening behind her startled her. Harper and the woman she supposed was Dr. Wetzel walked past her.

"You'll need help cleaning up the mess. This is Stella. She's your extra set of hands." Harper winked at her as if it were a little joke.

Great. I'm in a military dungeon, and I get to work with a scientific Cinderella. Stella was already thinking about the possibility of escape. If the pigs had done it, then she could too. She'd just have to figure out how. Luckily, the famed Dr. Wetzel had no idea who she was. The woman looked her up and down like she was a piece of machinery. Dr. Wetzel said nothing. She didn't even bother to introduce herself, but turned to face the pile of gore on the floor.

"We'll need biohazard buckets and gloves."

Harper's voice carried only the slightest hint of amusement. "That's my Miriam. Practical as always." Stella could feel tension in the air and knew it came from Dr. Wetzel. It was like the electrical crackle right before lightning struck. Harper winked again at Stella before he walked out of the room, but there was no sense of sharing in that wink. Instead, it felt like more of a warning.

Stella didn't know the history between the two, but she gathered the recent escape of their precious research had caused an enormous rift in their relationship. And the mess on the floor let her guess it was irreparable. She could use that in the future, and she wondered if she could convince Dr. Wetzel to trust her. How much had Harper said about her?

Probably nothing. He was the kind of man who hoarded information and dealt in secrets. He was the dealer at the table, and they were captive players. And he had the advantage of stacking the deck so that counting the cards in the game was near to impossible.

Near to, but not impossible. She hated this man who seemed to know everything. But he didn't know everything. If he did, he would have seen the potential for the pigs to escape and prevented it. She imagined that deep inside his calm outer shell, he was seething with anger.

Stella also guessed he'd taken for granted that she wouldn't tell Dr. Wetzel about her role with Chet and how she'd helped him steal the pigs in the first place. One look at the scientific woman's stony face assured her she'd find no camaraderie, no single bone of sympathy in that body. Harper was right. For now, she'd keep quiet. But she had to wonder why he'd decided to put them together. It was a terrible risk. Unless that was what he wanted.

She looked down at her pale-blue scrubs, identical to many of the medical personnel in the area. They'd made her change into them and had taken her other clothes to who knows where. Probably threw them in the garbage. It was the last she'd see of normal clothes. For a while.

"We'll need masks." Dr. Wetzel was busy dictating a list of items she'd require. A couple of technicians nearby were taking notes. When she was done, she looked at Stella. The scientist's dark-blue eyes were piercing and bore right into her.

"Do you have any experience with research?" The woman tapped her foot a couple of times while she waited for Stella to answer. She still hadn't even asked her name. It bothered her until she realized she wore her name on a badge they'd clipped to her shirt pocket.

Note to self: the scientist won't bother asking questions or chatting about the obvious. It was useful to understand what was important to Dr. Wetzel. It was a piece of the puzzle she might need in order to get free.

Miriam was seething beneath what she hoped was a calm and clinical exterior. Perhaps Ben and Binah had escaped, and she had no idea how Gevu would find his way to somewhere safe, but she took comfort in knowing his wounds would heal. It still stung a little that Ben hadn't told her about his genetic alterations. At Harper's request for a near indestructible being, he'd used a strange mix of gecko, stone-crab, and sea-cucumber genes to create a trait that allowed their research projects not only to heal rapidly, but to regrow their limbs and organs whenever they were damaged or removed. Remarkable really.

I should have noticed how quickly they healed. But she'd never really had the opportunity. They were completely healthy the first few months. The only injuries they had sustained were puncture wounds from the blood samples she'd drawn. And it was common to heal from those quickly.

In fairness, she'd had her own pieces of genius; she'd added in a biochemical solution of her own design. Something that bonded with DNA during the gestation process, subsequently increasing the IQ of their projects to far above any level they'd be able to measure. She'd given them innate rapid learning of complex concepts. What she couldn't control was their affinity for a topic or a subject. She might have produced a genius engineer or a brilliant writer or a supreme strategist. She was lucky with Gevu. Her studies of him suggested he was born for war. Born to become the greatest being the world had ever known. And if she could, she'd make sure he wasn't the last.

Miriam stared at the mess on the floor. Obviously, these clones weren't indestructible. And if they'd been born, Harper would have had no understanding of why they weren't as intelligent as Gevu and Binah. Pixie dust. Her own combination. They'd soon realize they were missing something, and when they did, they'd come for her and Ben, and rip it from their brains. Truth serum. Torture. Maybe both. Either way, she knew they'd eventually get what they needed. But the Cullers were running out of time. Her additional research told her that much. At least that was in her favor.

Chet struggled to pierce through the fog of his delirium, and gradually, his vision cleared. Then he remembered what had caused his vision to blur in the first place. Gevu's giant maw on his already injured leg. Teeth ripping away muscle from his bone. The unbearable pain. Screaming, fighting, tearing at the beast, trying to get away. Gevu holding him down. Two Chinese girls fluttering toward him. A needle. A syringe. A blur.

How had he lived through it? He looked down at his leg, or where his left leg should have been. It was missing. Approximately five inches below his groin was a tourniquet cinched tightly around his upper thigh. The tissue below it was a stub, perhaps two or three inches in length. At the end of the stub, it looked as if someone had cauterized it and pasted

QuikClot all over the flesh. He was surprised he wasn't in a great deal of pain. He felt pleasantly high, like floating on clouds. Still, his leg was missing. His goddamn leg!

Why didn't the fucking animal just kill me? Gevu would regret not doing him in; he'd see to that. At least he had a chance to make him pay. As long as he sucked air, there was the possibility of making the cocksucker suffer. But first, he had to survive. Through the fog of whatever drug they'd given him, he forced himself to make a vow. He would survive, and then he'd dole out more anguish than the pig had ever known. The fucking animal would squirm. Beg for death. That thought made him feel better, and he fell asleep.

TWENTY FOUR

October 19, 07:01

Binah stared out from the kitchen window. Ben was still asleep in one of his guest rooms. He'd given her the master bedroom. She explored the house and was surprised it was so big. Nestled into the face of the hill, hardly anyone would notice the building was there.

So much room here.

The morning sunlight was golden, and the rocks on the hills gleamed. Binah decided to step outside. See what there was to see. She went through the door and followed a tiny walkway around the side of the hill. Halfway along the path, she noticed a place covered with prickly bushes. Part of the path disappeared behind them.

Odd place for a path to disappear. She walked up to the sagebrush and other desert plants and tried to look behind them. She sniffed. Something smelled different here. Earthy. Moist. It was an odd odor to find since this was a desert. Her hand grabbed a rock as she pushed her head deeper behind the brush. She nearly fell over when a door-sized panel swung inward. Beyond the door, there was only darkness.

There must be a light switch somewhere. Binah entered the secret room. The door swung closed behind her. She felt along the wall and found a switch and flipped it up. Soft lights illuminated a large laboratory. *Ben? He built this?* She thought about the cartoons she and Gevu had watched on TV. It was like an episode of *Dexter's Laboratory*. A secret science room. But how had he managed it?

She moved forward. Laboratory tables equipped with gas lines. Bunsen burners. Various glass beakers. But what caught her eye was the 3100 Genetic Analyzer. Her gaze roamed around the room. Much of this equipment was state-of-the-art. Who the *hell* was Dr. Ben Skylar? She realized now that he knew much more than he'd ever let on. He was a scientist, but for some reason, she hadn't grasped how deeply he was involved in genetic engineering.

A noise behind her and the smell of fresh air let her know Ben had just come into the room. "You've ruined my surprise," he said.

She didn't turn around. "How did you manage all of this? This is incredible!"

"You'd be amazed at what a young man can do with a lot of spare time and imagination." His voice was quiet.

"And the money? Where did this all come from?"

"There's not a lot a scientist can't get these days. And as far as the funding, my parents were loaded. I inherited their estate when they died. It was...substantial."

Binah looked at Dr. Skylar. No. He was no longer Dr. Skylar to her. She was free now. Free to call him by his true name. Ben.

"But why would you choose to work with Dr. Wetzel?" There was so much she felt she didn't understand.

"You can only develop so much by yourself, Binah. It's easy to lose perspective. Ideas go dry. When you're on your own, you lack the talent of other intelligent minds. Miriam is a phenomenal scientist, and she excels in areas that I do not."

Binah looked back at the equipment. She thought of Gevu and what he'd told her about how humans farmed animals. She thought about how she'd nearly become a sacrificial lamb for the military. A replacement part. A replacement *brain*.

And Gevu had died to save her. Despite his dark nature, he'd sacrificed himself. His greatest fault was his bloodlust, his desire for flesh—not to mention his overwhelming anger at their mother's murder and at Chet who said he'd eaten her.

When she'd discovered that humans grew animals by the millions just for consumption, she'd become sick with disgust. And the odd thing was that humans suffered heart disease and a host of other ailments—not to mention an increasing resistance to antibiotics—because of their ingestion of flesh.

She'd done research on the Internet and learned how the meat industries contributed to animal torture as well as air and water pollution. And they were powerful.

Killing is money. Death is a commodity, and several men profit from the exploitation of it.

An idea tickled the back of her brain, but she didn't dare say anything to Ben about it just yet. She wanted to learn what the equipment in his lab could do first. And when she'd figured it all out, which shouldn't take long, she'd tell him what was brewing in the depths of her mind. Maybe, just maybe, he'd help her with her plan. A plan that could make the world a better place. God knows it was something the world could use, whether it wanted it or not.

October 19, 10:00

Zhu Bajie had started his life out just like myths. He was brutal, and after feasting on the flesh of his enemy, he craved even more blood. Sun Heung was pleased. Certainly, the gore was distasteful, but *the being* would grow past that eventually. What Heung needed to do now was to provide the god meat. And women. Lots of women to whet his appetite.

He'd had his men round up a few females from Sunset Boulevard. Easy to gather on the street late at night. He put them in a pen designed to keep them secure. They were loud with their sobbing and cursing, but he was sure *Zhu Bajie* would be pleased. Next to the pen, he'd arranged a few mattresses and made sure they were fitted together securely and covered in the thickest of plastic. He knew what would happen here, and he pressed the disgusting visions away from his conscience.

For the ultimate enlightenment. To travel to the beyond.

A door to the room opened, and Gevu squeezed through the archway. Heung hoped the God wouldn't grow much more or he'd have to enlarge the all of the entrances to his rooms.

"*Zhu Bajie,*" Heung extended his hand toward the women, "an offering to you May they bring you great pleasure."

The god looked at the women imprisoned in the pen and blinked. A dawning of understanding flickered in his eyes as he stared at them. He examined the mattresses and then gazed back at the women. All of them were naked. Heung provided one more brief instruction before he bowed out. "You need only to press your thumb on the panel of their pen, and the door will open. Close the door, and it will automatically lock." With that, Sun Heung walked backward and retreated from the room. He was glad it was soundproof.

Gevu had experienced an erection before. Many times in fact. The first time was when he'd watched humans mate on the Internet. He'd rubbed himself in his bed, late at night, and he'd shuddered with the orgasmic spurts of pleasure. He was never aroused when watching animals mate, and the only one of his kind was his sister.

    He stared at the naked women as they clustered together, their breasts heaving, their voices culminating in sobs of horror or words uttered in abusive and foul human language. He realized he was aroused, and his cock grew hard. What would it be like to put himself into one of them? He strode over to the pen and pressed his thumb to the panel. The door opened easily, and the women flocked to the far corner of the space, reminding him of the chickens he'd indulged in so long ago. His fingers wrapped around the neck of a fleshy, young blonde, and he dragged her out as she kicked and screamed. The sounds excited him further, and he slammed the door and threw her onto the mattress.

    The female rolled over and scrambled for the door. He stopped her easily, grabbing her up by her hair and pressing her facedown on the mattress. The fingers of his other hand explored between her legs, and he found the lips of her vagina. He remembered the word he'd heard ro describe that place on porn films. *Cunt.* He brought his fingers to his snout.

    Yes, her *cunt* smelled earthy, rich, and tantalizing. The thick flesh of his erection pushed against it, and he could feel her warmth. He thrust his cock inside her, ignoring her screams. He shuddered and grabbed her hips. She struggled wildly. He brought his fist down on her head, and then he moved freely inside her while she was dazed. His hips moved faster and faster, and he pushed his full length into her. She screamed once more and struggled. He hit her again, and she slumped forward on the mattress, her body unable to resist him any longer. She felt good.

    Pure sensation! He leaned against her. He couldn't believe his fortune, to escape from the lab, survive the blasts from the guns, and then fall into the hands of a human who worshiped him. Instead of fearing for his life, now he held life in the palms of his hands, and he had all of these women to enjoy at will. Then it dawned on him. He could enjoy them, but maybe he could also breed. Breed more of his kind. Create the species he only dreamed of having on Earth. If he could do that, then he wouldn't need humans. Except maybe for meat.

Gevu's stomach rumbled. Since feeding on Chet's leg, he'd gone hours without food, and now he was hungry. He looked at the woman who lay helpless on the mattress, then looked back at the pen. Perhaps he'd made the woman pregnant, but he decided he could do that to the others later. *This one will be an example.*

He reached down and lifted the blonde by the hair. She came to life once more, kicked furiously, and screamed as he dragged her across the floor.

"Look!" he bellowed, and he made sure all of the women's eyes were fixed on him before he opened his mouth and sank his teeth deep into her throat. The crunch of cartilage accompanied the spray of blood across his cheeks. The woman went limp. He looked up at the many faces gaping at him in terror.

"This is what will happen to you if you don't please me." He bent his head and bit off the blonde's breast, and chewed it slowly. It was soft and fatty. Tender and delicious. He tore off the other breast, then ate the muscle from her thighs and buttocks. Blood ran across his face and poured onto the floor. He lapped up as much of it as he could while it was still warm.

When he was done, his appetite was sated. But it wouldn't be long before he'd need flesh again. He looked at the women. He'd have to divide them into those he would mate with and those he would eat. Perhaps Heung could find him some fat ones to curb his hunger. He'd tell Heung what he wanted. The man would make it happen. He remembered when he'd watched dogs mate a few times on YouTube. Female dogs didn't care how many males fucked them at once. And these humans were dogs. Female dogs of the street. *Bitches.* But still, some of them could be the first mothers of his brood, so if they conceived, he decided he'd let them live. His flaccid cock stirred.

Suddenly, he had real purpose. *Breed and feed.* That's what he'd do. And when he'd finally created his species, he'd enslave mankind the same way they'd enslaved animals over thousands of years.

Heung thought he was a savior, but Gevu knew the truth. By the time Gevu was done, he'd bring hell to Earth, and Heung would help create the demons who would reign there forever.

He reached over and pressed his thumb to the cage panel. The females stood there wobbling on their feet weakly. Some crouched low to the ground. A woman with dark skin was closest to his grasp. He grabbed her by the hair and threw her to the mattress.

"Kneel," he said. She was trembling as she submitted to him on all fours, her ass stuck high into the air. Gevu was hard as he entered her cunt. He liked that word, *cunt*. It was a ragged word that imparted a certain disregard for women. It isolated the human bitches from his idea of the perfect mate.

He pounded inside her until he came once more, then tossed her back into the pen, taking care to remember her face. He'd have a go at her a few more times, and if she conceived, he'd leave her alone. If not, she'd go into the "feed" category, and he was discovering his appetite was larger than he ever imagined. He'd always be hungry, one way or another. He reached inside the pen again and pulled another woman out.

TWENTY FIVE

November 16, 06:03

Where the hell is she? Could she be working this early in the morning?

They'd been at the house nearly four weeks, and Binah had absorbed every shred of information he'd thrown her way. They'd reviewed biology, anatomy and physiology of humans and pigs, chemistry, and organic chemistry, and then they'd moved on to embryology, endocrinology, advanced cell biology, neurophysiology, and, finally, genetics and genetic engineering. When he wasn't teaching her, she spent time working in the lab or reading on her own. Her desire for knowledge seemed insatiable.

He'd gone to sleep late last night while she had been solving a particular genetics problem. She'd read all of the papers he had stored on molecular biology, theory of biological pattern formation, and cloning. This morning, she wasn't anywhere in the house. She was a voracious student. He figured she was probably still in the lab.

He began heating water for a cup of hot coffee, found some instant granules he had in the pantry, and then lit up a cigar. Groceries were getting low, and he'd have to head to town soon. He was glad he'd stored some major cash in the house just in case of an emergency, but when it was gone, he'd have to figure out a way to get to his money without the government tracing him. At any rate, it would be a while.

When the coffee was ready, he greedily took a sip, slightly burning his lips. It was bitter, since he rarely drank it black, but the caffeine load combined with cigar's nicotine did the trick. He finished his smoke and made his way to the cave to see what Binah was brewing.

When he found her, she was hunched over the eyepiece of an electron microscope.

"You been up all night?" He rested his hand between her shoulder blades and thought he felt a little quiver at his touch.

Binah kept staring into the eyepiece, but her finger reached over and pressed a button that turned on two of the nearby computer screens.

"Look," she said. Her ears twitched just a little. Ben noticed it was a habit she'd developed when she got excited. That, and a little extra curling of her tail.

Ben turned his attention to the screens. The cells of twelve clones were dividing. He'd seen this before, but he was amazed at how quickly Binah had put the pieces together. "Mouse?"

Binah looked up and smiled at him. He loved how her porcine nose wrinkled up along with the curve of her mouth. "Yes! I've been working with them all night. I was just about to do a transfer of the embryos back into the mother." She didn't ask if he wanted to help, or even if he wanted to watch.

"Let me know when you're done," he said. "We'll move on to more." Binah almost seemed to ignore him. A little flick of her tail, which poked out from a slit in the backside of her pants, was the only acknowledgment she gave him. He wasn't sure why she felt such an urgency to press forward with her training, but to her credit, she was excelling faster than anyone he'd ever seen.

I should be used to it by now.

A pang of jealousy bubbled up inside him for a second when he thought of the years he'd devoted to what she'd managed to learn in days. He watched her continue to work for a few more moments and then headed back to the house for more coffee and some food. She'd need him again soon, but for the first time, he wondered exactly how long she'd rely on him.

His thoughts turned to Gevu. He still hadn't told her. No time ever seemed to be right, but once she discovered his secret, she might never need him again.

November 16, 08:00

Stella took notes whenever possible, concerning the underground compound and the research. She concealed them inside her mattress but seldom had time alone to work on them. Dr. Wetzel managed to keep her continuously busy during the day, and she was still required to stay and clean up after the doctor's experiments.

This morning, the good doctor had constructed another set of artificial uteri already implanted with embryos. Amniotic fluid filled the clear cavities, and Stella could already see something small floating in the one. Dr. Wetzel was staring into a microscope. A computer and a pile of handwritten notes were beside her.

Stella started to say good morning but thought better of it when she heard the doctor mumbling under her breath. "Damn, damn it! How the hell did he do it?" She had no idea what the woman was cursing about. She discovered she usually learned more from the woman if she just stayed silent.

Temperature checks of each artificial uterus were her first duties. Stella learned yesterday that the Japanese excelled at creating acrylic uterine models, and Dr. Wetzel had perfected their design using stem cell tissue to assist in the creation of a fleshy inside on the back of the uterus where the egg attached. From there, it developed into an embryo and placenta. Through the fleshy placental tissue, she pumped nourishing vitamins and minerals.

All of the temperatures were normal except one. Did she dare tell the scientist now, while she was in the throes of irritation? *Sure. Why the hell not?* "Um, Dr. Wetzel?" Stella cleared her throat.

The woman looked up from her microscope. "What?"

Stella motioned with her hand toward the uterus with the suboptimal temp. "This one's reading a bit low."

Dr. Wetzel huffed under her breath and walked over to take a look. Moving around to the clear face of the uterus, she examined the embryo, then glanced back up at Stella. "Scrap it."

Stella had no idea how to go about "scrapping it," but the doctor was easily riled, and so she wasn't about to ask. She looked at the machine and hit what she guessed was the off button. The lights on the machine died. She'd probably need a bucket to empty out the uterus, and she went to look for a container, sure that the process of evacuating the manmade organ wasn't going to be easy. Still, leaving the area gave her a moment of reprieve from the tension in the room.

November 16, 13:00

"I can't figure out how he did it." Miriam hated admitting her failure to Harper. The microscope lenses were smudged from her constant observations, and she took a piece of lens paper, wet it with cleaning solution, and polished the pieces. She hated that he was the one in control, that he held the keys to her freedom, and that Ben hadn't shared the information with her ahead of time.

Ben, you loyal dolt. He was a man of his word, and when he made a promise, he meant it. Miriam figured it was exactly what the admiral and Harper had bargained on when they had asked him to find a way for the projects to regenerate. *Healing tissue. They could have shared that with me. Why didn't they?*

"It shouldn't be too hard to figure out." Harper's lips tightened. She noticed his hair was perfectly combed. Not a strand out of place. His suit was perfectly pressed. Hell, even his shoes were shined. They were glossier than those of any of the army men in uniform.

"If you'd let me know about it ahead of time, then maybe I could do it!" The accusation in Miriam's voice felt harsh in her own throat. *Regeneration! The things I could have done if I'd only known.*

"We couldn't do that, Miriam. It was too much power for one person."

"Bullshit. Ben had access to every one of my files. He knew everything I knew!"

"We took into account..." Harper paused to wipe a nonexistent smudge from the tip of his shoe. "...personality." He stared at her.

Miriam turned away from him. She was more than angry. She felt betrayed, despite the fact she'd done some gene tweaking without telling anyone. "So you think your placid doctor wouldn't dare to start something like this on his own? You think you're safe even though you don't know where he is?"

Harper didn't say anything.

She looked back at him. His face was almost stony, but the tiniest upturned corner of his lip clued her in.

"You know where he is."

"Yes, Miriam. We know where both he and Project Juliet are."

She noticed that he didn't mention Gevu at all.

November 23, 08:00

Binah was pleased. With a little fine-tuning, she had accelerated the growth rate of the pregnant mouse fetuses, and a week later, the animal had given birth. Eight out of ten of the pups had survived. Fairly decent odds. And each mouse was female. A carbon copy of the mother. She'd mastered cloning.

Next, she had focused her work on the cellular uptake of proteins, as well as what contributed to the histamine response in the DNA of a subject. Why were some humans and animals allergic to various substances and others not? What affected the severity of the allergy?

Ben sat on the stool next to her, and together, they looked at the screen. "See this?" She pointed to a group of cells. Some were processing proteins, while others were not.

"It would help if you let me know exactly what you are doing." Ben had been watching her all morning, and she'd been very careful with her experiments. She wasn't sure how he would feel when he realized what she was doing. A few days ago, she'd decided to do this work on her own. And it was almost time. Once she was done, if she succeeded, humans would have to live very differently.

"As you can see, these proteins can't be absorbed by certain cells."

"So?" Ben stroked his chin. He didn't seem significantly impressed that she'd discovered a way to install an allergy in a certain group of cells.

"They're animal proteins," she said. Ben gazed at her.

"So you spent most of the night figuring out what causes animal protein intolerance in humans. Great." His voice almost sounded sarcastic. Binah didn't let his tone bother her. He'd get it in a minute. She held up a bottle and lightly sprayed a glass slide.

"These are cultured human cells." She placed a drop of cloudy liquid from a bottle onto the slide, mounted it on the microscope, and focused. The cells came into view, and the change that occurred was amazing. Cells, which ordinarily had a mixed protein uptake, were metamorphosing before their eyes. Now, they accepted certain proteins and rejected others.

"Which proteins are they rejecting?" Ben was starting to look uncomfortable.

A wave of silence curled over them, as if they were facing a thirty-foot wall of water.

"Animal proteins."

"Wait. What's in that spray?" His hesitation at asking her was clear. Sooner or later, he'd have to know. Better now than later. He'd already been infected anyway. Not that it mattered.

She picked up the bottle and sprayed it into the air, a repetitive action she'd done more than once when she'd taken it outside earlier that morning and pumped it into the wind. "A virus that secretes a transgenic compound inside the DNA of human cells."

"You've altered the DNA of the cells? Why would you do that?" Ben's brow furrowed.

She could see he was trying very hard to catch on. "I did it for Gevu."

His face collapsed like a giant wave pounding into the ocean. Understanding crashed in his eyes.

"Yes." She was satisfied he finally got it. "No one on Earth will ever eat animals again."

Ben's lungs contracted, and his chest felt like he was two hundred seven fathoms below the surface of the Pacific Ocean.

Specifically, in the depths of South Sawyer, where icebergs were constantly being born into the tumultuous, swirling blue waters of the sea.

Every lesson he'd ever learned in school about research was the antithesis of what Binah had just done. Forget about World War II and the horrific experiments done on the Jews. Forget about Tuskegee and Project MKUltra. Ignore the Nuremburg Code and every aspect of the Belmont Report. Under his tutelage, he'd failed to teach her the most basic laws of human research and ethics—but then, he hadn't known she was planning on experimenting on humans.

"Binah, do you know what you've done?" They were the only words he could force from his throat. He pressed his face into his hands. *This is not happening.*

"Of course." She looked at him as though he were a school child. "I've just solved our problem. Humanity is thoughtless. They buy dead cow muscle at meat departments and turn a blind eye to the truth…that the cow was raised captive in a small pen, abused, and treated like garbage until the day it was painfully slaughtered. Its body is divided up, packaged in cellophane, and disguised as 'steak,' ready to grill and eat. But humans never think about the pain involved. Humans refuse to acknowledge the terrors of what they already know."

"And what is that?" Ben felt obliged to ask, but his mind was still reeling. She'd put a virus into the air, a virus that would infect humans and irrevocably change the course of mankind's evolution.

"That animals are living, breathing, thinking, and loving souls who deserve just as much happiness as humans."

God, how I've failed. This is all my fault. Ben wanted to lash out at Binah and make her see what she'd really done, how she'd violated all of the tenets of human research, but he realized he hadn't taught her these things. He'd shown her many methods of research in biology, genetics, and virology, and she'd learned it all. She was extremely intelligent and intuitive, so much that he hadn't considered she'd make a drastic jump from animal to human study and not to think twice about it.

"Binah, a scientist cannot perform research on human beings without their consent, much less introduce a virus into the world that will change their way of life and potentially threaten their existence!" He shivered. The lab was always the right temperature because it was burrowed into the earth, but just knowing what she'd done made it seem like a cold, dark, and almost-sinister place.

"Consent?" Binah's lips contorted oddly when she said the word, like it was both filthy and holy at the same time. "Which part of me were you researching every day when you and Dr. Wetzel studied me and Gevu, Ben?" Binah's eyes were glassy with tears threatening to spill over onto her cheeks. "I don't remember anyone asking for my consent to any of this." She took a few more steps toward him and looked up into his face. "Does that mean I'm less of a human, or much more than an animal in your eyes?"

Ben wanted desperately to reach out to her, to hold her and tell her things would be okay, but the challenging question she'd just asked him made him realize that no matter how hard he tried, he wasn't going to be able to give her the right answer. For now, the problem encompassed much more than the two of them. If Binah was successful with her virus, and success was her trademark, humanity would soon discover they could no longer consume animal proteins. But he had to make sure she understood the scientific rules of human research in case she decided to go further. She needed to understand the importance of a literature review, the development of a proposal, and how to obtain Institutional Review Board approval. It was important to show respect for humanity and to not conduct research without the individual's consent.

Less of a human or more than an animal? It was an uncomfortable—but excellent—question.

November 23, 12:00

Ben shuffled back to the house with Binah's experiment heavy on his mind. Her creation would render anyone who came in contact with the virus unable to digest animal proteins. No more steaks or hamburgers. No more fried chicken. No eggs or cheese. He didn't eat meat, but he still loved his eggs and cheese. By exposing him to the virus, what she'd done was render him incapable of any animal-protein absorption. And that was what she wanted to do to the rest of the world.

Because of Gevu. His death, his desire for revenge for his mother's death, and his anger at the slaughterhouses that murdered millions of innocent animals. This was her answer?

Not only would humans be incapable of absorbing animal proteins, but those proteins could literally be toxic to the human body, causing vomiting, diarrhea, and enlargement of the liver and the spleen. The worst effects could result in convulsions and comas. And she'd changed him without his consent by merely exposing him to the mist during her experimental processes. He might not have minded if only she'd asked. He struggled with the ethics of doing this to the world population, as well as the implications of what it would mean for millions of animals, the meat industry, and economies that thrived on the sale of meat products.

Because of Gevu. How was he going to explain to her that he was probably still alive? Not probably—most certainly. He thought about her transgenic experiment and then wondered, perhaps, if they worked together, they might find the answer to a peaceful immortality. Then the government wouldn't need animal or human replacement parts. They wouldn't need lungs, livers, or brains because they would simply grow back.

But not the brain, not fully. Not the memories of a lifetime. Still, it offered a partial solution to some global issues. But in order to bring it up, in order to even entertain the idea, he'd have to tell her about his gene-splicing techniques. He'd have to tell her Gevu was alive.

TWENTY SIX

December 1, 11:00

All of Gevu's attempts at breeding with the human females had failed miserably. Every pregnancy had ended in disaster. The longest a human female had managed to carry his child was twelve weeks. He'd done his research. A normal pig pregnancy was four months, and a human pregnancy was nine months, or more precisely, forty weeks. He wasn't sure how long the gestation of his genetic makeup mixed with the human species was supposed to take. He knew it had to be more than twelve weeks since all of the fetuses had died when they were born. They'd been either malformed or too small to survive.

He had to admit to the fun of trying to create his brood, though. Every human female they had captured and brought to him, he'd tortured and fucked, and he'd had a jolly good time. He had investigated every pleasure; he'd had them suck him off or he'd screwed their asses when he wasn't trying to breed.

Unfortunately for them, they hadn't enjoyed it. His long porcine cock was thick like a human male's but twisted like a corkscrew and almost twice as long, and it had caused them physical agony when he'd pushed all the way inside. And with every frenzied thrust, he'd taken immense pleasure in watching their faces contort as they'd screamed.

Gevu couldn't help but grin as he thought about it. There was nothing as satisfying as pushing them down on all fours, climbing on top of them, and plunging his cock in from behind. He'd set a mirror up in front of the spot he called the "mating mat" and forced the women to watch as he humped each one of them, their screams putting any wounded animal to shame. They'd squealed almost as loudly as when he had butchered them. And he'd butchered them when they had failed to produce a live child, which meant that he always had plenty of meat.

Gevu felt his pulse quicken and his body tingle. He was getting an erection already just thinking about it, and his tension needed a physical release. The mating mat had been freshly cleaned. He'd ordered the women to wash it after his last adventure. Since he hadn't waited to see if the female would get pregnant, it had been a particularly bloody mess he'd left.

The women in the cage were terrified. He'd heard their cries of fear mingled with those of the woman he'd tortured, fucked, and then eaten right there on the mattress. Oh yes, the women were afraid. And they should always be afraid.

He lumbered into the room and eyed the bitches clustered there. They were like hens hiding from a fox. Only four in the cage now, but Heung assured him there'd be more later in the day.

A buxom black woman stared at him defiantly, and he eyed her up and down. She was a fine piece of flesh. His stomach rumbled. The bitch would make a wonderful snack after he screwed her brains out. Maybe he'd even screw them out literally. Force his dick into her mouth and drill it right into the back of her head. And just when she was begging for mercy, he'd gag her to death.

Of course he'd have to knock her teeth out to keep her from biting him, but that wasn't a problem. He'd done that before after a couple of women had tried to bite him. A hammer was a great tool, in his experience, and Heung had provided every implement he'd asked for. Just a few swift blows, and the job would be done. And the bitch's blood would make it nice and slick for him too.

Gave grew harder at the thought of fucking as he moved toward the woman, a Taser in his hand. He would be gratified first, and then he would eat. Some part of him recognized now that trying to mate with human females to produce live infants was hopeless. But he'd solve that problem later. If he couldn't make babies, he could make pain.

Heung strolled along his private corridor and hoped the god made his transition soon. It was getting more difficult to collect women off the street without drawing attention. But he'd also sworn to endure all of the difficulties that came with the honor of housing *Zhu Bajie*. Serving a god wasn't meant to be easy. It was the ultimate sacrifice, and no person, no circumstance, would stand in his way.

And now he wants the female scientist. What help could she be to him? Heung contemplated the difficulties of acquiring the woman. She was still locked in the depths of the mountain at Point Mugu. He'd have to flush her out. *But how to do it and steal her away under the very noses of the US military?* He admitted to himself that he had no idea. He stepped into his meditation room and hoped the answer would come to him while he sat in bliss.

December 1, 13:00

Harper's muscles ached. He'd had a particularly vigorous workout last night, and the admiral's voice droned on like the quiet buzz of a bee gathering pollen from flowers. Persistent. Busy. Yes, the admiral was upset and impatient. All of them were upset. None more so than the Cullers. But the Cullers were prepared. And they had the advantage.

"Did you get that, Harper?"

He looked up from the command table where he sat. Admiral Blandy was eyeing him expectantly. It was odd to think that this man who wielded so much power in the military would, in a couple more years, be reduced to the humbling status of retiree. Of course, that was assuming he made it that long. Made it through the catastrophic changes that would soon happen to the world.

"Yes, Admiral. I've got it." Harper got up from his swivel chair and approached the electronic maps on the wall. "Dr. Wetzel claims she can't develop the creatures without two very important things. She needs Dr. Skylar to engineer the improvements you'd asked for in the first set of experiments. And, she needs Projects Juliet and Kilo as the original specimens. You want to move forward with your goal, but the unsettling truth is you can't."

The admiral shifted a bit uncomfortably and took a seat at the table. General Muttnic had joined them earlier, and there were other unfamiliar government members there whose names he did not know, and would probably never know. The admiral spoke. "The Projects are gone. All of our military efforts to find them have failed. We're depending on you, Harper."

Harper tapped the toe of his shoe slowly, took his dark jacket off, and rolled up the sleeves of his shirt before he spoke. "Dr. Wetzel is the only one who might be able to draw them out. Because of that, I suggest we use her as bait to get the others."

General Muttnic grunted. "How are we going to do that? We've got her locked securely underground. I can't think of a group or government who'd dare try to bust her out of here. Letting her go and following her isn't an option."

He tamped down his growing irritation at the man. *Let it out. Breathe. Idiots will always abound.* He looked at both the admiral and the general. "What we need to do is hand her over to the police."

"What? For what crime?" Admiral Blandy's bushy gray eyebrows knitted together. He seemed perplexed and intrigued. Harper could tell the man hadn't been sleeping. His uniform wasn't perfectly pressed. The wrinkles on his pants looked as if he'd slept in them.

"Murder." Harper couldn't have been more pleased with the wide eyes of shock on the faces all around. The hardest part would be convincing them his plan would work.

December 1, 08:15

Heung rubbed his palms together and allowed a relaxed breath to escape from his lips while observing the chaos unfolding before him. Dr. Miriam Wetzel's reddened face filled the flat screen for a few more seconds before the shoulders of law enforcement officers blocked his view. He read the subtitles at the bottom.

The research scientist was brought in for questioning concerning the murder of a man identified as Emmet Fisher from Green River, Utah...

So, the doctor was out of the impregnable stronghold of the US military and within his bribable grasp. *Zhu Bajie* wanted his scientist; well, the holy one would get her. Right now, Heung's greatest obstacle was the publicity over the crime. The media coverage would make it much harder to whisk her away.

It could be a trap. They want Zhu Bajie. Perhaps it's what they're expecting. Heung chuckled. He hadn't attained his power because he was an idiot. Only a shrewd and intelligent man kept his position in China, as well as around the globe. And with years of practice, he was a master at maintaining his position.

He checked his contact list on his computer. There were a few people who still owed him some serious favors. It was time to request their immediate assistance. If he was going to get the scientist, it had to be now.

Heung plucked a star fruit from the bowl on his desk, took a clean knife from a plate, and sliced some of it to eat. It was one of the few foods that hadn't bothered his stomach lately. He focused on a scroll painting that hung on the wall. The image of the Pig King stared back at him, his rotund form decorated with delicate pink brushwork and fine golden paint. His grandfather had been right. Years of listening to those stories, waiting for the true one to arrive.

His *Zhu Bajie* was definitely magnificent. Greater and more powerful than he'd ever realized. He'd retrieve the scientist for the fallen god, and then he would be that much closer to supreme enlightenment.

Heung pressed a series of numbers on his phone. He could have done it without looking.

Miriam felt as if she'd entered some strange twilight fog where reality twisted insanely upon itself. Awakened in the wee hours from the depths of her sleep, she'd been hastily removed from the belowground military base and transferred to a prison cell at the Federal Metropolitan Detention Center. In this place, Los

Angeles was a far cry from the home of God's winged children. Demons strode through the corridors. Devils cackled inside their cells.

She realized Harper was using her as bait to reel in his fish. It was Gevu he wanted. Perhaps someone already had him and was holding him for ransom, but if that were the case, then why would they need her? No, the Cullers wanted Gevu, and somehow they knew that he, or whoever had him, needed her too.

She was still puzzling over Ben's genetic recipe for regeneration, but now there was no time. The soldiers had handed her over to the US Marshals. *Fucking Harper. Always thinking he's one step ahead of everyone. Always plotting and planning.* Why had she ever trusted him?

You're the best I've ever trained, Miriam. She could hear the silky words coming from his lips. From days long ago, at a time when she had been young and oh so impressionable. And she had believed him with the innocence of a daughter holding her father's hand. Would have done anything for him.

"Your dinner, ma'am." A young guard pushed a meal through to her via a metal box in the wall. She regarded him as he walked away. He was no more than a child. Tall and lanky, with a walk that exuded arrogance and confidence. That walk would change with time, like all things changed, and she imagined his future before she decided to see what her dinner contained.

Young asparagus, new potatoes grilled to perfection, some sort of flat bread, and a stir-fry of beef and vegetables sat beautifully arranged on an aluminum plate. A fruit salad of fresh pineapple and blueberries topped with some coconut and a couple of walnuts sat in a little metal tin beside it. And a sealed bottle of water. At least they weren't going to starve her.

Despite the tension in her stomach, it was practical to eat. She'd heard how suspects were treated, often rising very early and going to bed late at night with only a sparse meal in between.

The warm food smelled delicious, but she maintained her discipline, chewing every bite thoroughly and sipping lightly on the water. She had no doubt there were cameras everywhere.

The guard returned for her dinnerware. "There's someone to see you." He waited until she'd shoved her tray back through the metal box, then he motioned with his hand at someone down the hall. She arched an eyebrow as a woman came into view. She was much shorter than Miriam. Asian. She bowed and handed her a card.

"Dr. Su Ling, ma'am. Your lawyer."

"I didn't ask for a lawyer."

"In this case, it's highly advisable." She turned to the guard. "Ten minutes please." The guard ambled down the end of the corridor and waited.

"I didn't think lawyers were called 'doctor,'" Miriam mused out loud.

The woman in front of her stood absolutely still. She was dressed in a black suit, a jacket, and a skirt, which all framed her small body perfectly. Her heels were black, sleek but simple.

"There's little time to explain," she said. "Your work is admired in many circles, even my own."

Miriam started to talk, but the woman's scrunched-up face made her stop. Her lips didn't move when she spoke next.

"Every motion, every word is recorded in this place." She handed her another piece of paper through the bars. "After you read it, I suggest you eat it." She stared into Miriam's eyes, and Miriam was surprised how lovely the woman's golden-brown irises looked even under the harsh fluorescent lighting. The lawyer stepped back from the bars. "Guard! I'm done!"

Miriam stepped away as well and turned her body toward a wall where it seemed least likely that a camera would see what she was doing. The sound of heels clicking on the floor receded into the distance. When she looked down and read the words printed on the paper, her heart instantly felt relief, like a boil when it's finally lanced to let out the pus. It was in Gevu's handwriting.

Friends arriving. Get ready. ~G

Gevu was not only alive and well, but he'd made friends. And apparently they were coming for her! She worried that this was all part of Harper's plan, and yet she didn't want to be in prison. There was no doubt in her mind she'd be found guilty of Emmet's murder.

The tones of a push-button device, likely some kind of cipher lock, made her shove the note into her mouth and swallow it. She turned to see a team of three men she didn't know enter her cell.

"Good evening, Dr. Wetzel." The smallest man stepped forward. They all wore blue polo shirts and khaki pants, professional but comfortable. The two larger men stood back, watchful. After her interaction with Dr. Su Ling, she couldn't help but find it odd that one of the men in the background looked Chinese. "You just received a visit from your lawyer, I understand?"

Miriam cleared her throat quietly and painted a smile on her face. "Yes. Yes, I did."

"Family lawyer?" He carefully watched her.

"No." She held the business card in her hand, the one the lawyer, or whoever she was, had given her. Her eyes glanced over it before she offered it to the man. It read *Criminal Defense Association*. "My family's back east. This firm has apparently taken an interest in my case."

He took the card from her and turned it over in his hands. "I'll get this back to you after our team takes a look at it."

She gave him a nod. When they left, she had the impression the Asian man stared at her a bit longer than necessary. God, she hated being a pawn. Nothing to do but wait for the hand to move you, never knowing whether you'd be sacrificed or turned into a queen.

Her stomach growled, and a sour taste filled her mouth. She laid down on the bed for a few minutes before she dashed to the toilet and threw up her meal. She hadn't felt sick like this in years. Had someone tampered with her food? Or was their kitchen just unsanitary? The meat hadn't tasted rotten. Her water bottle still sat on the desk next to her bed, and she took a few sips. After vomiting, she felt better, but now she was hungry.

The lights dimmed in her cell, and she lay down once again. One thing was for certain. It was going to be a very long night.

"You'll go with her and keep us informed when you can." Stella looked up at Harper when he spoke. He'd had her arrested, along with Miriam, for charges of car theft and a series of other petty crimes. She wondered what he was up to. He'd even let her bring her secret notes. The ones no one was supposed to know about.

"What do I get out of this?" She shifted her position on the bunk and realized she wasn't going to get anything out of it. Just a transfer from one birdcage to another. An opportunity to stay alive. Still, the more she kept him talking, the more she learned about him. She'd already learned a great deal from Dr. Wetzel in the Mugu facility, but only because the woman thought she was a dumb blonde and treated her as ancillary help on the level of a simple technician.

"I don't think I have to tell you that, Stella. You're smart enough to figure it out."

She couldn't help herself, and the words exploded out of her. "You've got everything all figured out, don't you? You're one hell of a bastard. You use people, and never think about how they feel." Her voice wasn't as steady as she wanted it to be, but she didn't care. Inside, she was seething. She hoped he had some idea of the fires that burned inside her, but he'd never come close to understanding how much she hated him.

"We're all users, Stella. The winners are the ones who take emotion out of the equation."

He left her cell, which was part of a "pod," as they called them, his gait smooth and steady. She inhaled the air as he left and realized he never carried a scent on him. The only odor that was barely perceptible on him was the smell of a freshly pressed suit. A starch maybe? She didn't know.

Her surroundings left a lot to be desired. Definitely not cheerful. The Federal MDC was not like most prisons she'd seen in her past. This place was much cleaner. Almost sterile. Her bed was a mattress spread over a knee-level concrete slab. A hard-cased television perched high on the wall, and below it was an immovable desk and a round poured-concrete stool. Next to that was a lovely stainless-steel toilet with a sink on top of it to wash her hands. Across from the toilet was a little showerhead. When she'd turned it on to clean her face, she'd noticed the shower was on a timer. *Probably to keep inmates from flooding the place on purpose.* There were no windows.

When she'd been brought here, behind all of the fanfare that had accompanied Dr. Wetzel's arrest, she'd seen the Federal Building from the outside. The prison cells were supposed to be above ground, but she got the distinct impression both she and Dr. Wetzel were in belowground holding cells. *They could have at least given me a window.* She thought about how weeks ago, she'd been riding free on the highway with a briefcase full of money, ready to make a new future. Her eyes stung with tears, and though she tried to blink them away, they surged past the boundaries of her lids and finally rolled down her cheeks. She quickly wiped them away.

She was a survivor. She'd do what Harper wanted for now, but when the opportunity came to be completely free, one way or another she'd take it.

TWENTY SEVEN

03 December, 03:00

Heung prayed to the Buddhas. *Success go with them!* Few people knew about the LA Underground. His men swarmed into the tunnels, which joined others near the prisons. They were guarded with cameras and security officers, but even the city didn't know the hidden places his men could go.

Zhu Bajie sat beside him in his private office, on a homemade chair fashioned from large, firm cushions. On the wall was a screen so they could see, from the point of view of the team commander, just how the operation was going.

Heung walked over and showed *Zhu Bajie* his map. "They'll need to go to the fifth belowground level here." The god said nothing, but studied the map. "From there, they'll rise to the reinforced tunnels that come up to the prison, here." Their route was that of a maze. It utilized portions of the city sewers, maintenance areas, and metro lines.

"The total length of the tunnels is approximately four miles underground, but they've entered here," he said as he pointed to a place near Little Tokyo. "Once they've obtained your doctor, they'll exit in the downtown area, then disperse. Your scientist should be here in a matter of hours."

Zhu Bajie grunted with approval. Heung admired his poise, and the god was wise not to ask questions. An American would have wanted to know how the tunnels worked, who put them in place, and how long they'd been operational. Any idiot with half a brain would realize the Chinese had had a hand in building much of this city. Particularly underground. It had taken years of careful planning. Now, that planning would play in his favor.

Together, they looked up at the screen. His men were moving into position. He only hoped his contacts on the inside did their part. In minutes, the camera was shaking, smoke billowed around them, and his men moved silently through a doorway that he knew led under the Federal Building. They moved along narrow corridors and past another sliding door. On the other side, a masked man stood with Dr. Wetzel and another woman with long blond hair. Heung was confused. He spoke through his transmitter to the team leader.

"Who is she? We only came for the doctor!"

"Our contact says she must come. She's the assistant!"

Something about her bothered Heung. He'd seen her before, but he couldn't quite place her. He looked at *Zhu Bajie*. The god stared at the screen intently and gave a slight nod.

"Take her." Heung looked over at the glorious being. "I'm sorry, your Excellency; this was unexpected. We will sweep her thoroughly before she enters the area."

The camera continued to track their retreat through another maze of tunnels. They rushed through the corridors, darkness pressing around the lights streaming forward from their headlamps. Minimal visibility. Minutes later, the team leader emerged onto a street alongside two figures wrapped in black coats and scarves. They climbed into a vehicle, and then the camera stopped transmitting. Heung's audio, attached to his ear, continued to work.

"We're on Wilshire. Fifteen minutes. No pursuit."

His team leader had done well. He said a prayer to the deities and sent mental gratitude to the man who had sacrificed himself to detonate the bomb outside of the prison. He would certainly be rewarded with another human life. No doubt the explosion had drawn a huge amount of attention, but at least he knew the scientist was unlikely to try to escape. She was now a fugitive, a federal criminal wanted for breaking out of a maximum correctional facility, in addition to the crime of murder for which she was accused. She wasn't going anywhere. The scientist was theirs.

Of course, it's a setup.

Having spent the time he did in the Point Mugu facility, Gevu knew the military had the means to track Dr. Wetzel and her assistant. The explosion outside the federal prison had been massive, according to Heung, but the government would suspect some sort of organized escape.

Gevu rubbed his chest. He'd taken a massive amount of firepower during his Mugu escape, and since then, he'd experimented with cutting his skin and allowing the women to bite him fiercely and scratch his flesh. His wounds healed quickly, often in a matter of minutes. It was obvious the government wanted him, not only for the replacement parts they hoped to grow and his brain, which they aspired to put into a soldier, but also for his unique healing abilities.

Gevu spoke to Heung. "Make them turn and drive in a direction opposite of the consulate. Drop the scientist and a couple of escorts at a tunnel entrance a mile from here."

Heung's eyes swept over him, and he bent his head with deference. "Of course."

Gevu rose from his chair. It was best he didn't meet the good doctor on an empty stomach.

"I will feed and shower, then meet her here in two hours."

"And the assistant?"

"Keep her in a solitary room. Go over both of them thoroughly. Remove anything under their skin that appears suspicious." Gevu lumbered from the room, barely squeezing out of Heung's doorway. *This place is too small.* He'd need somewhere larger to live, and soon. Especially when he had children.

December 3, 07:05

Miriam felt like she now knew what chickens suffered when they were stuffed into tractor trailers, cage on top of cage, and shuttled from one place to the next with no understanding of their fate. *Who are these men?* They moved her from the car to another tunnel, and then it seemed like they walked for miles. The men in front of her and behind her were Asian. They whispered in dialects difficult to make out. She wasn't a student of languages. The only one she had ever bothered to learn was dead. Latin was useful. It was the foundation of scientific prose. She also liked the language of numbers. Mathematical equations held secrets to scientific principles she could limitlessly explore.

Her captors blindfolded her before they exited a door. Their footsteps echoed on what felt like concrete floor, but instead of stale air, now there was a breeze. She stumbled along until they came to a standstill, and she heard the ding of an elevator chime. She was guided inside and felt the floor move her down, and then the doors slid open. The smell of incense greeted her nose. It was a welcome odor after the unsanitary surroundings of the prison and the moldy scents of the tunnels they'd traveled through.

She was placed in a room and stripped naked. Her blindfold remained in place as she was poked and prodded. They ran instruments over her, and with each little beep, they cut into her skin and removed a device. She remained firm through it all. It wouldn't do to struggle. Something inside her told her it was going to be okay. She was going to be okay. A rough hand grabbed her shoulder, and she shuffled into another room. There, a short Asian woman removed her blindfold. The woman's face was old, and dotted with age spots, likely from too much sun; her eyes were barely visible beneath her wrinkled lids. They were alone.

"You wash!" she demanded, pointing to a shower stall. On a stool next to it was a set of clothes. A pair of jeans, a blue shirt, and a red pair of slippers. And there were white granny undies that looked large enough to cover her own buttocks, plus one. She held them up by the waistband and waved them at the woman before she put them down again.

Not happening, lady. It's "commando" for me.

A new hairbrush, a new toothbrush with toothpaste, and towels, as well as a washcloth, sat on a shelf in front of a mirror.

The old woman just stood still as a heron, watching her every move. Miriam gathered from the woman's stance that her shower wasn't going to be private, so she stepped into the stall, turned on the water, and helped herself to the shampoo and soap. At least the water was hot. They'd even provided her with a new razor in case she wanted to shave, and it was a relief to remove the stubble from her armpits and legs.

Once she'd toweled herself dry, she put on the clothes and brushed her hair. She took a cursory glance at herself in the mirror. Her eyes looked tired, and among her long auburn strands, she could see glints of silver. She didn't mind seeing the gray, and the wrinkles at the corners of her eyes made her feel proud. *Little trophies of wisdom.* She'd worked hard for those marks of experience.

"Time to go, now." The wrinkled woman seemed impatient to get her to wherever she was supposed to go. They left the room and traveled along an ornate hallway decorated with plush carpets, elaborate teak tables, Chinese vases, and wall hangings adorned with golden paints. At the end of the hall, the woman stopped her in front of a polished wooden door. She knocked and entered first, then showed Miriam past the threshold.

Miriam was not prepared for what she saw. Behind a large mahogany desk sat a thin Chinese man in a sleek business suit. He sat upright, almost like he was at attention. On the left side of the room, on an enormous chair filled with cushions, sat her baby, Gevu. He was resplendent, draped in lush folds of red silk. He'd grown even larger since she'd seen him last. He was probably as tall as a grizzly bear and twice as wide.

The Chinese man rose to his feet. Gevu remained seated.

"Please come in, Dr. Wetzel." The door shut behind her. "You are unharmed, I trust." He didn't wait for her to answer, but showed her to a chair that sat on the other side of his desk. "My name is Sun Heung. I am honored to have you here."

Miriam noted his slight bow, and she bobbed her head in return but could not stop staring at the creature she'd helped design almost a year ago. Never in an eon would she have expected him to grow into such a gorgeous specimen. He exuded grandeur and power. And she had no doubt he was ferocious.

Gevu spoke to her with a grin that showed a row of very large teeth. "Not what you expected?"

"Not at all," she admitted. "I'd hoped you survived, that you escaped somehow, but you've done...very well." She looked around the room at the carved furniture, the flat-panel television screens on the wall, and the high-end electronics in various parts of the room.

"But you knew I'd survive." His eyes, dark and threatening as thunderclouds, bored through her.

Heung sat down at his desk, and Miriam glanced over at him before answering Gevu. "Yes, I knew. I just didn't know how well." She paused. The silence in the room was disturbed only by Gevu's deep respirations. "You've brought me here for a reason?" She wanted to get on with whatever he had planned, and she had no idea how or why this Mr. Heung was part of the equation.

Gevu's features took on a cold and calculating appearance, and he leaned forward when he spoke.

"I need you to help me have children."

Stella was processed, poked, and prodded. They removed two locator chips from her, and then she'd been allowed to wash while in the presence of a little old woman. When she was done, she was taken to an elevator that descended even farther into the ground, and then shown to a simple room that was a bit more comfortable than the prison cell. Barely. Still no windows. She gazed at the door, and the lock just below the handle.

Simple pin and tumbler. It was like a backward front-door lock, able to be locked closed with a twist of a knob on the outside and unlocked with a key on the inside. Except, she had no key.

There was a bookshelf on a wall next to the twin bed. Many of the books there looked like they were in Chinese, a language she wasn't familiar with, but some were in English. A couple of Tom Clancy novels, Stephen King's *Christine,* and *The DaVinci Code* by Dan Brown. She plucked up *The DaVinci Code.* She'd seen the movie, but had never read the book. From the size of it, she hoped she wouldn't have time to read the entire thing.

The main character in the novel, Dr. Langdon, had just made his faux pas by commenting to Captain Fache that the glass pyramid at the Louvre was "magnificent," when a rap came at her door. It was opened before she could answer. In front of her stood a thin man. Her throat constricted. She recognized his face.

"We have met before, I believe." He curtly nodded his head.

Stella said nothing, sensing it would be best to keep quiet.

"Let me show you part of our facility," he said without introduction. What had Chet called him? She racked her brain. *Something like Ching.* When she stepped into the hallway, two armed guards followed behind her. They walked a few paces until he stopped at a door.

"This is one of our control rooms."

She entered and was struck by the number of monitors on the walls. She scanned each of them. One view in particular was horrifying. Her host moved to a console and zoomed in on the face of a man who hung from shackles on a wall.

The enormity of what she saw crashed down on her brain. She barely recognized him, but it *was* him. Somehow these bastards had captured Chet. She stared at him and realized something even more shocking. Both of his legs were missing.

Stella's mind reeled. She remembered the day they had escaped with the money, taking this man's car for their getaway. This man, this *Ching*, hadn't forgotten her face. He knew who she was, or rather, he remembered that she'd been with Chet that day.

The man's face relaxed, and he smiled at her reaction. "Ah, it *is* you. I wasn't absolutely sure until now." He moved closer to her. His skin smelled of some kind of exotic cologne. Cloves and other spices. "Tell me how does one such as yourself disappear with my money, only to end up the assistant of a great scientist?"

God, I've been duped. If I hadn't reacted...

But she had reacted. Now he knew for sure. And there was nowhere to run. Nothing to do but wait and see what he had planned. She looked down at one of the desks. Paperclips. Scissors. An ink pen.

He didn't wait for her to answer. "Fate works in mysterious ways, I suppose. Let me show you something else." His hand gestured to another screen where a group of women were huddled naked together behind a wall of bars. She could see most of the room. A mattress. A wall of mirror. She didn't want to know what went on inside this room.

"If you don't cooperate with us, you'll join them. And your time there will be unfortunate," he said as he guided her away from the screen. He showed her back to her room, where a small meal waited for her, and he closed the door.

Stella suspected this room had at least one camera and a listening device. Sitting on the bed, she carefully removed the items she'd taken from the control room and slipped them under her pillow. If she had the opportunity to use them, she would. Meanwhile, she'd search for surveillance items so she knew where they were. When the time came, hopefully she could disable or block them.

She looked at the food. Some type of dumplings, a mixture of green vegetables, and fish. Although she hesitated to eat food from her captors, she eventually downed the meal. About an hour later, her stomach felt queasy. She wasn't certain if it was the food or the aftereffects of her guided tour. One thing was for sure; she wasn't going to stay here for another course if she could help it.

"It's all going as we'd planned." Harper still found it mildly disagreeable to keep reporting back to the military as often as they required. There'd come a day when he wouldn't have to.

"Have you located them? Pinned down their position?"

"No, Admiral, not yet. But we are working on it. As long as we know where Project Juliet is, there's no question we'll eventually get a bead on our scientist and Project Kilo."

"We're still having major difficulties with this virus outbreak. Our medical teams seem to think it has something to do with protein synthesis in the body. That's going to be a problem."

"That's one problem *you* need to figure out." He realized he'd just snapped at the admiral, and though he'd never give a hint of being contrite, he ended the conversation on a softer note. "Our survival includes the consumption of animal proteins, and we'll need to sustain the growth of those proteins for a year or more. Have NIH work on it harder. We only have a few weeks left."

Harper hung up and destroyed another disposable cell phone. He was bothered with the fact he'd been unable to track the male pig. They'd used phone monitoring, satellite imaging, and a good number of other spying devices, but they still hadn't been able to determine the beast's position.

Project Kilo has to be in the area.

Of course he suspected the Chinese. They were the ones who knew about the research, who had been interested in his projects in the first place. But none of his contacts had been able to dig up any information that led him to the animal. The Communist Republic denied being aware of the experiment, so if the Chinese weren't concealing him, then who was?

They'd returned to the underground parking lot and investigated the area. His men had come up with nothing. What if the man with the faux name of Wah Ching wasn't part of the government? He wished he'd obtained photographs of him, or fingerprints.

The money, which had been wired to his bank account, had completed the transaction, and shortly afterward, it had been withdrawn and the account had been closed. They still hadn't been able to trace it back to the original owner. He hated to think the Chinese had a similar organization to his own, but by the time the final days came, it wouldn't matter. Not for a while.

The other suspect was Chet. His old army compadre seemed to have dropped off the map since his getaway. But Stella's betrayal had ensured that he didn't have any money. And he had no friends in Los Angeles that Harper was aware of. He didn't see how it would be possible for Chet to get Project Kilo without some type of weapon. The only people he seemed to have a connection with were the Chinese. That Mr. Wah Ching. The missing puzzle pieces in his plan nagged at him, as well as the unexpected turn of events related to this new virus that was spreading across the United States.

He'd think more about those issues later. Time was closing in on him, and all of his assets had to come together soon. He pulled out his personal cell. It was time to check on Dulce and make sure the rest of his men were moving in.

December 5, 10:01

Ben logged on to his computer, thankful he still had a way to access the Internet. He'd kept his old account active with automatic payments to the satellite company under another name. He checked his secret email accounts now and then. Every day he checked one in particular, just in case he heard from Miriam.

The news of her prison break had been phenomenal, but it made him extremely nervous at the same time. She couldn't have done it alone. Assuming Harper was the one who had set her up to get arrested, he didn't have any idea who would have helped her other than Gevu. And if it was Gevu who had helped her, how could he be in such a position?

He scrolled through some of his obscure accounts hoping that somehow she'd be able to contact him. He found nothing, until he checked one last site. His heart banged against his chest when he saw a message in his in-box on deviantART.

If you're able, meet me at C-Street. It was signed, *Needle-Fingers.*

Ben sat back in his chair and lit up a cigar. If he contacted Miriam, it could be a trap, but he really wanted to see her again. And what if she needed his help? What if she'd found Gevu and needed a place to hide him? After checking another website, he figured he could meet her safely. His fingers remained poised above the keyboard until he finally tapped out a response.

S*urf today looks great. Surfer's point. This afternoon.*

It was a wide enough range of time to wait. He could go and do something he'd longed to do since arriving back on the West Coast, and still keep an eye out for her. There were surfboards and a wetsuit he could rent at the surf shop, of that he was sure. He left the house to find Binah and let her know he was going.

The lab was in full swing when he entered it. There were several projects running, but Binah was nowhere to be found. A note taped to the microscope told him she'd gone out exploring. He hoped she hadn't gone too far or that she wouldn't risk being seen. He scrawled another message to her on the back of the paper.

Gone into town for a bit. Be back soon.

If she knew he was going to meet Miriam, he wasn't sure of her reaction. She probably wouldn't be happy.

Perhaps it's best this way.

The sky was a brilliant blue when he set out on the dirt road headed for the main highway. He had friends who he hoped would lend him a pickup. It would make getting to Ventura, and carrying a surfboard, much easier. Not to mention getting back.

Suddenly, everything seemed right with the world. The birds were singing, the wind was blowing offshore, and the tide was going to be just right in a couple of hours. For the first time in a long time, Ben felt as if a giant rock had been lifted from his chest, even though he knew the momentary joy was only an illusion. Seeing Miriam again would bring reality crashing in on him, but until then, he might be able to catch a few waves and forget about the mess he was in.

Binah finished emptying another spray can. The droplets were even finer this time, since she'd aerosolized it. She stood on top of one of the highest hills, hidden by a few thick pines that gripped the dry, rocky soil. Her compound should be able to travel on the air currents for a long distance. All the virus had to do was spread out, much like when a stone plops into a placid pond and disturbs the surface. It would find a few human beings who would then come into contact with other human beings, and the ripple of her work would carry on.

Her eyes stung, and she couldn't stop the buildup of water in them before she felt the warmth of tears sliding down her cheeks. To add to her discomfort, her snout became stuffy, and she wiped away the mucous building on the end of her nose. She wasn't able to predict the exact consequences of her actions, but she was wholeheartedly convinced of one thing—the killing had to stop. The senseless slaughter of animals, the abuse of innocent souls, could not continue. Gevu would be proud of how she'd avenged him and their mother. And she'd done it peacefully, without taking a single human or animal life. Once they realized the change was permanent, the next steps would be theirs.

December 4, 15:24

How in the hell could anyone in his or her right mind get into that cold ocean, even with a wetsuit? Miriam sat on a park bench that faced the sea and watched the surfers on the point. The waves were rolling in beautifully. She would have expected the walkway along this side of town to be full of people on such a lovely day, but it was oddly bereft of beachgoers. Seventy degrees in the height of winter. Southern California was almost always nice this time of year.

A tall, lean man on a longboard paddled furiously in front of a swell and caught a wave just as it started to break. He rode the shoulder of it with finesse, his board slipping down in front of the curl to give him speed. He pivoted, swung back up to the crest, and slid down the wall once more. He rode the wave all the way to the shore and stopped in front of a pile of rounded ocean stones. She looked at his face, which was partially hidden by his long, waterlogged hair. It was Ben.

He grabbed up his board, let the next wave push him forward, and then crabbed up the rocks to the sandy shore. The surfboard was pretty battered. A rental or a loaner she guessed. He seemed transformed. Like every care had been washed away from his face by the sea.

"Hey, Em." The surfboard was a good nine feet long, and he carried it easily under his arm. He set it down beside them and sat on the bench. He looked out at the horizon while he talked. "You doin' okay?" She didn't know what to say. She wasn't okay. Far from it. "I heard about the prison break," he added.

Miriam wanted to tell him everything, but now was not the time. The goon squad would be back to pick her up near sunset. "I'm all right," she reassured him. "How's Binah?"

"She's...good. Learning a lot still. Keeping busy." Their small talk was awkward. It had never been this difficult before. But then, before this, she'd been the project leader of a cutting-edge research experiment. The fact that he'd used her to develop a side project, which was ordered by Harper, still left her with some bitterness. But it wasn't really his fault. He'd done what he was asked, and in her experience, Harper didn't really *ask*. Now she understood that Harper might have threatened him with destroying something he really cared about. The Culler was good at that. He could have threatened to hurt her in exchange for his silence.

"Are you...up for visitors?" It was a long shot. She felt his eyes move from the ocean and narrow at her in a sideways stare.

"Did you find Gevu?"

Though she hated to say it, the lie came from her lips like truth topped with honey. "No, not yet."

"Who broke you out of prison?"

"I don't know. One minute there was an explosion, and the next there was a group of men taking me out of the cell." *At least that part was the truth.* "I managed to get away, but I had nowhere to go. I emailed you from the library. Something in me said you wouldn't have gone far."

"How did you get here?"

"I stole a car."

His eyebrows arched in surprise. "How'd you steal a car?"

"Long story." She didn't want to have to explain a lot of details. They only led to more lies in a story and a difficult cleanup. "I'd like to see her."

"Sure. When?"

"A couple of nights from now?"

"Just leave me a message at the same place as last time. We'll be ready."

He got up and put the surfboard under his arm. "I've missed you, Em."

In seconds, he was paddling back out to the waves, and she stood up and strolled along the concrete path next to the beach until she came to a little roundabout with a small parking lot. There, in a sedan, the goon squad waited.

TWENTY EIGHT

December 7, 10:42

Gevu explained his attempts at breeding to Dr. Wetzel and described the poor fetal outcomes. He left out the details she didn't need to know, like his personal sexual preferences when trying to breed and his affinity for human meat. She had to have an idea of how brutal he could be, but something in him couldn't bring himself to let her know exactly how he mated or that he gorged on female flesh after he was done. And he couldn't risk her hesitation. What if she refused to help him? There was no one in the country better at genetic manipulation than her, except maybe Dr. Skylar. His hairs bristled at the thought of having to rely on him.

When he finished talking, Dr. Wetzel swept a calculating look over him before she spoke. "There's one way for certain that you'll be able to breed and raise children," she said. Gevu stared back at her, half knowing what she was going to say, but he needed to hear it from her lips.

"You need to mate with Binah. Your sister is the only proper match. With her, you could have dozens, maybe hundreds, of a fine new species." Her words were cool and clinical, but he caught a hint of excitement in her voice.

"And you'll help me?" Gevu had always suspected Dr. Wetzel possessed a dark side, and he was pleased to see it emerge. She seemed unaware of how conveniently she used the profession of science to mask her own desires and how she blurred the line of ethical boundaries in the name of her research. He realized that she was almost as capable of being cruel and merciless as he was. In that moment, he fully understood the scientist. In some ways, she was more animal than him.

"Yes." Miriam stood up and brushed some lint off her pants. "But we'll have to hurry. Binah will be vulnerable tonight after her meal, and then you can mate with her." She left the room, leaving him alone with his thoughts.

Gevu trembled inside but remained silent. Despite all of the foul things he'd done to humans, forcing himself on his sister was an act he'd never considered. Chet was paying dearly, in part for doing that very thing. He was Gevu's first taste of human flesh, and Gevu wanted to make sure Chet kept on giving. But even when he'd secretly watched in the shadows the day Chet violated his sister, Gevu had never considered having sex with her despite his own bodily betrayal. He felt sure the rage he felt against Chet and the bond with his sister, however tenuous, would make it impossible for him to feel lust for Binah, even when she was in heat.

But his assurance was short-lived. Incredibly, he was surprised to discover that the thought of fucking his sister did arouse him. His cock was growing hard. Maybe he *could* do it.

So be it, Binah.

Gevu raised an imaginary chalice into the air, a mental crystal cup traditionally filled with an offering for the Gods. He inhaled and pictured putting the offering to his lips, drinking down the sweet nectar, and then tossing the chalice to the floor. In his mind's eye, it shattered into thousands of pieces. He would grow more of his kind and do whatever it took. It was time for the dominion of *Homo sapiens* to end.

For the species.

December 7, 16:05

Miriam's drive to Ojai gave her some time to think. Participating in a rape, particularly in that of a sibling, would normally be unthinkable, but this case was different. Technically, a genetic pair couldn't hope to reproduce a viable species by interbreeding, but with careful gene manipulation and some cloning of Binah's children, she was sure she could help them survive.

Still, a question nagged at her.

Why is it so important for them to survive?

She didn't care about the military's needs, or Harper's either. It was the research that was important. Of course it was the research. To be the first scientist to usher in a new breed of intelligent life and watch them flourish against the odds—*that* was going to be amazingly satisfying.

She looked over at the bottle of wine she'd laced with a heavy dose of Ambien. It was a fantastic merlot. She'd make sure they drank the bottle at dinner, then Gevu would arrive. By her calculation of Binah's previous cycles, she should be approaching estrus. If so, then the pregnancy was almost inevitable. Yes, things were coming together nicely.

December 7, 20:30

The two days of waiting in her room were driving her crazy. Stella read the last page of *The DaVinci Code* and put the book down. The only person she'd seen the entire time besides her brief outing with the Ching guy was the little old lady. She came three times a day to bring her food. In the morning, she brought a change of clothes as well. Today's jeans were a bit baggy, but they fit okay.

Better than having them too tight. Especially today.

She'd listened to sounds outside of her door. Normally, people came and went at a relaxed pace. Voices at an even level. But this morning, there'd been tension in the air; voices had been louder than usual, there had been quick heavy footsteps, and around noon, the old lady who had brought her lunch hadn't given her the customary toothless smile.

In regard to her meals, the content of them had changed recently. More grains, vegetables, and soups. She'd noticed nothing had meat, not even so much as an egg. She'd eaten some of the food, and she hadn't become ill. That was curious as well. She hated not knowing what was going on. Hated not being able to hear the news and understand what was happening in the world.

Around what she guessed must be four o'clock, she realized the passageway outside her door was silent. It was agonizing not to have a cell phone, a watch, or a clock to gauge time. The best way she could figure out the time of day was by when her captors turned the lights off for sleep or on for waking hours, the numbers of chapters she read in a book, and how hungry she felt before her meals came.

Her stomach grumbled. An odd blanket of quiet surrounded the place and helped her make her decision. It was time. She chewed a few scraps of paper torn from a couple of books while she pulled out her paperclips, ink pen, and scissors. She'd worked on the paperclips under her pillow, when the lights dimmed for sleeping, until she'd had a couple of makeshift tools. She would use them if she had to, but hoped her next moves would work better.

Two different cameras were mounted on her bedroom wall in the vents just below the ceiling. She'd found another one in the bathroom vent right over the doorway. There were microphones hidden on her bed frame, on the bookshelf, and on the mirror above the bathroom sink. She tackled the cameras first, placing pages torn from the books between the vent and the cameras, and then she mushed the pieces of masticated paper over the microphones. Hopefully, she hadn't missed any.

The door unlocked, and the little old woman let herself in. She carried Stella's meal tray and shut the door behind her with a foot. The woman set the tray down on the bed, and Stella maneuvered behind her, reached around her neck, and pulled her into a chokehold.

Easy.

"I don't want to hurt you, but I..." Stella didn't get any further than that before the woman's foot stamped down on Stella's toes and her hands flew up to grab one of Stella's wrists. The woman twisted and pushed on her joints in such a way that Stella had to let go of the woman because of the pain. In a matter of seconds, the old woman had her on the floor. She let go and backed away to the door.

"You eat. Get stronger." Her gummy smile made Stella unsure if she should laugh or cry. The grandma had taken her to the ground without any effort, and she'd treated Stella's attempt at escape like a practical joke. She watched the old woman slip out of the room, still grinning, and heard the lock click.

She waited a couple of minutes before she went to the door and started to work. If there was someone still on the other side of it, she was doomed. If she waited for a while, she'd still be doomed. She was banking on the possibility that most of the security staff were gone for a reason. If they saw their camera view was blocked, they'd immediately come in, remove the books, search the room, and who knew what else.

She worked one straightened paper clip with a bend at the end into the bottom of the key opening and used it as a tension wrench. The other straightened paper clip had a "W" shape on one end, and the other end was shaped like an Allen wrench. She raked the "W" into the lock to get a sense of the number of pins inside. It seemed like a standard five-pin system. She worked to press each of them into the up position one by one. There was a *click*, and the lock turned.

Stella slowly opened the door. There was no one in the passageway. She started to run right, to where she knew the elevator waited, but she reversed her course and went left instead.

You're a stupid, dumb blond bitch. If you get caught, you deserve to die. She couldn't think of why in the world she was choosing to risk her own ass.

And for what? She hated the man. He was cruel and disgusting, and she had no fucking idea how she was going to get him out of the building. But the simple truth remained. Chet didn't deserve the torture he was suffering now. No human did. There might be some justice in it as far as Mr. Ching was concerned, and she didn't know if Dr. Wetzel even knew he was here, but she wasn't going to abandon someone being tortured, even if it was Chet. And it wasn't like he was really dangerous anymore. He was a slab of meat chained naked to a wall, his raw nerves exposed to the world in more ways than one.

Stella sprinted down the hall, avoiding the cameras. She was pretty sure she knew the way to the security room, but she didn't know how to find the door where Chet was held prisoner. She cracked the door open to the room, the one with all of the monitors, and saw no one there. Slipping through as quickly as possible, she shut the door and immediately stopped cold. In front of her stood the old Chinese woman.

She wasn't greeted with a smile, nor did the woman raise an alarm. She held out her palm, reached over to a table, and gracefully handed her a set of clothing, a sheet, and a blanket. On top of the pile was a car key.

"Go out. Go right. Pass four doors. Stop at yellow door. Take cart."

Was this woman actually helping her? It wasn't prudent to stand there and analyze the situation. She was committed to rescuing Chet, and hesitating would get her killed.

Stella took the pile of items offered to her. "Thank you," she said. The old woman bowed in return. Stella exited, dashed to the end of the hallway, and turned the corner, nearly running into a four-wheeled cart. On the cart sat a little key.

Take cart.

She grabbed up the key and pushed the cart until she came to a yellow door. It was made of heavy steel, but it wasn't locked. With a deep breath and a prayer, she slid it open. The stench in the room almost brought her to her knees. She shoved the cart into the room, wondering how in the world she was going to make their escape work.

The fucking pain. Fuck. The fucking pain! Chet opened his eyes. The sliding sound of the door woke him from his hazy slumber. He was so goddamned weak. Cold and naked on the concrete floor. Both of his legs were gone. Both of his goddamned legs!

He'd be festering with sores if it weren't for the old woman who had tended to him. She'd washed his body and sprayed away the shit and piss that had pooled around his stumps. Every now and then, she had injected him with something. It sure wasn't pain medication. Antibiotics, maybe. So he wouldn't get infected.

The manacles around his wrists had rubbed his skin raw. Flies had landed on the open places and laid their eggs. Whenever he could, he'd eaten the squirming maggots that grew there. It was protein. Nourishment. Any way he could get it, he had. He wasn't sure why he kept fighting, maybe if only to keep from giving the pig the satisfaction of watching him give up.

"Fucking pig!" His voice could utter no more than a croak. Waves of agony rippled through him. He saw a pair of pink slippers stride up to him. His eyes moved up past the ankles to a pair of blue jeans, then to a pink shirt and a pair of voluptuous boobs. He'd know those tits anywhere. Then he saw Stella's face.

This was the man I was afraid of?

Chet raised his head slowly, his gooey and watery eyes seeming to take in every bit of her until he got to her chest. They stayed there a second or two, then rose higher. She expected him to say something. After his previous outburst, she was sure there was nothing but hatred and loathing inside of him, but all she saw in his eyes was pain. The skin around his eye sockets was hollowed and dark. His cheeks were pinched, and his face was drawn thin.

He hung weakly from chains on the wall, his naked body squirming now and then, accompanied by sick mushy sounds under his buttocks. The putrid rot of his flesh caused her to gag, and she noticed the manacles had rubbed his wrists raw. Something moved just below his hands that looked like wriggling rice.

Maggots.

She heaved, almost vomited, and was instantly ashamed at the mix of satisfaction and pity she felt as she stared at him. He was nothing but a piece of flesh waiting to die, but death hadn't come. And it wouldn't come now. Not for a while. Not if she could help it.

She looked at him from top to bottom, trying to figure out the best way to move him. She could use the sheet to bundle him up and lift him onto the cart. That would be possible. It would be best to remove the metal cuffs around his hands first. If he had any strength in his arms or hands, he could help her.

"I'm gonna try to get you out of here." Stella hoped he was lucid enough to hear her and understand what she was saying. "I'm going to need your help, Chet. I'll need to you use your hands when I tell you." His only response was a grunt.

She put the key in the lock and released one hand, then freed the other. He flopped over on his side, and it was difficult to ignore the wriggling worms around him. The sheet was large, and she worked to roll him over onto it. When one of his stumps hit the concrete, he howled so loud she wanted to run out of the room, but she stayed. She worked to move him carefully, but she knew she didn't have much time.

Chet seemed to realize what she was doing, and she watched as a sudden burst of energy helped him use his hands to assist her. She didn't bother with trying to put clothes on him, but put the pile on top of him and covered the cart with a blanket. In just minutes, she was at the elevator and pushing the button to go up. The elevator dinged, and they rode to the parking deck. Stella hit the "lock" button on the car key the Chinese grandma had handed her, and she heard a beep from the back of the parking garage. She pushed the cart in that direction and pressed the button once more. The lights of a dark-gray, four-door Toyota blinked at her.

It was difficult to get Chet into the passenger side, but together they managed it. There was a paper sack in the back seat, and she was surprised to see it contained a cell phone, a buffalo belt buckle, and a Taser. She flipped the phone open. It was dead. She guessed it was Chet's.

Stella got in on the passenger side, and was just about ready to fire up the engine when two vehicles pulled into the garage.

Her heart pounded and she slipped low into her seat, motioning for Chet to do the same. *God, he has to be in so much pain.* He pressed his lips together and ducked his head. She hoped they hadn't been seen.

Looking toward the elevators, she saw one of the large pig-humans Chet had asked her to help him with the day they'd taken them from the farm outside of Bakersfield. He looked much bigger now than he had that day. He had to be at least seven feet tall, and nearly as wide as the car she was preparing to drive.

Dr. Wetzel walked on one side of him, and a thin Chinese man was on the other. What appeared to be a woman in a set of scrubs, carrying a small ice chest, stood with a group of men dressed in black who gathered around the elevator. The pig-human, Dr. Wetzel, and the thin man got on first.

Minutes clipped by, and her nerves were jangled. She had to get out of the parking deck before someone discovered they were missing. The rest of the men got on the elevator, and as soon as the doors shut, Stella fired up the engine. She drove up and out of the deck, bursting through a barrier gate, not even sure where she was going at first. Looking over at Chet, she realized there was only one place he could go—Cedars-Sinai. He needed emergency medical care, and he needed the best.

The street signs were hard to read in the dark. *Fucking Los Angles. City of the Stars. You'd think the city could afford some readable signs.* It took her a few wrong turns and asking a couple for directions to find the hospital. It was ironic that not too long ago, she'd ditched Chet there and now she was going to ditch him again. She pulled up to the emergency room entrance.

"Help! Please help!" Stella opened the passenger door and then got Chet's bag from the back seat.

A woman in a lab jacket and scrubs came out of the double doors, looked at Chet, and yelled for a gurney. Stella placed his belongings on top of him when they loaded him up, then hopped in the driver's side and pulled away before they could ask her any questions.

He was in excellent hands now. She'd done her good deed and still managed to escape. But where would she go? The gas tank was near empty, and she didn't have any money.

She could drive around a bit, park, and sleep in the car or stay in a shelter. The stink Chet had left behind didn't make the idea of snoozing in the vehicle too appealing, but it was better than dealing with the smell of a shelter. After turning a corner, a billiards sign caught her eye. *Stix n Balls.*

I could make some money here. Enough for gas and food. Maybe a decent pair of shoes and a change of clothes.

She pulled onto the side street and parked around back, then shut off the engine and checked her reflection in the mirror. She didn't look so hot, but by pinching her cheeks and biting her lips to add some color, she was a little more attractive. The center drawer of the car held five dollars and fifty-two cents in change. She stuck the money in her pocket and stepped out of the car, frowning at her little pink slippers. Luckily, most men didn't bother to look at a woman's shoes if her ass and her tits were in good form and her face passed for pretty. Hell, half the time they didn't care about the face. It was just an extra bonus.

Stella locked the car and walked around to the front of the building. The lights were on, and when she walked through the door, the joint was in full swing. She sauntered over to the bar and pulled out the five. The bartender came over with a practiced smile. His sideburns were gray, and his black hair was neatly trimmed on top. She could tell he was used to feeling people out but wasn't able to put her in a category yet. He was probably trying to pick from his personal list of prostitute, slut, or batshit crazy.

"Name's Geek. What's your poison, darling?" She gave him one of her winning smiles, the kind that said, *I'm new here, and this place looks cool.* She looked around at the numerous flat-panel screens, each with a different ball game or other sport playing.

She really wanted a Fat Tire, or maybe a New Castle, but had to play the part. "Bud Light, Geek. Small draft." The country accent she used worked like a charm. The bartender's mouth deflated into a thinner semblance of being pleasant. Maybe he was thinking she was a PAB, a poor-assed bitch, or that she'd just be a paint watcher at one of the tables. Either way, she wasn't good money and not worth a lot of his time. And that was just what she wanted him to think.

He brought her a frosted mug, and she wandered around the tables, watching the games. Now and then, she'd catch Geek measuring her out of the corner of his eye. That was okay. Better than okay.

Ball breaks filled the air. Some of the players were pretty good. Finally, someone took the bait.

"Hey, girlie! Yeah, you with the pink shirt!" Stella looked around. A few mixed couples were playing, but the man who called to her didn't seem to have a partner. He wore an open red flannel with a blue shirt underneath. His cowboy hat was conservative, not too crazy, and underneath it, she recognized the military haircut.

Bingo.

"Wanna play a game?" He motioned her over.

"Don't got no money, honey. And I'd be more a liability to you anyways." She wore her shy smile. The one that said, *Jeez, that was nice you asked, but I'm not all that good.*

"Aw, it's all good fun, babe. And I got enough to cover us. Just come be my partner. You'll do all right."

Stella breathed easier and let the beer relax her muscles. At least she knew she'd eat and sleep well tonight. And depending on how he treated her, so would he.

TWENTY NINE

December 7, 16:45

Miriam had trouble finding the house, and she was afraid she was going to be late. Ben had given her very vague directions, and she'd already traveled down two dirt roads and turned around. This was her third try, and if she couldn't find the house, she wasn't sure what to do. After another mile, she made out a pickup truck sitting on the right side of the road. Leaning up against it was Ben. She breathed a sigh of relief and pulled up behind him.

Ben walked over to her window. "We'll drive in the pickup from here." He was cautious, checking the road behind her.

"Sure." She reached beside her and grabbed the wine and two bags of groceries. "I brought dinner."

Ben's face softened. "Nice. Thanks, Em." He seemed unsure of what to say when she climbed into the passenger seat and buckled herself in.

"Did you tell Binah I was coming?" He hung his head and looked at the ground. "She doesn't know, does she?" Miriam figured as much. Ben was a softie. Too nice a guy, and he'd always shied away from head-on collisions or verbal conflicts.

His eyes rose to meet hers, and his lips pressed together before he spoke. "I couldn't. I thought it would be better as a surprise."

Miriam tried to play off what she wasn't feeling. Acceptance and understanding. "That's okay. It'll be fine." She placed her hand on his shoulder for a second or two, hoping her physical demonstration of tenderness would comfort him more.

He turned the truck onto another side road, one that barely looked like it had ever been used. They rode over scrub brush and weeds, and traveled for fifteen minutes before pulling up to the rock face of one of the hills. It took a couple of moments for her to realize they were at the house. It blended in so well with the environment, she hadn't seen it right away.

Naturally camouflaged.

Ben waited while she grabbed the groceries, and together they walked to the front step. "You should let me go in first. Explain that you're here."

Miriam didn't say anything but smiled at him hopefully. Inside, her stomach was twisting in knots.

What will I do if Binah won't see me? Ben disappeared into the house and came back in less than ten minutes. She shifted the groceries in her hands. Ben opened the door wide and let her in.

Binah stood in the foyer. Her eyes were red, as if she'd been rubbing them or crying. She shuffled her feet from side to side in apparent discomfort at seeing Miriam again.

Binah was so much smaller than Gevu, maybe a third to half his weight if she had to guess. The black shock of hair that had once been a patch of fur on her head was long now, and it flowed down her back. If it weren't for the pink ears that stuck out between the strands or the piggish snout on her face, she could almost pass for human.

"Hello, Binah." She felt Binah examining her from head to toe. *Is she afraid to see me?* Of course she was afraid. How could she not be? Miriam felt a pang of regret, knowing she was going to betray this woman, this half-human, half-pig piece of research with special genetic codes programmed into her DNA. If her kind were to survive, it was the only way.

"Dr. Wetzel." Binah paused and seemed to mentally correct herself in some inner dialogue. "Miriam. Come in."

"Let me take those into the kitchen." Ben lifted the groceries out of her hands, and Binah led her into the living room.

"You've been here all this time?" Miriam sat on a love seat. The cushions were worn, but comfortable. The fireplace crackled with fresh logs. She was amazed at how big the house was inside.

"Yes." Binah sat on the sofa across from her. "Ben's had this place for a long time. Apparently the government never knew about it."

Miriam hated doing the chitchat thing, but to win Binah's trust, she'd have to try. "It's good to see you, Binah. I'm glad you and Ben are okay."

Ben came back into the room and sat down on the sofa as well. Binah leaned forward. It was clear she couldn't contain herself any longer. Questions poured out of her like a waterfall. "So, where have you been? How have you been living? We heard about your arrest, and then your prison break. What are you going to do now?"

Miriam had prepared for these questions, though she had really hoped she wouldn't have to answer them. She'd used the long car ride to rehearse her answers.

"It's been tough." That part was true. Harper had taught her that long ago.

Weaving lies into truth makes a lie more believable.

"After you escaped that night and drove off with Ben, Harper caught me and took me back down to the lab." She looked over at Ben. "He wanted me to reproduce our experiments, but I just couldn't do it." She avoided mentioning what Ben and she both knew—that Ben held the key to regeneration. "Eventually, he got angry with me and handed me over to the US Marshals. I was really afraid I was going to prison."

"You did it, Em, didn't you? You killed Emmet." Ben's eyes begged her to confess, as if it would make her easier to trust.

Miriam made her eyes fill with tears, and she struggled to think of things in her past that had caused her deep sadness. Her childhood, the parents she'd never see again, her training with Harper and how he'd betrayed her. The love that had been shattered when she'd realized he had been using her. Suddenly the tears were real.

"Yes." She lowered her head. "The Cullers didn't want anyone knowing about Binah or Gevu, and when Emmet saw Binah's hands and feet at the motel, well...we couldn't take the risk. It was the hardest thing I'd ever done. When I refused to help the Cullers with growing more of our research, they used his death against me and had me arrested."

Ben leaned forward. "It's okay, Em. You're here now. You're safe." Miriam looked at Binah. Her child looked troubled. She wasn't so wholly accepting as Ben.

"How did you get away, Miriam?" Binah's question held a lilt of disbelief. Miriam worked to be more convincing.

"The explosion was a surprise." She wiped her eyes and took in a deep breath as if remembering something confusing. "A man came to my cell and took me out. They took other inmates too. We left through some underground passages. They hadn't shackled us or bound us in any way, so I walked with the group along the wall of a tunnel until I found an opening, and then I hid. There were so many of us, I guess they didn't realize I was missing until it was too late. I followed the opening along another tunnel until it exited into one of the subway tubes. It was easy to steal a car on the street. A skill I'd learned long ago."

She paused, hoping it looked like she was worn and tired, and like the memory brought back worry and fear.

Miriam could tell her story was working by the way Binah hung on every word. Ben's mannerisms were nearly the same. She looked at her watch. Now was as good a time to start dinner and wine. If she waited much longer, she'd run out of time.

"What I'd really like to do, if it's okay with you both, is fix some dinner. I'm famished!" She rose to go to the kitchen. "I've got some pasta and fresh vegetables for some primavera and French bread we can make into garlic toast!" It was a good thing both of them were vegetarian. They wouldn't notice the absence of meat in their main course. When she'd gone to the supermarket, all of the chicken, beef, and even the fish had been pulled from the shelves. The outbreak of whatever it was that was causing the epidemic still hadn't been isolated.

Ben followed along behind her. "Wine glasses?" Miriam held up the Merlot to emphasize her question. Ben pulled three from the cabinet. "Will Binah drink some?"

"Yes." Binah had come into the room and was watching Miriam take out a pot and two pans.

"Want to help cook?" Binah smiled at her, just a little.

Thank you, Einstein; she's starting to relax!

Ben pulled the cork from the bottle and poured them all half a glass of wine. Miriam held up her glass and made a toast. "To new beginnings!" They chimed their glasses all around, and Ben and Binah sipped the red liquid. Miriam pretended.

She handed some vegetables to Binah. "Can you chop?" The girl accepted them from her happily, like all her troubles were behind her and her cares were resolved. She pulled out a knife and cutting board and went to work.

Was I ever that innocent? Miriam didn't think so. Her entire life had been an education in disappointment and pain. But if Binah had ever thought she'd suffered in the past, she was about to learn a thing or two about what true suffering was. The first lesson on the education menu was that of betrayal, and lucky for her, Miriam was a very good teacher.

December 7, 17:02

The back of the van had been converted in to one large seat that faced backward and allowed Gevu to ride comfortably and still remain unseen. He took solace in the long drive, and contemplated his relationship with Binah and the meaning of their existence. Peering out the back window of the van, he felt an unfamiliar sense of peace, taking in the view of rocks protruding from the mountains framed by a wash of pink and purple sky. His sister had fled with Dr. Skylar to these hills, miles northeast of the cities of Ventura and Ojai. The sun was sinking behind the hills, and deep-purple clouds, outlined with flecks of red and orange, framed the last golden rays that were gradually disappearing behind treeless hills.

The vehicle barely held his bulky frame. It was snug, but comfortable. The two men in the front refrained from talking, which gave Gevu some much-needed peace and quiet. And time for thought. He'd see Binah again soon, and when he did, she wouldn't see him. It was a strange revenge, since she'd left without him the day they escaped, but almost satisfying.

She might not know you're alive. But it didn't matter. She should have waited; they both should have waited for him. *Instead, they took off, left me there, abandoned...*

The van switchbacked on the highway and bumped along a dirt road until they came to a house nestled in the hillside. When Gevu emerged from the van, he took time to appreciate the stillness of the country. Early moonlight made the trees and brush look as if they'd been painted silver, and a low breeze sang past the rocks with a gentle hum. Close by, the lonely hoot of an owl echoed around him.

Miriam stood in the doorway of the well-hidden home. The rectangular light looked out of place in this land of roundness. Fullness. Gevu made his way toward her. The driver and his companion stayed in the van.

He said nothing as he entered, managing to squeeze himself through the opening. The living room wasn't large, but it was big enough for him to move about freely. The ceiling rose up taller than the frame of the front door. Two supports for the ceiling in the middle of the room were carved in wood with Native American designs. The polished wooden floor felt nice and cool on his feet. He curled his toes against it and looked around the room.

Binah was asleep on the sofa. "She's out," Miriam said. "She shouldn't wake up for a while."

Gevu remained silent, but walked over to the sofa and looked at his sister sleeping on the earth-tone fabric. Her breathing was soft and easy. He reached under her shoulders and hips, and picked her up. She felt so light in his arms, and he marveled how the two of them had come into this world together. *Now we'll create a new world. Together.*

He looked up at Miriam, and she pointed to another door. He carried Binah into the room, which was decorated with Navajo rugs, southwestern pottery, and framed sand paintings on the walls. A platform bed was the central feature of the space, decorated with star quilts in earth tones and rich ambers. Gevu placed his sister on the bed and went to close the door.

"This is just in case she wakes up." Miriam handed him a syringe across the threshold. He took it and closed the door without a word. He set the syringe on the nightstand beside the bed and turned to regard Binah sleeping quietly. The rise and fall of her chest was comforting to him, and the sweet smell of her was heavenly. She smelled like *home*.

    Slowly, his fingers removed her shirt. It was large and red, with white patterns on it that looked like Sanskrit prayers. He examined her breasts, six of them now visible in the soft light of a glass lamp that sat on a table across the room. His fingers reached out and caressed them. It felt strange to see his sister, to touch her in this way. He gazed at Binah's face, slack in slumber. Her hair had grown long, and he could barely see the little piggish ears that peeked out beneath the strands.

    He reached down and undid the ties of her pants, which were large, roomy. No doubt comfortable. That was good. Gevu pulled them off her carefully, though he startled for a second when she moaned in her sleep. He rolled her over a bit to slide them away from her body. Now, she was naked, and his eyes roamed from her thick toes to her fine muscular thighs. An ebony tuft of hair covered her vagina. Her hips were round and ample, and the last set of breasts lay revealed for him to touch.

    Gevu slid off his black T-shirt, an enormous piece of fabric Heung had made specifically for him. It was plain, but the simplicity of it allowed him to move his arms and torso freely. His pants had a large elastic waist, designed much like martial artists' pants with a drawstring that pulled the light cotton material comfortably against his belly. He undid the pants and let them drop to the floor.

    The bed creaked horribly when he tried to climb on it. Although the mattress sat on a platform, he doubted the frame would tolerate his weight. He hesitated and realized he was not the least bit aroused. He stood looking at Binah, and stroked his long cock, but it refused to harden. Gevu paused in frustration.

    I can't do this. Not to her. He tried conjuring up mental images of the human women he'd fucked. He thought about their blood, the taste of their flesh. His cock stirred just a little, but it quieted again when he stared at his sister. What would he do if he couldn't lie with her? *It's for the species!* His rational mind went through all of the reasons this action was right, but still, his body refused to respond.

Gevu looked around the room. His eyes fell on the water cup and the syringe, which sat next to it, and he got an idea. He took the needle off the syringe and squirted the drug onto the rug. Drawing up some of the water from the cup, he rinsed it and squirted water out, then dumped the liquid in the cup onto the same rug where he'd discarded the drug.

Carrying the cup with him, he walked over to a wall, and closing his eyes, he once again imagined fucking the human women. Bloodying their faces, pressing into their asses. He stroked his cock again, and it hardened. He stroked it firmer and gripped his flesh with his palm, running it up and down his shaft until he was just about to come, then he let his semen pour into the cup as his orgasm spewed in hot spurts into the container.

Quickly, he rushed over to the nightstand, grabbed the needleless syringe, and drew up his sperm. It was whitish and thick, but he managed to fill it and then bent over Binah. His fingers found the entrance to her vagina. He pushed the syringe inside her and injected his semen. He did this two more times. She only once stirred and looked as if she might open her eyes, but she never did. When he was finished, he placed his sister under the covers tenderly. Almost like a mother might tuck in her child.

He put on his T-shirt and pants, grabbed the cup, and placed the syringe in his pocket. When he exited the room, Binah was still sleeping.

Miriam rinsed out the glasses and the wine bottle, and placed the bottle in the trash. Binah would never know until it was too late. Part of her wished she'd been able to watch Gevu with his sister. It would have been interesting to see how he'd responded sexually to mating within his own sibling.

She returned to the living room and had a seat on the sofa. Ben was still asleep in a lounge chair. She hadn't been able to encourage him to drink a lot of the wine, and hoped he'd stay asleep until long after they'd gone.

Still, she was excited. If Binah became pregnant, it would be overwhelming. The beginning of a species she could examine, test, and genetically manipulate even further. Ben groaned in his chair, and his eyes fluttered. Miriam paused in her thoughts and watched his face. His lips moved slightly.

"...in the lab. No...here..."

Miriam listened intently. Lab? What lab? Was he dreaming of their work together?

"Binah, mmhh, why? Don't...viruh..."

Binah? A virus? What the hell is he talking about?

On a hunch, she searched the house, all the while cognizant of how quiet Binah's bedroom was. She found nothing. Not a hint of a lab. Not a beaker, not a test tube. Nothing.

She went back to the sofa and sat on the edge, watching and listening as Ben mumbled in his sleep. While she watched him, she wracked her brain. Then an idea occurred to her.

The house is tunneled into the hill. Why not a lab?

Binah's door was still shut. Miriam opened the front door and looked at the scrub surrounding the area. A small trail wound its way to the left of the door and disappeared around the corner. She grabbed her iPhone, and using the flashlight app, she followed the path. It led to a dead end at the rock face of a hill, just behind some bushes. Some of the branches of the brush were cracked. She felt along the rock face and pushed against the wall in several places until she hit the magic spot. The door opened inward, almost silently with the exception of a small scraping sound. Her pulse quickened.

She'd found it! A secret lab. *Ben. How Batman of him!* She started to fumble for a light switch, but the lights automatically blinked on. Motion sensors. She looked at a panel on the wall. They were new. Probably recently installed.

The room could have been any biolab in the NIH, with the exception that there was more diverse equipment in one giant room instead of in separate departments. There were a couple of electron microscopes, benches with beakers, Petri dishes, test tubes, and a wide array of other machines. Two refrigerators and two incubators hummed in what would have been silence.

She'd always thought of Ben as a man with minimal resources, but standing here in the middle of this amazing laboratory gave her a new perspective of the scientist. Why had he sought her out? Why had he joined her research program? He had tons of equipment. He could have done anything he wanted.

And what have you been doing here, Ben? The computer near the closest electron microscope was still up and running. When she tried to access it, it demanded a user name and password. She made a few attempts before giving up. It was something she'd have to find out before they got on the road. Once she left this house, she knew she'd never come back.

She turned her attention to the refrigerators and the incubators. The refrigerators held nothing significant, but there were some samples of something visible through the glass door of one of the incubators. She pulled a couple of gloves from a box on the wall, put them on, and opened the door. Some Petri dishes were laid out on the top shelf, and test tubes sat in a rack next to them. The labels on each of them were printed with a series of letters and numbers in a code she didn't recognize. The handwriting was unfamiliar.

She'd have to go back to the house and see what she could find.

God, how long have I been asleep? Ben's neck hurt from the odd way he'd been sleeping in his chair. Everyone was gone from the living room. He stood up, still very groggy. Binah's door opened, and he started to say something but the words caught in his throat. It wasn't Binah coming through the door.

Large mounds of flesh pushed through the opening, and suddenly, he was face to face with a figure he'd been afraid to see again. He knew the bullets hadn't killed Gevu, but he hadn't expected or considered that he'd see him again so soon.

"Gevu." The name escaped from his lips.

What had he done to Binah? And Miriam? She was nowhere in sight. Just then, the front door opened, and Miriam stopped short as soon as she saw him. She looked from him to Gevu, and shut the front door.

"Miriam?" Ben was starting to feel like he was in the middle of a *Rocky Horror Picture Show*. And everything she'd told him had been a lie. Gevu shut the door to Binah's room. "What have you done with her?" Ben ran toward Gevu, intending to get to Binah and make sure she was okay.

Gevu grabbed him up and threw him across the room. He hit a side table and wall, and a lamp crashed to the ground. Miriam walked forward and stood over him.

"I found your lab." She said the words matter-of-factly, like she expected him to explain everything she'd found there. She couldn't have gained access to the computers, but Binah's research was still in the incubators. Ben said nothing. He scrambled to his feet and ran for the kitchen. There had to be something he could use there, but even has he rushed into the room, he realized nothing was going to hurt Gevu. He'd seen to that when he designed him.

The floor shook as Gevu's huge body lumbered after him. He whirled around only to receive a large fist to his face. Blood spurted from his nose. He heard Miriam's voice behind Gevu. "Bring him outside." Gevu grabbed Ben by his collar and dragged him through the front door. He dragged him all the way to the lab, where Miriam waited inside, then dropped him on the floor.

"You've been busy." She gestured around the lab. "What's all of this? What have you been doing, Ben?"

He could only stare at her in response. If she was with Gevu, what did that mean? The swineman was huge, and there was no way on earth she had a place to keep him secret. Was it a trick of Harper's, or something else? His mind was still muddy.

Miriam looked over at Gevu. "Get some rope." He lumbered back outside, and Miriam tapped her foot. "There's been some sort of epidemic spreading across the country. Are you aware of that? It wouldn't be due to anything you've done here, would it?" She pointed to the incubators. "There are quite a few Petri dishes and test tubes in there. Exactly what are you cooking up, Ben?"

Ben glanced up at her, then around the room. Was that all she had found? He wondered whom she was working for now and what would they do if they found the virus. They'd have a devil of a time trying to find a cure. Since it altered the DNA of those it came in contact with, the information wouldn't do anyone much good. All it would do is explain why everyone got sick from ingesting animal proteins.

Gevu pushed through the doorway once more, carrying a handful of cord, and Ben pushed away from him and stood up. "The information won't help you, Em. Why are you doing this? Why didn't you tell me about Gevu?"

The swineman's fist balled up and hit him again. Ben fell to the floor, slid across the tiles, and his head hit the edge of a counter. He felt the warmth of his blood roll down his neck and into his shirt collar. "Stop!" Miriam glared at Gevu. "Tie him there." She pointed to one of the building supports.

She looked down at Ben. "There are a lot of people who are tracking this epidemic. You know they'll discover the primary origin of it soon enough with some logical epidemiology. Your lab is going to be a CDC stomping ground. It will be more than that, once the press find out."

He was afraid of that and hadn't given that much thought. He and Binah couldn't stay here. He'd have to move to another place. Miriam was right, but he wasn't going to let her have Binah's work. God only knew what she'd do with it.

Gevu pulled him over to the post and tied him tight.

"What's the password to the computer, Ben? I need to know what you've been working on." Ben didn't speak, but stared at the floor. He couldn't let her know it was Binah who had done the research. From there, she'd discover it was Binah who'd let loose the virus. And then she'd conclude that Binah was probably more versed in genetics than she was. That was dangerous information.

"I'll get it out of you. One way or another. You and I have shared close time, but I need to know if what you're doing relates to my research or if it's something else." Although Miriam's voice was calm, he detected a threat in the undercurrent of her tone.

Gevu knelt beside him, and Ben was terrified when he heard him speak. "I'll gnaw you to a nub, piece by piece. And you better believe it." Ben thought about his words and listened to their intensity. He had no doubt the beast would do as Miriam said, but how could Miriam let Gevu hurt him? The answer rose quickly. Technically, she already had.

And she'd lied to him about murdering Emmet. The final threads of his faith in her disappeared when he realized

Miriam was not the woman he thought he knew. A sadness overwhelmed him, one that was not only filled with personal loss, but also piled with a new understanding of what darkness humankind was capable of. There was no sense in fighting. No matter how hard he fought this battle, he was going to lose. Eventually she'd get the password out of him. And if she didn't get it from him, then she might choose to hurt Binah.

"Kabbalah." He spat out the word, feeling he'd betrayed the meaning of it.

"Buddha2B." Now they had the password. Miriam typed the words into the computer and looked at the files that were already pulled up on the desktop. Her eyes glanced over the photographs they'd taken of the virus. Gevu stood behind her. There was no telling how much he understood from what he saw there.

Ben watched her send files to her personal email account. She closed up the computer. Pointing to the incubator, she asked the last thing she needed to know. "There's nothing in there that can hurt us anymore, is there?" He shook his head.

Ben watched Miriam go back to the incubator. She took the test tubes and the Petri dishes, made sure they were well sealed, and placed them into a plastic bag. Her footsteps sounded heavy as she walked toward him, and she squatted down to look him in the face. "You did a great job teaching Binah. I never would have known she was the one who'd done this work. But it's over Ben. If I were you, I'd get the hell out of here."

She stood up, turned, and walked away. Gevu was silent as he pushed his way out of the lab, and when the door closed, Ben felt as if the beast was disappointed he didn't get the chance to take a chunk or two out of him.

Miriam was dangerous. He realized that now. But he wondered if she knew what Gevu was really capable of. More blood dripped down his cheeks, then the lab went dark, and all he could do was sit hunched over on the floor and let his tears mix with the red corpuscles that trailed over his skin.

THIRTY

December 7, 22:13

The two drivers opened the back van doors for Gevu. During the trip back to LA, Gevu had nodded off and dreamed of Binah and the babies she'd have. When he woke, he wondered how many there would be. What would they look like? Dr. Wetzel parked behind them in her car. She got out of her vehicle at about the same time. She was wise to not begin talking to him right away.

Heung met them at the steel-door entrance to the elevator that descended to the rooms below. He bowed, but was also smart enough to remain silent. Gevu breathed in, thankful for the quiet. Only the doctor and Heung fit in the elevator with Gevu, and just barely. The rest of the men would have to wait for it to return.

Descending below, he thought about the creation of his *Porci sapiens* species. He needed Miriam's eyes and ears to make this work. He hated that he needed her, but in time, perhaps he wouldn't. And what of Binah's virus? It hadn't worked on him, but now he knew the source of the public health outbreak and he wasn't sure what that would mean for humankind. And what would it mean for millions of animals? Freedom from *Homo sapiens,* or more suffering of a different kind? There were a lot of factors to consider. Still, he was pleased.

Dr. Wetzel chose the right time to speak, as if she knew what was on his mind. He hated that she seemed to know him so well, but her words were important. "Their rooms are bugged. I don't know how long the devices will stay there, but we've got transmitters on their vehicle and a location transmitter placed directly inside Dr. Skylar. We should be able to listen in to their conversations and track them wherever they go, assuming they don't find everything we've placed."

Gevu was satisfied. The doctor had done her job. He decided not to question her yet about the virus. She'd been exposed to it. He assumed many more humans had as well. He'd have to watch. Wait. If Heung's men showed any sign of a meat allergy, he'd see it soon enough. His stock of women would probably demonstrate the allergy as well with their daily feedings.

Heung ushered him back to his room, which was newly cleaned. A king-size bed barely fit his needs, but it was comfortable. The sheets were fresh. His clothes were pressed and lined neatly in the closet. Gevu wanted a shower, but his stomach rumbled. First, he needed to eat. He left his room for the holding pen where his women were gathered. When he was done for the evening, a long shower, and maybe a bath, would be next on his agenda. He planned on gorging this evening. After all, the women were not necessary now, except as pleasure and food. And he needed both.

December 8, 07:47

Binah gradually woke from her slumber. Her fingers grabbed at the sheets and covers. Her eyelids felt heavy, as if someone had glued them shut. With difficulty, she opened them and inhaled the iron stink of blood.

Panic rose inside her. She couldn't remember last night. How did she get here? Her hand let go of the fabric and felt her body. She was naked. Not uncommon. She almost always slept that way.

With a sudden realization, she sat straight up. The motion gave her a piercing headache, and she almost vomited. She put her head between her knees and rubbed behind her ears.

What happened?

The last thing she remembered was sipping on the merlot. Miriam had made them dinner. A lovely pasta primavera. They'd drunk wine. Binah struggled to remember past dinner.

She looked between her legs and checked her sheets. There was no sign of blood. Just a sweet-smelling, sticky substance on her leg. She rubbed a finger over it and sniffed her fingertips. Semen? But it wasn't Ben's. She knew Ben's scent. This was deeper, richer. It was pleasant to inhale. Her head reeled with questions.

What the hell is going on? She rose from the bed, steadying herself. The smell of blood in the air was concerning. She wrapped a large robe around her body and went into the living room. Two lamps were on the floor. One with amber glass was broken, its fragments scattered across a braided rug.

"Ben? Miriam?" She paused. No one answered. She went from room to room. She found no one. A small trail of blood caught her attention when she entered the kitchen. It disappeared through the doorway, and small red speckles left a trail that led to the house entrance. Then she thought of the lab.

No. If Miriam knew, then what? The entire state may have been exposed to the protein virus, and soon it would be spreading across the country. It wouldn't do Miriam any good if she had found the lab.

Binah left the house and followed the trail. The scent of blood grew stronger, and some of the droplets along the way looked larger.

She pressed the concealed button on the wall behind the brush and entered the lab. The stink of iron flooded her nostrils. Her gaze swept over the room. Then she saw Ben, tied to a support beam. He was slumped over the rope that was around his torso. Blood ran down his head, and his shirt and his pants were soaked with brownish-red stains. Binah rushed to him and felt for a pulse along his neck. It was steady. He moaned.

"Ben!" She gave his shoulder a shake, and his head lolled up at her. His bottom lip was split. One of his eyes was bruised and swollen shut, the red, purple, and black spreading to his other eye in what looked like a raccoon mask.

"Immmh." He tried to speak, but she couldn't understand what he was saying. She untied him, then felt queasy when she recognized what he was bound with.

Five-fifty cord. Who in the world would use five-fifty cord, and where did it come from? She'd seen that kind of cord on the ranch near Bakersfield. Chet had used it to tie various things together, and Ben had told her it was commonly used by the military.

Had they all been attacked last night? Had Miriam been abducted? She shuddered at the thought of Chet and desperately hoped he hadn't been anywhere near the place. But if he had, she seriously doubted she'd still be here. Or even be alive.

She dashed to the sink, grabbed a rag from a nearby shelf, wet it, and returned to wipe away the blood so she could assess his wounds. He struggled to speak again, staring at the ceiling. "Ssssry."

"There's no need to be sorry, Ben. Shhh." Binah cradled his head in her lap. His hair was matted with blood, and she could see where a flap of his skin was peeled back from his skull. The bone seemed undamaged. She gently pressed the flap back in place and held some pressure on it.

Ben groaned and mumbled. She held a finger over his swollen lips and looked around the lab. Whoever had attacked him must have wanted something here. Her virus was already loose. In a matter of days, it would genetically alter every single human on the planet. No one could stop it. *Unless...*

She placed Ben's head gently onto the floor and found a few more rags to cushion it before she went to her computer. There, taped to the screen, was a hand written note. The handwriting was unmistakable. She read the words, and her body started shaking.

Sorry, sister, your virus doesn't work on me.

Resting on the counter below the note was a lump of fur. Her fingers trembled as she picked it up.

A small animal?

With revulsion, she realized it *was* an animal. Its head was torn off; the body had been crushed together like a tube of toothpaste. Not a drop of blood was on the counter. The tail helped her discern what animal it had once been. A rat.

Binah had the sensation much like that of being in a dream, the horrible kind of dream where she watched herself and wondered what the hell she was doing. She peeled the note off the computer, picked up the rat, and walked over to where Ben lay supine on the ground. She held the note and the rat body over his head.

"You knew?" Her body was trembling, and her voice grew louder. She shook the paper at him. "You knew?"

She watched as his mouth opened and shut, with nothing but soundless gurgles rolling out of it. Tears filled his eyes and rolled down the sides of his face. She realized she should be caring for her love, her dearest Ben, but she couldn't think of anything except the awful truth. It reached up to grab her from the ugly darkness, and it dragged her to hell. It was a truth that ripped away the fabric of everything she'd ever loved.

Gevu is alive. I created a virus to avenge him and forced the humans to change without their consent. I'm no better than them. Maybe I'm worse.

And admitting that truth led to acknowledging another, and another, and instead of reaching down to cradle Ben again, she spun on her heel and ran. Ran out the door and into the California sunshine. Ran across rocks, past sagebrush, and through sand. Ran until her body dropped from exhaustion, and she crumpled to the dusty ground, her lungs sucking in air as she rolled over and stared at the sun. She closed her eyes, and the waves of tears soaked her face.

A small pain in her pelvic region caused her eyelids to fly open. The full horror of what was happening enveloped her in sorrow, and she let loose an agonizing cry that echoed around the hills. Birds perched in a small pine took to the air at the sound of her shrieks. Her screams seemed to shake the earth beneath her.

It was incomprehensible, but there was no denying the feeling inside her. She was pregnant. And, she knew the father.

December 8, 11:52

When Binah finally returned to the house, she found Ben sitting in the living room. He'd patched himself up with some gauze, medical tape, and Band-Aids. He was injured, but apparently the wounds weren't life threatening. A pang of regret shot through her. She'd left him there on the floor, without any help. Still, she was angry.

Why didn't he tell me Gevu was alive?

Ben turned around to look at her as soon as he heard her footsteps. His eyes roamed her face, no doubt searching for traces of emotion. He didn't know yet, and she wondered if she should tell him about the life starting in her womb.

He held up a pocketknife. "It's a longtime habit to carry one. Ever since Boy Scouts."

She couldn't speak to him. A tight knot in her throat was growing larger and more painful.

"I'm sorry, Binah. Every time I wanted to tell you..." His voice cut off as his vocal chords visibly constricted. "I should have told you."

She quietly walked over and sat next to him. "Yes. You should have told me. I've started something. Something irreversible, in the name of my brother. In the name of my mother. Something I can't cure, and something I'm not sure I want to cure."

She gazed at his face. Misery emanated from his pores. His body slumped, defeated. His face looked like the old videos of the Berlin Wall, crumbling piece by piece as each realization, each truth, took him apart. Still, despite how miserable he looked, she couldn't let this pregnancy go on. She'd made her decision. Love of life or not, he'd have to help her end it.

Her eyes found his, and she laid her large hand over his smaller one.

"I'm pregnant. It's Gevu's, and I need you to help me get rid of it."

His eyes widened with incredulity. "But, Binah, how do you know already? They were just here...maybe you're not—" He broke off his sentence as she stared at him.

"I can feel it. And the sooner we remove it, the better." She couldn't believe she just verbally reduced a life to the word "it." She didn't want to think about what she was planning on doing and shoved the thoughts of the pregnancy into a small corner of her mind.

Ben seemed flustered. She supposed there were many thoughts flying through his brain. The logistics of ending a pregnancy such as hers would be challenging. It was a lot to process when combined with the recognition that Gevu and Miriam now knew all about their transgenic research and the virus used to introduce it.

"This will take time. I can't think of anyone who could do this."

"You can, and you will," she said confidently. "Make the calls and swear whoever does it to secrecy. And Gevu cannot know."

At the mention of his name, Ben's back straightened as if something had just occurred to him. He stood up and frantically started to search the room.

"What are you looking for?" He was acting odd all of a sudden.

He held a finger to his lips and pulled out a small black dot from the backside of a picture frame. She understood immediately and prayed they hadn't heard the discussion. Perhaps they weren't listening yet, but she had no idea where Gevu was staying. Ben crushed the dot under his heel and started searching for more bugs. After that, she expected him to find her a surgeon. She wouldn't just end this pregnancy. She'd make sure it could never happen again.

December 9, 15:30

"She's pregnant." Miriam took a sip of water from an Evian bottle. She'd debated telling Gevu so soon. But the threat of losing the child, or children, was too real. Never in her wildest dreams did Miriam think Binah would abort a baby if she became pregnant. She'd always been so vehement against killing anything.

Their phone monitors had picked up Ben's call to a local obstetrician. The surgeon was seasoned in his practice, and Ben had grown up with him. By the phone conversation, Ben obviously trusted him, which was a mistake. Miriam knew that obstetric pay wasn't that great in small cities, and money speaks louder than ethics to those who work hard and get paid next to nothing. The fact that Ben hadn't seen him since his early college days made her job much easier.

"She wants to abort it," Miriam continued. Gevu sat in a thick oak chair in the dining hall. It took up the entire end of the room, and the cushion of his seat was the size of a little Honda.

Gevu picked at his teeth with his fingernails. Miriam didn't want to think of what might actually be between his dentition. He never ate in front of her, and as time passed, she wondered why.

"Do we know where she's going?" His voice was low and rumbled like the beginning of an earthquake.

"Yes," Miriam walked over and showed him the transcripts from the calls. "We've contacted this Dr. Kevin Farley, Ben's friend. Apparently he's done several complex obstetric surgical procedures. He's really interested in this case and willing to do whatever we want as long as we're willing to pay him."

"Good." Gevu looked pointedly at Miriam and smiled at her. It wasn't a smile that made her comfortable. "And what about you, Miriam? Are you ready?"

It took her aback momentarily to have someone she'd raised from an embryo speak to her so boldly. And she had never thought she'd ever put herself in the position she was now considering. Scientist and subject. She was planning to cross the line, to delve into realms where researchers weren't supposed to go. It was scary, but exciting. The process went far beyond the bounds of scientific objectivity, but the idea of participating in groundbreaking science was too tempting. If she didn't do it, there'd be no opportunity to gather and analyze the data otherwise. The more she pondered her role, the more she was committed to their plan.

"Yes." She was surprised she said it with such conviction. "I'm ready to carry the child."

Gevu nodded approvingly. Something in the way he looked at her made her stomach lurch, and the serpent of hesitation reared its ugly head from the depths of her stomach. Then, like crushing a viper's skull beneath her heel, the feeling was gone. All that was left was her brutal determination. She was going to be a mother.

Harper removed his jacket, draped it over a lounge chair, and gently sat on the steel gray sofa. The plasma-screen TV on the wall showed a reporter interviewing witnesses of the LA prison break, and the scrolling print below the story listed a number to call if anyone had information concerning the fugitive scientist. After a commercial break, the news moved on to show descriptions of the comet ISON 2.

How long had it been since he'd actually been to his own home? Weeks? Maybe a couple of months? Good thing he wasn't married and didn't have children. He didn't have pets. Hell, he didn't even have houseplants.

They would have all died long ago.

He was the kind of man who eschewed caring for living things. And he made sure no one depended on him, and he never depended on others. The past few weeks of work might have ended in disaster, but what he'd learned during his covert years of life remained true. From the ashes of bumbling negligence, the fiery bird of opportunity often rose. No tragedy ever came along without the promise of a rose among the thorns.

The military's top-secret projects were gone. As far as the military still knew. But they hadn't vanished completely, because Harper and his men were always able to keep track of them. As a Culler, he'd learned to have backup plans on top of backup plans. And ultimately, although the military thought they owned these pieces of research, it was the Cullers who maintained control over them. The military was shortsighted, believing that Gevu, Binah, and any future clones of them would solve their problem of damaged body parts and brain-dead soldiers. Harper was almost glad they'd escaped when they had. It made some aspects of his job easier.

He looked over at the calendar. The final days were coming fast, and the facilities beneath the Denver Airport would soon be complete. He needed to call the Dulce facility and make sure everything was ready.

Doomsday. He'd laughed when he'd heard about the Doomsday Preppers. People who prepared for the end of the world. They'd all watched the fated day of December 21, 2012 come and go. When 2013 came, everyone was still here. And a couple of years later, they remained. For a while anyway. The Mayan calendar hadn't predicted the end of the world, and only a handful of people were aware of the truth.

The final days *were* coming, and every major government knew about it. They'd been building underground cities for years, preparing for the ending and the beginning of their brave new world. They kept much of their military unaware of this fact for many reasons. And when the time came to move underground, the defense forces would simply follow orders. That was the joy of handling the military. Keep them focused on conflicts, on military missions, and they were blind to anything else.

Once the final touches of the government plans were completed, the remaining troops would be detailed to the facilities, and the last supplies would be delivered. Luckily, the military officials trusted Harper completely. His record was impeccable. His behavior and his loyalty were without reproach. The independent agenda of the Cullers had been a challenge to conceal, but now the days of keeping secrets were almost over. However much he might mourn the loss of mankind, it was a waste of time. And he hated wasting time.

Harper switched on the radio. The signals from both Gevu's and Binah's hiding places transmitted. He homed in on Gevu's conversation with Miriam and smiled to himself. As much as she hated him now, she'd done so much to help him and hadn't even known it. And now, as he listened, he realized how she'd help him even more.

"Miriam. A mother." The words were comical. Ludicrous. And absolutely delicious. He chuckled out loud, as if he shared a private joke with the empty room. There'd been a time he'd considered Miriam attractive, but he'd always known that his mission and his men came first. And the mission took priority over all personal relations.

Over love, if there really was such a thing.

Through her, they'd get their first insight into how human bodies accepted organs of the *Porci sapiens*. And they'd learn more. Through her, they might even learn to become immortal. And through her, they'd find a way to repopulate the world.

December 13, 23:54

Ben ended the call to his friend, Jonah, in Ojai. He was thankful the man was willing to lend him his SUV to go into town overnight. All it took was handing over his genetic design for a stronger strain of weed. Binah rode in the back as they traveled to Ventura just after nightfall. Before they'd left for town, he'd had to provide Binah with a lot of reassurance.

"It will be okay. Kevin is an excellent physician and an old friend. He's seen some wild shit in his time, and he won't ask questions. He'll just need to do an ultrasound when you get there, to be sure of the structure of your anatomy. And I've paid for a staff that won't ask questions either."

"Let's just take care of this, Ben." He looked at her in the rearview mirror and worked hard to conceal his concern. Her face sagged with defeat, and her emotions were so radical. Up one day, down another. He thought about her motives.

Binah didn't want to just have an abortion. She wanted her uterus and ovaries completely removed so she could never get pregnant again. Ben had tried to talk her out of it, but she'd been so insistent on having a total hysterectomy that explaining the facts to her wouldn't have mattered. He knew that later she'd be surprised. And really angry. She understood that Gevu hadn't died, but she hadn't asked why. She assumed that somehow he'd survived the gun blast. And Ben still couldn't bring himself to tell her the truth.

THIRTY ONE

December 14, 01:20

"Clamp." Two nurses rolled a stretcher into the suite. Kevin looked over at the woman that rested on it. She was unconscious.

"Prep her." He was almost ready. The other OB/GYN, the woman Harper had brought with him, had scrubbed in and was putting on her gown and gloves. Kevin's eyes returned to the surgical site in front of him. Aside from the creature's many breasts, her odd external anatomy, and pink skin, the internal anatomy was almost identical to that of a human female.

"Bovie." His assistant handed him the instrument, and he cauterized a couple of bleeders.

The nurses rolled the woman across the room, transferred her to a second surgical table, hooked her up to the monitors, and placed restraints on her. The anesthesiologist intubated her, and the other physician stood at her side over the surgical site.

"This will need to be quick," Kevin said to her.

"Ready when you are," the other physician answered. She asked her attendant for a scalpel, and in minutes, he heard the patient's uterus plop into a stainless-steel pan.

Damn, she's fast. With that cue, Kevin made one more cut, and the creature's uterus was free. He stole a quick glance at the harvested eggs he'd taken from her ovaries earlier and then handed the uterus off to the other doctor.

"Coming to you." The physician took the organ carefully from his fingers. Kevin suspected it was larger than the one she'd just removed. She'd have to fit it in, restore the blood flow, and then close up the various layers. He didn't see how in the world the pregnancy would survive, but if it did, it would be amazing. But he could never talk about it. Never even write up a case study. If anything, it was something he could scribble in his journal. A remarkable event that might be discovered after he was long gone from the earth.

Kevin set about closing up the creature. He was surprised that she hardly bled at all. Each blood vessel seemed to seal itself off, barely needing any assistance from him. He let the field stay open for a few minutes just in case there were any more bleeders, and when he was satisfied she was stable, he sutured the layers of muscle and skin together and finished the job.

"She's clear to go to recovery."

The nurses busied themselves with moving the creature to a stretcher, which was a challenging task. She was at least six feet tall and weighed over three hundred and fifty pounds. They struggled to slide her over using a draw sheet, and finally accomplished the task. Kevin didn't watch anymore. He was eager to see what was happening behind him.

He moved over to stand opposite the physician. She was reconnecting the uterine artery, and in minutes, she undid the clamps and the grayish uterus pinked up.

"Excellent job," he said. Kevin admired how her fingers swiftly placed the sutures and connected the other vessels with expert accuracy.

"We'll see." She glanced up at him, her large almond-shaped eyes startling him with their golden beauty and intensity. "It will be a couple of weeks until we know for sure if she'll keep the pregnancy, and..."

"...that she won't reject the organ," he finished.

The silence in the room said what they both knew. This surgery was unprecedented. A physician's one chance in a lifetime. And they'd cut corners. There'd been no typing or crossmatching of blood. There'd been no careful preparation for the procedure. They'd done this with the expediency and caution of changing a car's oil at a Jiffy Lube. But because of this surgery, Kevin would be rich. He'd have enough money to pay off his student loans and his mortgage. Laura would be so happy. And his five-year-old son could go to any college he wanted in the future. Harvard. Princeton. And they'd never be in debt again.

He helped the doctor stretch the woman's skin over the muscles of the abdomen, and together they finished closing her up.

"I hope you'll let me know how she's doing." Kevin took off his mask as they both left the surgical suite. When he entered the scrub room, he nearly tripped over two bodies lying in the middle of the floor. His nurses.

In his horror, he slipped on a pool of blood, which had spread across the tiles from their necklines. In his panic, he reached out to steady himself on a sink. The doctor behind him caught him just before he dropped. Just in time to draw a scalpel across his throat and let him slide to the ground to join his nurses.

December 14, 04:11

Binah opened her eyes and felt a warm hand on hers. She looked over and saw Ben sitting beside her. *It's over. It's done.*

She filled her lungs. The pain wasn't so bad. She'd expected it to be worse.

"How do you feel?" The concern in Ben's voice was sweet. She gazed at him and realized he looked like a young boy, unsure, almost lost.

"Fine, I think." Her throat was sore, and she suddenly felt thirsty. She could drink gallons of cold water.

Ben held a spoon out to her lips. It was piled with ice chips.

"Really? That's all I get?"

"The nurse said you could have more soon. In a few hours." His voice hitched a little. It was clear he wanted to say more, but was unsure how to continue.

"What is it?" She was feeling better already. The irritation in her throat resolved when she swallowed some ice.

"It's almost daylight. We've got to get you out of here," he said as he looked around. "But I'm uncomfortable with moving you. I don't know what I thought, but this was serious surgery. Still..." He was staring at the sheet that covered her belly. It was as if he either wanted to tell her something more or he was afraid to ask a question.

She tried to reassure him. "I'm okay. Really. I actually feel pretty good."

A nurse came into the room. She still wore a mask, which Binah found odd. Perhaps that was the way they did things here.

Or maybe she's afraid I'll infect her with swine flu.

The nurse didn't say a word, but removed the IV from Binah's arm, pulled down the guardrail, and handed Ben a paper bag.

"Here are her antibiotics. You know the signs of infection?"

"Yes." It appeared Ben was mystified at her behavior as well.

"Is everything okay?" The words flew out of Binah's mouth before it hit her that the situation had to seem very strange to the human. But the nurse didn't seem surprised at Binah's speech.

The nurse looked at Ben, avoiding Binah's eyes. "There's some kind of epidemic going around. It's all over the news this morning. It started here, in California, they think, but now it's spreading across the country."

"What kind of epidemic?"

"They're not sure. Something with the food, maybe. People everywhere have had vomiting, stomach pains, and a variety of other symptoms." She handed Ben a sack of sterile pads for dressing changes, some medical tape, and a surgical facemask. Then she gave him some teaching sheets on wound care. "Be careful out there."

The nurse walked toward the door. Ben stopped her with a question. "Have you seen Kev...er, Dr. Farley?"

The nurse hesitated a second but continued to the door. "He's in another surgery." The door closed quietly behind her.

Binah noticed that Ben's lips were clamped together in a thin line. His brow was wrinkled, like he was puzzled about something. He glanced over at her.

"You feel ready to go? The sun's coming up. I hate to rush..."

"It's okay, really." She pushed herself up on the stretcher and slowly swung her legs over, glad she didn't experience the least bit of pain. Her abdomen felt sloggy and loose, and the emptiness of where her pelvic organs used to be made her giddy.

Mentally, she was lighter, as if someone had removed a ten-ton weight from the top of her head. *The pregnancy is gone. No mini Binahs.* She smiled.

Ben's eyes held no joy when she looked over at him. All she saw was worry mixed with fear. "Let's get out of here." He handed her a sack with her clothes, and she slipped them on, aware of how loose they were. *It's like I've lost ten pounds.*

They went through the back door they'd walked in earlier, to where Ben had the SUV parked for easy getaway access. Binah looked at the sky, where a few stars shimmered. She could clearly see a bright star with a tail. ISON 2. She'd meant to check the information on the comet a while ago but had never found the time. She wondered about it briefly as she helped pack herself into the vehicle. *I should look it up when we get home.*

When they drove past the emergency room at the front of the hospital, the flashing red lights of ambulances were lined up single-file at the drop-off point. The patient parking lot was stuffed with several cars, some blatantly sitting in no-parking zones and handicapped spaces. No one seemed to care.

Ben didn't say a word, but pulled out onto the street, and something in Binah couldn't help the strange conflict of emotions in her chest and the questions rolling in her head. The hysterectomy was successful, and her virus was working. But Ben didn't seem the least bit happy. She felt as if somehow she'd failed at everything she'd tried to accomplish, and her lightheartedness sank as the heaviness of guilt settled on her. She'd always struggled to protect life. Now she'd thrown it away.

So others could live! Her subconscious barked the words at her with insistent justification, and she chose to listen to it. It felt better than listening to the guilt.

She heard another siren in the distance and settled herself into her seat. She became more comfortable with the thought that her virus was spreading. Although the hospitals were overrun with sick patients, there hadn't been a human death yet. And because of her virus, animals wouldn't suffer under human hands again. But Gevu was alive, and the virus didn't work on him. With that understanding, her comfort turned to chills, and her entire body shivered.

It's good the genetic line will never spread. The aberration is a dead end. It dies with Gevu and with me.

Miriam heard voices all around her. It took her a minute to realize where she was. Then she remembered. She was being transported in a van to Mr. Heung's underground home. She opened her eyes. IV fluids still infused into her arm. The doctor who'd performed her surgery pumped up a blood pressure cuff on her other arm, monitored her temperature and pulse, and administered more pain medication.

"The surgery went well." She flashed a penlight over Miriam's eyes, and Miriam kept them open and let the doctor do a neurological check.

"Your pupils are reactive and equal to the light." She continued to talk while she checked Miriam's fingers and toes and examined her abdomen. "We'll go over your HCG levels when we get back. I've already given you another course of hormones to make sure your levels stay up, and some full-spectrum antibiotics. We may need to give you another hormone injection just in case, until your body starts producing the right levels on its own."

The physician still had her mask on. All Miriam could see were her beautiful almond-shaped eyes, golden brown irises, and little strands of ebony hair that had escaped from her surgical cap. The eyes seemed vaguely familiar. The woman removed her mask, and Miriam felt a jolt of surprise. *The lawyer.* She struggled with the name the supposed lawyer had given her while she was in the prison cell. *Ling. Dr. Sue Ling.*

The recognition must have shown on her face because the doctor smiled. "Many of us have a variety of jobs." She was reassuring, warm, and caring. Different than any other physician or scientist she'd ever known. "I'm very good at what I do, Dr. Wetzel. I'll take good care of you."

Miriam rested her head back on her pillow and closed her eyes. For the first time in a long time, she actually believed someone, and for some reason, she trusted this doctor completely. Maybe it was because they both had the same goal. To see this pregnancy through.

THIRTY TWO

December 17, 08:00

Harper's jaw hurt from grinding his teeth. Somehow, his men not only failed to follow Dr. Ben Skylar and Project Juliet, but they'd lost Stella in the process. His tracer on Project Juliet wasn't working either.

"What did I tell you?" He realized he'd raised his voice louder than usual, and he hated that. Yelling implied a lack of control, and in the face of utter chaos, it was important to visibly maintain control. "Find them, and find them now!" He pressed the "end call" button hard.

They apparently hadn't gone back to Ojai. He should have guessed Ben would be smarter than to return to his lab, but he'd figured the doctor would wait until Project Juliet recovered from her surgery.

Public health epidemiologists couldn't contain the outbreak, but they had already narrowed the viral origin to north of Ventura. Before they could get closer, his men had descended on the house to wait for Dr. Skylar and Project Juliet to return from the hospital, but they hadn't returned. He'd made sure the epidemiologists wouldn't find anything, and Dr. Skylar, well, he'd never have anything to return to ever again. Not that it mattered.

His men at the hospital had followed Miriam back to LA, but it hadn't done a damn bit of good. They'd lost her in the simplest of places—downtown—at a time when traffic was minimal. He suspected she and her prison break crew used some sort of underground system as their getaway route. That was the way he did things, of course. Except the system he used was on a much grander scale.

Now, his only lead to the projects lay in a hospital bed at one of the most prominent medical facilities in town. Chet had dropped off the grid after escaping with the money, only to resurface in the emergency room. He'd never have caught it except his men monitored hospital admissions, and the hospital personnel had used Chet's real name when they had admitted him. That, and they had recharged his phone. *Phones make such great locating devices.*

He'd have to talk to Chet soon. They were all running out of time. ISON 2 was already glowing brightly in the sky, but most people didn't know what else hurtled their way thousands of miles behind it. ISON 2 was projected to clear Earth, but what was coming behind it wasn't. The United States would only survive due to the underground world they'd created, thanks to the Black Budget. And most of the military were still none the wiser. He expected a call from the admiral as soon as he found out. But it wasn't Harper's position to brief it to him. That privilege went to the Joint Chiefs of Staff, and so far, they'd said nothing.

For decades, theories of US underground tunnels had been a joke in America. UFO hunters told conspiracy stories of deep underground military bases, laughingly called DUMBs for short, filled with aliens that the US government kept secret from the world. Truth was, the aliens were the only real joke. The tunnels and bases were not. His father had raised him in that subterranean world. He wasn't going to let something like losing Projects Juliet and Kilo stand in the way of making sure that those who deserved to survive did.

He held up the phone and dialed his man, Hudson. The phone clicked, and a raspy voice answered. Harper gave him the information on Chet and set up his next move to get the man discharged from the hospital. His people would take better care of him at the Dulce facility, and then Harper would get the information he needed to bring all of the missing pieces in.

December 15, 10:01

Heung was very pleased, despite the irritating escape of the female research assistant, along with *Zhu Bajie*'s man with no legs. The god had been furious at first, but he had soon settled down after hearing that his dream of procreation would become reality. Overall, he'd done everything the Pig King wanted, and he was rewarded with a god who was on the verge of becoming jovial.

If not for the god's occasional blood meals, he'd almost adore the being. *Zhu Bajie* was extremely intelligent, and Heung could not believe the next honor he was given. He was to personally oversee to the propagation of the god's children.

These certainly did not seem like degenerate times, as the Buddhist scriptures predicted. The days filled with dour faces of old monks who spread the word that enlightenment was less and less likely for someone such as him were over. With the children of *Zhu Bajie*, there'd be more and more converts. More people who would eventually find the way to their ultimate transition into supreme nothingness.

There were forty women in all. The unusable ones who were too old or infertile had been left in the pen for *Zhu Bajie*'s meals, along with a few homeless men who were picked up during his team's city rounds. He hoped the fertile women knew how lucky they all were to be chosen to carry the child of a god.

His own physician had worked diligently, maturing the contents of the ovaries, mixing the being's sperm with the eggs of his sister, and making sure that the embryos were implanted in the women at just the right time. He wondered how long their pregnancies would take. Months, or mere weeks? It was an exciting time, but he also realized he was running out of space in his underground home.

He entered the room where Dr. Wetzel stayed. It was one of his favorites, his meditation chamber, converted now for the birth of *Zhu Bajie*'s first child. Dr. Ling hovered over the woman with an ultrasound probe and turned to smile at him when he came into the room.

"She's doing beautifully." The obstetrician patted Dr. Wetzel's belly.

"And the child?" Heung didn't want to seem callous, but *Zhu Bajie*'s child was of the utmost importance.

"That's what I mean. Look! This is incredible. Only three days since the surgery, and the child is visible on abdominal ultrasound. See the heart, here? It measures the size of a twenty-week fetus."

Heung was taken aback. *So big? Already?* Dr. Wetzel's abdomen had a rounded lump under her belly button, the scar from the surgery just an angry red line, and the woman seemed enormously pleased. She looked up and chuckled when she saw his face. His surprise must have been apparent.

"This is wonderful." She rubbed her belly while Dr. Ling put the probe back onto the machine. Luckily, Dr. Wetzel explained without him having to ask. "The fetus is growing much faster than any of us had anticipated. When Gevu and Binah were designed and placed inside their host, it took the span of a regular pig pregnancy for them to gestate, but this time, the development is much faster."

Heung glanced at Dr. Ling. The news was good. Very, very good. And yet, where was he to put all of the deity's progeny? He couldn't transport them all to China in time, and he didn't have the room here. He'd have to make some calls to his advisors. Perhaps they could come up with something.

"Would you like a print of the ultrasound?" Dr. Ling held out a picture of the curled profile of the little god.

He bowed and took it reverently and headed back to his office, which was only a couple of rooms away. The Americans often said necessity was the mother of invention, and now he needed the birth of a usable plan. He'd keep careful watch over this little one. If she were truly a female, she'd be the key to many more like her.

Chet's main objective was to stay alive. He didn't know why in the hell Stella had come for him, or how she'd found him, but he didn't hate her quite as much as he had before. Still, he really hated her.

If she hadn't left me with any other choice than to go back and see the Ching-man, I'd still have my legs.

He rolled forward in his wheelchair, taking in the gigantic subterranean view. There was no way he'd ever have guessed Harper had something like this in his back pocket. The armed women at his side and the man in front of him escorted him along a vast passageway, and then down another corridor. He still had no idea where he was. They'd taken him out of the hospital and flown him from LAX in a private jet to some unknown destination. They hadn't said where. He'd figured it was Harper who'd rescued him, though God only knew why. Since he'd made off with the pigs, he was sure he wasn't in the Culler's good graces.

The male escort opened a door, and he rolled in to a black room. The walls were black, and there was a hint of a dark-colored desk in front of him. There was nothing on the walls. Nothing he could see. And the room smelled like a computer room, plastic and electronic. The only visible light came from a small red button on top of the desk. They waited silently for many minutes, and Chet started to get impatient. What did Harper want with him anyway? With no legs, he wasn't as good of a soldier as before.

A side door opened. "Minimal lights." It was Harper's voice. The room was gradually infused with a very dim, soft glow. It looked almost as if they were all encased in a heavy fog. The next sentence was directed at him. "You almost died."

Chet said nothing. His experience with Harper had taught him excuses were useless, and words were meaningless unless there was an answer to a question or a statement about an objective.

"You put everything at risk, you know that?" Harper's voice was loaded with scathing condemnation. Chet took it like the blows he'd taken from the enemies in Iraq. Harper continued. "Well that's over. Done with. It's time to move on. We've had losses, and so have you."

Harper strolled over to a wall and touched it. Instantly, a panel came alive and provided some more light. "When Stella brought you to the hospital, she dropped off some things. One of them was your cell phone."

Chet gazed at the lit panel. It showed several pictures and communications from his phone. "What I want to know is whether you can contact Dr. Skylar and bring him in. I've reviewed some of your texts. It looks like you might have something on him that he wouldn't want to go public."

Chet was confused for a moment, and then he remembered the video he'd taken of the doctor fucking the pig. He caught himself before he smiled. *Goddamn, I'm good! Always something in my pocket to keep me alive.* "Yes, sir. Matter of fact, I do."

Harper walked over and handed Chet his cell phone. "Make the call. Tell him you want to meet him."

Chet popped open the phone, and Harper gave him the directions to their location. Chet wasn't sure if he'd heard right until Harper repeated it. He dialed the number to the namby-pamby-assed doctor. His call was sent right to voice mail. He couldn't imagine Skylar taking a chance and ditching the phone. Not with what he had on him. At the beep, he directed Skylar to come to Los Alamos and hung up.

"Done." Chet ended the call and stared at Harper's half-lit shadow. "Good job. Keep the phone in case he calls you back. And in case you're wondering, no, you're not leaving here. Not for a very long time."

Ben's worries about Binah were put to rest when she asked him to pull over because she was hungry. He turned off the I-40 just past Needles and parked at a truck stop, far away from any of the other vehicles. He was anxious to start traveling off the highway. Once he got to Flagstaff, he'd head north. He popped open the back hatch to check on her wound. Her abdomen was healed except for a thin, little scar.

She looked at him sadly. "Where are we going, Ben? It's been two days, and you've barely said a thing." It was odd she hadn't questioned him before, taking their little motel stays in stride and sleeping most of the time.

He looked around the parking lot to make sure no one could see her. "Colorado. I've got some friends there who might be able to help us." He got ready to close the hatch when one of the bags he'd brought with him started to buzz. It wasn't a surprise. He'd expected it, eventually.

A green duffel sat right beside Binah, and he opened it and pulled out the phone. He listened to the voice message on his way into the store, and his hands shook as he bought coffee, Oreos, salad, fruit, water, and some vegan protein bars. The cashier eyed him suspiciously. "You're not sick, are you? Sick with that bug that everyone has?"

Ben shook his head. "Just a long day. Long drive." The cashier nodded. It was clear she was glad for the business, but cautious of contracting an illness. He carried his bagged purchases back to the SUV and opened up the hatch to give some food to Binah. He was surprised to see her typing on his laptop. Her skin was ashen, as if something had seeped the blood from her body.

"What is it?" He couldn't think of anything that could make her look so scared. Her virus was working, slaughterhouses had shut down, and grocery stores across America were stocking up on a huge influx of beans, corn, and other grains. She had every reason to be happy, particularly after her surgery. Their only burden was in finding a place to stay, a place to call home.

Binah jutted her chin toward the sky. "Can you see that light in the sky? The one just above?" He knew what she was talking about. The comet was in the news frequently these days. He looked up. Even though it was late morning, it was still visible.

"ISON 2." He hadn't paid much attention to the news; he knew the comet was going to bypass Earth and it wasn't a threat. Besides information on the virus, that was all of the talking-head information he'd had time to absorb these days.

She nodded. "Something bothered me about it a while back. I can't explain why, but I've wanted to look it up for the longest time and kept forgetting." She turned the computer screen his way.

Ben was always amazed at the capabilities of modern space technology, as well as Binah's ability to hack into encrypted mainframes with a simple computer. But he was puzzled. She explained further. "NASA has been tracking this comet for a while, and they've discovered it isn't in any danger of hitting Earth."

She typed a few more keystrokes and turned the computer back to him again. "But it's not ISON 2 that's the problem. It's what's following behind it."

Stella waited a few moments before following the SUV out of the parking lot. She hadn't been sure that the man who went into the store was Dr. Ben Skylar until he had returned and opened up the back hatch of the vehicle. Project Juliet, Binah, was in there; she knew it. And why should she care? She should leave, drive off in another direction, and let fate do as it willed, but in the end, she couldn't. From what she'd seen so far, Binah was a gentle soul, and if they were running from Harper, then perhaps Dr. Skylar was trying to do the right thing. It was obvious they had no one to protect them. They were alone.

Why am I doing this? Maybe the fact that she'd stopped at the very same convenience store at the same time they had meant something. Maybe there are no coincidences, and she was meant to be here. In the end, it didn't matter what reasoning she accepted. They were here, and she was here, and she'd had no primary destination other than to get away from the Cullers. Now, she wasn't sure if she was headed right back toward the people she was running away from, or perhaps, following two unlikely travelers on their way to sanctuary. There was no logical reason at all as to why she should follow them, but she made up her mind to do it. She stayed just out of sight of their red taillights and prayed that they knew what they were doing.

Heung almost sent the man away, but he insisted on seeing Heung and he'd demonstrated that he knew enough about his underground space to be a threat. Heung's men ushered him in. There was nothing special about him. Simple black suit, white shirt, and an ineptly tied tie.

The man strolled across the floor, his one-sided smile almost impertinent. When he stopped, he did not bow. Heung stayed cool and kept his eyes upon the stranger.

"Good evening." Heung waited for a response. The man only reached into his jacket and pulled out a piece of paper. One of Heung's men plucked it from his grasp and handed it to Heung. He unfolded the paper and wondered about what he read. He handed it to one of the females that stood behind him. "Check this."

The woman exited the room, leaving a ponderous silence among them in her wake. It took no more than ten minutes for her to return to the room. What she whispered in Heung's ear was nothing short of a crashing blow.

The man waited. Heung stared at him, then picked up a pen, scribed a note on the back of the paper, and signed it. If what the letter said was completely true, they had very little time. It was too late to fly back to China and make preparations. Too late to find somewhere well fortified in his homeland to prepare for what was about to happen. The most humiliating fact was that Heung was required to trust a stranger with his survival, and that did not please him. Not in the least.

THIRTY THREE

December 18, 07:15

Beads of sweat lined Miriam's upper lip, and her hair was damp. The contractions were coming more frequently, lasting longer, and intensifying. The room was dark with the exception of some ambient lighting and the glow of numbers and graphs on medical equipment screens. The fetal monitor showed a heartbeat of one hundred thirty beats per minute. It was normal.

"We could do a C-section, Dr. Wetzel. You've had recent abdominal surgery in order to carry this child, and now you have a different uterus. A bigger uterus. The uterine artery and ovarian artery attachments might not tolerate labor. The previous surgery puts the baby at risk." Dr. Ling's tone wasn't accusatory. She was simply stating the facts, but the implication was that Miriam didn't know what she was doing and that she wasn't capable of the task. The suggestion was that she'd be better off letting someone else call the shots during her delivery. *The hell with that.*

"I *will* go through the full process!" Besides, Miriam knew the mix of hormones she secreted both during and after delivery would give her the best chance at bonding well with the baby.

Another contraction hit, her stomach turning rock hard like a loose hand tightening into an angry fist. She focused on her breathing. *In. Out. Slow. Deep. Calm. Release.* She experienced a moment of peace before the next wave came.

Holy Minkowski, will it ever stop? It feels like I've been here for an eternity. But she didn't have an eternity. Not after the news Heung had given her only a few hours before she'd gone into labor. After that, she'd researched ISON 2 and the Black Comet and was shocked to discover that governments worldwide had managed to keep the other comet secret for two whole years. Luckily, most developed governments had contingency plans for imminent world destruction. Doomsday event planning was apparently big business.

Around her, people in blue masks and gowns came and went. A woman drew her blood. A man took her blood pressure. The next contraction sucked her breath away. A minute later, the one after it felt as if she were being torn to pieces inside. She yelled out from the ferocity of the pain. Not just a yell. It was a borderline scream. When the baby wriggled wildly, she not only felt the tearing of tissue inside her body—she *heard* it.

The baby's heart rate dropped to sixty and stayed there.

Dr. Ling didn't waste a moment. "Crash section!" She must have had anesthesia waiting right outside the door. A tall man rushed in and asked her a couple of questions, and before she knew it, she had a plastic mask on her face, breathing air designed to take her to dreamtime.

"I thought general anesthesia wasn't considered very safe..." The mask muffled her words. She inhaled and couldn't finish her sentence. Darkness reached out and grabbed her, but before it could drag her down, she thought she heard an infant cry somewhere in the distance.

"Little girl is big! What do you figure? Nine? Ten?"

The pediatrician humored the male nurse's questions just to get their minds off the weird circumstances. There'd be many more of these in the future. They'd better get used to it.

"At least nine pounds." She checked the creature, *the baby*, over from head to toe. Normal Babinski reflex, good suck, intact palate. She supposed the snout and the tail were normal. This baby would be what she compared the others to. In a couple more weeks, she'd know for sure.

The nurse looked over at the mother who was still under anesthesia, her uterus in the process of being removed. Uterine rupture was tough. The baby was lucky to have survived. The mother's constant bleeding, on top of her shredded womb, necessitated the hysterectomy.

"How's the baby going to feed?" The nurse grabbed a small white blanket.

"Bottle for now." The pediatrician finished up the exam. "We'll have to send for some formula." She hesitated. The baby had only cried once when she was taken from her mother. After that, she'd done nothing but quietly observe her surroundings. Her bright-blue eyes, goopy from the antibiotic they'd put there, stared at their faces. It was as if *they* were the objects of scrutiny, not the other way around.

Behind them, the nurses took bloody surgical instruments from the physicians and plopped them into steel basins. The doctors called for blood. Curse words followed, and an arterial spurt erupted from the body like Old Faithful. The cardiac monitor's telltale sound of a flatline filled the air.

"Code Blue!" A team maneuvered a crash cart into the room. They worked on the mother furiously, busying themselves between trying to stop the loss of blood and restarting her heart. The male nurse wrapped the baby in a blanket and put a hat over her ears to keep her warm.

Twenty minutes went by. Dr. Ling raised her hand, and the team stopped working.

She looked at the clock on the wall.

"Time of death, eight thirty-one."

The baby began screaming.

———

December 19, 05:11

Los Alamos. It had been a long time, but Ben still remembered the way. Chet's directions only confirmed what he'd suspected. The Cullers knew about the Underground.

Reporters discovered its veneer in August of 2013, and the government promptly declassified information about a 230-foot-long tunnel located at the base of Los Alamos Canyon. They said they'd planned to do it all along due to rising costs of keeping high security in the area. Investigations concerning the tunnel failed to uncover what he knew still existed beneath the network of labs and weapons-storage areas.

He drove past olive-colored piñon pines, tan and gray rocks, and red boulders. Ben turned onto a wide dirt road just as the sky was beginning to lighten, and there were a few feathery clouds scattered above. Sunrise would be beautiful. He wondered if it would be the last they'd ever see.

Ten more miles. Ben's eyes felt so heavy. He needed sleep, but he was glad Binah seemed to have slumbered quietly in the back. He heard her moan a little.

"We're almost there."

She hadn't asked him many questions when he'd continued taking I-40 to Albuquerque. They had headed north after that, and perhaps she had assumed he'd just chosen to go to Colorado via another route. A few miles past Pojoaque, he'd turned left and headed west. The dirt road they traveled on wasn't on any map.

"Where are we really going?" Her voice was soft, and yet it begged him to confide in her. To tell her what he was planning.

"Los Alamos." He heard her shift in her seat.

"Why?"

He was silent. Did it really matter now? The reason he was headed there made no difference in the face of what she'd shown him on the computer. Their world was doomed. The video of him with her would be a thing of the past. What mattered most was that they survived. And Ben was betting that Chet was with someone who could help them do just that.

"Ben?"

He'd avoided becoming emotional, but now the tears welled up in his eyes. He felt his throat tighten. The words wouldn't come. He wanted them to, but they were stuck in his windpipe.

"I *know*," she said. Her words were full of understanding, but he couldn't bring himself to answer her.

The forest closed in on them, and even though the sky was brighter, even though the sun was just starting to peek over the ridge behind them, turning the clouds ahead of them into a lustrous pink, the day seemed dark.

"Stop the car." He didn't want to stop, and ignored her. He wasn't sure he could keep it together if she insisted on talking to him. He continued to drive. The back hatch popped open.

"Stop the *car*!"

Damn.

His foot found the brake, and he stopped. Before he could open his door, she'd climbed out of the back, shut the hatch, and squeezed into the passenger side of the SUV. She could barely shut the door, but she managed. When the seatbelt warning chime kept dinging, he stopped the vehicle again, and she got out, fastened the seatbelt, and sat on top of it. He was amused at her antics and managed to smile for the first time in ages.

"What about safety? Can't have you getting hurt." Ben was teasing. He reached out to touch her hand, not caring what she, or anyone else in the future, would think. Binah was amazing.

Her piggy nose turned up, and her ears wiggled beneath her ebony hair. "The invincible don't need to worry about safety!" She was oddly playful. "Let's save the world!"

He wanted to smile again, but what came was halfhearted. He'd wanted to tell her long ago, but she'd figured it out on her own and probably felt he'd betrayed her somehow by not confiding in her.

His foot pressed the gas, and the SUV lurched forward. Red dust flew up from behind them, and the scarlet and ochre of the hills in front of them blazed with the fire of the morning sun. Vanilla pines rose in front of them like exclamation marks, emphasizing to him what she so poetically said she understood. Binah knew she was immortal.

Stella pressed on, the dirt road making it difficult for her to trail behind the SUV without being spotted, particularly when the sun started to rise. She had to travel slowly, or the dust from the road would tell the driver ahead that someone was near. Dr. Skylar and Binah might need her soon, but secrecy was of utmost necessity. She sensed that she wouldn't be able to help them if they knew she was close by. She'd have more of a chance of finding out what they were up to and discovering if they were going to be safe if she stayed hidden.

Los Alamos. It dawned on her that Dr. Skylar wasn't driving here to hide. It was in the middle of nowhere, a top-secret nowhere that most people didn't have access to once they reached the base. No, he was driving here to meet someone.

She didn't have a cell phone, and even if she did, she doubted she'd get a signal, so gathering more information was out of the question. She wasn't going to get it. Not out here. And it wasn't because it was too remote. This was a place of deep government control. It was likely that no one made a call or used the Internet without special communications or equipment. All other coms were probably blocked.

She thought back to the maps she'd seen on the walls during her training with the Cullers. Maps with large dark circles around certain cities. She'd never asked questions about them, but now she thought she knew why this place was special. What if the circles represented subterranean bases? She'd personally been inside the secret underground base at Point Mugu. Why wouldn't there be others?

The map's southwestern states of California, Nevada, Colorado, and New Mexico were linked by solid black lines from city to city, and in some cases, from military base to base. Vandenberg to Fort Irwin, to Los Alamos, Dulce, Denver, Tulsa, and Fort Stockton. And those were just the ones she remembered. The lines extended east across the United States and north to Canada, as well as south to Mexico.

Could there be a secret underground network that large? Stella didn't have the answer right now, but one way or another she had the feeling she was going to find out.

All of this beneath the city of Los Angeles, and I never knew.

Heung had relayed messages via the Silent Man and negotiated passage for forty women in addition to himself, Dr. Ling, Gevu, and his assistants. And as irritating as his mother was, he had to bring her too. An outsider might consider her an unnecessary burden simply because she was crazy. And troublesome.

But what kind of man could hope to pass into the Buddha fields if he neglected his mother and failed to help her survive otherwise-certain death?

It bothered him that she refused to recognize the Pig King in his glory, but she was stuffy and old-fashioned. And utterly deranged. He imagined that she expected the god to be dressed in the robes of a Shaolin monk. And he also suspected her of helping the two prisoners escape.

Things are different now, Mother. I am not deluded, like you think. I am awakening!

He looked around at the vast underground tunnel and the rails of the transportation system that would shuttle him, his family, *Zhu Bajie,* and the others to a safe haven. A place he hadn't dreamed he'd need to go in the future. *Zhu Bajie* took the news as if it were what he'd expected all along.

He'd taken it much better than when they had informed him of the death of the white scientist; his grief had incited a particularly bloody mess at the feeding cages. Heung marveled that the god had demanded the scientist's body be brought with them on the train. Perhaps, as his long-time protector and caretaker, he couldn't bear to leave her. Interestingly, her body did not bloat or stink. She had the blessings of the Buddhas for bearing a child of a god.

A small squeak broke him from his mental wandering. The new baby rested in the god's arms, dwarfed by the sheer size of his giant biceps and forearms. He hadn't let her out of his sight since they had brought her to him, demanding to take part in her daily feeding and cleaning. He was trying to feed her now, while they waited at the platform, but still the girl would not eat. They'd tried many brands of formula, but nothing worked. The baby only spat out the food. She was looking listless and very pale.

Heung eyed an attendant and signaled her to approach.

"Your Excellency, before we depart I have a gift for you."

Zhu Bajie said nothing, but reluctantly gave the child over to the woman with outstretched arms.

Three of Heung's men moved forward, carrying a long package wrapped in gold foil. Heung handed him a smaller package first, bowing low to present it. *Zhu Bajie* raised an eyebrow and tore the cherry-blossom-printed paper. Inside was a luxurious black satin jacket, large enough for *Zhu Bajie* to shrug on easily. A round patch adorned the left chest and rested just over his heart. It was bordered with several traditional symbols, but the design in the middle was just as he'd specified.

"Please wear it in good health, Excellency." Heung bowed low, and *Zhu Bajie* zipped it over his custom-made T-shirt. It was a perfect fit.

Heung's men stepped up and dragged the long package over to the god. He looked at Heung and tipped his chin in brief thanks, then he tore at the foil to reveal what was inside. The glistening silver handle was six feet long and three inches in diameter, with a nine-toothed rake at one end. The physical embodiment of the design on the patch.

"It is made of the strongest metal known to man."

Zhu Bajie grasped it, then swung it so it rested parallel in his palms. He gripped it once more and spun it around his body in a series of intricate moves, lifted it over his head, and crashed it into the concrete walkway. The ground shook. Shards of man-made stone scattered through the air, and when the dust cleared, the walkway bore a large hole where the pavement had once been smooth and solid.

He grunted and held the rake up to examine it. There was not a scratch on its surface. The god nodded, and Heung let out a sigh of relief. He'd rewarded the university scientists well for helping to make this weapon, and for agreeing to use their newly discovered metal alloy in its construction. He doubted they'd have much time to enjoy his reward.

Only a blast of air let them know the train was arriving. Heung felt the wind whip his hair and his jacket, and suddenly, the shiny, black train was there before them. Wide doors slid open, and men in black military uniforms stepped off, bowed, and ushered them in.

Zhu Bajie's car was perfect, the seating designed according to Heung's specifications. The god sat easily in the red cushioned chair built to hold his weight, and he snapped his fingers when he heard his daughter cry. The attendant brought her to him, and once again, he tried to feed her, but the baby girl spat out the formula and whimpered miserably.

"Let us hope that where we're going, they will solve her difficulty feeding." *Zhu Bajie*'s voice was a gruff rumble, filled with an unusual tenderness that caused hope to flicker brightly in Heung's chest. Perhaps the god's transformation was finally beginning. He bowed, walked backward, and bowed again before he closed the door and left the car.

Gevu stared down at his daughter and let his muscles relax.

Have I ever known a feeling like this?

All of his life, since the brutal murder of his mother, he'd been angry, seething with an internal rage that begged to be released. And he'd let himself release it these past months, over and over again. Rutting against and rending flesh. Killing humans and gorging on muscle and blood. He'd reveled in the fear he drove into the others, but none of this had truly sated him. Now, this little pink creation, this child made from his DNA and that of his sister, rested in his arms, and the anger was smothered with a sense of helplessness and, dare he think it—*love?*

The baby nuzzled against his chest, as if to find comfort in his warmth and, perhaps, his smell. She would need to eat very soon. He wondered if she were like him. Could she survive until they found food she would eat? Could she die?

The thought of her death shook his body, the bile of fear rising past his throat, coating his tongue with bitterness. It pained him to realize that now, after he'd acquired body mass, strength, and power, after he'd realized his invincibility, he'd actually created his own Achilles' heel. He was vulnerable, and powerless to help her.

Not powerless. The strength of the words came from somewhere deep inside him. They *would* help his daughter. Their lives, and the rest of those they hoped to save, depended on it.

THIRTY FOUR

December 19, 06:01

Gevu looked up with the soft knock on his cabin door. The train had only been moving for ten minutes or so. His door opened before he could decide if he wanted to see anyone, and a tiny, wizened woman shuffled in, a tea tray in her hands. He would have sent her away, except instead of tea, she had two infant bottles filled with a golden-colored liquid. She set the tray on a table by his chair and turned to go.

"Stop!" He hadn't had much interaction with this woman, but from her smell and her features, he had assumed she was Heung's mother. The woman came to a halt, and before he knew it, she was facing him. Had he seen her actually turn?

"Yes?" Her voice reminded him of the sound of wild prairie grasses dancing in the wind. It was soft, yet persistent. Gentle, but resilient. This was a very different human being. Very different from Heung.

Gevu gestured toward the bottles. "What are these?"

"Tea."

"For the baby?"

"Unless you prefer your tea in bottles as well."

"What kind of tea?" He was irritated at this woman who failed to treat him with deference. All others either bowed or cowered before him. This woman didn't act as if she were superior, not like the White Coats, but instead acted as if it didn't matter who he was.

"It will help the baby."

He looked over at the bottles and picked one up. It was warm. "What's..."

The woman was gone. Curious.

Trying not to wake the sleeping girl, he dabbed the nipple on his other hand and sniffed the wetness. Peppermint, lemon scent, and others he couldn't identify. He tasted a few drops. Slightly sweet. The baby stirred, her snout flaring, and her head stretched forward.

She must like the smell of it. He considered feeding it to her, but decided to test it further first. He snapped his fingers, and an attendant rose from a pillow on the far side of the room.

"Drink."

She accepted the bottle from him, her hands trembling, and placed her mouth to the rubber nipple and tentatively sucked.

"More."

He heard her swallow, once, twice, and with the third time, he held up his hand, observing that some of the liquid in the bottle was gone.

"Enough. Hand it here." He kept her standing there for two to three minutes, observing her balance. She was fine. He waved her away.

His daughter was now fully awake, staring at the bottle, her pink face screwing up into what would most likely result in an explosion of fitful cries. Gevu placed the nipple to her mouth, and she sucked on it greedily. In less than a minute, the liquid was gone.

The baby looked up at him, continuing to suck at the empty bottle. He tested the drops of the other bottle, sniffing and tasting, making sure they were the same, and then he gave her that one as well. She finished it more slowly, but drank every drop and fell asleep with the nipple still in her mouth. He gently removed it, experiencing another feeling he wasn't familiar with. The baby squeaked and cuddled against his chest once more. Gevu's eyes became cloudy, and he sniffed back the moisture that had gathered at the end of his snout.

Relief. And gratitude.

He dared not look the attendants' way. No one could be allowed to see this sudden weakness inside him. Instead, he stared at the baby and tried to imagine the species, and the empire, he would build with her. She was his instrument for success and revenge.

His eyes grew heavy, and the quiet lulling of the train pulled him into the most restful sleep he'd had in months.

"What do we do now?" Binah looked at the fence line, which was visible in the distance. The razor wire circled over the top of the main fence was fairly new. She could tell, because it was still bright and shiny, glittering in the sun.

Ben hadn't pulled to a stop, but was allowing the vehicle to creep slowly along the road. He was obviously trying to decide what to do next.

She placed her hand on his leg, and he looked over at her. His face was pinched, like he was in pain.

"It's okay. They know we're coming." She hoped her words would help push him forward.

He stared at the road, then put his foot to the gas and headed toward the gate.

While Binah understood his prior hesitation, the truth was, there were very few choices to make. The Black Comet would be here in a matter of days, and their only chance of survival rested with Chet and whoever was in charge. There was only one likely candidate. Harper. And if it *was* Harper, she wasn't looking forward to seeing him again. Last time, she had almost ended up inside the body of a brain-dead soldier. She shuddered.

What are his plans for me now?

The guard's office was made of rickety old plywood. It was rust colored, the same hue as the surrounding earth, and looked like it had been painted over and over again so many times that it was probably composed of more paint than wood. Their SUV crept forward. There was one guard at the gate.

Ben pulled up, and the guard came out.

"ID?"

Ben handed him his license. The guard looked it over.

"Wait here." He went back to the plywood shack, and Binah saw him pick up a telephone. He said a few words into the receiver, watching them the entire time. When he came back, he returned Ben's license and opened the gate.

"Pull through and stop on the other side. Someone will be here to meet you in a few minutes."

That was an understatement. Just before they could come to a halt on the other side of the fence, a Humvee pulled up in front of them. Two armed men in black uniforms got out, and one walked over to Ben's side of the SUV.

"Please get out of the vehicle, sir, and come with us." The other man was on Binah's side, motioning for her to join them as well. Binah glanced at Ben and then felt compelled to question the soldier. "Where are we going?"

"Just come with us, ma'am. We need to get you both below."

Ben didn't seem surprised. He must have expected where they'd be going. But then, he was the one with the underground home and lab. With what she'd learned about ISON 2 and the Black Comet, it made sense. But she wondered what good she'd be to the Cullers now. They couldn't eat her, thanks to her virus. And unless they'd transferred all of the brain-dead soldiers here, the contents of her head were safe.

Binah pressed the handle on the door and managed to pull herself out only seconds before she heard another vehicle gunning its engines behind her. She whirled around when a thunderous crash told her that something had hit the gate. It was a charcoal Toyota four door, and behind the wheel was a blond woman with wild, deranged eyes. She stuck her left hand out of the window and fired a few rounds from a pistol while aiming her car straight for them. The soldier guarding Binah couldn't fire his rifle in time and jumped to the side, and his partner aimed and squeezed off a few rounds before Ben launched himself at the man, knocking him over. The rifle hit the ground, and Ben snatched it up just as the blond woman screeched to a halt. Her pistol was pointed at the soldier next to Binah.

"Drop your weapon and move away from her!"

The soldier let his firearm drop to the ground and backed away.

The blond woman got out of the car and picked it up. "Don't worry, guys. We're going to follow you. We're just going to do it on our own terms." She gestured with her head. "Now, get in your Hummer!"

Both soldiers looked confused but moved slowly toward the Humvee. The woman fired a shot in the air, grabbing their attention. "Get moving!"

Ben got back into the driver's seat of the SUV, Stella walked over to ride shotgun. Binah climbed in the rear seat. The entire back end of the SUV sank low, almost touching the ground.

The soldiers got into their vehicle. Binah could well imagine the conversation they were having over the radio with their boss right now.

The woman looked at both of them. "Name is Stella. You don't know me, but I know a shitload about the both of you. What I don't know is why you're here. Hell, I'm not even sure I know why *I'm* here except there's something big going on, and, Binah, you're a huge part of it. You both have no reason to trust me, but it will be in your best interest to fill me in as quickly as you can. When we get where we're going, no telling what will happen."

The soldiers had turned their Humvee around and made their way across the compound while Stella followed. Ben gave the woman details, and Binah watched her eyes and listened to the lilt of her voice. She decided she liked this woman. Something made her feel as if she could trust her. Her scent was familiar, but she couldn't place where she'd smelled it before. Dilapidated buildings lined the streets of the compound. The wind kicked up dry reddish-tan dust and whistled around the rooftops. There was not a person in sight. It was a military ghost town.

Ahead of them loomed a large bunker set into a hill and sealed by a wall of steel. The Humvee kept moving forward, and as it drew nearer, the center of the wall parted into a huge gaping maw with rows of overhead lighting and small red lights lining the walls.

What are we getting ourselves in to? Binah remembered that day in the kitchen, when she had observed two flies trapped between the windowpanes at the Bakersfield farmhouse. One living. One dead.

Like the flies, they were trapped now. There was no place to run. Staying outside would only guarantee certain death in the coming days. Going inside might do the same, but their survival was dependent on it and they'd have to deal with whatever they found there.

Ben looked at her from the rearview mirror. "It will be okay."

She smiled back at him, watching her own reflection. What did he see in her? Whatever it was, her heart soared knowing that at least once in her life she'd known love.

Stella tapped the dash, and their attention focused forward. The Humvee was coming to a stop. Both men got out and walked toward them. Stella and Ben got out as well, and Binah followed.

"This is our stop." The larger man of the two seemed much more confident than he had before. "We need to take the elevator down. This way."

Both men walked past the Humvee to a panel on the wall. One of them pressed a button. When the elevator car came after a good two minutes, they all managed to squeeze inside, with Ben and Stella still keeping the noses of their firearms trained on the soldiers.

Long minutes went by. Down, down, and further down.

Jeez, how far does it go? It reminded her of Point Mugu.

The elevator slowed, and it chimed before the doors opened. The two men stepped out and moved to the right, and Binah immediately saw what she'd partly expected. There stood Harper with an entourage of soldiers behind him. What she hadn't expected was the person beside him in a wheelchair. Chet's grin was just as malicious above ground as it was below, and she wondered what had happened to him, but not enough to ask. Not now. Not ever. A sour taste sprung to her mouth.

Stella looked shaken, and Ben's fingers trembled near the trigger of the firearm.

"Harper..." His voice was shaky too.

"Let's dispense with formalities, shall we? Please hand back your weapons, and allow me to take you on a tour." He straightened his tie.

Four soldiers stepped forward and took the assault rifles from their hands. They'd entered the Underground of their own free will, but Binah suspected this was the end of any freedom they'd have for a while. A long, shiny tunnel, with walls that glittered like melted glass, stretched into the distance. It was very wide. Wide enough for six, or maybe eight, Humvees to drive side by side. Along the walls of the tunnel, there were rounded doorways, entrances to other tunnels.

Harper turned into the second one on the right, and that tunnel descended at an angle even further into the ground. He stopped at a thickly layered glass door. It was a good forty feet across. Maybe twenty feet high. He ran his identification card into a monitor that was much like the ones Binah had seen at Point Mugu. When the door opened, the acrid stench of chemicals and biologic fluids assaulted her nose. The rest of the group hadn't reacted, but the smell attacked Binah's senses, and she gagged.

"You are no doubt aware of the comet ISON 2 headed this way. And I'm guessing you know about the Black Comet as well?" Their little party was silent.

If I could just click some ruby slippers together...

The huge glass tubes caught Binah's attention first. There were hundreds of them lined up in rows. Inside, a fluid suspended the remains of a wide variety of creatures. Some with gross malformations, others not so clearly malformed. She examined one that looked like the spliced-DNA creation of an ostrich and a giraffe. Another resembled a black bear crossed with some kind of lizard. They walked past these macabre models until Binah realized that as they advanced, the bodies looked more and more human.

"There were so many failures." Harper stopped at one large glass tube. The small child inside had claws and tan fur. He seemed no more than four or five years old.

A mountain lion and human mix?

"And so, we realized we needed the brightest minds to help us solve the problem of survivability. We needed organ donors while living beneath the earth. Perfect matches. Unless we could manufacture them, we couldn't be guaranteed that our population would survive."

Binah felt a sting in her arm, and soldiers surrounded them. She dropped to her knees.

"Welcome home, Project Juliet. It's good to have you back." She looked up at Harper. His face started to fade. "You're finally where you belong."

"Binah!" It was Ben's voice. She loved him. But she knew the moment she saw Harper that this wasn't going to end well. Two men grabbed her under her arms.

They'll need more than these wimps to carry me. She closed her eyes, and the world faded away.

The baby cried, and Gevu woke. His attendant was already standing by him, ready. The low hum of the train stopped, and his cabin door opened.

"Take her!" The attendant reached for the girl and held her close. The car jiggled when he got up, and he grabbed his weapon. Four black-clad soldiers entered the room, their firearms aimed directly at him. They didn't move forward, but instead flanked the door. Gevu realized they were waiting for someone else. Steady footfalls preceded the man who entered the door, but Gevu knew who it was before he entered.

Harper stepped across the threshold. The man spoke at him, not to him.

"And now, we welcome Project Kilo back into our fold. He'll be happy to join his sister."

Binah! Binah was here?

His hand tightened on his weapon. Harper's eyes dispassionately flickered to the metal he held in his hands, and then zeroed in on Gevu's daughter.

"Project Lima. We've been waiting for her."

Two men moved forward toward the girl, and Gevu let loose a growl.

"You will not touch her!" He felt the hair on his neck stand on end. Adrenaline surged throughout his body. He could take these small men. His stomach rumbled. And, he was hungry.

One side of Harper's mouth turned up just slightly. "Let me explain something to you. In a matter of days, the world as you know it is going to end above ground. The only hope for everyone's survival is in *this* Underground. You were designed to help mankind survive. But, she and her kind are the key to *everything*. Do you understand? We have many more like her out there, growing inside forty other women, so your daughter is also...expendable. You can fight if you want, but in the end, it won't matter."

Gevu looked at his baby. Small, helpless, unable to feed. They would all starve without this man's help, if they *could* starve. He suspected Harper had scientists well equipped to develop a food her body would accept. Then he remembered Binah. *Perhaps Binah could feed her!*

Now was not the time to fight. There'd be time for that later. He'd learn their system. Learn their plans. He'd escaped before, and he could do it again.

But where would I go? He'd figure that out once he got the lay of the land. His fingers released the metal, and the rake clattered to the floor.

Harper's lips pursed approvingly, as if he were pleased that Gevu had made the soundest, most rational decision.

Gevu was determined to land at least one blow. "Miriam is dead."

Harper's eyes met his, the briefest moment of shock registering in the muscles around them. "Pity. She was a good agent." He directed his men toward the baby. "Escort the woman and the infant to the holding area." They took the attendant away.

"You'll follow me." Harper walked from the room.

Gevu bent down and picked up his weapon. No, now was not the time, but there would be an opportunity, of that he was sure. He didn't believe in a god. He was his own god. But he found himself swearing that when the opportunity came, he'd rend the man's head from his shoulders and devour his body. Drool dripped from the corners of his mouth, and he wiped it away.

He's gonna taste good.

THIRTY FIVE

December 20, 13:02

"Sir, the president has given the order. Most of the remaining troops are going underground. He'll be on his way here in two more days."

Harper stared down at the body bag. All of the pieces had come together. Everything had finally worked out just as planned.

Everything but this.

The stainless steel room was so cold he could see his breath. He wondered if he dared to open the bag, to see the woman he'd come so close to loving. As close as he had ever dared to love.

"Sir?"

Harper didn't look at him. He waved the man away to acknowledge he'd heard. A door shut behind him.

Alone at last.

His fingers reached for the zipper, then pulled away. Had something in the bag just moved? He waited. All was still. A trick of the brain. He grabbed the zipper's tab and pulled down, revealing the naked woman down to her navel. Her face was peaceful and appeared almost like a homemade doll's head right before the paint was applied to the cheeks and lips. Miriam's red hair beckoned to him, and he ran his fingers through some of it. It was slightly damp. He remembered how it had always smelled like roses.

There was no harm now exploring the aloof Miriam here. One of his best students, and one of the more enjoyable minds to toy with—now just a shell. He cupped her jaw and kissed her lips. They were not as stiff or cold as he had imagined. His palms moved over her breasts, and he stroked them, the nipples hardening under his touch.

"Shit!" His body shook with the realization of what had just happened, and what it meant.

He pulled out his two-way radio. "Operations!"

"Operations, over."

"This is Harper. Get a medical team to the morgue now!"

"Roger that, sir!"

Harper stood over Miriam once more and carefully zipped the bag back up, leaving only her neck and head exposed. His eyes watered, and he blinked back the wave that wanted to curl and break over his lower eyelids. He was beyond thrilled inside, knowing that his desire, his greatest goal, was still possible.

He'd waited for years, had groomed this woman to expect anything, to calculate, and to think in the direst of circumstances, so that in the future, she could still give him the thing he most craved. The thing he'd longed for, ever since he had met her. His fingers flexed in anticipation, and he thought about how he had almost been robbed of his dream—his dream of wrapping his fingers around Miriam's white throat and watching her die.

Binah looked around her prison cell. It was bare with white walls, white ceiling—even the benches were white. Her head ached. The bright lights didn't help. The video cameras in the upper corners of the walls reminded her of the captivity of her life. The disturbing thing was that it all felt so normal. Her time with Ben in the mountains seemed like a dream.

When will I ever truly be free?

A knock at the door startled her. It opened, and a short Asian woman shuffled in holding a blanket in her arms. The door shut behind her, and the woman moved slowly toward Binah. The blanket stirred and squeaked.

Binah's heart, which had, only moments before, languished with a rhythm of dull, dry beats, sparked to life. Adrenaline coursed through her. *No. Impossible.*

The woman's hand opened the blanket to reveal a small and lovely creature, and it stretched out its arms and legs, yawned, and rubbed its snout. Binah didn't want to rise up, to go closer, but some greater instinct pushed her forward until the little baby was in her arms. It cuddled against her. The woman backed away.

"It is girl." Binah heard the halted whisper just before the door opened and let the woman out again.

She sniffed the girl. *So sweet. So precious. But how?* She'd had the pregnancy removed. Her uterus. Her ovaries. And yet, this child in her arms was most certainly her daughter. And her brother's.

The baby's eyes fluttered open. Her abdomen gurgled, and a pained look crossed the girl's face. She opened her mouth and whimpered. The whimper became a cry. Binah looked around. There was nothing in this room to comfort the baby other than herself. No food. No water.

She's an infant. She needs milk. The thoughts pressed in on her. But, she hadn't birthed the baby. How could she be expected to feed her? She wondered who had birthed this child and how she had come to be here.

White Coats. The Cullers. How had they known?

The baby was still crying, and it rooted against her chest, seeking comfort. In her frustration, Binah gave in and lifted her shirt. The infant immediately found a nipple and latched on to it.

Shit! That hurts! She wanted to pull away, but the baby was satisfied for now. *Suckling on a dry breast must be better than none.* Her body tingled. She grabbed the baby securely, sat down on the floor, and then lay on her side. The strange tingling continued, but Binah felt warm, oddly placid and happy. Her eyes grew heavy, and she cuddled the child against her as it continued to suckle. Binah fell into a slumber, where dreams came to her filled with hundreds of babies all crying for her breasts.

Heung stared at the video screen and then looked over at the god. *Zhu Bajie* seemed unconcerned, and so Heung set his own mind at ease. If the sister could make the milk the girl child needed, then that would be good. Very good. Behind them, the man named Harper, the same man who'd first taken *Zhu Bajie* from him, watched the scene unfold as well.

"We'll need her for the first few progeny, of course. After that, both of you will go back to your testing until we need you."

Heung didn't know what that meant. What did they plan for his god? And what were they planning for *him*? It was unclear if they would let him live. For the time being, they seemed amenable to having him here.

"You and your sister serve higher purposes. You're, of course, aware of the Black Comet?" The god didn't answer, and Heung sat still, upright, and behaved likewise.

"That comet will strike Earth on the fourth of January. On that day, the world as we know it will be gone. We'd had plans to use your kind to help us with feeding the masses in addition to providing medical solutions for those in need, but your sister has...complicated things for us, and it is too late to change everything we've prepared for."

Heung wasn't sure what the man was saying. Was he saying that they'd planned to use *Zhu Bajie* and his sister as food all along? Food to feed the thousands housed under the ground? How were two of them supposed to feed an entire population? He thought about *Zhu Bajie*'s miraculous ability to heal and the babies growing in the women he'd brought with him, and a wave of nausea hit him. He'd unintentionally brought a substantial food supply to this man. One he couldn't use right now. So why keep them?

"Our scientists are working on an immunization against the virus. We may have a cure in a matter of weeks, or maybe months. Until then, we'll need you for other things." Harper didn't explain further. He let the comment hang in the air like a dangerous thundercloud.

The man touched Heung on the shoulder. The familiarity implied in his gesture was immediately offensive, but Heung tolerated it. He must seem accepting. He must appear understanding. It may help *Zhu Bajie* in the future.

"Mr. Heung, I will need you to help attend to the women you brought with you. You'll assist Dr. Ling with whatever she needs."

Heung maintained his silence, but inside he seethed. This man had reduced him to the role of a servant. Logically, however, it was preferable to being dead. He longed to ask what they'd done with his mother, but he dared not. They had no reason to guess who she was, *if* they'd found her.

Harper snapped his fingers, and his men flanked either side of *Zhu Bajie*. "My men will escort you to your room. As long as you continue your exemplary behavior, your sister and your daughter will be fine."

Zhu Bajie nodded and stood up from the floor. It was the only place he could sit because there wasn't a chair in the room that would hold his enormous frame. If only they knew who they were dealing with. *Zhu Bajie*'s stomach rumbled. Everyone in the room heard it.

Harper smiled. "Let's get you something to eat now, shall we?"

Without having the luxury of picking strays from the streets, Heung wondered what they would feed his god. At the very least, he hoped the meal would be worthy.

THIRTY SIX

December 26, 03:11

Chet chewed on a wad of Redman and rolled along the corridor until he reached a steel door. Two guards were posted outside.

"Here to see the prisoner!" God *damn,* he was happy.

"Sorry, sir. We can't let you do that."

He expected as much. Ah, the days when he had thought he knew what duty was and how important it was to follow orders. He lowered his chin and mumbled his next words. The guard closest to him bent down. "Sir?"

Chet lifted his head and butted the guard hard in the forehead, then grabbed the man's gun. *Man? Nah, this kid's a boy.* The boy fell to the floor, dazed. Having the advantage of surprise, Chet was able to point the weapon at the other guard before he could properly respond.

"Hand it over, boy." The guard stretched out his arm and gave him the weapon. Chet swung his rifle wicked fast and cold-cocked him in the head with the butt. He went down faster than a woman's slap from an insult. He knocked the other one out as well before he could fully recover.

"Yeah, I'm gonna pay for this later, but there's no time like the present for a little retribution."

He grabbed one of the guard's hands and pressed it against the electronic faceplate. A blue light scanned it, and the door unlocked.

"Much obliged."

He entered the room, wondering what condition the pig was in.

Holy shit on a shingle, this is sweet!

The pig bastard was in irons across the room. Judging from how they had him trussed up, he was barely able to move. The pig's eyes were trained on him from the moment he rolled in. Was there some amusement there? He'd show the pig some amusement. Chet pulled out his bull knife.

"You and I have some reacquainting to do."

"Yeah? Walk on over here then." The pig was ballsy even though he was bound tighter than a nun's asshole.

"Heh. You think you're funny." Chet neared Gevu's leg and plunged the bull knife into his thigh. Gevu growled, but the noise he made wasn't very satisfactory. Chet sliced a few more times and pulled a chunk out the size of a five-pound roast. Gevu groaned and then bellowed when Chet pulled the bloody chunk out. *Hell, if I had a slow cooker...* But he didn't have a slow cooker, and it wouldn't matter if he did. His meat-eating days were over until Harper's scientists found a cure for that pesky virus.

Chet tossed the chunk of flesh into the air and caught it. The pig resolutely stared at him, as if boring a hole through his head. But Chet knew how to really hurt him. He'd watched from the control room when Harper had met them at the train. He knew all about the pig's little bundle of joy. He settled the meat in his lap. He'd take it and freeze it. Soon as he could safely eat animals again, this would be the first thing he'd have on his plate.

His time was probably close to running out. Security would be turning over in a few minutes. He'd have a lot to answer for when they did, but in this place, all he had was time. Grabbing his wheels, he rolled back toward the door.

"Got a look at that baby of yours, Porky. Real cute. I'm thinking it's almost time for her to meet a real man. Too bad she'll never see her father again." He looked over his shoulder and winked at the beast. *One more thing. This oughta do it.* "Your sister's looking mighty sweet too. Time has made her ass look nice and cushy. I'll bet she's been waiting for me to plow her again. You got my legs, but you still left me what counts. Thank you kindly, ol' buddy. I'll be sure to use it again to make the girls scream."

His cock had grown hard just talking his smack and thinking about the things he could do to those sows. And the roar that came from the piggy's throat made his day. He almost spurted out some jism from the thrill of it. Tomorrow, he'd set out to find where Harper had the little girly and the sister stashed. After all, he never made threats without making them come true.

Binah is here. Gevu wanted to see her. Somehow, he knew that together, they'd find a way to escape. But she was also aware he'd raped her. He'd heard that on the bugs Miriam had planted at Skylar's place. He couldn't blame her if she never wanted to see him again. But, if he could just explain, he would tell her that it hadn't been like that—that in the end, he hadn't been able to actually do it.

But I did do it. Just not the way someone thinks of raping a woman. And they had a beautiful little girl. It dawned on him that if Binah was here, perhaps Harper had found a way for her to make milk for the baby. Despite the pain in his leg, it was a comforting thought. But did Binah know about Miriam's role? Did she know Miriam had grown the baby in her own body?

He looked down at his leg, trying to ignore the awful fiery sensation his nerves screamed to his brain. All in all, he'd had worse the day he was shot. He watched, fascinated as the blood stopped flowing. Little by little, the muscle knitted together from the inside out. It would be healed within an hour or two.

His stomach gurgled. Last night they'd fed him thirty chickens or so. He had been famished and had downed the lot, bones and all. They were nowhere near as satisfying as human flesh, but he'd survive. He'd play their little game until he had a handle on things, and when he did, then he'd finally eat human flesh again.

December 26, 05:30

Ben had short moments with Stella from time to time. Their holding cells were next door to each other; at mealtimes, the soldiers brought them into a common room. This morning, the TV on the wall showed the passing of ISON 2. It had come dangerously close, but in the end, it had whizzed by Earth, bound for its journey around the sun. But today, ISON 2 didn't have top billing. The news was finally out about the Black Comet. Its impact was plotted to strike the northeast side of Saudi Arabia, close to Jordan.

Pandemonium reigned in all of the large cities. People were taking what they could and heading to malls or underground to the subways—anywhere that could possibly be safe.

"They're only now getting the news? What took so long?" Stella ignored her breakfast, her attention more directed at the television. Somebody could have warned those people. If she hadn't felt protective and nosey about Ben and Binah, she'd be out there too.

"From what I read, a black comet is extremely hard to see. Its coma is dark and isn't illuminated by the sun. They've only been theoretical until now, and most astronomers haven't been able to see this one. They don't reflect light. There's been speculation about what it's made up of, but no one really knows. What they do know is that unlike typical comets that shed their mass as they near the sun, these grow larger and denser."

"How big is this one supposed to be?"

"The average comet is three to four miles in diameter. This one's projected to be six or more."

"Miles?" She looked up at the map displayed on the television. "Guess we won't have to worry about peace talks between Israel and Palestine in the future."

Ben took a sip of coffee.

She didn't have anything else to say and felt stupid making small talk, but she blurted out the obvious before she could hold it back. "So, after January fourth, we're trapped here like rats on a ship." *Damn. How does a gal not sound stupid in front of a guy like him? PhD. Scientist.*

"Something like that."

The door to their room opened. Harper walked in. He looked at Ben. "Come with me."

Ben shot her an I've-got-no-idea-what-this-is-about eyebrow raise, and she hoped she conveyed the it-will-be-okay look. Then she felt stupid once more because nothing about any of this was really okay.

———

The guard sat down and watched what would, sadly, be the last few days of TV. God, how he was going to miss it. Reruns of

Breaking Bad, his morning Fox News, the *Rush Limbaugh Show*. Had they saved the American icon and brought him below? Jesus, he hoped so. Just as much as he hoped they let people like Howard Stern, Rachel Maddow, and Jon Stewart burn in the coming hell. People like that didn't deserve a God-fearing community to live in.

He looked away from the TV and thought he saw a shadow pass by his door. "Hello?" He got up from his chair, wishing he wasn't on duty alone. His partner had come down with a stomach bug. *He probably tried to eat meat.* What an idiot. Hopefully they'd find a cure for the strange virus. He desperately wanted a real hamburger, or maybe some steak. Those foo-foo veggie patties just didn't cut it.

He looked out into the open weapons bay. There was some massive firepower there, by God. You name it; they had it. Although, he couldn't imagine whom they'd use it against once the topside world was destroyed. He heard a small noise by the grenades. Someone was in here. But no fucking way someone could be in here. This place had security. Those doors wouldn't open for just anyone.

The cleaning room door was open. The stink of old, sour mops was unmistakable. He stuck his head in to make sure it was clear before he shut it. A pair of hands grabbed his wrists and, quick as lightning, bound them together. *What the hell?* He wouldn't have believed it if he hadn't seen it. Who was that lady? She took his firearm and his radio.

The cleaning room door closed on him, locking him in. He'd have a fucking hard time explaining this, but maybe they'd provide a stand-in the next time a partner called in. At least he'd probably never have to work a shift alone again.

Harper hadn't called for him yet. That was a really good thing. Chet had been meaning to stop by the weapons depot and find some supplies. He could test out the security and see how good it was. Yeah, that's what he could tell Harper. "I was just testing out your security." Of course, that wouldn't explain the blood on the floor, and the piggy's wounded leg. But, if he were extremely lucky, the pig's leg would have healed by then. With the end of the world on its way, he sincerely doubted anyone had time to look at the security cams. That made him feel better.

There was no one at the security office of the weapons station. Chet would have just rolled in, except the doorway to the office was too small for a wheelchair. He had to open the main steel doors.

No fuss, no muss. He dragged himself out of the chair and into the main control room. The switch to the double door was labeled. Chet flipped it, and they opened.

Kid in a candy store and no parents.

He rolled in and found a machete, some grenades, and a couple of Colts. The semiautomatics on a rack looked like payday, but he doubted he could take more than one down the tunnels without being noticed. He grabbed one, then put a piece of green canvas he found on the floor over his lap. It covered his weapons nicely.

A sound in the closet caught his attention. What the hell? He might as well check it out. Security wasn't here. He rolled over to the door, opened it wide, and almost laughed out loud. Apparently someone else thought it was a good idea to have some firepower ahead of time. Chet kept his eyes on the man whose cheeks were redder than any ass he'd ever smacked. He put his finger to his lips. "Hey, bud. You were never in this closet, and I was never here. You got that?" He pulled his wheels in reverse, spun around, and rolled out of the weapons depot.

Things just kept getting better and better. Finally, he was on the upswing again.

December 29, 03:03

Stella's door opened. She might have slept through the soft click, except that sleep hadn't come to her easily tonight. Her mind was riddled with questions, anxious about the future, and she tried not to think of all the innocent people above ground who would die. *Billions.* Men, women, and children soon to be wiped out by a giant black rock.

Would Harper send someone in the night to dispose of her now? Probably not. Which meant her visitor was someone else. She lay still. Light footsteps padded over, just out of reach of her bunk. A small bundle dropped on the floor.

"Get dressed. Come outside when ready."

Impossible! But she recognized the voice.

As quietly as they came, the footsteps padded away, but the door did not click. Stella rose and put on the clothing on the floor. They felt like the uniforms she'd seen. She emerged from the room and almost bumped into Ben. The light was faint, but she could still see him. She looked down. They were both wearing soldier uniforms.

"Here."

The little old woman from Heung's underground home stood in front of her. Ben may not have seen her before, but Stella was sure it was the same woman. *What is she doing here? Had she come with Heung?* She had so many questions, but no time to ask them. She looked down at the woman's hands. Two uniform hats and two pistols. Stella wasted no time and put the firearm at the back of her belt. Ben fumbled with it after watching her, and then did the same. *God, I hope he never has to shoot anything. No time for range practice.*

The woman escorted them past two sleeping guards, and they kept to the darker sides of the corridors until they came to a door. The woman whisked in and motioned them to follow. The room was alive with electronics and screens, and there was even orange juice and cookies.

She pulled out a map and pointed to a location, circling it with pen. It was labeled Dulce. They were at the Dulce facility. A number of lines ran from the facility to different places, but one of the largest intersections was just west of Boulder. Apache Peak.

How much control did Harper have over that area? If they got to Apache Peak, would they be free?

The woman pointed to a screen. Stella recognized Binah resting on a mattress. She slept curled up with a small puppy, or something—she couldn't tell. She looked over at Ben. His eyes were huge, and he brought his face closer to the screen.

Ben's gaze flicked back to the old woman. "I need to zoom in." She shook her head. She didn't know how to do it. He squinted close to the screen again.

"We have to get her out of there. Quick as we can!"

The old woman flashed a smile; her crooked teeth made her look almost adorable, except in this situation there was little that was adorable.

She brought out a map of the compound. *Jeez, this woman was resourceful. How the hell did she manage to get all of these things?* Her finger traced a line from where Stella assumed they were at to where Binah was being held. It was fairly close. Just a couple of tunnels away.

The woman beelined out the door, leaving the final question on the tip of Stella's tongue. Assuming they got to Binah, assuming they escaped, how were they going to get to Apache Peak? Perhaps thinking was something she'd be better off not doing right now.

Miriam was hungry. She hoped they'd bring breakfast soon. Every day, three times a day, she'd had nothing but soy protein shakes blended with fruits and vegetables. They weren't the nectar of the Gods, but they had kept her alive. Her body had responded to the complex nutrients, and today she was feeling top notch.

Harper had visited her once or twice, just to see how she was doing. Otherwise, Heung's pregnant female attendants had waited on her, and each time she had seen their pregnant bellies, she'd longed for her own little girl. Harper assured her she'd see the baby in time, but he was vague as to how she was doing. Yes, she was feeding okay, he'd said. Yes, she was sleeping all right. But he had fielded her specific questions and whisked out of the door before she could ask more.

Well, it's time for me to get back into the business of living.

If Harper refused to give her answers, then she'd find them herself.

Hard to believe that just a few days ago I was dead.

She rose from the bed, curious as to what really lay beyond the door, and hesitated. She needed clothes. A full set of clothing, all black, rested on a chair beside the bed. She checked them over. Her size. Acceptable. On the floor were soft boots and a pair of socks. They fit well.

A digital clock on a file cabinet served as a makeshift nightstand. Red numbers glowed. 04:00. Well, maybe she could drum up some coffee or something. She flicked on a light switch; her eyes squinted from the overhead lights. She lifted her shirt and looked at her abdomen again. She'd been taken apart and put back together, and there was barely a scar to prove it. A gun holster hung on the wall. Was it hers? She checked the make and model. There was no mistaking it. She put it on and suddenly felt like her old self.

The next thing to consider was whether she was locked in the room, or free to come and go as she desired. The handle turned easily, and the door opened when she pulled it. A short hallway led from her room to a larger tunnel. She followed it, paying strict attention to her surroundings. Small vehicles drove in the center as if on miniature highways. People rode on Segways or walked along the sides. After close to a quarter of a mile, the tunnel suddenly opened up into a gigantic amphitheater. It was acres wide.

How could something like this exist underground?

There were stars overhead, and just like outside, she could tell the dawn was coming. A slight pink colored the roof of the eastern side. It was amazing. There were trees, except every kind of tree was a fruit or nut tree. Herbs grew in patches. Vegetables hung from ornate planters. People walked by the vegetation, picking a handful of berries or plucking a tomato. And above ground, it was winter! A waterfall splashed through the center of the area, and bridges crossed it. People gathered water at a shoreline; others cupped their hands and drank freely from it. This was paradise.

"Welcome to my home."

"Your home?"

"I grew up here." Harper's voice held a tone in it she'd never heard before. It was almost sad.

Miriam said nothing. She didn't ask how he'd found her. She assumed he'd placed a tracking device on her. He'd become so predictable.

"You're no doubt hungry. Let's get you food. Something better than those protein shakes?"

Miriam nodded. He pointed down another tunnel.

"We developed our cities similarly to modern day malls. It worked out better having certain districts, such as one for food, one for clothing, etc. Most things can be delivered. There's an underground computer network here, much like above."

They stopped at a noodle shop.

"Good pho here. I know you like it. Just no animal protein. We're still working on that. Project Juliet threw us for a loop with that one. Luckily, we've got millions of pounds of rice and bean stores, and other nonanimal nutrients."

"Where's Binah?"

"She's okay."

"Where's my baby?"

Harper sighed. "She's with Project Juliet. It seems she's the only one who could feed her." He paused and ordered two bowls of noodle soup.

Miriam had an intense feeling well up inside her, and realized it was jealousy. Binah had, for all intents and purposes, destroyed *her* child. She had decided on abortion. It was Miriam who had grown the baby, cared for her. She'd looked forward to raising and teaching her.

"It's just for now, Miriam. She'll be on solids before long. Then we won't need Project Juliet."

Why does Harper refuse to call Binah by her name? She supposed he preferred to see her as a creature. A continuing experiment. As she always said, "To name them is to get too close." And she'd crossed the line of objectivity, according to the world aboveground. But here, in this place where the world was new, perhaps she could help to write a new approach to research. One that should have been done a long time ago. There were too many rules and regulations right now. It was impossible to get a human study passed through an IRB without severe restrictions. Here, she could do the research she wanted. For an instant, she almost forgot how Harper had betrayed her. Kept her captive. Treated her like an animal. She continued to smile. He had to think she'd let bygones be bygones.

"Thank you." Miriam watched as the server scanned Harper's arm with a handheld device. He smiled at her. "Subcutaneous chip. We don't use money here. Everything operates on accumulated credits or on the bargaining system. It works very well."

She swallowed some of the soup the server brought her. It was tangy. Excellent! Harper watched her carefully. She ate the chunks of protein mixed in with the cilantro and lemon. Delicious! It was amazing. It tasted just like fish. She finished it quickly and almost wanted another.

"Shall we take you to see your baby?"

It was about time. Miriam ached to see the child. She felt odd about seeing Binah in her motherly capacity, but surely she'd understand that the child was now hers. And if she didn't understand it, there was still no cause for concern. Miriam would get the baby, and Binah would do what she was always meant to do.

THIRTY SEVEN

January 3, 22:05

Every hour that passed now, Binah lived in fear. It had been days since Miriam had come to see them. She'd wanted to take the baby then, but Harper had assured her the girl would be hers.

"Project Juliet is doing fine with Project Lima. She'll be finished nursing in just a few more days."

During Miriam's visit, she had barely glanced at Binah, but had taken the infant and held her close, tickling her chin. What bothered Binah most was that her baby didn't seem to mind. She hadn't screamed and cried for her mother, but instead, had nuzzled against Miriam like a longtime friend.

In the days after that visit, Binah had searched the room, explored every possible avenue for escape, and each day, she'd come up empty-handed. Her meals were delivered, and she came in contact with virtually no one. She was destined to lose her child, and her breasts ached with the knowledge.

The other thing she knew for sure was that tomorrow their world would change forever. She was fortunate, if it could be called fortunate, to have a small television in the room on which she was able to watch the news coverage of the end of the world. Humans panicked madly and beat on the doors of personal underground shelters. Several of those were breached and overrun with outlaws. There were shootings and horrific acts of violence—but then, some people were warmhearted and considerate as well. Heroic acts of kindness occurred everywhere.

Then, there were those who were simply resigned to their fate, who gathered with others to provide comfort and support. They prayed in churches and also outdoors in the communities. The poor and the well-to-do worked together to make the last day somehow bearable.

Binah brought her daughter to her chest, and the girl nursed vigorously, first emptying one breast and then another. *She will be taking solids any day now.* Binah trembled at the thought.

She realized this child was the love of her life. The only being she'd ever loved besides Ben. And where was Ben? She had no idea. Miriam didn't know, and Harper refused to say.

And what would become of her when they took her child away? Life wouldn't be worth living. She couldn't imagine it. What *could* she do?

You can fight.

Fight? But how? They were many. She was one. She looked up at the people praying to their gods. Who was her god? And if she prayed, would the god she supplicated to listen? She imagined a god who looked just like her. A motherly figure who embraced her and comforted her with love.

If you are there, dear Mother, I beg you to help me. Help me, and help my daughter to be free.

The power went out again. It was the tenth or eleventh time since he'd been here. With every occurrence, Gevu had heard the scramble of men trying to get controls up and running.

And with every power outage, *she* had come to see him. The woman was kind and seemed to genuinely care for him. Gevu could change his opinion of humans if all of them were like her. A warm cloth covered today's wounds. Yesterday's injuries were healing.

"Today, you leave."

Gevu wasn't sure he'd heard her correctly. Metal rattled. His shackles fell off, one by one. He could pound out of here—break this place! A small, aged hand touched him. It was illuminated by a glowing wristband. "No."

He looked down at her. Though he couldn't see her well in the darkness, he'd seen that face so full of wrinkles. She reminded him of a Shih Tzu, except she was much cuter. And he trusted her.

She handed him a map, and using a flashlight and a pen, she quickly oriented him to his surroundings. "No get distracted okay?" Her face was somber, her eyes wide and dark. "Get my son."

There was only one man who could be her son. Heung. Gevu couldn't take much time to ponder it, but he wondered how a man could be so different from his mother? She was wise. He was gullible. She was kind. He didn't know the true meaning of kindness.

"I'll get him. You have my word."

The electricity outages were plucking at Harper's nerves. They had occurred now and then, certainly, but since he'd brought Project Juliet and Project Kilo on board, they'd occurred much more frequently. He would check on the issue further, just as soon as he finished taking care of the leadership.

The power came back on, and the electronics flickered to life.

"Sir, the president is flying in. He's twenty miles out."

Harper experienced a moment of gratitude for his first man, Hudson. Hudson was not only trustworthy, but also dependable. Harper looked up at the screens in the command and control room. It was now or never, and there could be no hesitation on his part. He nodded to Hudson. "You know what to do."

Hudson made the call from the center of the room. "Team, operation realignment!" Ten men in black suits stepped up to various control areas.

Harper announced over the intercom, "The end of the world above ground is near! Our world has suffered over two centuries of poorly crafted government. When the comet hits, we will begin anew. Join me in the restructuring of our system! Together, we will continue to build a system that works!"

The room broke out in a cheer from many members, but others looked bewildered. Well, those members were new. They'd soon embrace the new world.

"Ten miles out, sir."

"Ready? Fire at will!"

Their screens showed the presidential helicopter flanked by many others. Some carried congressmen. Others carried billionaires. Missiles detonated. The sky was full of fire. Each bird went up in a burst of flames, and thousands of metal pieces fell to the ground. The President of the United States and the Congress—the US political system—were no more.

January 4, 01:33

Just like she'd done every night since the first time, the old woman picked the lock on his door and brought Ben his clothes. They were getting good at this now. He was surprised they weren't under such strict surveillance—but then again, where would they go? And the end of the world was probably more interesting to the security personnel than watching a couple of captives sleep.

He slipped on his uniform and met the woman outside. Stella was already there. He took a moment to ask a question, because he hadn't asked anything since she'd started all of this. He touched her on the arm. She was short and cute in a quirky sort of way. A little lady Yoda.

The Force is strong in this one...

"What is your name?"

The woman showed him her crooked teeth in response. She was amused, but he wasn't sure if it was because of the question or because he was just now getting around to asking her name. He looked over at Stella, and she shrugged. "We have to call you something."

She drew herself up, reminding him of someone preparing for battle. Her simple body language made him picture mountains and giant waterfalls.

"Mama Yang."

And like each night before, they followed her. They'd amassed several items and placed them in an odd storage room that never got used. It was as if someone had forgotten it was even there. It was the perfect hiding place. They'd even descended several levels below and found the subterrene vehicles used to travel lesser-known tunnels. Many of them had probably been used to dig those tunnels.

And tonight was to be the last of their outings. After this, they would live or, like the rest of the world outside, they would die.

Mama Yang stopped outside a door and picked a lock. The next door she stopped in front of required an electronic palm scan. She looked surprised for a moment, but hardly missed a beat.

"Wait here. Don't be seen."

She returned in less than ten minutes carrying something in a cloth. Ben backpedaled with revulsion when he realized what she carried was an actual hand.

Holy shit! She went out and got a human hand. She brought it back like she'd just gone shopping for, and returned with, a bag of onions. Who is this woman?

He made a mental note not to piss her off. Little Lady Yoda was sweet, but she had a Darth Vader lurking inside her, and she wasn't afraid to use him.

She pressed the hand to the panel. The door opened.

It had been so long since he'd seen her, and when he did, he realized just how much he had missed her beautiful face. Before Stella could stop him, he ran into the room, bent down, and kissed his beautiful Binah.

"Binah. Wake up." He wasn't even sure if she knew he'd kissed her. She rolled over groggily, the baby still clinging to one of her breasts.

"Ben?" Her eyes flew open, and she stared at him as if he were a dream. She looked behind him, and he realized she was looking at Stella and Mama Yang.

"Quiet." He put a finger over her lips. "They're friends. We're getting out of here." He helped her up. She hugged the baby to her and closed her eyes.

"Goddess be praised!"

January 4, 2:00

The Underground promptly halted every motion, every task, when the time came near. The comet, hurtling forty thousand miles per hour toward Earth, was projected to enter the atmosphere and hit at approximately 02:15 their time. Around the world, amateur newscasters continued reporting, although their predecessors had long abandoned their stations for privileged seats in underground shelters.

Satellites were trained on the comet. Every pair of eyes that could find a screen watched the doomsday rock come closer and closer until it fell from the sky, and at 2:16:03, the world, as they knew it, ended in a blank screen.

They all watched the world end from Binah's room, and before that, they'd learned with deep sadness about the death of the United States President and Congress. Their old world was gone. This was the one they had to live in now, and if they wanted a chance at freedom, they'd have to escape from Harper and the other Cullers. Maybe the president was dead, but the underground cities around Denver and Apache Peak had to have a different chosen leader.

Ben didn't want to stay around to see how it all worked out. They'd done some dry runs to practice their escape, and everything was ready.

"Here. Get your gear on." Ben brought over a pack for Binah. They all needed to help carry supplies, and this was the last of the load.

Binah was shaking, but Ben helped her pull on the pack. The baby was quiet, and while some children may have fussed at moving at the odd hour, this one silently observed.

"She's beautiful." Ben couldn't help but touch the girl, even if Binah might feel protective over her. He'd certainly understand if she didn't want him to. "What's her name?"

She looked surprised for a moment, like she'd really forgotten to name the baby. Ben found that curious.

"I haven't picked one." Binah's eyes brimmed with tears, and she hung her head.

"We've got to move!" Stella was getting impatient. She was right. There was no telling when they might be discovered.

They went as quickly as they dared. Nothing moved on the city streets. The entire world below seemed to have stopped in time.

Together, they raced to the elevators. Once they were gathered inside, Ben knew it would take them over three minutes to descend. He took a chance.

"Can I hold her?"

Binah smiled, hesitated, but then handed the girl to him. She was so big already. Her ice-blue eyes had a gaze that made him feel like she was piercing him to the core.

"Shekhinah." It was the perfect name.

"What?" Binah looked confused.

"That would be a good name. It's like yours. It comes from the Kabbalah, from the tree of life."

"What does it mean?"

"Mother of creation. Mother Earth." It was perfect for her really. She would be something like that if they all survived.

Binah tried the name out. "Shekhinah." She smiled. "I like it."

The elevator slowed to a stop. Once they were out, they traveled along their practiced route. Tall tunnels, much taller than those above, arched around them everywhere.

Stella and Mama Yang led the way.

"What are we doing? Where are we going?" Binah had no idea what they were planning, and she had trouble keeping up. At least they hadn't met any resistance yet. That was good.

"We'll explain it all later. Just know that for now that you both are safe and we're going to keep it that way." He took a moment to reach out and squeeze her hand.

"There!" Mama Yang pointed toward two enormous subterrene machines used to bore into the earth. Ben knew they left very little waste and carved the earth into giant tunnels perfectly. Most people had no idea they existed. The first time he'd seen them make tunnels, he couldn't believe something that huge, and manmade, could exist beneath the ground.

Next to the machines were some smaller vehicles. They looked like submarines, but with a rougher exterior. The problem remained: how were they going to use one?

"We have a driver!"

An old man stepped out from hiding and looked at Mama Yang kindly. Two younger men emerged behind him. Ben hoped the three men would be enough to run the earth subs.

Stella started barking orders. "Get in that one, closer to the tunnel…"

"Hold it right there!" It was Harper. How had he known they were here? They'd practiced this for days, careful to avoid being seen. They'd planned things down to the last detail. Every mission had been successful. Until now.

Chet rolled up beside Harper, a machete in his hand and grenades hanging from his wheelchair. He had a malicious grin on his face. This was not good. Not good at all.

Several soldiers in black, as well as suit-clad Cullers, stepped out. Ben realized they were almost surrounded. He hoped everyone on his team was on the same brain frame. He shifted his feet, stabilizing his stance. *Fight or die.* He wasn't going back into a box.

Stella must have picked up his physical cues. She immediately grabbed a grenade, pulled the pin, and lobbed it at Harper. Before the thing could land, both he and Chet were moving out of the way. They were quick. She'd have to do better next time.

Harper stood up and cupped his hands around his mouth. "You have nowhere to go! My Cullers control every place in this tunnel network. Any place you run, we'll be there."

Ben heard weapons lock and load all around them.

"You won't dare shoot them, Harper!" Ben found his voice. "They're your key to survival down here. You said it yourself."

The ground shook and continued to shake for over a minute. The rumble of the earth was deafening. *Some kind of earthquake? No, it had to be a from the comet's impact.* Just as the rumble started to fade, another one started. But this one was different. It had a rhythm. The rhythm of a run.

Gevu burst into the room, and his eyes found and locked on Harper. He held a giant metal pole in his hand, with some kind of rake attached at the end. It was an odd kind of weapon. He swung it over his head, but he missed Harper by inches when he struck downward. The earth quaked. Chet rolled around behind Gevu, and Gevu swung his rake weapon again. He connected with Chet's wheelchair and sent him flying toward the four of them. Chet was thrown from the chair and dropped his machete. It landed a few feet from his hand.

Without so much as a word, Binah handed Ben the baby, dashed forward, and grabbed the machete. She stood over Chet with the blade. Her voice shook, and the weapon trembled in her hands. "You deserve to die!"

Gunfire went off around them. Mama Yang and her new recruits were trying to hold the Cullers back.

Chet looked up at her with a sneer, and Ben could hear the hatred and loathing in his voice despite the surround chaos. "Go ahead and put me down, Miss Piggy."

Ben watched her hesitate, and then saw the ominous glint in Chet's eye. *No!* Ben handed Shekhinah to Stella, and he ran toward Binah.

"Binah!"

But it was too late. Chet used his hands to swing his torso around and swept Binah's legs from beneath her. He took the machete out of her hand before she even hit the ground.

"No!" Ben launched himself at Chet, but the man had already grabbed Binah's ebony hair, raised the weapon as high as he could, and brought the blade down. Binah's head came off right in Chet's hand, and her blood sprayed all over them. Ben screamed, and Chet laughed, crawled to his wheelchair, righted it, and pulled himself up in the seat. Binah's head dangled in one hand. He retreated back toward the city tunnel, but not before Gevu had seen what he'd done.

Harper spun his head their way after returning gunfire, looked over at Gevu, and frowned when he saw Binah's head in Chet's hand.

Binah! Ben pulled out a firearm, then aimed at and killed every target in his sight. He'd never killed humans before. They were much easier than killing rats, monkeys, cats, and dogs. Most animals didn't have a choice.

His brain felt numb, and each of his actions seemed to roll forward in slow motion. Between each shot, he had the time to think about it all. Humans were able to choose, in this case, whether to fight or die, but animals in the lab didn't have that luxury. They were innocent. Defenseless. And humans tortured and killed animals every day in the name of science. He'd done it before. He knew he'd never do it again. He reloaded his firearm, aimed, and squeezed the trigger over and over again.

"Chet! Get out of there!" Harper's voice was lost among the gunfire.

Gevu roared, and his tone was deep, visceral, and filled with anger—so much so that Ben almost wet his pants. Gevu roared again, and he gathered speed, racing at Chet like a runaway freight train. He was a juggernaut, pounding forward with the strength of a fifty-foot wave. All Chet did was laugh and swing the head of his sister in front of him. Her eyes were open; her face was slack. Ben felt a wave of nausea hit him. *Think of Shekhinah!* He had to protect her. He fired more ammunition with new resolve. Another Culler, a woman, went down.

Ben checked up on Shekhinah. Stella had laid her on the ground, out of harm's way, during the battle. She was firing at a group of Cullers who were using radios, probably to call for extra men. Oddly, Shekhinah wasn't crying. *All of this noise, and she's so calm. Maybe she's deaf.*

Gevu launched himself at Chet. In an instant, Chet brought up the machete, and with a yell, he shoved it right into Gevu's belly. Gevu crumpled on top of him, and Chet struggled wildly beneath his weight. In seconds, Gevu rose up again, pulled the machete slowly out of his own abdomen, and stared down menacingly at Chet.

Ben wanted to close his eyes, but he couldn't. He was riveted to the moment. In his mind's eye, he saw little Gevu, the squalling baby pig, the defiant child, the chicken eater, the rapist of his own sister, and the brother of Ben's true love.

Chet's eyes were crazy, filled with wildfire. "What are you going to do, fuckwad? Go ahead. Kill me! I'm not afraid to die!" His voice was infused with anger. *And fear.* Ben couldn't recall seeing Chet ever displaying a hint of fear.

Gevu raised the machete and bellowed when he brought it down. Ben heard bone crunch, and Chet's right arm was separated from his torso. Binah's head still remained in the hand's grasp, fingers tangled in her hair. Arm and head fell to the ground with a thud, and Chet screamed from the pain.

Suddenly, Ben realized the fighting in the room had nearly ceased. All eyes were riveted on the scene unfolding before them. Gevu raised the blade again and sliced it downward, severing Chet's left arm. He picked it up, sunk his teeth into the well-muscled tissue, and tore away a hunk of bicep from the bone. Blood dribbled down his chin as he chewed a few times, then spit the masticated flesh into Chet's face. The man in the wheelchair spurted arterial red from both sides, and his panicked yell became a howl, which rose to a deafening scream. He desperately looked around the room, pleading for help. Then his color turned from pale to gray, and the blood ejected with less force.

Before Chet lost consciousness, Gevu opened his huge maw and placed it around the middle of Chet's head. Teeth pressed into Chet's eyes—not quick, not merciful—and when he closed his lower jaw, Ben heard the slow crunch of bone collapsing Chet's skull. Blood sprayed onto the floor. Brain matter dripped from Gevu's teeth. Gevu looked up at the ceiling, and an agonizing howl of pain and loss ripped from his throat. Ben dropped to his knees. It was too much.

It was then that Shekhinah cried out, her wail echoing through the cavern. Ben ran to her and scooped her up in his arms. Stella hadn't missed a beat, taking down two more soldiers. Mama Yang came up beside him. "We must go!"

He called to Stella. "We need to get out of here!" He wondered if she had heard him over the noise. Stella nodded, and he assumed she was acknowledging and agreeing. The earth shifted, and rock and concrete fell from the ceiling. Part of the archway that they were standing beneath started to collapse. A portion of the ceiling crumbled in boulder-sized pieces and almost knocked Gevu over. If Shekhinah had any chance for survival, it would be with him. His strength would keep her safe. And she was his daughter. He'd guard her with his life.

Ben ran forward with Shekhinah in his arms. "Gevu! Get out of here! Leave!" He gave Shekhinah over to Gevu. A bullet whizzed by them. Another one struck Ben in the shoulder. He fell to the ground. The pain wasn't so great. But he could barely move. He couldn't go with them. He'd be too slow to keep up. The tunnels running from the main city rumbled, but this time, the noise was more mechanical. Revving engines echoed from the tunnel and warned of pending enemy reinforcements. Gevu looked down at Ben. It was the first time Ben had ever seen a flicker of emotion that looked like concern on the brute's face.

"Gevu. It's okay. Get her out of here. Get Shekhinah out of here!"

Gevu repeated the name. "Shekhinah?"

Ben smiled. "Yes, Shekhinah. Mother of creation. Mother of the world. It's from the Kabbalah, just like your name."

Gevu nodded, held the baby close, and sprinted for the subterrene.

Binah's head rested near Ben, her face turned toward him in a death mask. He didn't want to do this anymore. Not without her. He untangled Binah's hair from Chet's dead hand, touched her cheek, and sobbed.

Someone startled him by yelling in his ear. "Get the fuck up!"

Stella yanked at his shirt and pulled him to his knees.

"The tunnels are collapsing!"

They had nowhere to go. At least Gevu and Shekhinah were free. Ben caught sight of the subterrene disappearing into a tunnel, and suddenly, he had an idea. It wasn't a good idea, but he was willing to make a sacrifice if it meant their survival. Stella wouldn't like it. In fact, she might hate him. He grabbed up Binah's head tenderly. "Help me up!"

"Jesus! You've been hit!"

Ben ignored her, and after she'd helped him to his feet, he stumbled toward the city. Harper was still there, behind a stone column, barking out orders.

"What are you doing?" Stella's voice sounded panicked. She probably realized they had nowhere else to go. Freedom, it seemed, had to wait for another day.

Ben loped clumsily in Harper's direction, trying to wave his free arm to signal his surrender, but the pain in his wounded shoulder was excruciating. His motion was more of a feeble wave, but Harper must have caught sight of them.

"Cease fire! Stand down!" Harper's staccato words echoed around the room, and in seconds the firing stopped. All he heard were the occasional rumbles of the earth.

Harper's men surrounded him.

"I'll take that." He pulled Binah's head from Ben's hands and looked down at it, his face grim. "It didn't have to be this way."

More of Harper's men brought Stella forward.

Harper smiled, and Ben figured the Culler figured that not all was lost. He'd had a brief gain, even if it was only in the recapture of a scientist and an ex-agent.

The next shake of the earth brought down a major chunk of the ceiling, and it looked like it was on the verge of total collapse.

"Fall back to the city!"

The earth shook again while they retreated; Ben caught a brief glimpse of the world behind him come tumbling down.

THIRTY EIGHT

January 5, 08:10

Gevu held on to his little girl. What had Dr. Skylar called her?

Shekhinah. From the Kabbalah, he'd said. As was his own name and Binah's.

The mother of creation. He tried it out. "Shekhinah." The child looked up at him from the crook of his arm. It was a big name to wear for such a little girl.

Their vehicle traveled toward the new city, to an underground world he was sure, in time, he would rule. The women he'd brought with him after Mama Yang had freed him carried his other children in their bellies. It was lucky that Miriam had come to his prison cell when she did. If she hadn't, he might not ever have found her. He hoped that perhaps since she'd undergone the uterine transplant, having some of Binah's living tissue inside her body would allow her to feed them. He was certain she'd work to discover a mix of foods that would help them grow. He had no doubt.

Heung sat silently in a corner, and Gevu wondered at his usefulness. He was once powerful, with connections and resources, but now, he was nothing. Men would not follow him, whether human or swine. But Gevu had done as the woman, Mama Yang, had asked. He owed her his life, and so he'd saved her son. They were even.

Shekhinah started to whimper. She was hungry again. Miriam had explained to him how Binah fed the baby, and he was glad that at least the child had some sort of maternal bonding, albeit brief. The baby's rapid growth was amazing, and that was a biological advantage for his people. Whereas humans took years to mature, his brood would take weeks. Whereas humans were susceptible to so many diseases, his would be healthy. Almost invincible. Together, his species could survive anything.

He rested the palm of his hand on the baby's head. *Shekhinah, or better yet, Ki for now.* "Hush, Ki, we'll feed you soon." The nickname worked very well. It was short, soothing, and he remembered what it meant in Japanese. *Life force. Life essence.* And that was what she was. In Sumerian mythology, she was the earth goddess. It was the perfect title for his daughter to wear.

Ki.

What was it he'd read from a book a couple of months ago? A quote from the poet Aberjhani sprung to mind, and it suited this moment well. *A bridge of silver wings stretches from the dead ashes of an unforgiving nightmare to the jeweled vision of a life started anew.*

"We'll start life over, Ki. We'll build a place where our kind will survive, and in time, our people will be free to walk anywhere in or on the earth, and without fear."

His baby girl stared at him, and he could have sworn she was smiling.

She was beautiful.

EPILOGUE

February 15, 01:08

Binah woke. The room was a blur, and it was difficult to see. "Dim the lights!" A hazy face leaned over her. She struggled to focus, but the fluorescent bulbs hurt her eyes and they started watering. After the lights dimmed, her vision slowly cleared.

She recognized the voice, but her sense of smell was diminished. She could barely discern the scent of anything. In that way she felt almost blind. She had never realized how much her sense of smell told her.

"Ben?" Her own voice sounded strange, and her throat was cracked and dry. Everything about how she felt was unfamiliar. Someone was holding her hand. It had to be Ben. She brought his hands to her face so she could kiss him, but she noticed something was not right. She looked closer, then held his palm against hers.

A woman's voice across the room interjected a warning. "Are you sure this is a good time for this? She's just waking..."

"No time like the present," Ben interrupted. "She's always wanted to know the truth of things since the beginning. No need to hide it now."

Binah gazed at their hands. His was so much bigger. *That's odd. My hands have been larger than his for months.* Hers seemed well muscled. Manicured burgundy nails. Slender. Black skin. Smooth. She struggled to put the pieces together, and felt like a circuit hitting peak overload. Her last memory was of falling to the ground. Chet had grabbed the machete.

Oh Goddess! This is not my hand!

Her eyes trailed up the length of her arm, paying attention to the skin color, the well-defined arm, and the shoulder.

"Binah, wait." Ben tried to grab her hand, but she pushed him away. Why weren't they talking to her? Why weren't they telling her why her hand looked so different?

She almost yanked out the IV when she reached for her hair. Her eyes watered again. Gone were her long black tresses. Instead, there were bandages. And where she found hair, it felt curly, oiled, and cropped close to her head. Her fingers trembled when she explored the front of her face and discovered a rounded, very human nose.

"Binah, don't…"

She looked back at him, his features sharpening and becoming more defined. "What's happened to me, Ben? Where's Shekhinah? Where are we? Chet! I remember Chet! Is he dead?"

"Yes, Binah, he's dead. You should rest."

"But, I didn't kill him. The machete! He took the machete!"

"Don't force it, Binah. We'll explain everything in time. Just rest."

She started to shake her head, but she found she couldn't move it. It was secured firmly to the bed.

Shekhinah!

Her daughter was gone, and there was no time to waste.

Binah tried to rise, but her torso was strapped to the bed. She strained to prop herself up on her elbows and failed, but managed to look down the length of her body—and screamed.

ABOUT THE AUTHOR

Querus Abuttu, or "Q," loves writing what she calls "speculative bio-horror," as well as other types of fiction. Her work has been published in the online magazine *69 Flavors of Paranoia,* the fiction magazine *Pantheon,* and an anthology titled *Hazard Yet Forward.* She was awarded second place at the Gross Out contest at Killercon 4 in 2012, won first place at the Gross Out contest at Killercon 5 in 2013, and placed third at the Gross Out at the World Horror Convention in 2014. Q has served as a Nurse Corps officer, certified nurse-midwife, and forensic nurse with both the Indian Health Services and the United States Navy for over twenty-eight years. She holds a master's degree in fine arts (MFA) from Seton Hill University, as well as a master's of public health (MPH) degree from George Washington University and a master's in nursing from Case Western Reserve University. She currently lives in Ventura, California, with her most understanding husband, two resilient teenagers, her junkyard dog, and rescue cats. When she's not writing, she's surfing the wild Pacific waves or dabbling in a little local ghost hunting, which has yet to result in locating real ghosts. Despite her failure at tracking the paranormal, she still hopes to capture the phantoms one day and make their stories her own.

If you'd like to connect with Q in her quirky world, you can write her via her author page on Facebook, or visit her website www.querusabuttu.com .

A deliriously dark blend of blood, sex, and mutant pig people. You'll need industrial-strength brain bleach after you read this one!
—Tim Waggoner, author of *The Way of All Flesh*

Sapient Farm is "...clever, imaginative, loaded with conflict (!), and repeatedly engaging."
—Timons Esaias, author of "The Children's War," in *Sherwood: Original Stories from the World of Robin Hood*

Made in the USA
Middletown, DE
03 February 2019